An Internat
(Ra

DEAD FIX

You Bet – They Win

- Douglas Stewart -

WHAT'S THEY'VE SAID
ABOUT THE RATSO SERIES

"Gripping, action-packed thriller."
  - Peter James – Voted the Best Crime Author of all time.

***** "A brilliant start to meeting Ratso. A story you can believe in and a gritty style of writing that works."

***** "Could not put it down!"

***** "Wow! A definite 5-star from me!"

***** "Fantastic read, great characters, gripping storyline. Roaring success Mr Stewart!"

***** "Engenders the same get-to-the-end compulsion as does a *Harlan Coben* crime suspense novel"

"People just love your books – you are getting an unusual percentage of high rankings."
  - M J Rose – New York Times best-selling author.

TABLE OF CONTENTS

-1-

London

The lean and fit looking man blinked as a tear splattered across the scrap of paper. Mark Rayner was seated alone on a comfy white leather sofa, a crudely scrawled message shaking in his hand. While parked at his local hospital, someone had tucked it under a wiper-blade of his Porsche Turbo. Of course, he had dreaded what *they* might do – somehow, some place, some time. Yet never in his lowest moments had he considered them stooping to this.

Mutilation.

After wiping away the worst of the tears, he glanced out as the sun set behind the silhouetted trees in his spacious garden. Of one thing, he was sure. Some bastard had been watching and waiting for him at the red brick hospital. Or had followed him there.

Maybe the evil bastard had even tailed him home.

Might now be lurking somewhere in the shadows.

At the front or round the back.

Perhaps be peering through a window.

Watching and waiting.

You were warned.

The words on the note haunted him. He let out an anguished howl as he relived what the surgeons had told him. The sound reverberated round walls lined with Impressionist artwork painted by his wife Yvonne. At the sight of them, guilt swept through him, making his body shake. For the third time since reaching home, he reached for the Grey Goose bottle and glugged down a generous swig. Then, as the note fell from his chinos, fluttering to the pine-wood floor, he rolled sideways on the sofa, arms clenched around his knees, head tucked into the foetal position, shoulders heaving.

There was no choice now.

Not after this.

He had to go on.

Play their game.

Dance to their tune.

Unless…

-2-

New York City

Alex Anderson waved London's Daily Mail. "A hammer! That's what they used." He jabbed at the article. "Mark Rayner's baby was eight months old. Now, five weeks later, Rayner say she'll never walk, talk or do anything meaningful again." He glared at the placid features of the Indian before switching to the truculent face of the New Yorker.

For Enzo Pagano, Vijay Chetri and Alex Anderson, this was just another regular meeting – at least on the surface. Today though, the atmosphere was electric. Typically, they had worked well together, though they had never been friends. This was business, no more, no less.

The clipped sentences, the restless hands, the alcohol, the sideways glances and lowered eyes revealed the tensions. What never changed was the five-star opulence of their meeting-places like the Mandarin Oriental in Las Vegas, the George V in Paris, the Bel Air in Los Angeles and the Hermitage in Monaco.

Today, they were at the Pierre on East 61st Street with an elegant suite overlooking Central Park. Not that any of the trio gave a toss for the view. Sure, they liked the discreet ambience but they chose the luxury for the simple reason that they expected nothing less. Extravagance was their norm. Mainly they talked betting and money – horses, cricket, American football, baseball or basketball.

After neither listener showed any concern about the brutality,

Anderson rose to his full height topping six feet. He advanced towards them, towering over them in their separate chairs. "His wife Yvonne – blinded for life. Acid thrown in her face." His dark eyes bored into each listener in turn. "Sure, Rayner did not deliver the fix." He leaned forward to smash his fist on the table. "Cost us a wad but does that make this okay?" Again he waved the pictures of mother and child. "Like hell it does!"

He went to the window. Down below, a horse towed a carriage of tourists into Central Park. Vijay spoke gently with a sing-song accent. "Alex, this was nothing to do with us." He sounded sincere but no way did Anderson believe him. The short but tubby Indian joined the Englishman looking down to the park entrance. He was too short to put a friendly hand on Anderson's shoulder but he clasped his elbow before continuing. "My guess? The heavy mob from Pakistan wanted Rayner, shall we say, *encouraged* never to fail again. They probably lost multi-millions."

Anderson said nothing. It was Pagano, sprawled sideways on the sofa who spoke. "See Alex? Nothing for us to feel bad about."

As Anderson looked round, he caught Pagano's condescending smile. He returned to stand over the corpulent figure, his voice raised. "Crap," retorted Anderson, stroking his hand over his thinning black hair, cut short and covering his ears. With the chiselled features and wide-set eyes, he looked both handsome and yet someone not to be messed with.

Pagano, though, had survived and thrived in the toughest parts of the Bronx and along the New Jersey shore. As if Anderson had not said a word, the New Yorker continued, rubbing his hand down his stubbled cheek, a chuckle in his voice. "Alex, Alex – we were *victims*. We trusted Rayner to fix Surrey Patriots to lose. Bigger fish than us lost so much more."

Anderson turned away to sit down with measured assurance,

very aware that four eyes were staring at him. He was in no rush to contribute. He had not got rich without being calm under fire and cunning to a fault. "Whatever. Hammering a baby's brains, I mean that is fucking sick, so count me out – no more fixing cricket. I'm out of all that. I'll stick with HOSS." He brushed down the lapel of his grey suede jacket. "And Jupiter. I'm up for that."

It was just what Pagano wanted to hear. "Take a hike, Alex. You ain't picking and mixing in a candy store. You are in or out."

"Mark Rayner has got the message. He won't let us down again." Chetri sounded sincere but he addressed the words as much to his black tasselled loafers as to Anderson. "At his next televised match, he'll deliver the result we want."

Alex leaned back and clasped his hands behind his head but said nothing.

He knew it was better that way.

Play silent ... and deadly.

The long game.

-3-
London

Det. Inspector Todd "Ratso" Holtom was unsure just why he had received the call to meet the Assistant-Commissioner at New Scotland Yard. His last major investigation, *Operation Clam*, had been successful so he knew or *thought* he knew that he was not being carpeted.

He always walked when he could, his stride long and brisk, part of his desire to keep in shape for his remaining days as a club cricketer. Now pushing towards forty, it would not be long before clapped-out knees and weary muscles would prevent him from racing in to bowl at over 70mph.

After crossing the Thames, he passed the bell-tower of Big Ben. There, he quickened his pace with the intensity of the beat from Black Sabbath filling his ears. After passing through security at Scotland Yard, he took the elevator to the A-C's office where he was not kept waiting. As Big Ben struck eleven, Wensley Hughes offered him a coffee and a seat. "Prosecutions following *Clam* in good shape?"

"I believe so, sir. Both here and in Spain."

"Good. Excellent result." His fingers, touching as if in prayer, added to his monk-like appearance. "But you were lucky. Nailing Boris Zandro became an ego trip." He sucked in air through his narrowed mouth. "Not on. The risks you took – brave ... but unacceptable." He fixed Ratso over his gold-rimmed glasses. "No room for glory, no need for heroes."

Hughes had been a loyal supporter and Ratso had no answer to the criticism, so he just nodded. It was pointless defending the indefensible.

"So, if you want further promotion, I want no repetition. Sticking your neck out on theories, I can live with. Results aren't achieved by blinkered thinking. Your enthusiasm serves you well. But becoming a maverick?" Hughes shook his placid features. "Not on. Not these days in the Met. Understood?"

"Understood, sir." Ratso waited for whatever else was coming.

The AC glanced at his monitor. "You've become an invaluable team-member in the drugs war." Ratso sensed an almighty *but* coming and his spirits drooped. He fought unsuccessfully to keep a poker face. He tilted his head sideways and tried to look away as Hughes nailed him with an unfaltering stare. "Relax, Todd. I can see what you're thinking. I'm not putting you out to grass." He placed his hands, palm down across the desk. "I think you'll like what I'm going to say." He topped up their coffees. "You like cricket."

"Love it, sir. Are you inviting me to captain the Met Police veterans?"

It was a facetious remark and Hughes smiled. "At your age? Get real. No. Let's talk match-fixing."

"It happens."

"Then your role will be to stop it. You read about Mark Rayner's wife and baby being attacked."

"Disgusting."

"The local police team are dealing with this as a personal matter. That or some local nutter."

"But you don't think so?"

"Rayner captains Surrey Patriots."

"You think this thug got at him by attacking his family? Something to do with fixing?"

Wensley Hughes spoke in a matter-of-fact way, never showing euphoria or despair. From his facial expressions to his hand and arm movements, every sparse ounce of the man spoke calmness as he continued "Big money in fixing. Murderous guys too. Big time criminals from the Asian sub-continent."

Hughes was telling Ratso nothing he did not know. "You think he crossed them?"

As he often did, Hughes strolled to the window, his tall and narrow figure far from filling the frame. "I don't know. So I want you in the Organised and Economic Crime Command. You'll be based in Vauxhall, Cobalt Square. Rayner may lead us into what's going on."

"If he's not too scared to talk, sir." Ratso's arched eyebrow gave away that he guessed the answer.

The AC's eyes showed no reaction as he continued. "Research his background, all his recent matches. Work with the bookies." He smiled. "Oh and meet up with Craig Carter."

"Carter – the Chief Super? He retired, didn't he, sir?"

Hughes nodded agreement. "Now works for the ECB at Lord's cricket ground. Special subject – match-fixing." The slight nod of the head and pushing his cup aside were familiar moves to signify Hughes was finished.

"Do I get to bring any of my team? If they want to move, that is." By now, Ratso was by the door.

"Who?" Already the AC's mind was elsewhere.

"DS Strang, DS Watson and DC Petrie."

"Ask them. I won't decide. That's one for the Deputy."

—4—

New York

"**In or out,**" repeated Pagano, his turkey-neck wobbling. He helped himself to an oatmeal cookie and chewed greedily while he spoke. "You quit cricket, then no more HOSS and like fuck you'll still get a cut of Jupiter."

"I paid my share for the HOSS software *and* helped fund Jupiter." As always, Anderson spoke quietly but each word was emphatic and delivered in his pronounced Newcastle accent. His clean-cut masculine features gave him an air of authority as he pushed aside the last of his mac-cheese.

"Alex. We're a syndicate. You can't dip out. Got it?" Pagano's face was flushed with anger now, the more so because Anderson was so composed yet defiant.

Chetri shifted uncomfortably as he listened. "Don't be too hasty, Alex. It was a shocking attack. I've got kids and grand-kids, so …" His voice trailed away.

Anderson's eyes were so dark brown as to be nearly black. His glare stopped the speaker in mid-track. "Rayner may spill everything to the cops." He flourished the newspaper and then read from it. "The police have an open mind on motive. Mrs Yvonne Rayner saw nothing of her attacker. One theory is a random attack. Even an assault by a lone fundamentalist cannot be ruled out. However, there is no reason to connect it to Mark Rayner's captaincy of Surrey Patriots T20 cricket team."

Vijay Chetri shrugged. "Given the attack, I'd say he'll keep his mouth shut. Come on, Alex, hang on in." Chetri was Indian by birth but had lived around London for most of his life. Aged in his late fifties, with near silver hair, his face looked carefree and younger despite being fully grey-bearded with a close-cut trim.

Anderson bought time by pinching his chin before replying. His mind was racing through the history of their relationship. It had started a few years back when Anderson and Chetri had met over cocktails at Churchill Downs while watching the Kentucky Derby. The Indian had persuaded him to invest in predictive software that would pick race winners. "The beta version proves it works. I've got the contacts to write and maintain the programme. I'm calling it HOSS – Home Operated Sophisticated Systems. I'd like a co-partner even though I am wealthy enough to fund it myself." Chetri leaned forward and whispered. "Bet on Nobel Rot."

"An outsider?" Anderson looked puzzled. "The tipsters don't rate him a donkey's chance."

Chetri shrugged. "HOSS says go for it."

An hour later, as Nobel Rot won by a short head, Anderson was over two-hundred thousand richer and agreed to invest in the software. Over the next few months, relations were business-like but rising costs from the programmers had led Chetri to let Pagano become a third investor. For reasons that Anderson never understood, the little Indian seemed impressed and in awe of the cigar-chomping New Yorker. Anderson had resisted. "We don't need him. I don't like the fat slob. I'll pony up 50-50 with you to keep him out. He'll be a cuckoo in the nest."

Chetri though had ignored the warnings. A Gibraltar company including offshore trusts was set up to handle the bets and winnings, together with four bank accounts in the tax haven of Monaco. Just one month later, HOSS was delivering big wins on both tight and long odds. Betting their millions at low odds or sometimes on a commission basis, they had won steadily so that an uneasy harmony ruled.

Particularly betting on lesser race meetings, they usually cleaned up. Additionally, on more unfashionable tennis tournaments, the software's algorithm tracked down conflicting odds on offer from different bookies so that they could back both players to make a win inevitable.

Anderson recalled another meeting in Boston from two years back. Pagano had announced he was *bored to hell* with winning so easily. "Heck, I'm nearly sixty. We're all stinking rich. We don't need no more money. I want some *action*, like in my scrap metal days on Long Beach. Y'know – winning deals. Screwing the other guy. Negotiating. Bribing. Arguing, cheating, fucking doing whatever it takes to win."

"Problem solved." Chetri had enthused. "I can cut you both in on something I'm into." He looked sly. "I have contacts in Dubai and India." Over crab claws and Chablis while looking out over the Charles River, he continued. "HOSS is great but suppose we *know* who will win matches or tournaments? I mean *really know*. Like a fixed result." After seeing he had their attention, he continued. "Obscure tennis tournaments, televised cricket and soccer in Eastern Europe – they're all rife with fixing."

Pagano, his mouth full of crab, said nothing but Anderson remembered being cautious. "If we bet say a couple of million on some upstart novice to beat Roger Federer at Wimbledon, hell the bookies would go apeshit." Anderson tossed the remains of his crab aside. "Alarm bells everywhere."

Chetri laughed, his small and even teeth shining brightly from his light-brown face. "You're thinking big name bookies and big name players. I'm not." As he often did, his head shook from side to side like a nodding dog as he emphasised his point. "Forget them. I'm talking of the illegal betting market operating from the Middle East and throughout Asia. On cricket alone, it is worth multi-billions every year. These guys set the odds. If a fix is on, they clean up. So would we! Exciting enough for you, Enzo? Pretty damned good, eh?"

The American worked his finger furiously in his ear as if he had lost something deep inside. "Bribe players? You kidding me?"

"I'm not going round bribing," added Alex.

"No problem." Chetri's head nodded sideways. "The fixed cricketers are in place. But if somehow *we* could deliver these guys a big fix, the return would be enormous. Like netting maybe one-hundred million each.

"Jeez! Real money! Sure. I'll get my rocks off on that. Count me in," Pagano enthused. "But cricket. That's a crazy game."

"You doing these fixes Vijay?" Anderson had sounded doubtful despite the big numbers.

"Not me, Alex. My contacts."

Anderson's face broke into the faintest of smiles as he nodded yes. Not that he believed the smooth talk. From his wild days growing up in Byker, one of Newcastle's tougher inner-city areas, Anderson liked to know anything and everything – lessons that had served him well during his rise to wealth. Were Chetri and Pagano crooked, greedy, gay, straight, violent? He did not care about their life-choices. What mattered was *knowing*.

He knew.

Private detectives had delivered.

In a dozen pages, they had Pagano and Chetri well-sussed. Besides getting rich by selling out his scrap metal and waste business, the American, who preferred hookers to marriage, had served time for fraud. Chetri's company had been bought out by an

American giant from Silicon Valley and he had no known police record. In contrast, Anderson liked to play in the dark, volunteering little or nothing of the shadier side of his property deals around Newcastle. He doubted they knew the square-root of fuck-all about his past. By thirty-five, Anderson had made it big. Now, at forty-one, he was worth well over three hundred million with a mansion in Florida and a sprawling villa overlooking the Adriatic in Trogir.

The grunts as Pagano heaved his bulk from the chair brought Anderson back to the present. Now, he knew he was being watched for his decision. *Sod them! He'd bought in to Jupiter. In under three months if it worked, his share might be another twenty, maybe even thirty million.* He looked up and smiled at each listener in turn. "You're right, Vijay. Maybe I was too hasty over the cricket. Let me think it over. For now, count me in on everything." Anderson knew it was a lie. He needed to buy time – time to uncover how Jupiter would work. Only then could he quit.

"Can we get on now? Pagano's voice was gravelly and aggressive. He slurped his coffee as he stared at the Englishman from his stance across the polished table. He then tilted his head back as if sniffing the air which smelled of new carpeting and Chetri's expensive after-shave. "I want to talk Jupiter. It could be … the biggest fix since the Black Sox game about one hundred years back. Ain't that just something!"

"Maybe!" Anderson tried to sound less enthusiastic than he was.

Pagano was mainly bald but with hair tufting around his ears. For a moment he tugged at his drooping earlobe. "So what's news Vijay?"

"We got lucky." In a few pithy sentences, the Indian briefed them on how the plan was nearly in place.

"Holy shit!" With a whistle, Pagano flopped back to his

sprawled position. To Anderson he looked like a fat and contented toad. Beneath bushy brows, his deep-set eyes showed that hundred-dollar bills were filling his brain. "You're not shitting us? Your guy will deliver?" The tone of Pagano's voice showed incredulity.

If it were possible, Chetri looked even smugger as he nodded yes. "Glad you stayed, Alex?"

He was.

-5-

London

Five weeks and two days had passed since the attack in Richmond Park as Mark arrived at the hospital in Yvonne's 4 x 4 Mitsubishi. After stepping out and looking around, he saw nobody or nothing suspicious, just the usual toing and froing towards the end of visiting-time. If the paparazzi were lurking or if he had been followed, it was not apparent.

He bounded up the steps and within five minutes re-emerged leading Yvonne slowly and carefully out to the waiting vehicle. This was her first taste of a world she would never again see. Beside him, a nurse had Emilia-Jane in a carry-cot. She was wrapped in a pink blanket, her tiny body still and almost lifeless, her head swathed in bandages. Another porter carried a small Gucci suitcase and a Pooh Bear bag with E-J's bits and pieces.

The West Indian nurse gave husband and wife a big hug of farewell. "See you on Tuesday with E-J," she confirmed, her emotions nearly getting the better of her. From the rear-seat, Mark produced a huge bouquet of flowers and an envelope. "There's a donation for the hospital's charity. Thank you."

Moments later, they exited the precincts and after passing through a couple of traffic lights, he turned into Richmond Park where he parked with a view of the pond. He pulled out his phone and checked that it was switched off. "Aren't we going straight home?" Yvonne asked, turning her head to him but seeing nothing.

"A surprise for you, darling! Your Mum's putting us up for a couple of nights. She's desperate to do whatever she can. So I said yes."

She fumbled to grasp his hand in pleasure. "Thanks darling! I'd love that! Super surprise!" She turned to the still silent baby. "We're going to Grandma's. Isn't that fun E-J!" There was no reaction and Mark was unsure whether the tiny shape was asleep or awake beneath the bandages.

"Your mother's in a right old state. Only to be expected. I said we'd reach Eastbourne by about 11pm. So I picked up sandwiches, your favourite Mars Bar. There's a flask of cocoa for you and coffee for me. What about E-J? When will she need feeding?"

Suddenly, Yvonne twisted towards him, her arms reaching out to find him before she broke down, her tears and sobs barely muted against his navy and green hooped sweatshirt. "I'm so scared. For me. For you. For Emilia-Jane." She faltered, trying to be brave. "How will I cope? Looking after any baby is …," she sobbed. "I mean – now with me like this and E-J's … special needs." She couldn't bring herself to say the words *total dependency*. Her voice trailed away into nothing as her body heaved and trembled against him. Mark bit his lip to fight against his own emotions as guilt and despair hit him like a falling brick. His tears soaked the nape of her neck. Eventually, Yvonne struggled to answer his question. "I just fed E-J, so she'll last till we get there."

He pulled away from her. "Here are the sandwiches and I've unwrapped the Mars bar." As he spoke, he placed a sandwich in her hand which she sniffed.

"Smoked salmon and cream cheese. Perfect."

"You eat while I fix your drink." He grabbed a red thermos and from his pocket, he tipped in two crushed sleeping tablets. After closing the lid, he shook the flask and then poured a cup for her.

"Hopefully you'll sleep on the journey while my coffee keeps me awake. I haven't had a decent night's sleep in weeks."

"Poor you," Yvonne responded nodding her head. "And still no idea why we were targeted?"

"None," he replied softly. "Detective Sergeant Trasker is at a loss. The attacker never spoke. You saw nothing. The detective is not even sure whether she's looking for a man or a woman. Me, I think it was a man. Someone strong enough to grip you from behind as you sat looking at the pond." As he spoke, he glanced to his left at the simple park bench. His eyes welled up with tears again. Then suddenly, in his mind, all he could see was the scrap of paper and the words *You were warned.*

Between bites of her chocolate bar, Yvonne spoke slowly, the muscles in her once beautiful face taut. "I've re-lived it so often. Look, if it was some crazy woman who had lost a baby, she would have confronted me. Wouldn't she have said something? Like *you bitch* or *I hate you and your happiness.* Least, that's my take."

For a moment neither spoke while Mark turned to see E-J lying peacefully, scarcely any of her pink features to be seen. Every day he had re-lived the secret meetings, the cash payments, the fixed results, the guilt flooding over him. This was the worst yet. His stomach churned and he fought back feelings of nausea.

"We're at the spot, aren't we," Yvonne suddenly volunteered, sitting up sharply and looking round as if able to see.

"Clever girl! The bench you were sitting on is right beside us. I've been coming here every day, hoping to spot someone hanging around or maybe find some clue." He gazed over the open spaces. "There's a young roebuck grazing close to us. So young, so peaceful, so beautiful and at ease, just like you were that afternoon." He handed her the cocoa with a long sigh. "Here, right here, is where some sick bastard destroyed everything we had."

Lost in thoughts, Yvonne drained the cocoa and he topped it up again. "We ought to be pressing on. It'll be about two hours." He fired the engine as she clasped the last dregs of cocoa. "Let's get going. I can't wait to see Mum." There was a pause as she realised what she had said. Then she laughed but without pleasure. "Well, so to speak." She leaned into him but could not see his wet cheeks. "And cricket? You'll start playing again soon?"

"I'll play in the big 50 over match at Lord's." He pulled away. "Nice evening for the drive but you get some sleep before E-J needs feeding." He headed south towards Brighton taking the M25 and M23 before heading east towards the genteel coastal resort of Eastbourne. Long before passing Gatwick Airport, Yvonne had fallen into a deep sleep, her peaceful breathing soothing Mark as he sped along in silence at 70 mph. Only the whiteness in his knuckles gave away his inner turmoil. When at last he reached the outskirts he turned away from Sovereign Harbour where his mother-in-law had a penthouse with great marina views. Instead, he turned west.

Across the Atlantic, at the same time, during a meeting in the Coronado Hotel at San Diego looking across the blue of the Pacific, Vijay Chetri was updating Pagano and Anderson on the latest news from London about Jupiter. It was all good. As he listened, Alex Anderson was ticking off the details he needed to know, yet showing his usual casual indifference, leg slung carelessly across the arm of a well upholstered chair.

If Pagano wanted him out, he now knew enough but more would be even better. He popped a shrimp into his mouth and chewed contently.

-6-

Sussex

A glance across to the passenger-seat showed Rayner that Yvonne was still in a deep sleep. In the back, besides an occasional tiny sigh, EJ had never stirred. He nodded in satisfaction. Fearful that Yvonne or E-J would awaken, he kicked down hard on the accelerator and surged the Mitsubishi forward, skilfully manoeuvring the bends as the road climbed higher and higher towards Newhaven. With a grim nod of satisfaction, he saw the distant hoarding that he had seen on his reconnaissance trip.

The powerful vehicle roared further up the hill. In the powerful headlights and now clearly legible, was the sign for Beachy Head. He also spotted the notice for the Samaritans that he had seen the previous day. It meant nothing to Mark now. His mind was made up. The damage he had caused could never be undone.

There would be no turning back.

He had picked the spot, checked the route with precision. To his left beyond the grassy slope was the sheer drop of the white chalk cliffs – the UK's most notorious suicide spot. Yesterday, he had strolled beside the sometimes unstable cliff edge. He had walked as close as he dared to take in the sheer majestic beauty of the white cliffs and the almost vertical 500 foot drop to the rocks and sea below.

He could have jumped then. Escape from his guilt had been just a five second free-fall away. For a moment he had been tempted to dive head-first into glorious oblivion. The closer he had got to the edge, the stronger had been a near magnetic pull. But to leave Yvonne blinded with a brain-damaged child. No. That was just too cruel. *Better for them to know nothing.*

He slowed down as he neared the place where he could quit the road and head for the mighty drop. No way could he live any longer with his guilt. No way should E-J suffer the existence that he had brought on her. For the infant, this was the kindest way. For Yvonne too.

For me?

Escape from guilt.

Escape from the bastards who had suckered, trapped and tricked me into match-fixing.

I begged to be let go.

No.

So I fixed them, not the match.

Big mistake.

Vengeance had been swift.

Poor Yvonne.

Poor E-J

He swerved the car off the road, bumping over the chalky grass towards the drop, not far from where, far below, the red and white lighthouse defied the crashing waves.

I wish you dead, Lee!

One day!

Some day!

Rot in hell, Lee.

Rot!

Rot and burn!

For a second he glanced back at E-J. Soon her suffering would be over.

Soon all their suffering would be over.

With a surge of power, his eyes fixated on the black emptiness ahead, he sent the 4 x 4 rocking and jolting over the rising chalky grass.

Just seconds more suffering.

He clicked on the CD and Adele's voice filled the car with the lyrics of *Skyfall* which he'd carefully selected. Yvonne stirred, her mind confused by the strength of the sleeping tablets.

"Are we there yet, darling." Her voice was thick with sleep.

"Won't be long now." He patted her thigh as he pressed harder on the accelerator. The Mitsubishi roared and soared over the huge drop into the night sky. It tilted forward in the nothingness, its headlights picking out the white foam around the rocks. He let go of the wheel and rolled across to cling to Yvonne's body. "Yvonne, darling – I love you, love you. And I'm sorry, so sorr…"

The heavy vehicle slammed into the rocks in an explosion of flying metal, landing upside down. The passenger compartment was crushed into a contorted mass of torn scrap. A wheel flew through the air, bouncing and crashing between the rocks and white foam. There was a roar as the fuel exploded engulfing the wreckage in a fiery inferno

The sweet sounds of Adele died with the family.

-7-

London

L ee Westdale was a troubled man but his burden could be shared with nobody – especially not with his wife Mandy. Now, as he breakfasted with Jason Varder, a tabloid journalist, he tried to focus on the interview. They were seated in the packed Wolseley restaurant on Piccadilly, the room full of media gossip and banter.

As he played with scrambled eggs and tomato, he was finding it impossible to blank out the headlines and photos of the crushed Mitsubishi. Since Yvonne and the baby had been attacked, he had been tormented. But right now, the trick was to keep his mask in place and trot out all the usual crap.

A few moments before, breakfast had been interrupted by a request for a selfie by a middle-aged woman who had loudly proclaimed that she was his number-one fan. *God! How often had he heard that line!* But would she be a fan if she knew the truth? Like hell she would. More likely she would have spat in his face.

And deservedly so.

Varder looked at his notepad. "So Lee, here you were, former England and Somerset Hawks cricket captain. Your world fell apart. Tell me about it." The enthusiastic sports-writer had finished his full English while Westdale's food was barely touched.

Westdale had been asked the question dozens of times before. This time at least it kept his mind off images of his pal Mark trapped in the burned out vehicle. "I blame myself. Someone told me of this Parabolic Investment Club. It was based out of New York. Big returns were being made by investors – like 14 percent big. I was unmarried back then. With my earnings from cricket, product endorsements, my TV job and public appearances, well I'd saved up a chunk of money. So I invested four million quid."

"It was a scam?"

Westdale's poster-boy looks broke into a rueful and boyish grin. "If it sounds too good to be true, it probably is." Now aged forty-one, he retained the super-fit image that fans around the world had all adored. "It was a Ponzi scheme. I lost the lot. My only consolation – and it is no consolation really, was that hundreds, probably thousands of others had also been conned like me."

"Big names?"

"The Parabolic was like a Who's Who from sport, politics, Hollywood."

"Is it true you were ruined financially?"

Lee Westdale's eyes gave away the painful recollection. They were close-set, deep blue and with gimlet-like penetration, qualities that had enabled him to open the batting for eighteen seasons. "House, car, lifestyle. All gone. Parabolic went tits-up shortly after I married Mandy." He turned away to stare out at passers-by on Piccadilly. The smell of more hot coffee being poured by the journalist brought him back from his thoughts. "That was tough. Mandy and me, we nearly split. But somehow we got through it."

"Your book?"

"That helped our finances. It went to number-one here and in Australia." He played with the cold egg. "I worked harder and did even more rubber chicken dinners. I wrote more articles and upped what I charged for appearances. That's how I traded out of the doo-dah." The glib answer flowed freely.

"Will you get anything back?"

"From Parabolic?" Westdale laughed and shrugged, his whitened teeth perfect for a TV cricket pundit. "Hot-shot attorneys in NYC are running a class-action lawsuit."

"Humiliating times for you?"

Westdale winced at the word. "Yeah! You could say that."

"You captained England. You were one smart guy – nicknamed the *Egghead* or *The Prof* in the media. Yet here you were – destroyed by Parabolic."

Westdale fingered the collar of his lilac shirt which he wore beneath a tailored grey suit. "Different skill-set." He glanced at his Samsung Galaxy as a text pinged in. "Being a successful cricketer was no grounding for the sharks in Parabolic."

"Sharks?" The journalist mused, liking the word. "Like guys who are into match-fixing. What's your take? What do you hear in the TV studios, the commentary-box? Mark Rayner?"

"Look, Jason – you do see hard to explain things, curious decisions during matches. It doesn't mean there's a fix in place. But there might be. The convicted Pakistanis showed that. As to Mark Rayner? Tragic end of a good mate." Westdale ran his hands across his well-groomed black hair. "Mark was squeaky clean as far as we all know. Can we go off the record?" He saw the reluctant nod. "Look, after this tragedy, I can't say this in public. Understood? Agreed?" He waited for the yes and the closed notebook. "Mark was a bit fragile, brittle. He'd had a bad trot with his batting this season. He didn't like media criticism. He had been really down. Nothing I could say seemed to get through. So when tragedy struck his family. My take? He just couldn't cope."

The smooth-talking lies flowed seamlessly. "I saw Yvonne. I took flowers to the hospital. But what the hell do you say? I was Best Man at their wedding. That day, she was drop-dead gorgeous. When I saw her in the hospital, I wanted to throw up. I mean hell, she was blinded and had lost half her face."

"Well at least she never saw what they had done to her. Or to the baby."

Westdale looked at the black and gold of his Rado watch. He had no wish to be quizzed any further. "Sorry Jason but I must dash. I've another meeting."

As he left the crowded restaurant, his face was sombre as he recalled how everything had started – with the visit from the Indian businessman. What had seemed harmless chit-chat about team selection and pitch conditions had taken a sinister twist with a proposition that had attracted his greed.

He had been groomed.

Like he had then groomed Mark.

Now, the bastards owned him.

He danced to their tune.

Had to.

Mark's family had proved it

There was no escape.

Now the fixers were bleeding him dry. As a former England skipper, he had opened doors the Indian never knew existed. Step by step, with generous bungs, he had created and corrupted a network of contacts – cricketers like Mark Rayner, Amrit Segal and some Australian and South African umpires.

Mark had kicked back, wanting out.

Never an option, Mark.

As I told him – "These guys? Mark, don't mess with them."

And me?

Now? Kick back like Mark?

Tell the cops?

Fess up to Craig Carter at the ECB?

Get real.

Anyway, I've got Jupiter to fix yet.

If I deliver that this morning, then maybe, they'll let me go.

Dream on, Lee.

Dream on.

Overhead the mid-summer skies were oppressive. It was only 10-15a.m. yet the London air was humid and reeked of fumes from cars, taxis and buses trailing along Piccadilly towards Eros. Besides not liking the journalist's questions, he wanted thinking time before the Jupiter meeting. He saw a Caffè Nero and popped in.

Using an anonymous offshore company, his paymasters had hired a hotel suite in the nearby Cavendish. Not that they would be there. It would be just the two of them, sorting the fix, the money, the pay-off arrangements.

As he stood in line for a latte, he was recognised and smilingly signed a page in a diary for another middle-aged woman who told him *she was his number-one fan.* He passed the time laughing and chatting to her until his drink was ready and then sat down alone in a corner, facing away from the room. There were times when it was good to be well-known and there were times when it was a pain in the butt. Right now, he wanted to gather his thoughts.

He pulled out the narrow slip of paper revealing his list, all in small, neat writing. After checking that he had every agenda item covered, he folded the note and tucked it away. With dreams of his biggest payday yet if Jupiter succeeded, it was easier to forget Mark and the funerals next week. Already, his paymasters had gifted him an apartment at The Palm in Dubai and a five-bed villa on the west coast of Barbados.

But was it worth a burned-out Mitsubishi with your mate and his family cremated inside?

Ostensibly, he rented the properties but hidden beneath a complex company and trust structure was evidence of his ownership worth several million. Besides the properties, there had been brown envelopes delivered to the usual place, sometimes brimming with sterling, sometimes with US dollars. Cash would somehow reach his London security-box. From there he would distribute pay-offs to Mark Rayner, the Essex guys, a groundsman or perhaps an umpire who had helped in the fix.

His thoughts turned to a cosy lunch with Mandy at the Bleeding Heart. Much as he loved his noisy twin boys, a quiet hour or two with his wife was a rare treat in his packed diary. And just maybe, after a good lunch, they might slip back to the suite at the Cavendish for a couple of hours. *Two secret assignations in a day?* The thought was pleasing as he drained his latte.

-8-

London

At much the same time as Westdale was supping his latte, Todd "Ratso" Holtom was striding out along Park Road towards Lord's Cricket Ground. There was a rare smile on his face following a conversation a few moments before. He had been passing the Sherlock Holmes Museum at 221b Baker Street, the beat of Guns 'N Roses thumping in his head-phones when an American tourist had stopped him. "Did the great detective die in there?"

Ratso did not have the heart to tell the guy that Sherlock had never even been born let alone die there. "I'm not sure. You'd better ask inside." He assumed the chat was over but the man in his tartan jacket and yellow trainers was peering at him intently.

"Say, are you, yes you are, Al Pacino? I saw you in *Sea of Love*. Terrific movie."

The comparison floored Ratso for a moment and he wondered whether the tourist needed new spectacles. "I'm flattered. When did he make that?"

"Maybe 1990, I guess."

"It's not me, pal! I'm a Brit. Al Pacino is from New York and about thirty-five years older." He raised his hand to about shoulder level. "And I reckon he's six inches shorter. Unless he's shrunk carrying all those dollars he earns."

The man blinked behind his black-framed spectacles before high-fiving. "Yeah. Maybe that explains it. His height, I mean."

"Same with Tom Cruise and Sly Stallone," Ratso added deadpan serious.

The man looked at him again. "Carrying all that dough, eh? Awesome!" He gave a near military salute and turned into the store.

Ratso switched tracks and hummed along to Queen as he anticipated his first meeting at the ECB – the HQ of the England & Wales Cricket Board. Not only was the agenda intriguing but ten years previously, he had enjoyed working under Carter. Now they would be meeting as equals.

For Ratso, any visit to Lord's was a privilege. Bitter-sweet memories flooded back, even though today the great stadium was silent. The long history and sight of the mix of old and new stands, always made his blood pump faster. Even as a kid, cricket had never been far from his mind. In days now gone, he and his wheelchair-bound father had been regulars at the big matches.

He could feel his heart beating faster. An air of heightened expectation showed in his stride, in the set of his jaw and the rapid arm-swinging. Today he would start bringing down the bastards who corrupted the players, cheated the spectators and enriched the gangsters … who lurked? He was not sure *where* the Mr Bigs lurked. Craig Carter would know.

He was admitted via the famous Grace Gates wondering how many times he had pushed the wheelchair through the entrance. He sighed as he looked over to the area by the pavilion where he had always wheeled his father to watch. Never again, not with the old man now passed away.

Though casually dressed in a pale green shirt under a denim jacket, he felt hot and clammy from the thundery clouds that hung low overhead. He removed his jacket and felt better for it. In the ECB's reception area he gazed at the pictures as he awaited the appearance of his former boss. "As ever. Right on time, Todd."

Carter appeared from round a corner. "Tea? Coffee? Too early for anything stronger. Come on in."

Ratso accepted the offer of coffee and followed the well-built figure into a meeting-room designed for many more than the two of them. "I've been looking forward to this."

Carter sat down beside him. "Couldn't agree more. It's been too long. Me? I've been chasing too many shadows. I need a breakthrough."

"You mean," Ratso paused, "we have one?"

Carter shook his head. "I thought you had something for me." He enjoyed the blank look on Ratso's face for a moment. "Just kidding! But there's something we might get our teeth into. Besides these biccies." He grinned as he pushed over a plate and Ratso selected a chocolate digestive. Six hours before, breakfast had been a hurried bowl of cereal topped with semi-skimmed beyond its sell-by date.

"Hey," grinned Carter, "how about this joke I heard over in the Long Room last night? So the village team's best batsman was on the phone to his captain, explaining why he couldn't play the next day. "No, I can't let you off the game," the captain retorted. "If I did, then I would have to do that for any other player whose wife dies.'"

Ratso had heard it before but still laughed. "It's like ex-Liverpool manager Bill Shankly's opinion that a football result was more important than life or death. For many fans, he was right. Life begins and ends with the next big match."

"We don't need cheating bastards throwing away their wicket or umpires taking bribes for outrageous decisions." Carter frowned. "But y'know, some young players who get hooked, they deserve sympathy. Others, the ringleaders – hell, I want to crush them." He took another biscuit.

"Mark Rayner?" Ratso looked at his former boss. "What do you know?"

Craig Carter stood up and patrolled a circuit of the table. Old habits die hard, Ratso thought as he remembered the trait from years back. "I don't buy all that stuff that one lone nutter hammered the babe."

"Or that some jealous woman attacked them." Ratso put down his cup looking appreciative. "Better than the coffee in Cobalt Square. I must come here more often. Anyway, I've spoken to DS Trasker. She's no fool. She's banking on me ... well on us. She can't even hint at match-fixing because of lack of evidence. The media would have a feeding frenzy."

"I'll drink to that." Carter pushed his half-glasses up his bulbous nose. "Bloody journalists are always sniffing round about fixing. Speculating. Bad for the game. Report facts, not hunches."

"You've no hard facts. Right?"

Carter sat down in a different chair, hands clasped behind his head. At fifty-three, his tired eyes and reddish face were pointers to long hours and the hard living of a former senior detective. "The players have a confidential hotline to report approaches or to whistleblow. But hammer and acid attacks on a player's family are not helpful."

Ratso fought against accepting a second biscuit. "When the Assistant Commissioner appointed me, Mark Rayner was to be my starting-point."

"He left no message? Confession?" Carter munched his third digestive.

"Not that we know. Trasker reckons Yvonne was a sweet young woman but with more beauty than brains. Not an enquiring mind. She simply expected their high-living lifestyle. She had a point." Ratso ran both hands over his Caesar-style wavy hair.

"You don't sound convinced." Carter swept some crumbs off the table, which smelled of lavender polish.

"I'm not. He had a Porsche Turbo and a new 4x4. Okay, he captained Surrey Patriots but we'll be checking out his finances."

Carter spread out his arms in an expansive gesture. "Even before the attack, I didn't trust him. No evidence though. He made some unusual captaincy decisions but nothing that would stick with a jury. If he *was* bent, then he was cunning too. He joined our watch-list after a very curious game between Surrey Patriots and Somerset Hawks. If you want to fix a match, the best guy to nobble is the captain. Better still, both captains."

"Or a groundsman. Or an umpire." Ratso poured more coffee for himself.

Carter nodded. "There were no signs of a doctored pitch. The Patriots were strong favourites to win. They had the best batting line-up in the twenty-over games this season. But their batsmen played like demented trout – all out for 47 chasing 189 for 6."

"No ludicrous umpiring decisions?"

Carter shook his head. "There were three gifted catches on the square-leg boundary and two ridiculous run-outs. It was laughable stuff. On a seaming wicket, it was ideal for a bowler like you – yet Rayner opened with a spin bowler who never turned even one." Carter leaned forward and tapped a slim folder. "In here, it's betting data mainly" he opened the file. "Here's another odd one. Just a week before the babe got hammered and Yvonne blinded, the bookies reported too much money backing Mark Rayner's lot to lose. That info came from the big bookies and from our contacts watching the black industry operating in Dubai."

"And?"

"Mark's team romped home – as they should have done against weak opposition."

Ratso flicked open the first page of the file and saw a photo of Rayner in his England shirt. "So you think …?"

"Could be. Mark Rayner didn't deliver and his family paid the price." Carter leaned back, hands clasped behind his head. "Remember a Pakistani player called Haider?"

After a slight pause Ratso nodded. "Didn't he quit while touring here?"

Carter pointed to a picture of the young man. "Scared as hell, he was. Death threats to him and his family." He tapped the table top in a rapid rhythm. "A single match between India and Pakistan attracts over 500 million US dollars in bets."

Ratso's hooded eyes showed his shock. "Worth fixing a result for just some of that."

"An Indian player claimed he was paid over one million dollars for his part in a fix." Carter's head swayed as if weighing up his thoughts. "If Mark Rayner welshed on a fix that would cost the bookies and gangsters a ton of money. Revenge is an obvious reaction."

"So, Some bastard taught Rayner a lesson." Ratso scribbled more notes. "Ideas? You must …" Ratso's sentence died as the entire room shook. A picture of an England cricket squad tumbled from the wall. The windows rattled as if in a Storm Force 10.

"Christ! What was *that*?" Carter checked his watch, a habit he had never lost. It was 12 noon precisely.

-9-

London

Lee Westdale closed the door after his guest departed leaving him alone in the suite. Immediately, he left coded Voicemail messages on two Pay-as-you-Go numbers that would never be used again. "All boxes ticked," he murmured after exhaling a long ye-e-es.

He tucked his flimsy note behind the protective cover of his Samsung Galaxy before flopping back onto a comfy grey chair. He stretched out his long legs, kicked off his loafers and called Room Service, the picture of relaxation. It had been eight years since he had led out the England team in his final Test match but he had kept his figure trim through a ruthless keep-fit regime. Usually, a drink at this time was off-limits but what the heck! He deserved a celebration. Moments later, Room Service delivered his double gin-and-tonic and a bowl of Pringles.

Jupiter was go!

He took the first icy sip, his smile wolfish as he anticipated his three-million pay-off. He was in good time to meet Mandy and for twenty minutes, he day-dreamed of taking her and the twins somewhere special like Necker Island in the Caribbean.

When it was time to go, and hoping to return later, he gave the suite a final look as he stood beside the door. For a moment, he imagined Mandy sprawled across the bed, beckoning him with a crooked finger. *Yes, there much to look forward to.* Once outside in Jermyn Street, he felt stifled by the humidity. Even in his light-weight suit, the near steamy air reminded him of Orchard Road, Singapore. This was London at its summer worst. Overhead, an angry purple tinged the scudding clouds. He knew the signs and reckoned there would be thunderous rain before too long.

In these conditions, no way was he going to walk to the restaurant – far too sticky with sweat already trickling down his cheeks. For a moment, he stood on the corner of Duke Street beside Fortnum & Masons and debated whether to take a taxi. The traffic heading east looked almost gridlocked, an endless line of red buses, cars and taxis. Reluctantly, because he hated the Tube, he decided the stinking heat down there would be the quicker option.

He could feel beads of sweat now trickling down his back. In a swift but elegant move, he removed his jacket and draped it over his shoulder as he wondered whether to pop into Fortnum's and buy a colourful silken scarf for Mandy. No! Much better to buy it together later. He turned away, not hurrying but avoiding eye-contact with the throng of other pedestrians who might want selfies with him. He headed for Green Park Tube, his thoughts now on a romantic lunch … and that crooked finger inviting the come-on.

-10-

London

The ground had barely stopped shaking as Ratso and Craig Carter raced outside. People were appearing from offices around the Nursery End, exchanging worried looks and staring for signs of what had happened. Standing well clear of any building, Carter checked with Lord's Security who confirmed that there was no known problem on the premises.

The pigeons that normally waddled around the green turf were flying in random circles, swooping and soaring after the huge shock-wave had disturbed their normal routines. Ratso meanwhile had his phone pinned to his ear. Carter beckoned him with a waved arm. "Come on. Top of the Mound Stand. There's a great view from there."

Ignoring the clammy air but both jacket-less, they took the elevator to the top tier where on match days, the debenture holders enjoyed a prime view. Normally, Ratso would have gazed lovingly down at the immaculate and gently sloping playing-area. His quick glance showed just a couple of ground-staff scurrying across the outfield, both gazing skywards.

In the other direction, looking south beyond three towering cranes and an array of drab buildings, the skyline normally took in a distant view of the top of Big Ben and the London Eye. But today they were invisible behind a spreading pall of thick black smoke that was now billowing into the thundery sky.

Ratso pointed towards the West End as he clasped his phone to his ear, waiting for news. "See – beneath where the smoke is coming from! My God! That fiery red – flames everywhere. London's burning." Suddenly and eerily came the first distant wails of siren after siren. "Pity the First Responders," muttered Ratso. "This is not going to be pretty."

"Will you stay? I'd booked lunch in the Tavern pub."

Ratso waved Carter a silent no as he listened intently, his eyes showing concern. The last time London had been attacked, on 7th July 2005, Ratso had also been on duty. He had been sent to Tavistock Square where a double-decker bus had been blown up, one of several bombs detonated that morning. Now, as a veteran of 2005, and having spent two years in Security Command, he knew he could expect to be front-line. "I've been called back to base. Immediate reports are that something exploded in the West End. Buses are on fire and there are blazing buildings on both sides of Piccadilly. Multiple casualties are expected."

-11-

London

M andy Westdale looked at her watch and called Lee's number for the umpteenth time since arriving at the Bleeding Heart. She turned to the waiter, her usually friendly eyes now flashing irritation from her oval face. "My husband's obviously running late. Not for the first time. I'd better have a drink." She tossed her chestnut brown hair. Everything about her oozed panache – matching her eye-candy image that ensured that she was singled out by the paparazzi at A-List functions.

"Of course, madam – but it's chaotic around the West End. There was a bomb. Public transport is shut down. Where is he coming from?"

Mandy thought for a moment. "A bomb? I never heard it." She tapped the side of her delicate pink cheek. "I must have been deep down on the Tube when it went off. These bloody extremists!" She pursed her lips in thought but then shrugged. "Where's he coming from? It sounds silly but I have no idea. He goes all over the place – meetings everywhere." She laughed dismissively, showing her expensively whitened teeth in a generous mouth. "I can't keep up with him."

"I'm sure he's fine. In the meantime, what can I get you?"

"A vodka-tonic would be very welcome. Make it a large one. Thanks."

Until the twins had been born nearly three years previously,

Mandy had worked for American stock and commodity analysts at Canada Water in Docklands. As a high-flyer, she had been reluctant to stop work, especially as she and Lee were still getting through the fiasco of Parabolic.

Mandy's creamy pink features, so beautiful in repose, hardened as she relived the recollection, her gentle eyes showing her bitterness. Still riled all these years later, she gazed at the menu without even seeing it. The worst thing had been Lee making the investment just days before the wedding – but without telling her,

I'd have seen through the fraud in a nano-second.

"Your brain's in your cricket bat," she had shouted when he confessed what he had done. "Never ever take decisions affecting my future without my agreement." She looked round for the waiter and her drink, her sharp movements revealing her tormented emotions. There had been weeks of sulky silence.

The rift between Lee and her parents had never been repaired. Again, she tossed her head as she relived the humiliation of the financial chaos with bounced cheques, their heavily mortgaged home being sold and the keys to the Ferrari handed back. Only the return of the waiter broke her unpleasant memories. A few sips of the icy Absolut soothed her. She had to credit Lee. By working his arse off, he had turned things around remarkably. After returning from meeting the attorneys in New York, he had been almost euphoric – seemingly hopeful of winning what he had called megabucks in compensation.

But it had yet to happen.

She checked the time on her phone. Now he was very late – even by his standards. An unpleasant tightness gripped her stomach. She called his number again but there was no response. Normally he turned on a voice message rather than be interrupted at meetings. Now it was simply ringing unanswered. Her fingers fumbling on the keys, she clicked on the Sky News app and trawled through sketchy reports about a bomb-blast "with casualties."

He was an hour late now.

Moments later, a reporter appeared on screen with a backdrop of flames and black smoke. "Unconfirmed reports are that a coach proceeding east along Piccadilly exploded beside buses waiting at traffic-lights. Londoners are asked to be on high alert as the capital is being checked for further devices. So far, it is understood there was no warning and no group has claimed responsibility. The Commissioner of the Metropolitan Police is due to give a statement at 4pm and the Prime Minister will speak from Downing Street at 6pm. For the moment, no public transport is operating and all mainline railway stations will remain closed until they have been declared safe. All public buildings are in lock-down."

Yes, that's it.

Lee's stuck somewhere underground on a Tube.

"Would you like to order something?" The waiter ended her train of thought. Typically, Mandy would have relished the Dorset Crab followed by rib of beef but now she was not hungry. As the waiter hovered politely, it was as if someone had grasped her throat so that she could not breathe and her chest started to heave. "Just … sparkling water … for now, thank you." She struggled to get out the words and was relieved to be alone, telling herself to be calm while she sipped the remains of her vodka.

Don't panic.

Not your style.

Lee's going to be just fine.

Moments later her phone rang. Excitedly, she grabbed it.

$-12-$

Las Vegas

Five thousand miles away in Las Vegas, Enzo Pagano was in high spirits. He had been gambling all night in the giant darkened sports-betting arena at Caesar's Palace. With a tumbler of Jack Daniels on ice beside him, and comfortably seated in his well-padded brown chair, he had been whiling away the night with fun bets while watching the action on the array of big screens. Just ten minutes before had been the call he had waited up for.

"Vijay here." Chetri was speaking from his luxury mansion in Enfield, North London. "Our guy had a great meeting. Jupiter is go. No, nothing else for us or him to do."

Pagano coughed throatily through his cigar smoke. "Okay but wait one! Alex is bugging me. The guy's a wuss, all girlie about Rayner driving over the cliff." He took a deep draw on the cigar. "Fix a meet. The Beverly Hills Hotel. We'll get him out." He chuckled. "That way, you and me, we share fifty-fifty on Jupiter. No three-way split."

"Alex won't take that lying down. I just spoke to him."

"I don't give a flying fuck. Look Vijay – you and me, we can fund this and Alex don't get nothing back from what he put in neither. A deal is a deal. We don't need all this shit. Your guy set up the whole Jupiter thing. Now he's clinched it. And Alex? What's he ever brought to the party? I'll tell you. Apart from whingeing and griping, a big fat fucking zero."

Vijay peered out of the window at the stormy rain now beating down, the water bouncing off the statues on the huge expanse of his lawn. From the direction of central London came a rumble of distant thunder. "Alex is a decent guy but he'd be a bad enemy."

"Huh! Alex don't scare me none. We send him to outsville. He loses his investment. We fund the rest. Period."

Chetri was unconvinced but was in no mood to argue. "You heard there was a bomb over here? Two hours ago?"

Pagano checked the time. "It's just turned six a.m. here. No. I ain't been watching TV. Better things to be doing, buddy. Ciao."

He ordered a treble Jack Daniels and puffed contentedly. Alex would soon be gone. Jupiter would deliver maybe two-hundred million while in the penthouse suite, Helga, the busty brunette he had left asleep, would be ready for more action. He scuffed his feet on the thick carpet in anticipation.

Boy! Did she know some tricks!

The day had started well and was going to get better.

-13-

London

M andy swirled her sparkling water, the ice tinkling in the glass as she grabbed the phone. Her face fell when she found it was Nena, their Austrian nanny calling to check if she was okay. "I'm fine but Lee is not answering his phone. Did he tell you where he was going to be?" She listened to the negative response. "I'm not surprised. If he rings, let me know. Oh – and take the twins to the park but keep away from busy areas. Public transport is on lockdown. Looks like I'll be back late. Give the boys a hug from me." There was a catch in her voice as she spoke, already imagining telling the children that Daddy is not coming home.

Ever.

By 2-15pm, she could sit still no longer. Doing nothing was not an option. Where to go? What to do? Call the police? The hospitals? Which one? There were at least three-hundred dead and countless more casualties. Survivors spoke of glass showering down from buildings, even 400 metres away. Maybe Lee had been injured. Maybe he had just lost his phone in the blast.

Walking to Piccadilly would take about forty minutes. She set off, teeth clenched, eyes unblinking, desperate to quash her hot flushes of panic. As she passed Litchfield Street, she spotted Le Beaujolais, another favourite haunt. As memories of laughter and shared intimacies in the restaurant-club downstairs hit home, her first tears flowed, turning to uncontrolled sobs. After drying her eyes, she impulsively entered a corner-shop and bought cigarettes and a lighter – her first smoke since she had been twenty-five, seven years ago. Then, as the first heavy drops of rain started to spatter the street, she took shelter in the doorway of a derelict store and lit up, feeling both guilty and light-headed at the same time.

After stubbing out the butt, she headed for a hotel on Leicester Square, not too far from the blast. All the while, as she scurried against the flow of pedestrians, she kept her head lowered, avoiding eye contact, her umbrella held low. Every stride made her increasingly aware of the smell of burning – maybe timber, cars, buses, God knows what. The pungent aroma seemed to fill her lungs as her high heels splashed through the filthy streets bringing her closer to Piccadilly.

And perhaps to Lee.

As the rain eased, she stood outside the hotel looking at the damage to the famous square. Several hundred metres away, the angry sky was fiery red beneath the drifting pall of thick smoke and drifting ash and debris carried on the swirling wind. She could hear the roar of flames mixed with the constant wail of sirens and shouted commands or instructions. As she looked towards Piccadilly, she watched charred paper, burning debris and blackened timber falling around the Swiss Glockenspiel.

She glanced at her soaked red shoes now ruined by the ash and filthy puddles. Her surroundings were like a TV shot of a war zone in *someone else's* country. Plate-glass windows had been shattered. Discarded shopping-bags, newspapers and fast-food wrappers lay amidst huge shards of glass. Here and there, she saw pools of blood where pedestrians had been struck by falling debris. The few pedestrians now remaining seemed to be heading towards the stations at Charing Cross and Waterloo where she guessed they would have a long wait.

In Piccadilly, there must be hundreds just injured.

Not dead but needing treatment.

Lee would be a survivor.

She entered the five-star hotel and joined a small crowd grouped round a TV screen in the bar. Armed with a single malt whisky, Mandy grabbed a seat and waited impatiently for the News Conference. On impulse, she speed-dialled Ricky Mather, a journalist friend of Lee's. Though he covered sports, Ricky fed the call through to a colleague on the News Desk at the Radio Station and he promised to broadcast that Lee was currently among those missing.

Right on time, the Commissioner appeared looking grave. "It is too soon to speculate on total casualties except that the death toll is likely to be exceptionally high due to collapsed buildings on both sides of Piccadilly." As to who bore responsibility, he confirmed nobody had yet come forward. "The massive explosion suggests this was a well-planned attack designed to cause maximum death and destruction." By the time he had taken a few questions, he had added little to Mandy's knowledge except confirming that at least four office blocks had collapsed onto ground-floor cafés and stores. Other countries were sending in blood supplies, emergency workers and sniffer dogs. Then at last he gave out the Emergency Number which Mandy tapped straight into her phone, her fingers shaking.

Having no wish to join in the chitchat that was now breaking out around her, Mandy went outside and immediately lit up, drawing the smoke deep down inside her and exhaling noisily. The storm had eased the humidity but the stench and noise of London burning still drifted across the square. Eagerly, she called the emergency number and after holding on impatiently, her call was answered.

"Ah, yes. Thank you. Is there any news of Lee Rupert Westdale?"

"Please hold on while I check."

-14-

London

"Go straight to Green Park." The message a few minutes before had stopped Ratso on his long hike back to Vauxhall. Whatever lay ahead he reckoned a full stomach would help. He stopped to pick up a toastie from a busy caff by Baker Street tube station.

Before he had finished the hot and dripping cheese and ham, he got another call from his new boss, Det. Chief Superintendent Mick Tolvey. He and Tolvey had already forged a good bond, unlike the contempt he still felt for Arthur Tennant, his former boss down in Clapham. "Todd, I've just see the first pictures. This is ten-times worse than 2005. Meet me by the Ambassador Hotel. Two minutes from Green Park Tube."

Ratso's memory flashed back to the Tavistock Square bus-bombing where the roof of the number 30 had been blown open, killing thirteen and injuring too many others. "Give me fifteen minutes, boss."

"And Todd, I suggest you don't eat anything."

As he picked his way over the thick carpet of broken glass in Berkeley Street, his ears were filled with the mounting noise as acrid smoke and falling dust swirled around him. He dodged between abandoned vehicles, many of them smashed by falling masonry. The fashionable street, usually so busy, was now almost deserted, the office buildings empty.

As he reached the Holiday Inn, a brilliant flash of lightning ripped through the black smoke ahead of him. Almost instantly, a fierce crack of thunder directly overhead brought the rain belting down. In seconds, Ratso was soaked, the rain dripping off his dark brown hair and running down his cheeks. *At least the fire service will welcome this divine intervention.* Pools of blood that had stained the pavement were soon being washed away by the rain that bounced from the debris to form streams running along the gutters.

Despite Tolvey's warning, until Ratso reached Piccadilly and saw the carnage, he had reckoned he was ready for pretty much anything. But not this. The famous street was in ruins with fine old buildings collapsed on both sides and fires raging everywhere. Hot dust seemed to fill his nostrils and clamp his throat. He held a spotted blue hankie against his nose and mouth, trying to stifle the stench of toxic fumes and worse. For several seconds, he stood unable to absorb the scale of the devastation.

He took in the fire crews hauling hoses or sending jets of water over the burning rubble as stinking smoke rose from the remains of unrecognisable vehicles or from burning buildings. The cloudburst added to the filth beneath his feet, his shoes, designed for heavy-duty walking, already fit only for the trash-bin. Every step was rewarded by squelching or crunching. Everywhere were flashing blue lights and people shouting. A couple of paramedics hurried past, carrying a man on a gurney who was struggling to breathe. Fire trucks manoeuvred beside and between ambulance crews who were listening for cries for help against the relentless roar from the flames that in places soared thirty metres high and more. Other emergency personnel sloshed their way across the sodden mounds of concrete, twisted metal and office furniture, most of it smashed or crushed beyond recognition. Rescuers in yellow jackets and paramedics in their green tunics were shifting debris in a desperate search for survivors concealed beneath small and giant chunks of concrete and the bricks of old London.

Gaping spaces had destroyed the ornate skyline of properties that had stood for generations. There were new and different smells now – ones that had haunted him since 2005. Waves of nausea swept through him. Besides the lingering smell of explosives, he could detect gas, diesel fuel, burned-out rubber, flaming timber and a smell like a summer barbecue. But this was not chicken and burgers. This was the smell from blackened remains of the poor sods that had been closest to the seat of the explosion or burned beyond recognition as their offices had crashed down into the fiery furnace. He recognised with distaste the distinctive smell of burning hair, mixing with the almost fog-like dust and ash that cast a shroud between the remains of the once proud buildings.

To his left towards Eros and Leicester Square, the burned-out remains of at least three London buses were close to what seemed to be an enormous crater. The magnificent front of the Ambassador Hotel, just across the road, no longer displayed its enduring image of permanence. Curtains flapped like shrouds behind glass-less windows.

The line of flags that usually fluttered above the ground floor entrance had been ripped to shreds or burned. Though the historic building was still standing, the ageing stonework was now scarred and gouged where flying metal had ripped into it. Beside him, Ratso saw nails and bolts that had been packed around the explosives – *shipyard confetti* as it was known to bomb experts. Each one had been used to cause maximum carnage.

Across the street and dimly through the haze, he saw Tolvey standing by the remains of the hotel entrance. Steeling himself for what lay ahead, Ratso clambered between several crushed and burned-out cars. Office desks, melted printers, an espresso machine and reinforced concrete pillars surrounded him, reminiscent of scenes after the collapse of New York's Twin Towers.

As he neared Mick Tolvey who waved him onward, his foot kicked something heavy and on looking down, he realised he had just hoofed the head of a young woman, her eyes staring into a future she no longer had, her once black hair, singed and flecked with concrete dust. Of the rest of her body, there was no sign. Ratso swallowed hard. Just over an hour before, this had been someone's wife, friend or daughter going about her daily life, full of hope and expectation.

"God knows what it's like closer to where the coach exploded," said Tolvey over the wail of sirens and the distant but muted screams from injured persons still trapped beneath a building on the south side beside the remains of some traffic-lights.

"So what's our role?"

"There are people dying under the rubble we could save. We need to get stuck in." Tolvey pointed to what had once been five floors of offices above a store selling mobile-phones. "We're to start there." Some of the building's fascia had crashed into the middle of the wide street but mostly it had simply crumpled, each floor crushing the ones beneath.

And everyone within.

Ratso swallowed hard and put on a yellow jacket and heavy duty gloves that Tolvey handed to him.

-15-

Wimbledon

Exhausted, her make-up blotchy from tears and eye-wiping, Mandy got onto a packed train at Waterloo just after 9-15p.m. She was beyond caring about her appearance. She stood, eyes lowered, swaying with the motion of passengers crammed around her. There was more chat between strangers than usual. Everyone had a story, an opinion or speculation about what they had picked up from TV, Twitter and Facebook.

She wanted to shout out that her husband Lee Westdale, the famous cricketer and TV personality, was missing but instead she locked herself away, staring at the floor, listening to Andre Rieu through her headphones. It was a relief to tumble out onto the platform at Wimbledon, the evening air now chilly after the stormy cloudbursts of the afternoon.

It was just a short walk to their rented four-bedroom home. On arrival, Mandy called *hi* to Nena but went straight to the boys' bedroom. Biting her lips to fight meltdown, she stood for several minutes, watching them sleep peacefully, so innocent of the cruelty of the world into which they had been born. After changing into a pink slopping-about onesie, she headed for the kitchen where Nena's face asked the question.

Mandy sat down at the black marble-topped counter and accepted the offer of coffee. "Nothing."

Instinctively, Nena came across and gave her a hug, the first time ever. Mandy turned and lifted her head to smile weakly. "The TV reporter said that Lee was among the missing – but there's plenty of others – big name actors, that Irish rock singer and a couple of famous jockeys who were going to a charity event."

"Goes with the Mayfair area, I guess." Mandy's normally expressive face and vibrant voice were devoid of emotion. She rose and paced round the room, desperate for action yet helpless to do anything. Phoning the emergency hotline again was not an option.

As Mandy circled the counter-top, Nena stretched out and clasped her hand. "But there's still hope. He's not confirmed dead."

Mandy winced at the word but then nodded. "As they say in sporting interviews, I'll take the positives." She went to the wine rack and poured them both a glass of Chateauneuf du Pape while Nena set out a plate of French cheese and pickles. After 10-30pm, with Lee's picture on the news, she started receiving text messages and calls from friends. Her parents also called having just awoken to the story during their trip to New Zealand.

The bottle had long been drained when at shortly after one a.m. Nena took a call. "It's from St Thomas' Hospital, Westminster." Immediately, Mandy grabbed the phone, hungry for news. She listened in silence.

"I'll come at once."

–16–

Enfield, North London

In Boca Raton and Las Vegas, Alex Anderson and Enzo Pagano each joined in the Skype call from Vijay Chetri at 11pm London time. "This was on the TV, Vijay?"

"Correct. His meeting was very close to the bombing. But look, my guy being killed is no big deal. Everything was in place." The Indian tapped his hand-made leather shoe on the thick pile of his Oriental carpet. "We got lucky. After his meeting this morning, he was dispensable."

Alex was sitting in a golf-buggy beside the 17th green at the Boca Raton Resort & Club. The sun would soon be setting and he was anxious to finish his round. "You wanted to meet, Enzo. Get the air cleared, right?"

Pagano coughed throatily as he listened from his bubbling Jacuzzi on top of Caesar's Palace. "Hey. Now your guy's gone, we ain't got no need to cut him in. More for us."

"Nice one, Enzo." Vijay laughed, in a fawning and silly tee-hee way.

Anderson's jaw tightened in irritation. "This is Lee Westdale you're talking about – the guy who brought Jupiter to Vijay. We owe him. Is there a widow? Kids?" He spat out the words in mix of exasperation and anger. "Christ. He's not even confirmed as dead and you're dancing on his grave. You're a pair of shits.! This meeting you want. Where? When?" He took a swig from a chilled can of

Newcastle Brown Ale to combat the humidity that surrounded the buggy. "Let's meet in London."

"Fuck fucking London. I ain't coming to London." Pagano grinned at Helga who caressed the nape of his neck. "The Beverly Hills Hotel. Vijay – fix a bungalow. Next Tuesday morning."

-17-

London

As Mandy's Uber dropped her close to the modern buildings, she had no interest in the rich history or traditions of St Thomas' Hospital. All she wanted was to reach Lee. She turned left at the main entrance and ran around the exterior until she reached the A & E entrance on the south side.

Reach Lee?

Easier said than done.

A noisy throng was jammed outside a reception area not designed for a disaster on this scale. Almost lost in the babble of raised voices, from across the Thames came the deep and resonant tone of Big Ben chiming two. The panic surrounding her was infectious. Every second counted to reach him but her route to the admissions-desk was blocked by a mob of anxious relatives and friends.

Never had she seen a hospital's surrounds so packed with frightened, angry or frustrated people – all pushing and shoving on the concrete walkway outside the A & E entrance. A turbaned group standing in a huddle seemed close to hysteria, arms waving as they consoled each other in some foreign tongue.

Mandy joined them, pushing and jostling her route through the bottleneck into the building, squeezing and weaving in her race to reach Lee. At last, breathless, she was inside where she edged towards the team seated behind the counter doing their best to cope. The usual calm and smooth-running machine was close to meltdown.

As she fought to be patient awaiting her turn, she took in the hospital smells of disinfectant and air freshener but they were fighting a losing battle against the stale sweat from dozens of hot, emotional and nerve-racked bodies. To the right of the counter, another seating area was standing-room only, filled by with those summoned to the hospital and waiting for news.

Suddenly, she was there, quicker than she had feared though it seemed much longer. "Lee Westdale. He was admitted at 6-30pm." She held her breath, waiting for the dreaded words that she was too late.

"Follow the signs for Urgent Care and then head into the Admissions Ward."

Her spirits rose as she forced herself not to run along the corridor, its air smelling faintly of Alpine pine-forests. Everywhere in the white-walled corridor there was movement. Gurneys were being pushed back and forward; exhausted looking nursing staff, porters and paramedics in their aubergine or green scrubs hurried about their duties with no pretence of dignity. It was unprecedented to have hundreds dead and thousands injured, many critically and all from a single event.

At the Nurses' Station in the Urgent Care ward, she joined a line of three other people seeking to visit their loved ones, their faces taut and shoulders drooping. "Lee Westdale," she said to the Malaysian nurse when her turn came.

"Oh no! Not *the* Lee Westdale?" The elderly gentleman behind her spoke gently.

"Terrorists don't pick and choose, do they," Mandy responded with a nod, hoping to sound more gracious than she felt.

"I hope he pulls through."

The young nurse led Mandy into a ward that was a flurry of activity and then into a side-room. As she entered, a short doctor aged perhaps sixty with a round and rather jowly face was just leaving, his eyes and furrowed brow showing he was deep in thought. His grey wavy hair seemed to add to the impression that here was a man who preferred to see the glass as half-full rather than half-empty. "Dr Premadasa, this is Mrs Mandy Westdale, come to see her husband."

"Mrs Westdale, hello, I am Dr Ranil Premadasa." His voice was distinctly Asian sub-continent but his accent was crisply English, consistent with his degree from King's College and his medical training in London. In fact, he came from Kandy, high in the Sri Lankan hills. He said nothing more at once but simply clasped her arm and led her into the room.

He motioned the Asian paramedic, who had been dismantling a drip, to leave. After he had gone, Premadasa eased Mandy towards the chair by the bed but her eyes were transfixed by what she had seen already. Her husband's entire body was covered in a crisp white sheet. A smell of dust and rubble in the small room came from his torn and filthy clothes stacked on the bedside cabinet. "I'm sorry but I'm afraid we lost him. Barely five minutes ago. It was a losing cause right from admission. He had lost so much blood. He was very weak and had ..."

"No, no. It can't be, Not Lee. Not gone. There must be a mistake. You're sure it is him?" Her voice was suddenly dry and husky.

Dr Premadasa moved towards the top of the bed and pulled back the sheet. Mandy saw at once that it was Lee, an eerie calmness on his pallid face as he lay on his back. Instinctively, she dived towards him to clutch his body which she found was still warm.

Dr Premadasa said nothing as he let her clutch Lee's body as if willing it back to life. All the while, she was sobbing and murmuring *no Lee, no, no, no.* Only after she twisted to peer back at the consultant did he speak. "I knew it was Lee as soon as I saw him.

I'm an MCC member at Lord's. I've watched him play many, many times. A fine captain and a great batsman. An interesting commentator too. But anyway there was ID in his rather damaged wallet."

Mandy pulled her tear-stained face further away from his body for a moment. "But he looks so ... so okay?" She looked at him accusingly. "Why did he die?"

"He was admitted with multiple injuries – a blow to the back of his head, probably struck by falling masonry. That's only my unskilled guess. That alone would not have led to this ... sad end." He paused to pick his words with care. "Your husband was conscious intermittently, even coherent but he had been struck by several pieces of shrapnel. Two large nails had penetrated his abdomen and thigh. He had lost so much blood."

"So he was ... er," she faltered, "close to this coach that exploded?"

Dr Premadasa shook his head and removed his glasses to polish them. "Those close never knew what hit them." He could have said more about bodies blown apart, smashed beyond recognition.

Her face hardened and her tone was sharp. "So why wasn't he found quicker? They could have saved him."

"He must have been some distance away when he was struck by the shrapnel. Had that been all, he might have been found before he had lost so much blood." He stroked his chin thoughtfully. "Just too much internal bleeding."

"So? You mean precisely what?" Mandy's bitterness showed through her sobs.

"The admission notes said he was found partly immersed under a collapsed building." He moved beside her and clutched her icy cold hand. When he continued, he again seemed to be cautious about every word. "I'd guess he was partly buried. He must have missed the worst of the falling rubble because, as I said, his head injury was not severe."

He watched as she gasped for air, her chest heaving beneath the pink onesie. He poured her a tumbler of water. "Don't blame the rescuers in Piccadilly. The scene there is too awful for television footage." His face turned hard and the dark brown eyes showed his strength of feeling. "Blame whoever hated our civilised society." That was his cue to release her hand and turn to the door. "I must move on to save others if I can."

Silence fell on the brightly lit but sparsely furnished room. She blew her nose on an already soaked hankie as she turned and nodded sheepishly. "Of course you're right," she sobbed "but it's hard to be fair when life is so … cruel." She stared at her husband's face. "You said he was coherent. Did he mention me?"

Dr Premadasa turned towards the wall for a moment and debated his answer. *Why make things worse for her?* "He said all kinds of things as his mind wandered but his final words were – *tell, Mandy I love her.*"

"And Jason and Justin? The twins."

Premadasa's inventiveness could not stretch that far. "Not by name, no." He paused thinking about the mix of incoherent and coherent. "Well, perhaps he did but I didn't catch it. After the emergency surgery, he was drifting in and out while I assessed his head injury."

"That … that means a lot." Once again she dabbed her eyes and blew her nose.

As he listened and watched her, Dr Premadasa looked anything but comfortable, his eyes restless behind the black-rimmed spectacles, his mind racing. "My dear, I'm so sorry. He was a giant of a player," he paused briefly and thought carefully before adding "and no doubt a loving husband and father. Now I have to go. There are others fighting for their lives."

"Of course, of course. I'm sorry. Very selfish of me." She leaned over the bed and kissed Lee on his mouth with the barest of touches before the surgeon pulled up the sheet. Then he steered her slowly out to the main corridor. "Can you get home?"

Mandy nodded. "I'll be fine." She was about to leave when she had another thought. "Can I see Lee again? I mean, not here?"

"Yes. Contact the hospital tomorrow. By arrangement, you can visit him alone in the mortuary."

"And his belongings?"

"Leave all that for now. So much paperwork and the staff are overwhelmed." His kind and soothing tones were persuasive and Mandy's slight nod of the head showed acceptance. "The Patient Affairs Officer will sort the death certificate and any other details."

Death Certificate!

Christ!

Me.

I'm a widow.

For a moment the word widow seemed to reverberate round her exhausted brain. "Thank you, doctor."

Looking troubled, the surgeon watched her hip-swaying departure along the busy corridor before he hurried back to his office. In there, and armed with a strong cup of tea, he needed to scribble some important notes before rushing to the next patient.

It was going to be a long night.

-18-

London

Twice during the past ten days, Craig Carter had phoned, sounding mysterious and wanting to meet but for Ratso, match-fixing had been off the agenda. Only now had the top brass agreed to him returning to normal duties. During those ten days, ISIS had claimed responsibility and the counter-terrorism team had announced that a hired coach had been crammed with explosives and shrapnel in a lock-up garage in Hounslow, West London.

Though Ratso had been enthused tracking down his old contacts to help destroy the ISIS cell, the relief in being away now from the hot-house intensity showed in his confident stride as he headed for Lord's. For August, there was a chilly breeze and Ratso walked briskly, lightweight tote-bag over his shoulder, swinging his arms to the beat of Eric Clapton. His pace was geared more to excitement about Carter's sly tone than the chill in the wind but he was still glad of his gunmetal-grey leather jacket.

Throughout the West End, he had glanced at shop windows with photos of missing persons, each one a personal tragedy for loved ones left behind. The death toll had now risen to over eight hundred and many more were barely clinging to life. But he knew that among these claiming to have lost someone were the lying bastards faking death to claim on life policies or to escape to another life. He had uncovered two fraudsters already. There would be many more just like after 9-11. Around him, he saw London going through the motions of stiff-upper-lip and business as usual but with rumours of more attacks to come, everyone was on high alert. He viewed fellow Tube passengers mumbling prayers or carrying bulky rucksacks with particular suspicion.

After Ratso had bounded up the steps into The Tavern, he found the mood sombre. Carter delivered none of his usual repertoire of old jokes to warm up the meeting. The daily news diet of funerals and horror stories of blinded or dismembered victims still cast a pall over everything. "I see they've named some persons of interest," Carter prompted as they settled at a discreet corner table.

Ratso nodded as he slung his bag to the floor. "A missing Pakistani is the hottest target. He's a bomb-maker from Luton but it's never that simple." He leaned back on the chair. "Fixing a bomb like this needed quite a team. Getting hold of so much shrapnel, fertiliser and other explosive materials." He nodded his head. "Big task. To say nothing of involving a top, top bomb-maker."

Carter was quick to agree. "One Pakistani could hardly buy a ton of heavy-duty nails in a hardware outlet." He sighed, his face flushed, the jaw-line sagging.

"It needed big money too." At the word money, Ratso noticed the sharpened intensity on Carter's face. "With so many household names killed or maimed, we forget all the ordinary folk who were wiped out that day."

Carter nodded in agreement. "Kevin Groom, the English rugby international and that entire Irish rock-band. Those names sell newspapers."

"Hard to blame the media," Ratso continued. "But everybody else became mere statistics. Celebs like that American tennis player Dick Hollinshead and Lee Westdale. They hogged the headlines."

Carter gave Ratso a curious glance and there was an overlong silence as if he was debating what to say, his eyes revealing that something important could follow. Even though nobody was in ear-shot, he leaned forward. "Match-fixing funds terrorism. No question. Some of the black-market mobsters in India and Pakistan have a terrorist agenda."

Stunned, Ratso peered over the creamy froth of his Guinness. "Go on…"

"These guys – you name it – smuggling, drug trafficking, extortion, contract killing, gun-running, terrorism, political corruption and of course murder and illegal betting. We've picked up some strong leads but with their billions, these bastards are above the law. Arrest them? No way. Their money talks. Or just one word of warning and they can scare officials shitless."

"And they fund ISIS?

"No direct evidence yet." Carter looked at the menu and summoned the waitress. He paused to order a mutton T-bone with a bottle of Rioja and Ratso went for the sirloin steak and salad. Then he continued. "Naturally, young cricketers who get corrupted don't get near these top guys or know who they are now involved with. But that's where the profits end up. They're at the bottom of a complex web that spins everywhere."

"Quite poetic, Craig." Ratso's eyes laughed for him. Then, for a second, Ratso relived the sight of the young woman's head, eyes staring and lifeless. He wondered who she was and what she had left behind. Ratso cupped his chin in his hands and tried to sound upbeat. "In the end, life goes on. Normality *will* return. For now, we must clean up cricket. You've opened up new avenues. I had no idea about terrorism." He ran his fingers across his Caesar-cut.

"Wait one, Todd," his face creased into a wide and warm grin. "That's not why I got you here."

"There's more?" Ratso's throaty London accent showed his enthusiasm.

"Of course. But never forget, it's not just cricket either. Most sports have been hit by betting scandals. Here and in the USA."

"Mark Rayner. That's where we reached last time. Give." Ratso looked round but nobody could hear their conversation.

"We will talk about Rayner. You'll have read those betting patterns I gave you last time." Carter looked across the table, a mischievous look on his face. "But even that's not why we're here."

"Go on then."

"New evidence. It's credible ... but incredible." He watched the crusty bread arrive. "But first, let's turn the clock back to 2000. Who'd have thought back then that Hanse Cronje was totally corrupt?"

"Yeah. South African captain. Ultra-Christian. A paragon of virtue – except he was a mega-cheat. Corrupting youngsters in his team."

"After the Cronje scandal broke, other big names from England, Australia and the West Indies emerged whether fairly or not."

"So who policed this back then?"

Carter shrugged, his sardonic smile saying it all. "There was nothing joined-up internationally." Carter drained his Rioja with obvious pleasure.

"After he was caught, Cronje was killed in a plane crash, wasn't he?"

"In 2002. That led to all types of conspiracy theories. Like he was going to name names and so was silenced to protect the big guys, y'know the usual shit."

"Sounded like bollocks to me," muttered Ratso sounding dismissive.

Carter doodled with a finger on the table before continuing. "Remember Bob Woolmer? Of course you do. Played for England but years later ended up dead in his hotel room in the West Indies.

Conspiracy theorists ran amok. That was 2007. By then, he was coach to the Pakistan team. The Jamaican police called it murder but the evidence of poisoning followed by strangulation was contradictory. His blood and urine *may* have contained cypermethrin. An anonymous tip-off named aconite poisoning."

"Your view?"

"It looked like a fix but show me the evidence. His Pakistan team had just lost to Ireland. This had been a huge chance to back the Ireland minnows at great odds to beat one of the best teams. There were suggestions that Bob was silenced when he got uppity about the players letting him down. Others alleged he was involved and pointed out, *nudge-nudge, wink-wink*, that he had been coach to South Africa when Cronje was captain."

"So? Inconclusive evidence."

Carter nodded. "Not a shred. Just rumours, rumours. Nothing to hang your hat on. Maybe the Pakistan players just had a bad day at the office. Maybe poor old Bob just collapsed and died. The jury returned an open verdict."

Ratso's eyes closed as he weighed up the implications. "But the *jury* didn't buy natural causes." Ratso fell silent. "You're saying Woolmer and Cronje might have been murdered – but there's no evidence."

"There have been other murders linked to cricket but insufficient evidence."

Ratso raised his eyes and realised that Carter had been watching with an amused look on his face. "Call me naïve but until Rayner, I had an open mind about threats – let alone murders involving fixing. Your take?"

"How's the steak?" enquired Carter and on seeing Ratso's contented smile, continued. "The guys who sucker in the players are middle-men and in it for the money. These are smooth operators and not likely to be murderers. These middle-men report to the real fixers who hook into the illegal bookies operating from India and Dubai. These puppet-masters," he paused for effect, "are utterly ruthless. They give the orders."

Carter leaned forward, steepling his fingers. "Look – billions are staked in a year. This isn't about Ranji in Chennai betting his few rupees on India to lose. This is about *millions* of Ranjis whose illegal bets are channelled through a layering system of unlawful bookies. The gangsters at the top either keep the risk or lay it off into lawful markets. Multi-millions are bet on a single match or on scores at different stages of longer matches."

Ratso's watchful eyes widened. "And these gangster bookies, they want inside information from the players? Want to fix odds knowing the result?"

Carter nodded. "The middlemen mix with the players. They might chat *by chance* in a bar, get friendly and buy drinks. As the relationship develops, it might be dinner. Sometimes there is entrapment with pretty women. Bollywood movie stars have been involved. Whatever, the middlemen slowly sucker in the players. At first, they want pretty basic stuff – weather conditions for the match, team morale, injuries, who will play. They pay good money for this. It all seems harmless enough." He scratched his fingers across the table. "But once the claws are in, they tighten the noose."

"You mean blackmail?"

"Exactly. These new-found friends then show their true colours by threatening players with exposure. Force them to fix results."

"And I guess some get attracted by the offers of hefty bungs."

Carter's eyes rolled skywards. "Tens of thousands, hundreds of thousands. Millions for a bent captain." Carter declined port or brandy but with a show of reluctance. "On the funny side, there can be a comedy of errors." He laughed, loudly enough to attract an irritated glance from the nearest but still distant table in the sombre room. "In one match, I'm convinced *both sides* had been bribed to lose by different gangs. Can you imagine it? I watched the match. It was funnier than Robin Williams at his best." He showed a moment of despair. "But proving it was fixed?" Carter shrugged as he signalled for the bill and turned serious. "This illegal market is all about thinking you know more than the rest."

"So if a fix goes wrong, these gangsters catch one helluva cold?"

Carter's cheeks reddened as he continued. "As do the bigger punters who thought they knew the result. Any one of them might take revenge."

"Nice people to do business with." Ratso shook his head slowly. "In context then, smashing a baby's brains with a hammer…"

"If Rayner screwed them…" Carter waved his arm dismissively. "To these thugs, a hammer here or there? A mere blip." He peered over his half-glasses, his cheeks now even more florid with frustration. "Once hooked, there's no escape. I'll lend you a book by Ed Hawkins called *Bookie Gambler Fixer Spy*. He explains how this vast illegal operation works." He signed for the bill before continuing. "We have our confidential hot-line for a player to come clean or whistleblow. It helps but mainly, players are just too shit-scared to come clean."

"So what happened to Rayner's family…"

"Does not help. I see our prime role as prevention – educating the players. Making them street-smart to spot a fixer trying to hook them. But if there is fixing, we're there to stamp it out."

Ratso tilted his head to one side and tapped the side of his nose. "I'm still waiting for whatever you brought me here for."

"Before showing it to you, you needed to understand that background – what we're fighting against."

"We?"

"The ICC. The ECB. Other sporting bodies. Bookmakers. Governments. We work together through endless committees."

Ratso sniffed disapprovingly. Committees and Ratso did not mix. "Come on Craig. What's the big news. You're playing with me."

"No committee has seen what I will show you. This is toxic."

$-19-$

Wimbledon

The house seemed deathly quiet. The twins were at a kids' party along the road and it was Nena's afternoon off. Mandy opened the door to the walk-in closet off the entrance hall. The air smelled musty after weeks without being opened. It needed sorting. In there, they had kept luggage, tennis-rackets, Lee's golf-clubs and his cricket gear for the occasional charity match. With a sigh, she turned away. She had no stomach to sort it. Trembling, she leaned back against the oak-panelled wall.

I'm a widow.

That thought still haunted her. Before Piccadilly, widowhood was what happened to other people or only in old age. Now it was reality. Somehow life had to go on – more grooming the boys about daddy. More worries about debts and dealing with creditors. More folding away his clothes for the last time. More handling the same well-meaning but banal comments from sympathisers and well-wishers.

Slowly, she eased away from the wall and entered Lee's study. The air was stale so she opened a window. A keyboard and monitor lay on the spacious maple desk, exactly as when he had last sat there. She stroked the arm of the chair where *his* elbow had rested. She looked at his mementos and framed photos, some unique to his past, others where they had shared moments of happiness.

Christ! I never knew how much I wanted him, needed him. His quiet laugh, his silly jokes, his April Fools, the surprise gifts and loving touches like stroking my neck, his whispered suggestiveness. The excitement of putting up the Christmas tree with the twins. The christening, when Mark Rayner and Yvonne had been godparents.

Gone.

All gone!

Memories of things never to be repeated or shared.

Her knees felt weak, so she seated herself at his desk staring mindlessly at the garden view until she could contain her tears no longer. She pushed aside the keyboard and folded her arms on the desk to cradle her slumped head and stifle her tears of helplessness. It was twenty minutes or a little more when her composure was restored sufficiently to take in her surroundings. On the floor beside her stood his Dell computer tower. Dumped in a cardboard box were his personal effects she had brought back from the hospital – car and house keys, his blood-stained wallet, his Samsung smartphone, a couple of credit cards and a few pounds in petty cash. In the filing-cabinet was his paperwork, stuff their solicitor on Gray's Inn Road had said he would need for probate. She sighed at the prospect of delving into his life and again turned to a cigarette and coffee for comfort.

Later it would be a ciggie and gin.

But not much later.

With the Rayner family funerals and Lee's now behind her, it was reality check time. Friends, neighbours and relatives had done their bit but now she found herself too often chewing her lip as she wrestled with a future without Lee or his income. She strolled into the kitchen and spotted their wedding photo on the wall, their faces shining with excitement. She unhooked it, kissing his face and then clasped the photo to her chest. He looked like a walking advert from a style magazine – not a hair out of place, the wide smile, the perfect teeth and the tailored grey morning-dress. Yet at that moment, behind Lee's dimpled smile and innocent look, she knew now that he had been concealing Parabolic.

Deceiving me.

She perched herself on a red-topped bar-stool beside the central counter-top. Had she dragged the full truth from him? He had sworn that she had. Did his old Dell have more on it than he had ever told her? "These days, I only need my Samsung," he had once volunteered. "I could dump Dell-Boy except for stuff on it going back to when I skippered England. Sentiment really."

Would there be skeletons? Evidence of flings with other women? Like that flirty breakfast TV presenter he always smooched with at parties. Where had he been before the bombing? Had he been shagging? Nobody seemed to know anything since he had breakfasted at the Wolseley. And how had he got four million to invest in Parabolic anyway? Did it come from advertising a wrist-watch, a range of sports shirts and promoting a pension company? Do I believe that?

It was history. Don't go there. No need.

She checked the wall-clock. It was gone three p.m. She needed another ciggie. Janie, her neighbour had been right – she *should* sort everything and move on – and fast too. "Close the door on the past. You'll find it cathartic," Janie had volunteered yesterday after their second shared bottle of red. "Dump the past. It's crap. History. *Carpe diem.* Sort the finances with lawyers and accountants PDQ. Then move on."

It had seemed so easy the way Janie had sold it. Now, as she re-lived Janie drawing heavily on her cheroot while grasping Mandy's arm, the imponderables seemed enormous. Too many unanswered questions. "Look, Mandy, everybody knows Lee meant the world to you. He felt the same about you. He told me that, more than once. But he's not coming back through that door. Not now, not ever. Treasure the memories but start now – get a new life. When my ex walked out, that's what I did."

"Death's different, Janie, especially a sudden death. Your ex was a right sod. Moving on was a no-brainer. But Lee?" Her voice had faltered as she wiped away some tears. "I loved him rotten."

Janie had poured the remains of the Chilean merlot. "Lee was not the only man in the world for you. With your looks, your style, that panache – you'll be in big demand." She moved her manicured hand to rest on Mandy's jeans. "Anyway, Mandy, it's not cheating when Lee's dead. I mean … a woman has …needs." As she spoke, Janie had started slowly stroking between her own thighs. "Time to move on, darling. Start with the clear-out. Then get the sex. Big, thumping, yelping and moaning sex. Against the wall. On the stairs. On the carpet." She pointed to the table-top. "Right here or in discreet hotels with satin sheets. Like I said, you'll find it cathartic."

Cathartic.

She shivered again as she realised she was slopping large measures of Bombay Sapphire onto ice-cubes.

What the hell!

I deserve it.

After topping up with a sparse amount of tonic, she flopped onto a chair in the sitting-room. Beside her was a photo of Lee chatting with the Duke of Edinburgh. She blew a perfect circle from her cigarette.

Cathartic.

I'll start sorting tonight.

But a couple more gins would help.

-20-

London

"**I hate committees,**" Ratso emphasised as he watched Carter opening a slim black folder. "Pompous civil servants or experts spouting psycho-babble – drivel like *thinking out of boxes*, telling me *to square the circle* or even warning me *not to try to boil the ocean*! Then they distort the minutes or leak the confidential stuff." His voice showed he spoke from bitter experience.

"Last week, an American suggested to us that we *open up the kimono*, whatever that meant."

"A Japanese pubic hair fetishist perhaps?" Ratso grinned.

"Actually, he was an on-line gambling expert based on the Isle of Man. Kimonos apart, he talked horse-sense about identifying fixers and launderers." "But now this." Carter's eyes flashed excitement as he looked at the documents in his hand. "What I have here is not for any committee. Not till we both agree."

"I hope it's worth all your hype. I've waited less time for a London bus."

"It is." Carter pushed across a short letter written on Marylebone Cricket Club notepaper displaying the MCC logo in red and yellow. Attached was a longer document running to several pages. Ratso saw that both were marked *Private & Confidential* in bold black type.

Gingerly, and out of habit, Ratso picked them up by their very edge. The covering note was signed by James Mellows, the Chief

Executive of the Club and addressed to Carter at the ECB. Before even reading the attachment, Ratso looked up, his eyes and furrowed brow revealing his shock. He flicked through the five pages of closely typed material. It was a letter addressed to Mellows. As he raced through the contents, he fingered his slightest stubble, eager to get to the end.

"Well?" prompted Carter as Ratso slowly handed back the paperwork which Carter immediately returned to the folder.

Ratso looked around and saw that the bar and dining-tables were filling up. He lowered his voice. "As bad as it gets. Dynamite."

"If true."

"What do you think? Is this believable? Mr Squeaky-Clean?"

Ratso found his relationship with Craig Carter to be odd. Even calling him Craig seemed cheeky. Back along as a keen youngster, he had always deferred to Det. Chief Superintendent Carter. Now, they met as equals except for Carter's unique knowledge about sporting corruption. Ratso thoughtfully ran his fingers down his cheek. "Maybe we should discuss this elsewhere." As they pushed back their chairs, Ratso added. "You realise what this means?"

"That we have a major problem?"

Ratso suggested Carter try again.

"There's going to be another fix?"

"Yes but more than that." Ratso spoke slowly putting emphasis on each word. "It means that unless we get lucky and pretty damned quick, someone, presumably a player could be murdered."

Carter suggested they stretch their legs by taking the long way around the playing-area to his office. Ratso, at just over six feet, was considerably the taller and leaner. When in the Met, Carter had never been overweight but now he was developing something of a paunch. As they strolled behind the grand Victorian red brick pavilion, Carter walked much slower than when they had once worked together on a bullion job in Leytonstone.

Somewhat breathless, Carter resumed the sensitive conversation in the empty spaciousness beside the fragrance of the Rose Garden. "When we spoke just before the bomb, we both agreed Rayner's wife and kid were targeted."

"Correct. And that the attack was linked to Mark Rayner's captaincy of the Surrey Patriots." They entered the chilly gloom of the walkway beneath the silence of the giant Grandstand. To Ratso it seemed appropriate to be talking of the dark side of professional sport away from the light of day. "Now, if this note is true..." Ratso grasped Carter's arm in emphasis. "Rayner had several guys he called in when he needed a fix." They emerged into the blustery wind and daylight beside the Compton Stand. "So, Craig – any other pointers?"

"Let's revisit Surrey Patriots' televised matches and study the other captains too. And see if Westdale, well ... er Lee, was always present too."

"Let's still call him Lee," agreed Ratso. "As we all did when he was everyone's super-hero. If we're right, Mark double-crossed Lee and paid the price. Is that why Lee was saying sorry, sorry?"

"Guilt-ridden. Full of remorse." Carter nodded as he looked at the statue of a batsman by the Nursery Ground. "Can't turn the clock back to the days of Hutton, Cowdrey and Compton. No T20 cricket. No internet and no on-line gambling. Fixing as we know it never existed."

"This is our chance to rid sport of this scourge."

"I can't share your optimism." Carter saw the disappointment on Ratso's face and hurried to explain. "We might win this battle but the war can only be won in Pakistan and India. This goes way beyond cricket. Bringing down the Mr Bigs is not going to happen." They had paused beside the entrance to the futuristic media centre prompting Carter to continue. "Good things *are* happening

– like media access, indeed *any* access to players is now difficult during matches. Here in England, we have a strong accreditation policy. The days of uncontrolled access to players during matches has gone. Even mobile phones are removed. Lee, though, as a commentator and presenter was in a prime position at televised matches."

A concerned frown carved its way across Ratso's rugged features. "But Lee would never have taken a hammer to a best mate's baby. Or have ordered it."

"My take? Lee's job was to sucker in guys like Mark who had looked up to him. The thugs are elsewhere. Who fixed Lee? That's your starter for ten. Who was he working for?" Carter opened the door into the ECB's offices. "You'll need to interview the widow…" Carter's face almost split in two with the size of his grin, a throwback to when he had been the boss telling a young Ratso to do the dirty work. "I'd like to be a fly on the wall for that one. Rather you than me, matey."

-21-

London

At precisely 7-15 a.m. Det.Sgt Jock Strang and DC Nancy Petrie joined Ratso for breakfast in the basement canteen. "Welcome to Cobalt Square, both of you." The burly Scot's plate was overloaded with a monster fry-up while Nancy's tray had only granola and green tea. He looked the Glaswegian up and down, debating whether he had added a few pounds to his waistline since they had last met. Perhaps but still not someone to mess with. "So Jock, what's with the huge moustache? You look like a Frenchman who's lost his accordion. All you'd need is a black beret."

Jock laughed as he dumped his mug of tea on the table. "Jealous, boss? I reckon it makes me more ... more exciting, mysterious even."

"A Scottish Fu Manchu who's pushing fifty? And with that stomach? Exciting? Mysterious?" He pointed to the spreading paunch that rubbed against the table. "Will you tell him or shall I, Nancy?" Ratso paused but saw she was not risking banter with her superior. "Look I'm delighted you've switched to Cobalt Square but Jock you know more about the number of pot-noodles in a pot than about cricket."

"Right enough but I can name every Glasgow Rangers player for the past forty years." Jock's eyes bulged as he looked at his three eggs, bacon and all the trimmings. "Is cricket thon game played with mallets and hoops?" Jock's joke brought a rare smile to Ratso's face which turned to a laugh as Nancy took it seriously and told him he was confusing cricket with croquet.

"No mallets or hoops involved, Jock."

Jock chuckled, deep and throaty. "Och, I ken fine about cricket – you soft posh-boy southerners hit a ball with a wee bit of wood. And the supporters wear their daft wee hats and stripey blazers. That enough, boss?"

"Grade A, Jock. Tell him about T20, Nancy. You said on the phone you'd been swotting up."

"Twenty-two players in two teams. Two umpires to control the game. Each team bats for twenty overs of six balls. Right so far?" She saw Ratso's nod of approval. "The bowling team has to get up to ten batsmen out in those one-hundred and twenty balls. They can knock the stumps down, catch the ball after it has been hit and something quite beyond me called LBW."

"Leg-before-Wicket is a tough one. Useful tool in the armoury of a bent umpire. Anyway, go on."

"Then they swap round and the team that was bowling has to get a higher score."

"I'm impressed." Ratso finished the last of his scrambled egg on brown toast. With her streaky blonde hair and chubby but smiley face, Nancy looked more like a small town hair-stylist than a detective. She ate with eager but delicate mouthfuls, her posture and jawline revealing her enthusiasm for some action, to get things moving. Back in the Cauldron during Operation Clam, he had rated her as a high-flyer. "You still grinding through the promotion process?"

Nancy coloured slightly adding to her allure. "I'm hoping for the nod for stage four."

"I'm with you on that," Ratso was quick to add. "You're ready for the twelve month temporary rank." He looked at her, impressed with everything about her. These days with budgets being slashed by Government, morale was falling and resentment mounting. At twenty-nine, Nancy's upbeat demeanour and her enthusiasm were welcome, rare and infectious.

Jock broke off from mutilating a blackened sausage. "And the players wear white flannels and stop for tea."

"Not in T20, Jock. It's all coloured kit and big hitting. Think of T20 as fast-food compared to a five-day gourmet dinner." Ratso guessed from the mischievous look on the Scot's face that Jock knew much more than he was admitting. *Whatever*, the guy's experience, courage and dogged determination would be invaluable. Better still, Jock Strang was as loyal to Ratso as a blind-man's dog.

"When I told Nancy my move had been approved," Jock continued "she then said she needed to escape the fug down in the Cauldron." As he listened, Ratso was reminded of the stale smell of empty pizza boxes, curry take-aways, sweat and silent farts. He made no comment but his antenna sensed a message somewhere in Jock's rasping tone. Unable to decipher it, he let it pass.

"I told the Deputy AC that I read Wisden, the cricketers' bible, every night and so my move was approved too," Nancy enthused. "That's left poor old Tosh Watson to carry on the drug war."

Ratso sighed. "I like Tosh. He's a solid enough detective but being side-lined now, he can only blame himself. Disobeying my instructions during *Clam*. Damned near buggered everything." He shrugged. "The top brass don't forget quickly."

Ratso watched Nancy's delicate movements as she spooned up her granola. During the Cauldron days, he had spent more time than he cared to admit watching her. Though she wanted to be treated as one of the boys, drinking and whooping it up on wilder nights down at the Antelope, for all that, Ratso had found her to be teasingly attractive too. Occasionally, he had detected a suggestive glint in her oval shaped eyes, heavy on the mascara. But he had never put it to the test. A debacle nine years earlier had taught him that bedding another officer, senior or junior, was not a good career move. And anyway, imagining Nancy in the sack had been before he'd hooked up with Kirsty-Ann.

"Some of these cricketers in their tight flannels look tasty – good-looking hunks compared to the rugby players with their cauliflower ears and broken noses." Nancy paused. "Pity about Lee Westdale. He could have bowled me over any time."

Ratso gave her an enquiring look. *Surely she had not got wind of Lee's corruption? No. Impossible. Just a throwaway remark.* "Read this." He handed each of them the five-page letter sent to the MCC. "This is from Dr Premadesa who tried to save Lee Westdale's life. Reading it was like driving a dagger through my heart."

"We didna' know ye had a heart, boss," laughed Jock as he fumbled for black-framed glasses. Nancy though said nothing as she held the typed letter and started to read with obvious care. While he waited for them, Ratso's thoughts turned to Kirsty-Ann Webber. Last night they had skyped for over an hour, trying to keep their long-distance romance going against the reality of the Atlantic dividing them.

K.A was a detective in Fort Lauderdale, Florida and a widowed mom. Her FBI husband had been murdered on duty in Atlanta. They had met when Ratso had been working in the Bahamas. A few months later, she had visited London and they had spent a near magical week together finding togetherness in cinemas, theatres, walking by the Thames, over dinners and smoochy late night dancing. Despite that, they had agreed that total commitment was not on. Ratso was not ready to quit the Met and K.A could not consider shifting her mother and young Leon from Florida. For now, Skype was as good it got.

While he waited for Jock and Nancy to finish reading, he fired off a couple of texts and even managed a crafty peek at a picture of his leggy blonde in a skimpy red bikini.

"You believe this, boss?" enquired Nancy Petrie, her nostrils suddenly flared and her cherubic features looking fired up.

Ratso nodded. "This doctor had no reason to make it up."

The smell of Jock's fried bread and hash browns filled the air as he shook his head, his florid cheeks wobbling. "Och, I'm no so sure." His Glaswegian accent hung heavily as he continued to shovel away his full English with extra black pudding. "Firstly, look at his name. Did he understand what Lee was saying?"

Ratso pursed his lips. "You'll be interviewing him. My worry is whether Dr Premadasa will understand *you*. Unlike Lee, you've *never* spoken English. Every word you say sounds as if it has been through a mincing-machine – backwards, at that."

"Aye! Right enough" Jock laughed, slapping his hefty thigh cheerfully, his right eye drooping lower than his left, the legacy of a late night arrest in Glasgow.

"Check him out before meeting him. Premadasa says he admired Lee."

"Didn't we all!" Petrie looked thoughtful. "No reason for the good doctor to do Lee down, then."

Ratso rubbed the side of his strong nose. "He's a top notch neurosurgeon. Born in Sri Lanka. Conspiracy theorists would say that coming from there, close to the seat of cricket's corruption industry, he invented all this to throw us off the scent. But me? For now we regard his notes of what Lee Westdale said in hospital as *bona fide.*"

"As our learned legal friends in their wigs and gowns would say," Nancy chimed in.

Jock had not done yet. "Aye! Acid test then – would his evidence survive an attack by some slippery Queen's Counsel?"

"You mean like the case about Viagra that was dismissed because the evidence did not stand up in court." Nancy Petrie's cheeky grin fixed each listener in turn. Ratso had heard the joke before but Jock laughed over-enthusiastically.

Ratso brought them back to the matters in hand. "Jock – I agree, normally our job is all about what a jury will buy. This is different. Mark Rayner and Lee are dead. We're not going to prosecute them. We're looking further up the chain."

Nancy flipped over a couple of pages. "As an MCC member, Premadasa would hate what he was hearing. The doc says he was angry, furious and so scribbled his notes immediately Mandy Westdale had seen the body. He then typed them up later."

Ratso was staring at Jock's mug which he had not seen since the Cauldron days. "I see you've kept that souvenir mug Tosh gave you."

Jock slowly twisted it round so that Nancy saw the slogan – *Ivor Bigun – the World's Biggest Liar*. He tried a wink but the drooping eyelid wouldn't manage it as he took a slurp and pointed at Premadasa's notes. "See here boss – Westdale had been struck on the back of his head. These ramblings were after emergency surgery from the shrapnel. He had been doped up and was barely out of Recovery."

"Can't disagree with that, Jock." Ratso's hooded lids lowered in acknowledgment. "But *someone* – someone with credibility had to be the middleman, fixing the players. Lee fits the mould.*"

Nancy patted her hair before pushing aside her empty cereal bowl. "Past England captain. TV Quiz Show panellist. Smooth operator." Petrie crunched on a Nutrigrain snack pulled from the pocket of her black slacks. "He would have known Mark Rayner well."

"Lee had access to players from all the main countries – West Indies, Australia, New Zealand, India, Pakistan, Sri Lanka."

"Don't forget South Africa," prompted Nancy. "I've read about the Cronje scandal."

Ratso yet again was impressed with the young detective. "You're right. Craig Carter reckoned any fixers' Plan A would be to nobble team captains."

"Ye mean they used Lee Westdale like a can-opener?"

Ratso liked Jock thinking positive. "Craig is checking back to when Lee skippered England. He's never been under scrutiny before. No reason. Maybe that's how he had four million to invest in an American Ponzi scheme." He saw the blank looks and promised to explain later.

Nancy wiped her mouth with a paper napkin. "So Lee fixed his mate but later was tormented by what happened at Beachy Head."

Ratso listened to the young detective with respect. "If we believe Premadasa, Lee repeatedly said *I'm so sorry, Mark*."

Jock reached for a doorstep of buttered toast before commenting. "The guy was dragged from the Piccadilly rubble, near dead and *del-usion-al*," he emphasised the word. "He was away with the fairies." Jock tapped the table with a meaty finger. "He was rambling as if Mark was beside him in the ward."

Ratso's slight toss of his head showed he was not buying into it. He pointed to a paragraph in the doctor's notes. "Lee thought someone had tried to murder him. He never knew it was a bomb blast."

"Right enough boss but the guy was under the effects of anaesthetics." Jock flipped a couple of pages and read aloud: "*I always thought they might get me. Now they have. And they'll get the others too.*"

"See, Jock. Someone was blaming Lee for Rayner not delivering a fix."

"So from where he was coming, Lee was not delusional," Nancy chipped in. "And his dying words – saying he loved Mandy. To me, that's a clincher. Mandy didn't arrive till after he had died, so Premadasa must have got the name from him."

Jock drained the last of his strong brew. "Boss, the doctor might have invented that to cheer up the poor woman. He'd have got her name when she arrived."

"Embellishment?" Ratso studied his sergeant's lived-in face with obvious respect. "Premadasa invents those comforting last words? Possible. But the rest? For now, I buy it." Ratso polished an apple. "Top priority is to prove who corrupted him."

"And who he thought had tried to murder him," agreed Petrie.

"Ye'll ask the widow?"

"I will Jock. It'll be a bloody tricky interview– and then some." Ratso saw his listeners wanted an explanation. "Look – Mandy Westdale is a grieving widow. Since her marriage, probably since she first met Lee, she has idolised him – he was a trophy husband. Rich, famous, successful. And I come tramping into her life suggesting her beloved husband, murdered by a terrorist, had orchestrated match-fixing on a grand scale. "Mrs Westdale, I've got to say it – based on his dying words, Lee was a crook and by corrupting Mark Rayner, he almost literally drove that family over the cliff." Ratso looked at each of them in turn. "Do you want to tell her that, Jock?"

The Scot looked sheepish. "I see what ye mean. A wee problem there."

Nancy Petrie dabbed her mouth with a paper napkin. "I'd like to meet her. You might find a woman's take on her to be ...?"

"You mean Mandy might have *known* what he was up to?" Ratso's eyes disappeared for a long moment. "You're right. Let's keep an open mind. You Nancy will come with me but we will not go alone."

"I'll sort that boss," Jock laughed, understanding what his boss meant.

"You mean we take the heavy mob, like a raid?" Petrie had not heard Ratso use the expression before.

Ratso gave something close to a smile. "No, Nancy. Not the Territorial Support Group. Not yet. I meant a search warrant – to use only if Mandy cuts up rough."

"A search? A bit heavy, boss?"

"Not at all, Nancy. We need his phones, computers, paperwork, bank accounts, just as if he were alive. You Jock will spend ten minutes on Wikipedia swotting up on cricket before meeting Premadasa. He really understands the game, remember."

Petrie's round face broke into a wicked smile revealing small but even teeth. "Will I get to see any cricketers some time soon? It's quite a turn-on, when they rub the ball up and down their thigh."

"You mean when we polish one side of the ball on our buttocks?"

Nancy leaned forwards and winked. "Give me the chance, boss, I'd do it for them."

Ratso nearly joked about inviting her to watch him play one Saturday but just stopped himself. *Avoid sexual familiarity with fellow officers.* A sudden thought flashed across Ratso's mind. "Your son, Jock? Still with Glasgow Rangers? They were looking after him last I heard. I should have asked."

"Thanks, boss. The laddie is doing just great. He faced the inevitable after thon leg injury. The club was good to him but he felt he needed a future away from the game. He's taken a job in Paisley fixing mortgage loans."

"Shame! Not quite same as scoring a winning goal for Scotland in the World Cup."

"Aye, it's been a tough time but he's moving on."

"I'm glad. By the way, Jock. I heard that the lads in the Cauldron had a whip round to buy you a musical mirror. It plays The Beatles singing *I am the Walrus*."

-22-
California

As he did every morning when at home, Enzo Pagano looked out of his picture window to make sure that Tyler, his African-American servant, had raised the American flag beside the curve of the pavered drive. With a grunt of satisfaction, he saw the bold red, white and blue flag hanging limply in the still of the morning air.

The New Yorker had bought the mansion in Monovale Road for twenty-six million dollars three years previously having quit his apartment on New York's Upper East Side. Here in Bel Air, the up-market area of Los Angeles, he felt best able to enjoy the pleasures of life without the noise, traffic and aggravations of his native city.

Close by were former homes of Elvis Presley and Michael Jackson. Like his own property, little of them could be seen from the road. That did not prevent the endless lines of gawping tourists who were shuttled by for a glimpse into the lives of Hollywood's rich and famous.

For a moment or two, he stood on the balcony, savouring the endless blue sky against the backdrop of palm trees and flowering shrubs. The summer fragrances of the abundant flowers enhanced the early morning birdsong. To him, this was what made the USA great, the way the country should be. The rolling lawns, the servants, the *objets d'art* and fountains around the grounds proved how a kid from Hoboken could live the American dream through hard work and ingenuity.

He despised the weak and corrupt politicians on Capitol Hill and the filth-ridden street corners thronged with illegal immigrants waiting to be taken to building sites. What counted was betterment through self-help.

Being a creature of habit suited him. He liked everything pigeon-holed. Downstairs, Tyler's wife, Mary-Lou, would be setting out his breakfast on the shaded patio. It never varied: juice, scrambled eggs, Canadian bacon, a low stack of pancakes and her home-made strawberry jam. Coffee would be in a silver pot and the flower-patterned china was from Limoges in France.

His folded newspaper would be beside the bowl of mango, pineapple and papaya. In front of his breakfast on the portable TV, Fox News would be running, giving him the only view of the world he wanted – one in which the broadcasters wanted America to be great again, not pussyfooting about.

Having seen his parents' marriage end in punches, shouting and tears, Pagano had never married. His father's three Convenience Stores had been lost through alimony claims. He had vowed to avoid that trap, preferring to pay for sex with no commitment. In New York, he had left behind folk he had steamrollered or conned while getting rich at their expense. Some had trusted his word; others had worked their butts off for him or perhaps had got the dirty end of legal small print. Nothing had stood in his path that he had not crushed or fixed. The only setback had been those years in a penitentiary but that had been airbrushed from his recollection.

He knew little of Alex Anderson but a scowl came over his face whenever, like now, he thought of him. This guy with the strange limey accent contributed little with ideas or contacts – but was quick to grab every last cent of the winnings. Now, he wanted to back out because some cricketer and his family had gone walk-about over a cliff.

The guy had no balls.

The sooner he was out, the better.

Especially out from Jupiter.

With a rolling gait, Pagano descended the wide amber carpeted staircase. Ornate black and gold railings lined either side of the sweeping curve. If filled with singers and dancers, the lobby would have looked like a set from a 1950s Hollywood musical. As always, his arrival on the sunny patio was timed to catch the news headlines where he would read fast, eat slowly and watch with occasional glances.

After finishing every last scrap, he turned off the TV and checked the bank balances from Monaco. He grunted happily on seeing that HOSS had delivered its usual quota of winners. As to the rest of the day, he could reach the Beverly Hills Hotel in less than fifteen minutes and could prep Vijay – give him some back-bone before handling Anderson. Pagano turned to go back inside, his smile unpleasant. Unwittingly, he was rubbing his hands as he left the patio and the shade from the spreading branches of a large maple tree.

The meeting was going to be rough. Just the way he liked it.

At that same moment, Alex Anderson was reclining on his white leather seat during the flight from Florida. He was scheduled to land just before 9-30 a.m. So far, he had not slept, his mind filled with thoughts of the meeting ahead. During his youth in the filthy streets of Byker and later in his edgy dealings in Newcastle, he had learned various ways to deal with bastards like Pagano. Knife crime, shootings, bare knuckle fights – he had seen them all. But a hammer to a baby, for God's sake? Blinding an innocent woman.

He sipped his coffee.

Should I take Pagano head-on?

Or play a long game?
What about my investment in HOSS?
And the million I paid towards Jupiter.
Write it all off?
No way.
Do I know enough now?

Despite the early hour, he asked the flight attendant for a second schooner of vintage port. As he savoured the smooth roundness, his mind cleared. He produced a small notepad and in scratchy writing assessed what he knew about HOSS and the plans for Jupiter. As the pilot announced their final approach, Anderson's mind was made up. He added the final option to his list with a satisfied smile.

That I like.
If it comes to it.

-23-

London

" **T**hat was Jock," Ratso volunteered as he put down his phone. "He interviewed the doctor." DC Petrie was driving him to Wimbledon.

"Premadasa convince him?"

"Well, almost. Jock won't ever admit he got it wrong. Seems Premadasa speaks perfect English. As a cricket fan, he understood what Lee said while he was dying … and the implications. It gets better though. Jock got a statement from a nurse who was monitoring Lee at the time. She was second-generation from Ghana and confirmed the gist of what was said though she had had not understood the significance."

"The noose tightens then, 'cos I was impressed with Craig Carter. Those clips of captaincy decisions that Mark Rayner made in those four matches looked well suspect."

"Yeah. And each match was televised with huge sums being wagered." Ratso stifled a yawn after his early start.

"Lee Westdale was commentating too."

"Bet you didn't notice this though."

"Boss?"

"Lee never commented once about Rayner's unusual captaincy. Yet he must have spotted it."

"That other commentator did. The West Indian with that golden treacly voice."

"You're right." Ratso fell silent, thinking back to the rest of his conversation with Jock. "We called what Westdale said *rambling*," Jock had explained. "Not so. The doc was so intrigued it was almost like Q & A. It gets better, right enough. Premadasa showed me the hospital records. It was not his decision to shift Westdale from the Recovery Room to the private ward. That's where Premadasa first saw him for the head injury. A patient only gets released from Recovery after extensive observations tick the boxes."

"Did anyone tell Westdale he had been blown up?"

Jock shook his head. "No. He was sure someone had tried to kill him."

"Did he name anyone?"

"Sadly not."

"How bad was the head injury?"

"Westdale died before Premadasa did any formal assessment but apparently he would have scored highly."

"Go on."

"Something they call the Glasgow Scale. It covers three different headings which each score points – motor response, verbal response and eye opening. Low scores point to serious brain damage."

"So Premadasa reckoned?"

"At least thirteen and possibly fourteen."

Ratso knew a little of the assessment process but not the detail. "Give."

"Premadasa reckoned six for motor response – obeying commands though he was very, very weak from his injuries. Four for verbal response. The conversation was rational except that Westdale had assumed someone had tried to kill him. Take that away and his admissions were good enough to be called an *orientated response*. He also got four for eye response. In total, he was almost top of the class. He assessed the injury to the skull as nasty but transient."

"I get it. Lee Westdale's only confusion was how he came to be in hospital at all." He looked through the window and saw where they were. "We're just arriving in Wimbledon."

"Oh I say! Do bring me back strawberries and cream," Jock put on his best English accent.

"Sorry, Jock. The Wimbledon tennis is finished for this year." Ratso's thoughts turned to the interview ahead but were interrupted by Nancy as she deftly swung the Honda into tree-lined Lingfield Road. She pointed to the expensive detached homes, several of them set behind substantial burnished brick walls.

"Posh area, boss. Lee must have been coining it in."

-24-

Wimbledon

The detective constable parked the pool car outside the house in Lingfield Road. "Cool pad, eh!" Nancy's eyes rolled. "That'll be me when I win the lottery."

Ratso agreed as he looked up and down the narrow road. "You wouldn't get much change out of four million." He gathered his tote bag and climbed out, stretching his arms as he did so. "Westdale didn't own this. I checked at the Land Registry and with local agents. His rent was more than I earn in a year."

For a moment they both stared at the substantial Edwardian detached property. It was made of brick and on two levels. An extra room had been added into the attic with an eyebrow window cut into the roof. At ground-floor level, the main entrance was between two large reception rooms – each with protruding bay windows.

The musical chimes sounded and they heard a woman's voice yelling at Nena to answer the door. From somewhere, came the sound of a child crying. "Yes?" The door opened and a slender figure volunteered nothing more. The child's screams turned louder. Ratso and Nancy produced their ID but the young woman seemed not to understand.

"Police. We need to see Mrs Westdale." At that moment Mandy appeared from the kitchen carrying a screaming two-year old with another a few steps behind her. She glanced at the identification, looked puzzled but then smiled.

"Sorry about the noise. You'd better come in. Nena – please take the boys into the garden – well out of earshot!" She handed over the kicking and struggling child with a smile of relief as she led them into the sitting-room at the rear. It overlooked about eighteen yards of lawn bordered by shrubs. *Not quite long enough for a cricket pitch* was Ratso's immediate thought.

Mandy offered them a seat on a rusty-red sofa and was about to sit down when she changed her mind. "Tea? Coffee?" After seeing their shakes of refusal, she elegantly lowered herself into a matching easy chair just opposite. For a moment as she wriggled into a comfortable position, she looked expectantly, assuming they would open the conversation. On nothing being said, quite deliberately, she smiled at each in turn, her eyes showing curiosity as she spread her hands out to lie on each arm-rest. "This is about Piccadilly, I assume."

"Yes and no. I'm assuming you are Amanda Eliza Westdale and were married to Lee." Ratso spoke slowly, like a vicar delivering his best point in a sermon. He hoped it showed respect.

"Mandy, yes."

"I, well I mean, we, are both so sorry for this tragedy," Ratso was surprised at how nervous he was, revealed by the fluffed intros. "This must have been a terrible time for you." Ratso had rehearsed the words but looking across at the fresh-faced widow had made getting to the point even harder than he had expected.

"What a great picture and happy memories no doubt," chipped in Nancy looking at the large framed photo of the couple standing beside some palms on a sunny beach.

"Our honeymoon. Barbados, yes." It was said flat, deadpan, her face in disconnect and almost disinterested. *Like don't drag me back to those happy days.* As a copper on the beat, Ratso had encountered similar responses when dealing with battered spouses.

"Do you work?"

Mandy answered Ratso's question with an explanation of how she had given up work in Docklands just before the twins were born. As he listened, Ratso noticed that he had been shuffling his feet and stopped at once. "So, Mrs Westdale, let me get straight to the point. There's no easy way of starting this discussion and I can't even tell you that we're here for a friendly chat. We are not."

"Oh?" Ratso saw apprehension cross Mandy's disarmingly open face. "Is this about me? Or Lee?"

"It's about Lee, I'm afraid. Had he been alive, we would have been here to question him about corruption in cricket."

For a moment, Mandy hesitated before tucking her legs up beneath her. "Oh, Lee knew about that. He could have told you a few rumours. He often talked about it. He reckoned it was the scourge of the game, something that had been going on for over twenty years, especially involving..."

"I'm sorry to interrupt you Mrs Westdale but we have cause to believe that your husband was actively involved in match-fixing." Ratso watched the widow intently and let the words hang heavily between them.

Mandy's face screwed up in horror. "No. No, surely not. Lee had been England captain. He's been to number 10. Buckingham Palace too. He had an MBE. Head Prefect at school. No. Lee would never ever ...." Her voice trailed away and for a moment Ratso thought she was going to cry. Once again, he said nothing. Silence was a good weapon. So often the person volunteered a loose remark. Ratso watched her steel herself, fighting to control her emotions.

Then she rose in a flurry of movement. With the wiggle of a catwalk model, she crossed the spacious room to a coffee-table displaying a photo of Lee holding the Ashes – the tiny urn that symbolises the intense cricketing rivalry between England and Australia.

She grabbed her cigarettes and lit one. She re-crossed the spacious room, her movements lithe and graceful. Only after she was again seated and had taken a couple of deep drags, did she then respond. "Lee encouraged use of the hot-line for players to *squeal* as he put it. Telling them to whistleblow if approached by fixers."

"Look Mrs Westdale," Nancy Petrie spoke gently, though in her London-Kentish accent, her tone could never be called soft. "Maybe, just maybe, Lee was clever and cunning enough to fool you and everybody."

Ratso spotted the flinch at the suggestion that anybody could dupe her, Mandy's eyes flashing more than indignation. "I hadn't smoked for years. Until, y'know." She lowered her eyes and took a deep breath. "Mr Holtom, believe me. I would have known. We shared everything. True soul-mates." She took another deep drag and then continued as if an idea had just struck her. "Who made this allegation against Lee?"

Ratso had been prepared for this. "We have convincing information."

"Someone, whoever it was, must be mistaken." She blew a perfect smoke-ring and admired it rising above her groomed chestnut hair. "Look, inspector. You and me – we have very different starting-points. You have a job to do and I respect the way you have tried to handle this." She paused as she fixed him with a hardening stare that told Ratso that however seductive her smile and movements, she could be a ball-breaker. "It's all so unfair – hurtful. Who could say these things about Lee? Anyway," her tone sharpened, "tell me – what do you want to achieve? Lee's not going to grace the Old Bailey whatever your evidence." For a moment, there was a catch in her voice as her emotions fought the permanence of death.

Ratso rubbed the end of his strong chin as if thinking of a response to a tricky question but he had rehearsed most answers.

"Well, obviously, I needed your frank reaction to what I had to tell you. Secondly, had your husband been here, I would have wanted his help." He lowered his eyes to show respect. "Sadly, Mrs Westdale, you now stand in his shoes."

"Help?"

"Lee must have told you that match-fixing is no one-man show. He might have been able to point me in the right directions – particularly over Mark Rayner. Had he ever mentioned rumours about the Surrey Patriots skipper?"

Mandy stubbed out the cigarette in an ornate green ashtray. "Mark? You shock me. No. Not at all. Never mentioned. I mean he's English ... was English. Poor Mark. *Poor all of them.* No, Lee blamed foreign players."

"With names?" Ratso was quick to seize on the point.

Mandy shook her head. "He said it was wrong to speculate. A loose word from him in the commentary-box or anywhere, might spread and be unfair. As I recall, *defamatory* was a word he used. As a commentator, he had seen players get out to dumb shots or by giving simple catches. He had seen crazy run-outs or stumpings." She tossed her head dismissively. "In tense situations, *cock-ups*, his description, do happen. He said it was almost impossible to prove anything."

"Mrs Westdale," interjected Nancy, "would you mind if we took a look around and if we find anything useful, take it away?"

"Take Lee's things?" For a moment she looked irritated. "The place is a bit of a mess, especially the bedroom. For the past two days, I've been having a real clear-out. A friend said it would help me get through, y'know..."

Ratso eyes and voice showed warmth and sympathy as he leaned towards her. "We understand. We just need to study his finances, his phone, his laptop, his paperwork, notebooks. We need to get these allegations resolved. And quickly. Better for you too."

"I won't say no. There's nothing to hide."

"Thanks," said Ratso forcing himself to give her a smile of encouragement. "Cooperation makes our task easier."

"So others? You're on the trail of others?"

Ratso stood up and nodded. "This is a very heavy investigation. Lives may be at stake."

Mandy lit another cigarette. "Lives! Christ! Surely you don't mean … murder?"

"Early days, Mrs Westdale … but yes. And it's good that you knew nothing of what Lee is alleged to have been doing." Ratso paused as he approached her, trying to look friendly whilst his eyes showed concern. "Because if *you* had known something, one life at risk might have been yours." Ratso debated whether to add more. "Look at Mark Rayner's wife and babe."

"You think that attack was linked to cricket?" Mandy's voice choked as she slumped back deeper into her chair as if cocooning herself. "I know nothing," she responded, sobbing for the first time. "Like I said, Lee knew nothing or he would have gone to the guy at the ECB. Craig somebody." She stopped to dab her eyes with a tissue removed from the sleeve of her crimson blouse. Ratso watched her intently, waiting for her composure to return. It was several moments and a couple of nose-blowings before she continued. "You carry on. Search anything, everything."

Nancy, who had moved across to stand beside her, put a friendly hand on her heaving shoulder. "We'll need his laptop and phone."

Slowly, Mandy uncurled herself and stood up. "I need a vodka-tonic." She looked defensive. "Does that sound awful so early in the afternoon? I never used to. Now…" She shrugged. "Can I get something for you two?" She saw Ratso decline for both of them. "Lee never had a laptop. Way back, he used a clumpy old desktop thing with a tower by his desk. When I started the clear-out, that was among the first things dumped."

She stood up, standing taller than Nancy, emphasising her more flattering figure and stance. "Funnily enough, not long before he was ..." Mandy faltered. "Before the bombing, he had considered buying a new lightweight laptop and then backing up his smartphone." She flicked ash with precision using her manicured finger. "Then he decided he could do without. He used his smartphone for everything – communication – emails, Twitter, photos."

"You have it?"

"His Galaxy? Yes. It's in a box with stuff from the hospital. I haven't got round to touching that yet. It's in the office." She faltered. "The Galaxy was ...with him when the bomb went off."

"What happened to the old computer?" Ratso was still interested in the desktop "Can I retrieve the hard-drive?"

"You're only just too late." She shook her head. "I worked for an American corporation at Canada Water. The house-rule was never to dump computers with data on-board. Lee's Dell went to the dump but only after I had removed the hard-drive. That went to Nivens, the car repair place, the one near the dog-track. They crushed it in a vice." She laughed for a fleeting moment. "Much cheaper than those Docklands disposal companies that my former bosses used."

Ratso was not happy that possible evidence had been destroyed, however old it was. "Unfortunate, Mrs Westdale."

"Lee hadn't used it for, oh I don't know, three or even four years since he got the smartphone. Everything will be on that."

"Only everything since then," muttered Ratso abstractedly. "What else have you dumped?"

"Clothes mainly. He hoarded souvenirs, like his first contract to play for Somerset Hawks. A battered cricket ball from a tour of Australia. It meant nothing to me. All that stuff was dumped." She led them into the hall and opened the walk-in. Besides a variety of suitcases, it was crammed with sports equipment. "I'm sending his cricket bats, tennis gear and golf-clubs to the Lord's Taverners charity to be auctioned."

Ratso waited for her to close the door. "We'll look round now then. I'll take his study. Nancy you start in the bedrooms and work down." Mandy pointed him towards a compact room at the front with leaded windows. From there, he watched her climb the stairs, her cute backside swaying in shapely white jeans. He was sure she had known he was watching.

Lee had certainly picked a real beauty.

For a moment, Kirsty-Ann seemed much, much too far away.

With a swift U-turn, he entered the study which smelled unused and stale with just a tinge of lavender polish. Whatever Nena's role was, it had not involved hoovering or dusting because the outline of where the computer tower had stood on the floor was clearly outlined, as were places where the keyboard, monitor and mouse-mat had stood on the light oak desk.

He strolled around the room. The walls were lined with photos of Lee with team-mates or Prime Ministers. Besides a cardboard box, on the desk there was merely a desk-lamp, a cheap pen and an empty notepad. He held it up checking for indentations. There was nothing. Ratso flicked the lamp's rocker-switch. The bulb had blown and not been replaced. There was no land-line. A dark green filing-cabinet close at hand held two unlocked drawers. A glance inside confirmed he would need to examine every bulky or battered file.

He plonked himself onto the black moquette swivel-chair and slowly spun round 360 degrees. The windows were grimy and the curtains were cheap and badly fitting. The carpet beneath the desk showed no signs of major scuffing from Lee's feet. Everything pointed to an unloved room in a rented property.

Ratso glanced at the box Mandy had brought back from the hospital. It was scarcely big enough for a few cans of baked beans. It looked pathetic – Lee's final worldly goods, mainly stained by blackened blood. He pushed it to one side and for nearly two hours, ploughed through the files. The bank statements, invoices and sundry correspondence revealed nothing to suggest that Westdale had a pivotal role in fixing.

Only then did he return to the box, picking out each item with care. After going through everything twice, he awarded himself a grunt and a nod of satisfaction. As he stacked the credit card statements to take away, Nancy appeared with a gloomy expression. She was carrying a polythene shopping-bag brimming with unseen small items. Almost immediately, Mandy trotted down the stairs, her make-up now restored. "Well?" Her tone was somewhere between aggressive and defiant.

"Too soon to say," murmured Ratso with a sideways glance at Nancy. "We'll quickly list everything we're removing and then be gone."

Twenty minutes later, Nancy eased the Honda away. "I saw your glance, trying not to look like a cat that had found the cream."

"That bad, was I? No Oscar for me this year then? I'm disappointed."

"Upstairs, I found several years' diaries and an i-Pad. But the diaries simply had family dates marked – y'know, birthdays and anniversaries. The i-Pad was full of downloaded books and movies. Mandy opened the email programme for me. Nothing. I've got the password. It'll need to be checked again." She was driving them towards Wimbledon Village. At the traffic-lights, she turned to him, her eyes asking the question that was burning up inside her. "And you?"

"You'll never guess what I found."

-25-

Hammersmith, West London

Still feeling exhilarated, Ratso had suggested Jock and Nancy join him at one of the riverside pubs, not too far from his dreary apartment in Hammersmith Grove. The Dove, just upstream of Hammersmith Bridge, was full of history dating back to the 17th century. It was small but fun if you could beat the evening rush of locals chilling out in its photo-lined rooms. They had arrived just after 6pm with his promise of dinner at Sagar to follow. He hadn't yet volunteered to Jock that the Indian restaurant was vegetarian. No doubt afterwards the Scot would be complaining that he was still *fair famished* and needed a fish supper or a meat pie.

The late summer sun was starting to sink towards Heathrow as they settled in with pints of Guinness and a spritzer for Nancy. On the small balcony with its iron railings topped with flowers and shrubs, they had a corner table where Ratso now pulled out a photocopy of a note he had found folded inside the protective cover of Lee's Samsung Galaxy.

"Sheer chance, Jock," Ratso acknowledged modestly. "I'd checked out everything in the box. I was waiting for Nancy, messing about really, so I decided to remove the cover." He produced a photo of the Samsung inside its protective cover and then with it removed. "Lee had replaced the bog-standard rear cover and fitted this clip-on fancy job which flips over to protect the screen. At some point, and maybe even that final morning, he had removed the cover, folded the note into a square and hidden it in the back."

"Must have been important," Nancy smiled. "I mean it's fiddly."

"Agreed. He didn't want the note lying around ... and yet had to keep it."

Nancy put down her spritzer in a decisive movement. "He didn't want Mandy to find it. That would make her as clean as she said."

Ratso's eyes fixed her. "Give!"

"If she knew Lee was a fixer, wouldn't she have known where he hid his sensitive stuff? And of course she'd have removed and destroyed it."

"Aye, sounds right enough."

Ratso's face showed his respect. "Unless Mandy couldn't bear to touch it – all plastered in blood and dust. There was no urgency. She had no idea we were dropping by."

"Without knowing we would be coming, she had destroyed the hard-drive. Innocently enough. I believed her – nothing sinister." Nancy helped herself to a cheese-cracker. "But I didn't like her. I don't know why. Maybe she just turns it on for men."

"She certainly oozes flighty charm." Ratso's screwed up his eyes before putting on a pair of shades as the sun sank lower. "Despite myself, I found her convincing. If she was hiding something, she never put a foot wrong."

Jock scratched his iron-grey hair. "Why a bit of paper? He could have typed or scribbled or even talked this stuff straight into the smartphone – a permanent record."

"So he didn't want to do that," suggested Nancy.

Ratso shook his head. "That's a leap too far till the IT boys have salvaged everything on his phone. Maybe he was going to dictate it into the Samsung later."

Jock studied the note. Even on the photocopy, smears of near black blood showed up, partially obscuring two corners "It looks like an agenda but it means nothing to me."

"And you were Sudoko champion in the Cauldron?"

The Scot grinned as he wiped some beer from his lips before pushing the note back to Ratso. "Sudoku plus years sorting out the heavy boys around the Glasgow bars – no help. Whit's it all about, boss?"

Ratso twisted round the piece of paper. "I'd say an agenda or a shopping list for a meeting. It's about fixing – that's a given." The three gathered close to study the details

Jupiter
TV
Final
September
WC?
Weather
Playing Conditions
Who will play?
Order?
6 – 2
10- 6
Tie
30% upfront, balance after
Dubai
Bishopsgate
Surrey
+409WGG =SJW 4878903
NO PERSONAL

"Boss, before you decipher this, what about the hand-writing? You know? The note Detective Sergeant Trasker found screwed up in Mark Rayner's briefcase saying: *You were warned.*"

Ratso stared at Lee's notes looking for inspiration. "Yup. Not destroying the note was Rayner's only mistake."

"Meaning?"

"I spoke to Lilian Trasker. Before he drove over the cliff, he had dumped his phone or phones and computer. Everything gone. Destroyed or buried somewhere. He'd stripped the house of files, everything. If he had cash stashed there, he'd removed it."

"Sanitising his legacy." Nancy breathed the words as if thinking aloud. "He'd planned the suicides carefully then."

Ratso switched screens and an image of the message from the briefcase appeared. "Very different writing. No surprise there. Lee's looks more educated. Jock, get the originals compared. Not just the writing but also the paper. Finger-prints." He drained his Guinness. "I'm assuming some hired thug mailed it to Rayner – or got it to him somehow."

"Jupiter? Is that something cricketers shout like *Geronimo or Howzat*?" Jock was unsure whether or not he was joking.

Ratso shook his head. "Means nothing to me." He pointed to *Weather*, *Playing Conditions*, *Order* and *Who will play*. That's obviously connected to fixes. As to 6-2 and 10-6, those are ones for Craig."

"Betting odds, boss? Just a thought." Nancy eased her slim navy trouser-suited figure on the slatted seat. "September's two weeks away. I'll check what's being played."

"Not dates." Ratso spoke with authority. "I'd say these are brackets linked to spot-fixing. That's a bit curious because Craig says that's almost dead in the water. The bookies don't usually accept bets like that now. Too easy to fix. Say if the fixers *knew* a batsman would get out for under or over ten runs or that wickets would fall at defined stages of the match, they'd clean up. Make a killing."

"A Tie? Is that easier to fix than a result?"

Ratso looked thoughtful, his brows knitted together. He sucked his teeth before shaking his head. "Not easier Nancy, no."

"You'd need both captains involved then." Nancy looked at each listener in turn. Jock was out of his depth but gave her a big and admiring smile.

"Craig Carter reckons someone like Lee delivering results could get millions. Sometimes cash, sometimes real estate tucked away somewhere." Ratso pushed his empty glass towards Jock hoping for a reaction but got none. "We need to check Lee's movements that morning. Mandy should know. Maybe there's a diary in his Samsung. He may have been meeting a replacement for Mark Rayner – perhaps another corrupted captain."

"Or may have been *going to meet*," Nancy prompted. "But he was blown up first."

The thought hit home. Ratso looked at the blue sky tainted with the grey of pollution from the traffic on the A4. He shifted uneasily. "That would mean this note means nothing. There'd be no fix. That would make our job a bloody sight harder."

"WC? Water Closet. Do the fixers need to ken the number of lavvies?" Jock's rasping Glaswegian hung heavily as they chuckled, while Ratso stared again at his empty glass.

"It can't be World Cup. There's none imminent, so let's backburner that. I reckon it's initials – someone like Winston Corveau, a great West Indian batsman who Craig suspects has been on the take." Ratso turned to Nancy. "Craig will get you a list of every cricketer from every country. You can check out all the WCs."

"He means flush them out, Nancy," Jock laughed as he saw Ratso looking at his empty pint and got the hint. "Same again, then boss?" He rose to get in another round before turning to look over his shoulder. "Winston Churchill. A pub maybe. Must be dozens of them."

While they waited for Jock's return, Nancy asked about the finances. "Living there, Lee wasn't short of money."

Ratso swayed his head from side to side as if weighing up that opinion. "Appearances can be deceptive. You can be seen in a Rolls-Royce but have never owned one. We need to check the detail." He leaned forward and beckoned her to do the same, her perfume now apparent over the cigar smoke drifting from the next table. "Craig told me Westdale only narrowly avoided bankruptcy a while back. Something to do with a scam in New York. He more or less lost everything but fought back, paying off his creditors."

"Good PR. How did he do that?"

"If you believe the spin, he worked harder. If you're a cynical Detective Inspector, you might say he fixed matches and got bungs in brown envelopes."

"New York?" mused Nancy as she stood up beside Ratso to watch a pleasure-boat chugging up the Thames with a steel band. It was playing *Yellow Bird*, one of her favourites. She swayed her hips to the lilting rhythm, something not lost on Ratso. As the music faded, she sat down and continued. "When I was searching the bedroom, Mandy mentioned New York." She paused to gather her thoughts as Jock returned with the drinks and bags of pork scratchings which she and Ratso declined.

"All the more for me," Jock enthused. "Any roads, a bit of history for ye," Jock's florid features looked smug. "Which King used to come here?" He sat down and took in the blank stares. "Call yerselves English and it takes a Scot to teach ye! It was King Charles the Second. Used to chat up yon orange seller here – Nell Gwynne."

"No doubt treating her to pork scratchings to get his wicked way," suggested Ratso.

Nancy gave a thumbs-down. "Wouldn't do it for me, boss. I'd want at least an entire wild boar."

"A wild boar?" Ratso's face broke into a broad grin, all the better for it being a rare sight. "Sounds like Jock. But maybe he's not so wild these days." He and Nancy exchanged high-fives. "Back then I expect they ate at least an ox or two, a couple of swans plus a dozen of her oranges before hitting the sack." They all clinked glasses. "Anyway, New York. Carry on, Nancy."

"Seems like there was a meeting for the victims. Billions had disappeared in some Fund. Parabolic, she called it. New York attorneys are running a lawsuit to recover the losses. She said that signing up to sue had got Lee out of his depression. Apparently, he'd lost four million. Parabolic was supposed to deliver a 12% return – well over four-hundred grand a year. They were heavily borrowed – mortgage, cars. The lost cash-flow destroyed their lifestyle. Till he bounced back."

"12%? Lee believed that? Crazy." Ratso's eyes blinked as he chopped his hand across the table. "Sounds like a classic Ponzi. Okay I get this bit – a lawsuit might give the losers hope. But if she's saying that was the turning-point in Lee's fortunes and his mindset, I don't buy that. All he had was a distant chance of compensation. So why so cheery? Makes no sense."

"I read somewhere. These US lawsuits can take years."

"You're right, Nancy." Ratso glanced at Jock who was patting his belly which bulged over the top of his jeans. With his extra weight, the Scot was looking his age tonight and the drooping grey moustache did not help.

"Give the guy a wee break, boss. It's whit Lee Westdale *perceived* that counts. Mebbe he'd swallowed the slick lawyer talk"

"*Perceived*? That's a long word for you Jock. Been studying your Scottish – English dictionary again?"

Jock paused for a moment before replying. "Learned it from Tosh Watson." This was an in-joke because Detective Sergeant Tosh Watson struggled with any word longer than four letters.

"I'm with Jock, boss. *Perception* might have been a straw to clutch at."

Ratso looked at Nancy's narrowed eyes and her raised eyebrow. He was unconvinced but was not going to dampen her enthusiasm. "For now, assume you're both right." He raised his glass to each of them. "Check out this New York scam. Who were the victims? Who are the attorneys? What did they promise? How did Westdale get into an investment over there? Was it really his money that went in? How did he happen to have a cool four million?"

"Got it." Nancy sounded enthusiastic. "So, according to this note, something is going to happen in September." She tapped the note. "And involving WC."

"Craig can tell us the fixtures. There are still some one-day games here in September but the fixed match has to be televised to attract the mega punters."

"Where are the biggest matches, boss?"

"In September? The biggest games for the punters? I'd say in India, Sri Lanka or Bangladesh – or maybe Dubai." Even as he said the word, his hand was thumping the table. "Of course, of course, the note mentions Dubai. I thought that was linked to hot-money transfers but maybe Pakistan are playing a home match there."

"Boss?"

"National teams no longer go to Pakistan since eight police officers were murdered and several cricketers injured. Terrorists shot-up the Sri Lankan team bus. So Pakistan play their so-called *home* matches in the UAE – that includes Dubai."

"With no so much cricket next month, it shouldna' be difficult to find the right match then." Jock drained his pint as if from a thimble. "That curry, boss. My stomach's rumbling worse than the night train to Glasgow."

Ratso agreed but absent-mindedly. "But Bishopsgate?" he mused.

"The payoff was 30% upfront and 70% on success." Nancy checked the note again. "Reckon the pay-out is in Bishopsgate?" She looked and sounded hesitant to push her limited knowledge too far.

"And the number looks like a code or password."

Ratso looked into the distance, a faraway look in his eyes. "I went to Bishopsgate way back in 1993. The IRA had set off a bomb there. I wheeled my father along it a few days later." His eyes closed at the difficult memories. "It's quite long. Full of tower blocks. With expensive City rents, there aren't many small shops, pubs and places to grab a coffee. Not ideal for a secret divvy up of the winnings. We'll need to check it out."

Nancy stretched back, raising her hands above head so that her summery-thin white blouse beneath the navy jacket emphasised her small but shapely breasts. As ever, she was keen to keep on message. "Would there be banks? Maybe Lee's bank?"

Ratso thought for a moment. "Don't know but I guess so. London bankers are pretty damned slack over handling hot money but they're getting better. A big fat wad coming in from Dubai might prompt questions. *It ought to.* Nancy, ask Mandy Westdale where they banked. The statements I glanced at today only gave sort codes and account numbers."

"Mebbe a money-changer on Bishopsgate running hawala on the side?"

"Bang on, Jock! That's what I was thinking too. A poky newsagent fronting for hawala transfers – or a money-exchange joint. There's a few of those not far from Liverpool Street station." They rose from their seats and for a moment watched a rowing coach in his tiny motor-boat use his megaphone to bellow at eight rowers as they skimmed their way upstream.

As Ratso turned away, his phone rang. "Yes, oh hello Craig." His face lit up. "Interesting, interesting."

-26-

Beverly Hills, California

Vijay Chetri paced nervously around the sofas and deep-padded armchairs. He was in Bungalow 5 at the Pink Palace, otherwise known as the Beverly Hills Hotel. It was his preferred bungalow of the many tucked in the grounds behind the hotel's frontage and all reached via verdantly lined walkways. Pagano was due any moment with Alex Anderson joining them about thirty minutes later.

He loved the hotel and its place in Hollywood history with ghosts of Marilyn Monroe, Frank Sinatra, Elizabeth Taylor, Elvis Presley and President John F Kennedy being just a handful of the rich and famous who had savoured the pale pink and green décor.

The previous afternoon, Chetri had been picked up from the airport by the hotel's limo. At the Villa Blanca restaurant he had agreed a College Basketball fix with a former star but since then, his mind had been full of today's Pagano and Anderson confrontation. Just thinking of the meeting gave him dagger-like pains in his stomach. He felt like an uneasy pig-in-the-middle – wary of Pagano's wrath but hesitant about how Anderson would react.

Right on time, there was a knock on the door. One of the front-desk team had escorted Pagano to the bungalow. "Enzo! Come in." The small Indian waved a dark brown hairless arm towards his guest. The Indian had chosen a black silk shirt with short sleeves to match his tailored slacks and his usual highly-polished tasselled loafers.

Pagano ignored shaking hands but his curt nod was just about friendly as he waddled in. His tough physique gone-to-seed was not designed for his faded jeans or indeed anything casual. He needed to wear just the type of clothes that he spurned – a double-breasted jacket cut long might have concealed the broad leather belt skulking beneath the rolls of belly. As it was, he looked bulky and uncomfortable but Pagano had no interest in his appearance. With the tufted grey hair now slightly overlong above each ear and a face that could smile with the duplicity of a tiger, experience had taught him that he could still get whatever he wanted.

"Outside or in? I thought outside."

"The patio if we can't be overheard," Pagano growled.

Without speaking, Chetri led Pagano to a white circular table with three chairs already around it. On it was an oversized fruit platter. Guests using the patio could relax behind pastel pink walls, surrounded by tropical shrubs and the reds and whites of flowers that mingled with the lush green of the trees. The noise and fumes from Sunset Boulevard were lost in the soothing calm of the cloistered yard. "We've a bottle of chilled Krug."

"Save it till after the Brit has gone. That won't be long." Pagano rolled his bulk onto the chair with something between a sigh and a grunt.

"You living so close, I thought we'd maybe meet at your home. More convenient for you."

Pagano raised his eyes beneath his wild and wiry salt and pepper eyebrows. For a moment, they flashed irritation. "You said it. Monovale Road is my *home*. I don't run a Super 8 Motel – or rent out through Airbnb." He jabbed a stubby finger towards the listener.

"My home gets treated as a hotel," laughed the Indian showing his white and gold teeth. "My wife is one of nine. They're always visiting. Their husbands, kids and even grandkids drink, eat, spill, crawl and fart everywhere." He laughed again though Pagano could sense that behind his rimless glasses the Indian was nervous. "Maybe you're right, Enzo. Perhaps my home should be my castle."

Pagano softened for a moment but he too was like a coiled spring waiting to pounce on the Brit. Nervous he was not. That's the way he wanted it – no niceties. Just tell the fucker the way it was and kick him out. There was nothing the wuss could do about it. "Leave the talking to me. Right?"

Chetri had serious reservations about messing with Anderson, so he just nodded without enthusiasm. "Enzo, I'm not backing off … but, I mean," his head wobbled back and forth, his eyes looking startled, "we don't know much of Alex's background. Only what he's told us."

Pagano glared at Chetri, taking in the perfect symmetry of his face and head. His plentiful silver hair seamlessly joined his neatly trimmed beard by each ear. The beard circled under his chin before joining in with his moustache. It was all close-cropped and matched his manicured eyebrows precisely. "You chicken? Alex don't scare me none. The guy's done good, real good from HOSS. Now he's raised a white flag 'cos some jerk-off cricketer who cost us a bundle went over the cliff … tough shit, baby! No way is he getting his snout in the Jupiter trough." He bit angrily into a juicy pear before continuing. "You don't like it, then you can quit too."

The Indian was too edgy to sit down and he circled the table uneasily, all the while rubbing his hands together in front of him. "Maybe as a fall-back, we should, er, I mean cut him some slack on Jupiter. Give him ten percent and we get forty-five each. Keep him onside. Buy some insurance, if you will."

"You crazy? No way. Alex has made over thirteen million through HOSS and the cricket. The guy can take a hike."

There was an over-long silence as Chetri hovered, debating whether to speak or shut up. "Alex may not see it that way. He's invested in Jupiter. Maybe he could cut up rough," The Indian grasped the chair-back to stop his hands from trembling. "Maybe, he'll see only what he's going to lose. We had a deal on Jupiter."

Pagano snorted at the word *deal* and took another bite from his pear before hurling it against the tiled floor where the juicy remains exploded, spattering in every direction. At that moment, there was a rap at the door. Chetri hurried towards it, his mind still in turmoil. "Ah, Alex. Good to see you. Come on in. Enzo's just arrived."

-27-

Hammersmith, West London

After leaving Jock muttering about lack of meat at dinner, Ratso turned into the soul-less anonymity of Hammersmith Grove. The best feature was the large trees that lined it. He had never liked the street or his rented first floor apartment with tenants above and below him. On the other side of the road, some houses had been gentrified for one-family occupation. Unfortunately, his pad had no view of their chi-chi front yards and palm trees. His window looked across to a derelict shop, one window broken and the paint faded.

Towards Shepherds Bush were what the local realtors called *prestigious double-fronted family homes* but as he climbed the twelve cracked stone steps to the brown front-door, *prestigious* was not a word that sprang to mind. Even in the twilight, it was obvious the windows had not been washed in years. A dead plant in a pot was all that remained of a line of four, the other three having been stolen last year.

Once inside, he was hit by the usual smell of garlic drifting from the neighbour's ground-floor kitchen. It was mixed with the stench from the battered pram that the family kept in the hall next to a kid's trike. It was no place to impress guests. *Bleeding miracle I ever get my end away in this dump.* He tried to ignore the brown lino and the worn but stained green carpet on the stairs.

He cheered up after entering his two-bedroomed apartment.

Before Kirsty-Ann had flown in from Florida, he had spent a couple of weekends and occasional evenings decorating the place in contrasting colours, trying to add feminine touches with subtle lighting and new furnishings from Ikea.

It was the best he could afford and a big improvement but on looking at the ragbag assortment of cutlery, mugs and plates, he had still felt embarrassed. In a moment of panic, he had busted his budget by booking them into the cosy ambience of Bailey's Hotel on Gloucester Road, something he had never regretted.

He poured himself a Guinness and settled back on the new sofa to watch the recorded T20 match between South Africa and Sri Lanka. When he had phoned, Craig Carter had encouraged him to study it. "Shit happens," Carter had told him. "It's pretty damned suspicious but not evidence. We've got to get to the guys hidden deep down."

As he debated a final can of Guinness, Ratso noticed the South African quick bowler's initials – WC.

Willy Corretty.

He wrote down the name to check out. Corretty seemed an unlikely candidate. As a specialist bowler, he might as well have batted using a stick of rhubarb for all the good he was. His highest ever score was only seven but as a devilishly quick and dangerous bowler, he could be pivotal in influencing a result – but not on his own.

Ratso swigged a final mouthful of stout as he replayed a particularly curious over bowled by Corretty. If he had intended to bowl badly, he got a straight A.

Where would Corretty be playing in September?
Would he be touring in India?

He kicked off his shoes and flung his long legs onto the sofa, wondering whether he could persuade his boss, Mick Tolvey, to support a trip to India. The ringing phone disturbed his thoughts but his irritation disappeared when he saw that it was Kirsty-Ann.

His face broke into a warm smile. "Heh! Great to hear from you."

"You too, Todd. I can't skype. I just wanted to hear your voice."

"Call us quits on that!"

"What's going on? Still nothing bringing you my way?" She spoke in a slow southern drawl. "Y'know I'm missing y'all."

"Make that two of us. But no. Nothing. I'm still working on cricket stuff and you Americans aren't into that. Too slow and too subtle." He enjoyed the little dig. She laughed and Ratso could imagine her head rocking back and her natural blonde hair swaying around her ears.

"From that clip you showed me, it seemed to be all about men in white coats waving their arms and everyone stopping for a few drops of rain."

"You learn fast, sweetie! But here's the good news – I'm saving for a trip to Florida. Maybe in November. I want to meet your mum and Leon."

"That'll be just awesome. You can stay here. Leon will so love having someone to do boy-stuff with him."

"So long as he doesn't get too used to it. You understand."

"Hey, you know I understand. What we have is wonderful. Sure it's too long distance. But it's the best … since…" Her voice died away with memories of her newly-wed husband being gunned down four years previously.

Ratso dived in quickly to stop her train of thought. "How's Bucky?" He was referring to her larger than life waffle-eating Chief at the Fort Lauderdale Police Department.

"He's doing just great."

"What's keeping you busy?"

"A celebrity Pro-Choice couple were murdered yesterday. Feelings are running pretty high here."

Ratso was confused. "Pro-Choice?"

"You got Pro-Life – they are anti-abortion. You got Pro-Choice – freedom to make your own decisions. The airwaves are full of it. My worry is retaliation – revenge killings."

"You take care, Kirsty! Your country is too full of gun-carrying crazies!"

"Hey, don't let it stop you come visit. Oh Lordy! That's Leon shouting for his pizza." She blew a couple of kisses down the line and was gone leaving Ratso wishing the September cricket had been in the West Indies. He might have wangled a routing via Florida.

-28-

Beverly Hills, California

S howing no signs of fatigue after his five hour flight, Alex Anderson looked the most relaxed of the three men grouped round the coffee, juice, fresh fruit and giant double-chocolate cookies. He sat, arms lying loosely on the table, legs stretched out whereas Vijay never stopped moving, arms and legs fidgeting. The blood vessels around Pagano's cheeks looked fit to burst as he waited for a chance to let rip at the Brit. It wasn't coming soon, not the way Anderson was playing it.

Anderson was deliberately small-talking about the flight, the golf in Florida, the UK's political scene and the previous day's racing. Though he knew he was in the hot-seat, he was damned if he was going to show it. In his Ralph Lauren pink shirt and immaculately pressed white trousers, Anderson might almost have passed for one of the hotel staff. It was calculated nonchalance, a determination to let the other two seethe as he strung out getting to their purpose of the meeting.

It was over thirty-five minutes before Pagano could keep up the pretence of civility no longer. "Okay Alex. Fuck all this bullshit. Let's cut to the quick. We're here to decide about you and Jupiter, not talking shit about the weather or room service at the Beverly Wilshire Hotel."

"Remember where we left off before?" Chetri tried to soften the harshness.

"Of course," Anderson responded as he crossed his legs and smiled at each in turn. "I've decided. I vote we continue with HOSS and Jupiter. No more T20 cricket."

Pagano selected a strawberry with care. "You don't like what happened over the cliff. Some guy who stiffed us? We sure as hell don't shed no crocodile tears over that shitbag. If you do, that's your call. But nothing changes. T20 is easy pickings, brings us big bucks."

"Is that it? Your final word?" Anderson's reply came after a long silence while he sipped some juice.

Hopping from one leg to the other, Chetri was now studying a creeper clinging to the wall. Anderson spotted at once that the Indian was distancing himself from any violent reaction. Then he turned around, his tone wheedling, his small and delicate hands clasped in front of his chest. "The deaths of Rayner and Lee Westdale haven't screwed us. Alex, we've other assets in place."

Anderson said nothing but gave each man a nod and a smile.

"Here's the deal," continued Pagano. "Going forward, we fix *anything* we can – basketball, maybe the occasional baseball game, soccer, you name it. Cricket is in. You are ...OUT!" Pagano's voice rose to a crescendo as he barked out the final word.

If he had hoped for a strong reaction, Pagano was to be disappointed. The Englishman said nothing, simply smiling at each man in turn before stretching out for a second cookie. Pagano was wrong-footed. He had expected anything but this. The silence confused him and as the seconds ticked away, he had to fill the vacuum. "You are in breach of our deal — this ain't no pick and mix. We were in this together."

Silence.

This time, there was no smile, no sign that the Englishman

had even heard what was said. Chetri watched Anderson's hands, wary that a gun was about to be pulled. Uncertain how to cope, the Indian could think of nothing to say.

Pagano jabbed a finger towards the Englishman. "You break our deal, you face the consequences." To Chetri, this sounded lame.

Silence.

"Like, you can go fuck yourself before we'll repay you a dime of your one-million in Jupiter or your investment in HOSS." Pagano's pudgy hand finger-pointed across the table in a series of rapid jabs.

Silence.

Anderson did not move.

Pagano looked at Chetri as if seeking inspiration on what to say next. But the Indian was just as confused at the deadpan reaction. Eventually, when he judged the moment right, Anderson brushed aside a cookie crumb from his thigh in a dismissive gesture. Then he rose to his full height and stretched out his tanned arm to shake hands. "Cheerio."

Pagano ignored the gesture and stared pointedly into the branches of a tree that towered over the pink wall. Chetri however after a moment's hesitation, shook hands. Formalities done, Anderson turned with a slow swivel on his white striped sneakers and strolled into the bungalow. He then exited, closing the door gently behind him.

After he had gone, Pagano crunched noisily on a cookie, still confused by what had happened. In his experience, confrontations were noisy and sometimes violent. Victory had never come so easily. At last he stood up and scratched his spread of backside. "Played that well. Took the wind right outta him. Got him goddamned speechless. I told you the guy's a wuss."

Chetri was standing by the barbecue, clutching the framework as his head spun. "I don't like it. That was too easy. Alex has just walked away from millions."

Pagano stood close to eyeball him. "Open the Krug. Like I said all along – that guy is flaky. Now we share 50-50. What's not to like?" With an almost imperceptible nod, the Indian turned away to fetch the chilled champagne and glasses, his thoughts filled with the disconcerting image of the menace in Anderson's parting smile.

Not far away, Anderson ambled slowly to the Polo Lounge's shaded patio. He felt like a glass of champagne with smoked salmon sandwiches. A smile of quiet satisfaction still lingered.

-29-

London

Munching a jumbo-sized hot dog with onions and mustard, Ratso took his seat in the vast bowl of Wembley Stadium in north-west London. Normally the home of English big occasion soccer, today it was hosting American Football, so different to what Americans know as soccer. Beside him was Craig Carter who had got freebie tickets from a good mate.

"How long does this game last?" asked Ratso.

Craig laughed. "That depends how you look at it. One answer is sixty minutes."

"So an hour plus maybe injury time?"

Still laughing, Craig spluttered and almost choked on his burger while Ratso looked utterly confused. "The ball is in play for an average of just eleven minutes."

"Christ! I won't have even finished my dog."

"Oh you will … believe me. A typical match lasts over three hours."

"For eleven minutes action?" Ratso pointed to the whirling movement beside the pitch. "No wonder they have these stunning cheerleaders to provide the entertainment."

"I came last year and got really into it. Just like cricket, you need to understand what each team is attempting. There's huge strategy involved."

Ratso nodded. *That* made sense but how eleven minutes action could take three hours was beyond him. "I heard the sport was catching on here but it's passed me by."

"There's been fixing in this sport – not this match though," Craig added quickly. "Least not that I know about," he laughed. "Baseball, basketball, ice-hockey, tennis. They've all had scandals. We shouldn't get too blinkered to cricket."

The stadium was packed but without the passion that normally preceded a Cup Final – no partisan fans singing and chanting from each end. Ratso shivered in the evening air. There was an unusual nip and he was glad of his large tea. "Nancy said you'd tracked down nine WCs."

"Since then, I've ruled out all the English ones. They're only playing games not televised. I'm going to India for meetings but on the evidence we have, the WC links are pretty damned flimsy." Carter leaned slightly closer. "These illegal bookies are no mugs. On TV, there's a delay in transmission between when a batsman hits the ball and TV viewers actually seeing it. *Latency* I think it's called. What you'd see on TV can be one, maybe even two balls behind the action."

"And?"

"The bookies will have spotters on their phones at the match paid to report ball by ball. Get the drift?" Ratso did but was too busy devouring the last inch of his dog to respond. "The bookies can change the odds knowing something *has already happened.*"

Ratso pursed his lips in a tuneless whistle. "That … plus fixed players … makes setting odds and insider betting a no-brainer!" He looked at Craig and could tell there was more to come. He was right.

"It gets better or worse, depending how you look at it. Suppose there's a fix that a bowler will concede say fifteen runs during his six-ball over."

"Go on."

"The bowler will give a pre-arranged signal like tying a boot-lace or complaining to the umpire about the shape of the ball. This causes delay which is what the fixers want. The spotter sees the message and tells a bookie thousands of miles away the fix is on. He then bets his millions knowing what is likely to happen."

"Tonight's game is being televised globally. So, it could be happening here?"

Craig shifted awkwardly on his seat and spoke quietly. "Why not? This is an Exhibition Match – nothing depends on the result. Well, maybe bragging rights but it's not as if the Superbowl hangs on every move."

"Do the Indians, Bangladeshis and so on, do they bet on American Football?"

"Of course – these gangsters operating in Dubai or Mumbai, they run a book whenever they can get an edge and the punters pile in. Plus I'm told there's plenty enough wealthy Americans who would mortgage their Gran to buy a result." Craig realised they had got side-tracked. "Oh yes – WCs – none of the Indian team has those initials. So there's only Winston Carmichael. Bats number four for the West Indies. He'll be in India."

"The last two?"

"A couple of South Africans who will not be in India and who have no big matches in September."

Ratso's lack of enthusiasm showed. His lips narrowed as he thought it through. "If a fix is on, you'd need WCs in the Indian team, surely? So what next?"

"India ought to be strong favourites against the Windies. The best odds should be on India to lose," Craig poured coffee from a flask which smelled suspiciously as if he'd slipped in a tot of brandy.

"Maybe WC meant what it said on the tin. A meeting in a WC to pass information? To hand over some dosh."

Craig offered coffee but Ratso declined. "Open mind on that, Todd. What about Jupiter?"

"Isn't Jupiter a pretty damned big planet?"

"The largest. Could be a pointer to something big."

Unimpressed, Ratso at first said nothing as they both stood to cheer the appearance of the teams. "The pieces don't seem to fit. Plus the note said *Final*."

Craig was now more interested in the scene below. "So maybe just the last match of the three in India will be fixed?"

Even though he usually avoided fast-food, Ratso wiped mustard from his lower lip approvingly. "*Final* sounds more like a cup game, not something from the best of three." Ratso was applauding but with less gusto than Craig. More important to him was trying to make sense of the oddities – *WC, Jupiter, Dubai, Bishopsgate. Final*. Both men sat down. "If we're right so far then the fix has to be on India to lose to the West Indies – maybe in the final match."

"September is the only link to the list."

Carter looked at his phone as it buzzed. His face showed no big reaction but from the way he gripped Ratso's arm, it seemed to be important. "New information from India. I think you'll find it … rather interesting. I'll explain after the game."

"Christ! That's hours away! Wake me if I'm asleep."

-30-

London

Vijay Chetri had not been sleeping well since the Beverly Hills confrontation. Not that it had been confrontational in the classic sense, not the way Alex had played it. Yet behind that parting smile, Chetri continued to sense something deep and disturbing. Now, as he waited for his guest to arrive, his eyes were lowered, his hands restless showing his troubled thoughts.

When he did not want to be spotted, Chetri avoided the West End's famous Indian restaurants like the Tamarind or Gymkhana. Anyway, if he wanted good Indian food, nothing could beat his wife's naan bread, her succulent Butter Chicken and her Rajma. This evening, as the American football was being played a few miles away at Wembley, he was meeting his gofer, Eric Sommer, in Belsize Village. He liked the Italian restaurant's discreet lighting, intimate booths and great cooking. He was not there often enough to be known and anyway, most of the couples who used it had eyes only for each other.

He thought back to Pagano. In a sharp move, he broke a breadstick and prodded it into the butter, still pissed off at the guy's arrogance.

Was Alex now history?
He had better be.
He had been very quiet.
Too quiet maybe?

Think of better things – like Jupiter.
At least Lee Westdale had sewn that up.

It was a solitary cheering thought as Eric Sommer appeared. He was below average height but with an ungainly frame. Though his face was unprepossessing, he walked with a swagger, rolling his shoulders back and forward to add what he hoped was a *don't mess* image. His ferret-sharp eyes peered furtively round the small dining area, all red and green furnishings, till he spotted the Indian.

"Eric, good to see you. It's been a while." Vijay's surprisingly long and slender fingers wrapped around the meatier grip of the Englishman's fist. He sounded more enthusiastic than he felt.

"Not since before …" Sommer's gravelly voice with its Essex accent trailed off. "Helluva shock. You been up Piccadilly since then?"

Vijay shook his head. "Been travelling." His diction as usual was perfect, contrasting to the rasp of the Essex boy done good.

"Besides them buildings what collapsed, more is being pulled down or shored up. Right old mess. Gonna take years."

Vijay caught the waiter's eye. "Your usual, Eric?" He saw the smile on the thirty-something's face. "Make that two gin and tonics, twist of lime and plenty of ice."

"Good holiday then?"

Vijay paused before answering. "Good enough."

Eric Sommers guessed the Indian was lying but did not care. *Think of the money me old son.* He looked at the menu and struggled with the Italian. "What you reckon?"

"It's all excellent. I usually go for the fish or the veal." He tapped his watch. "Shall we order? I've another meeting to get to." It was not true but mixing with Sommer was business, never pleasure.

Twenty minutes later they were into their starters with a chilled

2012 Chardonnay between them. "Tell me about Dubai," Vijay prompted.

"I saw P.T. Stopped off there on the way back from Mumbai, didn't I?"

Vijay's face broke into a warm smile. P.T. was their key contact, an abbreviation for a shadowy figure they had nicknamed Pigeon-Toes. "Was he scared about the Jupiter figures?"

"Nah! Piece of cake. P.T. said one-sixty mill easy. More even. Maybe over three-hundred. Plenty liquidity." These days, as Sommer would tell people, he *lived alone and posh* in an Edwardian house overlooking the Thames Estuary at Leigh-on-Sea. But his childhood had been very different – a rough school in Chingford. Since then, several of his mates had been jailed. Sommer could have been one of them but at his right turn, left turn moment, he had taken a job in a Dagenham betting-shop. There, till his mid-twenties he had learned the business, listening to mug punters and spotting the occasional shrewd ones who ticked over a steady profit.

His first lucky break had been meeting Anant Tomar, a bent Indian cricketer who was playing for Essex Foresters. Sommer had noticed that his bets on cricket were uncannily successful, even in games where he was not playing like the Patriots v Hawks. Having won Tomar's trust, he had been introduced to Chetri, someone Tomar described as a *top, top man*. Now nine years later, Sommer drove a Jaguar and lived well. He was a snappy dresser always buying designer suits that merely emphasised his awkward shape.

In Eric Sommer, Chetri had spotted the qualities he was looking for – street-smart, devious and ruthless for easy money. Chetri had set him up to oversee a chain of six betting-shops around London but otherwise he was the go-to man. A few years back, Sommer had travelled to Dubai with Vijay for the first time and been introduced to a dark-skinned Indian who they referred to only as P.T. Over cocktails in the Fairmont, Sommer had learned of the billions being gambled in the illegal betting market. "This is where the real money is made," Chetri had explained. "And with contacts who fix matches, we can all make real money."

As if reading Sommer's thoughts, Chetri glanced across the starters. "We've come a long way." They clinked glasses, misty with condensation. "Now to the other business. The note? Did Mark Rayner keep it? You were watching I assume?"

Eric shifted his buttocks in a manner that left Vijay unconvinced he would get the truth. There was also something in the sideways glance and the quick lick of the lips. "He never saw me. 'Course he looked round the hospital car-park but he ain't seen nix." Eric grinned. "Why? I'll tell you why. 'Cos I was only watchin' from inside the bleedin' hospital wasn't I? Upstairs window. You with me?"

"Yes – but the note?"

"It was getting dark. Hard to see."

"You looked for it after he left?" Vijay sounded anxious and his normally calm wrinkle-free features looked troubled.

Sommer gave a dismissively hostile look. Despite his full-moon-face and toothy smile, Chetri had always sensed he was not someone to cross. Now, when his good sense was questioned, Sommer's eyes were mean and unflinching. "I didn't find it. Mind it was a windy night. Might have blown away but my take? Rayner trousered it." He flourished his fork. "Meaning the Old Bill could have it by now."

Vijay looked puzzled.

Sommer laughed. "The Old Bill? The cops, the rozzers, the Sweeney, the cozzers, the filth, the pigs, the law. Them lot down at Scotland bleedin' Yard."

The Indian fell silent as he weighed up the risks while the

waiter set out their mains. As Sommer grabbed his knife and fork with all the finesse of a starved baboon, Vijay continued. "So you wrote it?" He saw the nod. "Your DNA on the paper?"

"I wore gloves."

"You always told me you have no criminal record?"

Sommer laughed. "Clean as a whistle me old mate."

Vijay flinched. Sommer was useful but old mates they were not. Vijay did not believe in mates whether old or young. "We've lost Lee Westdale. No Mark Rayner. What's Anant Tomar doing about it?"

"He's still got eight or nine guys." Sommer grinned. "Relax, Vijay. It's all good mate. Full on." Sommer had a *didn't-I-do-good* look on his rounded cheeks. "Me and Tomar, we got, y'know, all bases covered. Before that effing bomb got Westdale, we had all them ducks in a row." He lowered his eyes briefly. "So yeah, it's business as usual, no sweat."

As he raised his hand to pat down his unruly mop of brown hair, a tattoo momentarily appeared on Sommer's right wrist. For a sickening moment, Vijay wondered if that was the last thing Yvonne Rayner had seen when the acid had been hurled into her face. He wiped his mouth and hands as if cleansing himself of any involvement. Suddenly, he no longer wanted to be with Sommer and started to eat faster.

He had found out what he needed anyway. Get the odds right after Day One and Jupiter could be worth two-hundred mill. At least.

-31-

London

As he waited for Ratso to drop by, DCS Mick Tolvey wondered what made Detective Inspector Todd Holtom tick. Was he ambitious? After promotion? Desperate to prove his worth? Or did he prefer being a maverick, sometimes irritating to superiors but inspiring loyalty from his own team?

Tolvey looked at Todd Holtom's record. The man didn't like to be called sir and rarely dressed in a suit or tie. He couldn't be faulted for effort – the guy was obsessive, worked all hours. But for all Tolvey's uncertainty, so far, they had bonded well, seemingly because he had given Ratso the freedom he wanted. One thing was certain – Todd Holtom got the best from those around him... even when, like now, his efforts and investigations were getting nowhere.

He flicked through his DI's latest report but his thoughts were still more focussed on warnings from the Assistant Commissioner about Holtom's tendency to ski off-piste. It was a risky pastime in the Met. *Unless you got lucky and nailed the bastards. And not always then.*

And, as his record showed, Todd Holtom had not always been right. He was not infallible, nobody was.

Tolvey turned away from Holtom's report and stared at the photo of his three kids, all early teens now and living with their mother since the divorce. True, he got to see them often enough but nothing could bring back what they had shared until their mum had taken off, sick to death of being a copper's wife. *No one else involved* as she had said. Almost made it worse really – her preferring to have no man, rather than be with him.

Perhaps Ratso's determination to remain single was an example of his good judgement, at least on that. His uncomfortable thoughts were interrupted by the tap on the door and Ratso's immediate entry without waiting for any request. Tolvey signalled towards his personal cafetière. "Morning, sir. And yes, a coffee would be good. Rather a late night with Craig Carter. Watching American football certainly makes life seem shorter. But I got into it – well a bit anyway."

"Give me rugby at Twickenham any day. Anything to add to your report?"

Ratso knew at once that Tolvey had not been impressed. "I want to go to India, sir. Delhi."

"Who doesn't, Todd? Interesting place for a holiday – and especially for someone like you – all that cricket." Tolvey's smile was foxy. "You could even do the Taj Mahal if you wanted some culture."

Ratso fumbled inside his bomber jacket and produced his smartphone. "See this, sir." He handed it over and Tolvey took in a high quality picture of a table stacked with food with Lee Westdale leaning over towards someone Tolvey did not recognise.

"Who? Where? When?"

"Chutney Mary, London. Nitin Mithi, the Indian team captain. Last April. There's another. The Bombay Brasserie taken the week before the bombing."

"Conclusion besides sheer conjecture?"

Ratso's voice showed he did not appreciate the negativity. "The smartphone, *sir*. Look at the phone he's using." The hidden subtext of *get real arsehole* was not lost on Tolvey.

"Yes. I can see Lee is holding one ... and in the second picture he's tapping into it."

"An Indian photographer took these. Craig Carter no doubt tipped him a good lunch to get hold of them. The snapper reckons Lee was scribbling into the phone. Making notes."

"So?"

"That is not the phone he had with him when he died. That was a Samsung Galaxy and the IT boys found nothing useful on it. All routine stuff – calls to his folks, to Mandy, photos of his kids. Crap basically. Like for example, sir, he did not have Mark Rayner's contacts in there. Yet they had been good mates." He tapped the photos in emphasis. "And Mandy, the widow, she told us he used the Galaxy for everything."

"He had two phones? So was Mandy duped or lying to you?"

"Open question, sir," Ratso nodded. "The Galaxy was found on him in the rubble. The other one? Either not with him or lost and dumpstered away with all the other debris."

"Maybe abandoned. Or left at home that day."

"Agreed, sir." He nodded his head in emphasis. "We never found a second phone at his home."

Tolvey raised his left hand as if to pat down his hair but he was completely shaved, the only visible hair being a grey shadow across his skull. "Nothing in his bank records about running two phones?"

Ratso shook his head. "The Samsung was paid on direct debit monthly. This other one must have been off-the-books. Cash job."

"Maybe he had several phones."

Ratso laughed as he agreed. "Fixers and drug dealers change their phones more often than ... than an incontinent vagrant changes his underwear."

Tolvey's angular face almost broke into a grin. "I'll remember to use that one over breakfast with the A.C." He turned serious. "So we have a link to a key figure in the Indian team. Good … but it proves nothing."

"Sir. The IT boys found nothing in Westdale's phone about meeting this guy. No phone numbers or calls. No mention in his electronic diary."

"I see. You're telling me his missing phone contained his double-life."

"Correct. Sir, I want to go to India. Support Craig Carter."

"Todd – I've read your report. You can't explain Bishopsgate, Jupiter, WC. From the rest of the note, you're jumping to a conclusion using September as the part of the jigsaw that fits. The rest you've chucked away. Now you want to charge off like a bull to India."

"Over-simplification, sir but you're right – we've found nothing definitive. We got Doc Premadasa's evidence, the Jupiter note and now these photos."

"Home phone records?"

"DC Petrie checked. Zilch. No pattern. Nothing unusual."

"Reliable? She would spot something?"

"Yup. Nancy's a smart kid." He refrained from telling Tolvey that on the way back from Wembley, he'd spotted the young detective outside the Red Cow in Shepherd's Bush. She'd been waving her arms and belting it out to *Knock Three Times* coming from inside the pub. As Craig had waited at the lights, Ratso had considered surprising her by joining in till he saw Jock's puce face the other side of the pub window as he too stomped feverishly, matching her movements, head rolling from side to side.

Amazing what a droopy moustache could do.

"Mandy?" Tolvey's enquiring tone brought Ratso back to the present.

Ratso put the image of the wild dancing from his mind. "Woman's take? Petrie reckons she's a tough nut, a ball-breaker. Kept him in line."

"Evidence?"

"Impression, sir. Sure, she's a genuine grieving widow. No evidence of him playing away from home. Nor her. Not yet anyway. But there's something between me, her and the naked truth."

"Todd, you're sounding like a late night condom ad."

"The difference is that it's her that's holding back." Ratso's retort was instant and Tolvey laughed.

"You reckon she knew what her hubbie...?"

"Can't prove it ... but she's one smart cookie."

"And?"

"I'll lean on her." Even as he said it, he remembered he had to press Nancy for her report about the New York meeting.

"That's more useful than swanning about India drinking Cobra beer."

"Is that a no to India, then sir?"

Tolvey rolled his eyes beneath the creased brow. "Yes. Far too flimsy." He pushed his coffee to one side. "Look. Back to basics. What are we trying to prove?"

"A fixed match in India, sir. Maybe code-named Jupiter."

"Wrong. Try again."

"Lee Westdale's corruption?"

"So what? The guy's dead."

"But we expose everybody he's corrupted – like maybe the Indian captain. Like Mark Rayner. Then we look the other way to uncover the gangsters."

"Who may be based in India or Pakistan and not our problem." Tolvey's tone hardened. "Two cricketers having dinners? Big deal!" His downturned lips added to the sarcasm. "Why should UK taxpayers pay you to prove a bent game in Delhi? Even if it is. That's for the Indian CBI."

"Because, because," Ratso was floundering, "because we might bring down an entire network."

"Mark Rayner? Another one we're not going to see at Southwark Crown Court, whatever you prove." Tolvey waved his arm towards the computer screen. "You won't learn anything in Delhi you can't get from watching on TV and from quizzing the bookies."

"With respect, I think you're wrong, sir." Ratso's tone was muted whereas with Arthur Tennant back in the SCD7 days, he would have exploded and walked out. But Mick Tolvey was different. Ratso respected his new boss. Tolvey was no nose-picking time-server like Tennant. Down in the Cauldron, they'd often joked that Tennant was so lazy it was amazing he hadn't asked someone to pick his nose for him.

Tolvey placed his elbows on the desk to get closer – a gesture of solidarity. "Look, Todd," he could not get into the *Ratso* thing, "I may be wrong. Make it easy for me to say yes. Bring me more on why the big fix is in Delhi."

"Other ideas, sir?"

"This Jupiter note doesn't join any dots pointing to this Nitin Mithi guy. Your only WC in Delhi plays for the wrong team. Besides, I've seen Mithi play. I've seen him being interviewed. Looked like a regular guy."

Ratso was not impressed with that comment but said nothing.

"Work on it, Todd. Otherwise, let Craig do the heavy lifting in India." He changed screens on his monitor. "Mandy's quite a stunner. Go and lean on her... and I don't mean over the kitchen-table."

"As if I would, sir." Ratso laughed dismissively though the thought had crossed his mind at least twice on the first visit. Her flashing eyes, wiggles and leg-crossing had all seemed designed to attract attention.

"Think phones, computers, banks, Rayner's team-mates. Other commentators who worked with him. Stick close to home."

"Can I claim for the tummy-bug tablets I bought for Delhi?" Ratso put on a look of injured innocence, his head tilted to one side, his eyes smiling enquiringly.

Tolvey knew it was a wind-up. "Out of here, Todd."

~32~

Wimbledon, South London

"You don't mind if I take Lee's passport?" Ratso was skimming through the pages that Nancy had looked at on their first visit.

Mandy crossed her shapely legs in her rather short and tight pale blue skirt and smiled her consent. "Go ahead. Do you want mine too?"

Ratso was about to say no when he thought – why not? He shrugged. "Thanks."

"What are you after?" Mandy's dulcet tone was very much the grieving widow lost in a world of which she knew nothing. Ratso was not buying it. Not yet anyway. She leaned forward to offer the two officers the plate of assorted chocolate biscuits. Both accepted.

"Open mind," volunteered Nancy.

Ratso laughed and intervened. "That's true but it makes us sound as if we haven't a clue what we're doing. Like we're prodding about in the dark." *Not far off it.* He placed both passports on the low-level coffee-table beside a photo of Lee shaking hands with Her Majesty at Lord's. "Look, Mrs Westdale..."

"Please call me Mandy."

"Well, Mandy, we need to know who wanted matches fixed and who paid Lee to help. Then we need to identify players who performed in matches to orders." He saw her puzzled look which turned to one of irritation. Ratso had no intention of backing off.

The agenda note, uncovered since the first interview, had stiffened his attitude. Pointedly, he leaned forward to focus his stare even closer. "You must know who he met that morning?"

Mandy curled her legs up under her and shook her head slowly. "Lee wasn't like that. He never bored me with every minute of his job. If he had to go to Buckingham Palace or Downing Street, he'd tell me." She flicked her hair dismissively. "As to his daily meetings, frankly I was never interested. If I asked, he would tell me." She twisted a strand of hair in her left hand. "I trusted him. He was meeting people all the time. I didn't track him." Her pink lips pouted. "Mr Holtom, I didn't need to."

"You told us he only had the Samsung?"

"Yes – but I'm sorry? I don't get this. " Mandy looked puzzled. "Why on earth do you think Lee might have had two mobile phones?"

"So your answer is still no, then," confirmed Nancy, sounding more irritated than Ratso preferred. "You think you knew him well? No secrets." Nancy waited for the nod of yes but changed tack on seeing Ratso's hurried glance warning her not to mention the second phone.

"We've had his Samsung checked," Ratso explained trying not to be distracted by Mandy flashing a child-like and wheedling smile as she sat opposite him. "For such a busy man, there's not much on it."

Mandy lit another cigarette as if racking her brain before answering. "He only used the Samsung – the one you took away with a protective cover."

Ratso returned her disarming smile and decided to move on rather than confront. "Sometimes desperate situations make people behave out of character. Lee had lost a fortune in the USA. That could have made him turn to crime. How's the lawsuit?"

"No end in sight." The tone was resigned yet bitter, her eyes showing frustration.

Ratso decided to ratchet up rather than pussyfoot any longer. "Lee had turned his misfortune around. Quickly too." He could see that Mandy understood the drift.

"After he got over the shock and humiliation. Well, once we *both* got over losing a lifestyle. He chatted up old mates. He got favours returned and worked flat-out to rebuild our lifestyle." Her eyes welled up and she looked towards the window to compose herself. "Working long hours. Racing round the UK to speak at events … that's what got us back." She looked round the expensively furnished room. "He wanted us to live like this again, the way we used to before Parabolic. But nothing's paid for. It's all on credit and somehow I've got to keep up the monthly payments."

"Is that a problem?" It was Nancy who tried to sound sympathetic.

"What do *you* think?" she snapped, her mouth now thin and mean. "I've two boys to bring up." Just as quickly, her eyes turned soft and doe-like as she tapped her lips. "A life policy may kick in but there's an issue about missed premiums." She twisted to confront Nancy full on. "Do *you* understand what it means to wake up every morning and worry about money?" She paused and saw Nancy look away. "I can see you have no idea." Her tone was bitter and she made a point of looking down, studying her nails. Then her moist eyes faced each listener in turn. "Every night, I cry myself to sleep aching for Lee's love. In the mornings, I cry with worry."

The difficult silence that followed was broken by Ratso. "Look – Mark Rayner murdered his family. Others have been murdered because of match-fixing. Lee's name is in the cross-hairs as someone who could have given us names." Ratso picked his next words with extra care. "We realise how hard this is hitting you but we cannot be diverted from our wider duty."

"Mandy, we need to check for more bank statements than were in Lee's filing-cabinet." Nancy got the nod from Ratso before going on. "There was nothing suspicious so far, paying the rent, the HP, car instalments, Harrods, Sainsbury's, the usual."

"We think he had other offshore accounts," Ratso continued. "And property abroad given to him by these gangsters." Without any evidence, Ratso enjoyed lobbing in the grenade to test her reaction.

"Rubbish. I would have known." Her tone was no longer defensive.

"He followed the England team. Plenty of chances to open an account in the Caribbean. Dubai. Did he ever go to Switzerland?"

"Yes to Geneva, a romantic getaway when we were not long married." The slow shake of her head caused Mandy's shoulder-length hair to sway in unison. "As to elsewhere? Lee and I shared everything. Like I said, we had no secrets." She exhaled loudly while Ratso thought of all the cheated wives and husbands who thought they knew everything within their marriage.

Ratso glanced at Nancy indicating he wanted to continue. "Lee made the Parabolic investment without telling you. So he did keep things from you."

Mandy's face changed. When her lips narrowed and her eyes hardened, Ratso was reminded of the mugshot of Myra Hindley, the Moors Murderer. She jumped from her chair to pace back and forward. "True," she snapped. "That was before we married. When he confessed, that's when he got it between the eyes." In full flow, Mandy was formidable and Ratso could imagine Lee cowering from the volley of flak. "Any secrets and I would walk. That was the deal."

Both listeners could almost believe that. "Have any strangers contacted you since he died?" Nancy tried to catch Mandy's eye but with her pacing around the room, it was impossible.

After frowning for a second or two, Mandy said no. "I mean all types of people have been in touch. Strangers to me. Well-wishers, cricket fans. But nothing … sinister." As he saw her clenched fists and heard the edge in her voice, she was certainly convincing. But Lee had plenty of secrets – *unless he had confided in her.*

Was she a scheming little minx?

Or had Lee been able to dupe her?

"The bank statements we took didn't show the address of the branch." Ratso was hoping to hear Bishopsgate.

Mandy crossed the room in her stockinged feet, her anger gone so that her movements were again smooth and feline. The sway of her tight buttocks seemed designed to impress. She stopped beside a Georgian style chest with five drawers. Ratso had checked it on their first visit and had stripped it of anything half-interesting. From the top drawer she produced a letter. "It arrived from the manager yesterday. Lee chose the bank long before I knew him."

Ratso's disappointment was hidden behind his heavy eyelids as he and Nancy glanced at the details. "Carnworth Private Bank," he read aloud to nobody in particular. "Carnworth House, Fleet Street. They're a blue-chip outfit, aren't they?"

"They charge enough, I know that." Mandy's laugh was genuine. "Lee reckoned they were good to him when … things went tits-up, as he used to say." At this memory, her composure failed her. She leaned against the wall for support, her shoulders heaving. Nancy started to get up to console her but Ratso motioned her to stay seated. They watched and waited while she wiped her eyes on a delicate hankie with embroidered edges. "Sorry. Sorry about that," she faltered. "In public, I try, try so hard, to pretend I'm over it – but …. anyway, carry on. Where were we?"

"Did Lee know Nitin Mithi?" Nancy prodded.

Mandy sashayed her buttocks back into the chair.

"Everybody knew Nitin. I knew him. Very personable. A fun guy. But never eat any curry that he recommends. Fiery hot! Why do you ask?"

"Did you or Lee ever have dinner with him?"

"Me? Once or twice. Lee? Probably several times. I mean his life revolved round these famous guys. It was his job, f'God's sake."

Ratso turned to the passports again, picking the aubergine documents from the table. "Did you ever go to Dubai with Lee?"

"Maybe a couple of times."

"I see he went quite often. What was he doing there?"

"Meeting the International Cricket Council. He would interview their guys for his newspaper column. Also, Pakistan play there."

"Makes sense," Ratso agreed, his eyelids lowered as he scanned the passports again. "Where did you stay in Dubai?"

"We rented."

"Different place each trip?"

"Lee liked a place on the Palm, so he always rented that."

Ratso liked the answer but gave no sign of interest as he continued. "The Caribbean?"

"The same – a rented villa in Barbados. He used it as a base last time the England team toured."

As a planned ploy, Ratso looked at Mandy's passport. Now was the moment to pursue what he had spotted a few minutes earlier. "Miami? What was that about?"

Mandy looked puzzled for a moment, staring at the ornate

ceiling and then out of the window at the stone bird-bath. "I've never been to Florida."

Ratso remained poker-faced as he swapped passports in a slow but ostentatious move. "Not you. I meant Lee. He went there at a time when, in his words, he was *tits–up* from Parabolic."

Mandy's brow frowned. "What do you mean?" Both her face and voice showed shock. With no wiggle this time as she walked *towards* Ratso, she asked to see for herself. As she leaned close beside Ratso's shoulder, he was intensively aware of her breath on his cheek, an expensive fragrance and a lingering smell of cigarettes.

She grabbed Lee's passport and stared at the open page. She stood very upright, back arched in defiance, impatiently tapping one foot as she flicked through every stamp. "You're correct, Mr Holtom. He seems to have flown back from Miami after he went to New York." She rapped the passport thoughtfully against the back of her hand. "The sneaky bastard! The lousy, sodding bastard! I never knew. What the hell was he doing?" Her almond eyes were on fire, the fury burning her up. "Well … I *thought* I knew everything." She opened and then snapped the passport shut. Her mouth twisted into a snarl as she flung it onto the low table. "It seems I did not. What in hell was he doing there?"

"It happens, Mandy." Nancy's smile was soothing as she moved forward as if to give her a reassuring pat on the arm – which she did not. "We've all thought our men told us everything."

"Come on," Ratso beckoned to Nancy. "Mrs Westdale needs to think this through alone. It's been a nasty shock." He turned to Mandy who was almost hyperventilating. "I hate to say this, Mandy but I'm sure there are more nasties that Lee never told you." They both rose from the comfort of the Harrods' settee and crossed the nearly new carpet and out to the front door. "We'll need to speak to you again."

Mandy's jaw was quivering and her hands trembling as she shook her head in tacit agreement. Slowly she closed the door behind them and placed her back against it, breathing heavily. Gradually the shaking stopped as her nerves calmed. Armed with a stiff vodka-tonic and her pack of cigarettes, she went through to the conservatory. It smelled of the colourful flowers that she had arranged on a marble pedestal. The sun beating in made the temperature uncomfortably warm, so she slid open the door to the garden before settling.

There was just one place on her mind.

Somewhere she had never been.

Somewhere Lee had never mentioned.

Miami.

-33-

London

A fallen crane had blocked traffic south of the Thames
and so they were heading across the river to the Lower King's
Road. As they drove down Putney Hill into an even worse than
usual snarl to get across the traffic-lights by Putney Station, Miami
was very much in Ratso's mind too. "So he went to New York but
came back via Miami."

"And unless Mandy was play-acting, she was gobsmacked." Nancy
was driving giving Ratso the chance to browse the passports again.

"She was shocked, no question. If he'd been in the room, she'd
have set about him with a frying-pan." He looked at the exit stamp
again. "Check with the airlines. He went into Newark so my guess
that was Virgin Atlantic. He returned via Miami, so it could be
them or British Airways."

"Your point, boss?"

"Did he plan Florida before he left England? Or did something
happen in the Big Apple that made him change his itinerary?"

"You mean like," Nancy turned her head to grin broadly "maybe
meeting a leggy blonde from Florida? *That* can happen."

Ratso laughed at the dig about Kirsty-Ann Webber. His relationship had caused many a joke since taking her to the Cauldron.
"Cheeky," Ratso gave her a playful punch. "For Lee, that was an
expensive detour. He was ragged-arse poor, selling his home, handing back his car. Fair enough visiting NYC. Important meeting,

signing up for the lawsuit. There and back in two or three days max."

Nancy turned right after Putney Bridge heading for the West End. "Go on."

"Yet he returned from Miami after two days down there."

"And Mandy thought he was in NYC? He must have been a great liar."

"So go in-depth on his credit card statements, his bank statements for that time. Pin down where he went, hotels, restaurants. Cost of meals – was he paying just for himself or ...?"

"Westdale was quite a hunk – sexy, charming and famous. Maybe he got lucky and got shacked up in a freebie."

"Whatever. Not telling Mandy. That's what makes it tasty."

"Puts her in the clear, maybe, boss?" Nancy wanted to catch his look but needed to keep her eyes on the traffic. She saw his slight tilt of the head as if to say *not proven*. They continued the journey in silence, each weighing up impressions of Mandy, though Ratso was also checking the latest score from the second one-day match in Mumbai. There was no sign that anything hooky had happened. "Craig Carter's in Delhi. India should walk the final game of the three. They romped home today again. They're two up, so the bookies will make them strong favourites."

"You confident there's a fix on in the final match?"

"Lee's good mate Nitin Mithi is captaining India. Now India can't lose the series, the temptation to throw the match for megabucks could be ... irresistible."

Nancy sounded hesitant. "You're sure of this?"

"It's our best shot. This is the closest fit." Ratso saw Nancy purse her lips in disbelief as her fingers drummed on the steering-wheel. He decided to change subjects. "Maybe Jock will have turned up something about the crushed hard-drive. He was visiting that repair-shop by the dog-track."

"I hope he didn't bump into Arthur Tennant," Nancy laughed. They both knew their former boss spent most of his spare time watching the greyhounds.

"Don't know what Arthur will do with his spare time except golf and pick his nose. Wimbledon dog-track is closing." Ratso stretched as far as the low height would permit. He yawned loudly having started his day with a jog round the darkened streets of Shepherd's Bush just after four.

"Tolvey's worth ten of Tennant but he'll have me eating crow if I'm wrong about Nitin Mithi."

On reaching Vauxhall, Nancy parked deftly beside another anonymous looking grey Honda. As she switched off the ignition, Ratso turned to her, only his eyes revealing his anticipation. "I suppose when Jock got to the repair shop, he knocked three times to get in."

"Boss?" Nancy sounded confused as her mind raced in every which direction.

"Jock likes that old hit. Ratso broke into the catchy lyrics: *Knock Three Times on the Ceiling if You Want Me.* "Jock always sings along something rotten, waving his arms like a Zulu warrior."

"Boss?" Nancy's face reddened as she turned away to grasp the door-handle.

"One of your favourites too, I believe."

-34-

Richmond, South-West London

Alex Anderson's flight into Heathrow from Miami left him plenty of time before his meetings: Despite several warnings, there had been no further attacks on London but Anderson avoided staying in Central London anyway. The chauffeured 7-Series BMW whisked him elegantly across the back-doubles between the airport and SW14. Conversation en route had been non-existent – he with his Geordie accent and the driver from the Czech Republic had given up on each other. Instead, he browsed The Sun and Daily Express newspapers, occasionally thinking *that's why I quit England.*

Anderson had often stayed at The Trumpeters Hotel, loving the spacious parkland and restful views compared to the madness of Central London. On arrival, he felt instantly at home, relishing the familiar and comfortable surroundings. The country mansion, set on the crest of a tree-lined valley, looked down on the Thames above Richmond and its quiet aura always soothed him on arrival.

He declined the offer of a late lunch downstairs and opted for room-service in his suite. Now, wearing well-cut slacks, a dark green golfing shirt and tan suede loafers, he lay back on the navy-blue rocker, the epitome of carefree. Yet beneath his neatly trimmed black hair that receded just slightly at the temples, his mind was in overdrive.

Tomorrow he was returning to his native Tyneside, back to his old haunts. There, he would meet Walter Harvey, a mucker from his schoolboy years. As teenagers, they had kicked footballs, watched the Magpies, stolen bikes, shoplifted and watched out for each other when confronted by gangs of bigger boys from the next streets. Those teenage years now meant Anderson had no fear. His experiences had served him well in his rise from the Victorian backstreets to massive wealth. His purpose in going north to Newcastle was brief and clear. His investigators had reported on Harvey and he was confident he could handle him, even twenty-five years on. Hopefully, Harvey would still be the same evil bastard who had served time in Durham jail.

This afternoon's meetings were different. He was entering a world where he was out of his depth. But it should be worth it. His knuckles whitened as he thought of Enzo Pagano, sitting *oh-so-smug* and toad-like in the Beverly Hills Hotel. Getting the bastard was going to be so pleasurable.

If do-able.

How computers worked, he had no idea and even less interest. What was exciting was discovering if his plan for HOSS was workable. As he stared at the ceiling, he felt he knew enough about the software to brief the geek. He swung his legs to and fro as he rehearsed his script for the second part of his plans. Different skills were needed for that – charm, soft talk and then winging it.

The Byker backstreets had given him the confidence that nothing and nobody would scare him. In business, he had used his swagger and self-confidence to be cool under fire – but above all, he valued careful preparation and anticipation. *Think like the enemy.* If his ideas backfired and someone put a contract on him – *let them try. Bring it on.*

As a bachelor in Florida, he lived alone in a stunning three-bedroomed villa. Every day he compared the ocean views to the Victorian terraced house where he had spent his childhood. Outside his Byker window, he could watch fast-food empties being blown down the street or see a rat scuttling through the trash. Now, when hanging out in the singles' bars in Boca Raton or Palm Beach, his swarthy and almost-Slavic good-looks attracted casual dates. He wanted nothing more.

After room-service had cleared the remains of his Steak Tartare and a robust half-bottle of 1995 Hermitage, he dabbed on some cologne before watching a mindless quiz on the TV. Almost instantly, he nodded off to be awoken ten minutes later when the phone rang. "Mr Toufiq has arrived."

"I'll come down. We'll meet in the Orangerie." He checked his appearance in the mirror and headed downstairs. His steps were eager, his jaw set in a confident smile.

The fightback was starting.

The following day, after a long lie-in, Anderson ate a leisurely full English breakfast, revenge still filling his mind. As he savoured the fluffy scrambled eggs, his quiet smile showed satisfaction at yesterday's progress. By 3pm, he was in his first-class seat on the express to Newcastle expecting to arrive just before 6pm. During the journey north, he looked at the dog-eared business card of Youssef Toufiq. The card had not been the greatest advert but the Moroccan youngster reckoned Anderson's idea to be straightforward. He had promised to deliver on Anderson's return from Newcastle in under forty-eight hours. As to the rest of his plans, Anderson's chiselled face showed quiet satisfaction as the train hurtled north through Peterborough and on towards York.

Now for Walt.

Looking for his limo outside Central Station, he breathed in the Newcastle air, so different from what his dad had told him. Now, it was just fumes from cars and diesel vans trapped by the drizzle. Back in the fifties, sooty smoke from the thundering steam trains and blackened plumes from the heavy engineering had polluted the air, choking the lungs of the thousands of starlings that gathered each evening. As he took in the familiar surroundings, he saw a silver Mercedes glide up and stop beside him. He handed over his carry-on to the driver and took a front-seat. "The Malmaison, isn't it, sir," enquired the driver.

"Why aye, man." Anderson found himself slipping straight into Geordie. The Malmaison stood beside the Millennium Bridge over the Tyne, barely a mile from his Byker home yet its luxury was more than a million miles distant. For a moment, he relived his childhood, wearing his black and white striped shirt, kicking a ball against a wall with his mates. Life had been simple then. A word out of place and you sorted it, head-butt and all.

Would the next part of the plan be as simple?
Would Walter Harvey be up for it?

-35-

Hammersmith, West London

Ratso's normally healthy skin was pallid after another long day but more due to the cricket news. It was mid-evening and the kitchen smelled of sodium glutamate from his Chinese dinner. He looked and felt drained as he scraped burned potato from the top of the cooker. The unwanted task had nagged at him for days. With sharp jabbing movements, he let rip his frustration while unknowingly grinding his back teeth.

The sound of his phone brought hope that it was K.A but he then saw that the Carter was calling from Delhi. "Craig, I've already sunk two cooking brandies. What the hell went wrong? India cruised it."

"So you saw it?" He sounded pretty deflated.

"If this was the big fix then something's gone very, very wrong."

Craig sighed. "I just don't get it. This was the final game, India two up anyway – a dead match. It was the obvious one for them to throw."

Ratso fingered an empty can of Guinness and knew he would have to open another after the call. "Looks like we read too much into the pics of Lee with Nitin Mithi."

"You saw the odds? A West Indies win was worth 4 -1. Mithi could have cleaned up."

"Yeah! Winston Carmichael top-scored for the Windies too." Ratso chucked the empty can into the bin. "Maybe the fix was never on. Maybe the bomb got Lee before the big meeting. Jock established that Nitin Mithi was in London the day of the blast."

"What did the widow say about that morning?"

"Mandy claims not to know where her husband had been."

"You believe her?"

"Yes … probably, well, maybe," Ratso replied slowly and thoughtfully. "She knew he had a meeting or meetings before they would get together for lunch."

"Nobody contacted her to ask why he had been a no-show?"

"She said not. She denies any sinister callers or visitors." Ratso leaned against the recently decorated wall of the cramped sitting-area, his body aching with disappointment. "Seems like Mick Tolvey called this right. We read too much into the tea-leaves."

"Agreed." Craig's voice was somewhat faint but the message was clear enough. "There was no street-chatter over here. No buzz. I gotta say that none of my contacts had sniffed a fix."

"Any new ideas? I need something positive when I get my arse-kicking from Tolvey."

"He'll be chuffed at saving your fare to India." Craig fell silent for what seemed an age. "New ideas? No. I'm beyond thinking of anything except a kip. I've had enough of Delhi. It's hot. Crowded. Noisy. I never got to the stadium. I watched on TV, mainly while seated on my private white pedestal."

"Delhi Belly?" Ratso guffawed at the image.

"Despite drinking only bottled water."

"Back to square one then," muttered Ratso, his shoulders slumping until his chin rested on his chest. He felt like a kid caught hammering a piece of a jigsaw to make it fit. "So you've no posi-tives for me then?

"Well at least you haven't had to raise the Japanese flag."

-36-

London

DCS Mick Tovey was a good detective and a decent man, one that Ratso instinctively felt comfortable with. They could talk almost as equals though both knew who was boss. But just after leaving the Chief Super's office, Ratso felt like a whipped pup. Every word of the expletive-ridden tirade had been justified. Indeed, he had put his hands up in surrender, accepting Tolvey's rant that Ratso's theory had been a five-star fuck-up.

Now, as he stood beside his desk, Ratso's immediate instinct was to head for the White Swan to drown the pain with several pints. But today, he was not even up to that. When he told Jock about Tolvey's message, the Scot offered him a pub lunch which he declined. "I'm going home. I'm due time off. I've got to fix the transport for the charity golf on Saturday."

A year before, Ratso had been elected to the committee of Action for Victims of Spinal Cord Injury. He had been a supporter for as long as he could remember. Ratso had just turned seven when his old man had tumbled from a ladder. Until his death, his dad had been confined to a wheelchair. Unable to cope, Ratso's mother had vamoosed to Magaluf with a toyboy while Ratso had shouldered the burden with support from an endless stream of carers.

Jock shuffled his feet, barely turning away from his computer screen as he spoke. "We were thinking, me and Nancy, well we might support the event." Nancy wandered across on hearing her name.

Suppressing any sly digs at the burgeoning friendship, Ratso gave them the details. "Tickets are twenty-five quid each. We're expecting a huge crowd if it stays dry. But I didn't know you liked golf."

"Right enough – but I like the cause," muttered Jock looking a bit embarrassed.

Nancy, all perky and cheerful, studied the poster advertising the event. "All these celebs! I've played Crazy Golf at Lyme Regis but it's seeing all the celebs, that's the big turn-on."

"You won't be disappointed. Plenty of selfie opportunities." He felt better not thinking about the debacle in India. "Thanks to events like this, we'll find a cure for broken spines. It's getting close, y'know – there's a guy in the USA now walking using a mix of his brain and computer technology." Ratso sighed. "Till then, thank God for the celebs and the public coming to support us. Including the auction, we hope to raise at least five million quid."

Nancy brushed back her hair in a suggestive manner. "If you need chauffeurs for the big names, count me in. If it's for David Beckham, I'll even clean out the back-seat of my car."

Ratso managed a weak smile. "Sorry, no David Beckham. Anyway, I doubt he'd want to travel in your clapped out Mini. It's only the rust holds it together."

"It's seen some action though."

"The car or just the back seat?"

"Could be both, boss." Nancy gave a laddish laugh and Jock looked embarrassed but whether through guilt or just at Nancy's humour, Ratso was unsure.

He pointed to the poster on the wall. "See. We ran a competition for wheelchair users to be there, pride of place. I'm arranging their minibuses. After that bollocking by Tolvey, it'll be a better way to spend my day. I'm sick of match-fixing, mysterious notes, crushed hard-drives. All blind bloody alleys everywhere."

Jock had rarely seen his boss so deflated. "The darkest hour boss. We'll find the missing link. This charity kick – is it all about yer dad?"

Ratso's sad nod said it all. "Too late for him. We take a lot for granted, y'know. See you there."

"Aye, ye're best away from here. Clear yer head. But that wee note? It's the best route-map we've got."

"We just read it wrong," agreed Nancy.

Ratso was touched by the word *we*. "*I* read it wrong. *I* screwed up. On Monday, we'll brainstorm the evidence again."

"Oh and boss," Jock continued. "That repair-shop I visited. The place was a tip – everything oil-stained and filthy-dirty. Anyroads, they phoned. Somehow among the bald tyres, monkey-wrenches, chipped mugs and spunk-stained girlie-mags, they found their copy of the invoice for crushing Mandy's hard-drive. They charged her a tenner. I'll pick it up later."

"That's another door closed then." Ratso slung his leather jacket over his shoulder, his irritation evident in the sudden move. He turned sharply as an afterthought hit him "The date on it?"

"Two days before ye first visited her."

It was not what Ratso wanted to hear. Nancy yawned as she stretched back, her black high-neck tank-top straining across her modest chest. "You think she was telling the truth? That Lee didn't use it?"

In his present mood, Ratso was not interested. "I don't know. Right now, I don't even care. What I do know is that I don't like *any* evidence being destroyed." With that, he was gone leaving Jock and Nancy to share a look.

-37-

Surrey, England

Seventeen miles from Central London, the Royal Kingsweir golf-club was perfectly positioned not far from the multi-million homes on St George's Hill. This exclusive enclave provided seclusion to celebrities, Russian oligarchs and for those with old money or more probably, those who had recently struck it rich.

Besides the wealthy club members, a radius of thirty miles brought in many of the noisy revellers who annually brayed and guffawed in the champagne tents at Royal Ascot, Henley Regatta or Wimbledon. Today, for those with almost unlimited wealth, the Royal Kingsweir was the place to be seen, especially for those seeking social acceptance or a knighthood, by supporting a worthy cause.

The huge special car-parks were filled with Aston-Martins, Bentleys, Ferraris and endless lines of well-groomed BMWs and Mercedes, many with chauffeurs and some with bodyguards. Incongruously, among them was a 2002 red Mini with a pair of fluffy dice dangling in the rear window. On the rear bumper was a giant fake Elastoplast.

With the sun still warm but dropping lower in the late afternoon, the Celebrity Pro-Am tournament was over. Nancy and Jock stood by the putting-green and were taking in the pleasing smell of wood-smoke and barbecuing which drifted towards the first tee.

"Paid twenty-five quid and we canna get nearer the food than this," moaned Jock for the third time. He patted his stomach in emphasis. "The poor only get to drink and eat peanuts."

Nancy looked across the barriers to the elite section and the long lines waiting for hot-dogs or roast-beef baps. "There's plenty enough rich guys around prepared to pay a hundred quid in a good cause."

"After the raffle, we're away. I'm fair famished." Jock pointed to the clubhouse. "Get this! In there, for twenty-five thousand a pop, you get free champagne, savoury biscuits with bits on and the chance to spill your drink on some famous golfer's fancy shoes. One hundred grand buys you a sit-down dinner with the celebs."

"It's called charity, Jock." She was met with a snort as she checked her watch. "Anyway, it's raffle time. Feeling lucky, are you?" She saw Jock's shocked frown at the very notion. "I bought five tickets," she continued in a chirrupy way. "Great prizes like three nights in Paris, golf at Troon, grouse-shooting in Scotland or a Caribbean Cruise."

"And the boss, I suppose he's with all the celebs, swilling the bubbly."

"I took a peek – they're shoulder to shoulder, crammed in circling the podium. Gawping at the Duchess. Ratso's in the front with all the wheelchair winners."

"Anyroads, I'll fetch ye another drink. I'll just take a cuppie tea for mysel'. I'll drive."

"Vodka and Red Bull for me then." While Jock was gone, Nancy flicked through her selfies and was still beaming when Jock returned. "Fourteen pics — golfers, Premier League players, two Wimbledon champs. Sex on legs, the lot of them."

Jock did not look enthused. "They're just rich and famous, that's all." He was about to add something when his mobile phone alerted him to a message. He looked down and saw it was from Ratso. He groaned expecting to get a reaction from Nancy but she wasn't listening.

"I've won. I've won." She was waving a pink ticket. They stood gazing at it, almost unseeingly, as a cultured voice came over the sound-system. "I'll repeat that. Two tickets for the Ryder Cup – pink ticket 291834K."

Jock was about to comment that the trip to Paris would have been better but Nancy had gone, weaving slightly drunkenly towards the double-doors, her pink ticket held high. Then he looked at the message again as he sipped tea from a throwaway beaker with the club crest. Ratso wanted to meet them by the 18th Green in ten minutes.

Jock had a vague awareness that the Ryder Cup involved golf played every two years between a European team and the USA. His old mate, Det. Sgt Tosh Watson, followed it avidly. So long as there was a lavvie nearby to cater for his weak bladder, Tosh would give anything to be there. He saw Nancy returning, her usual cherubic face almost split in two by a dazed and silly grin. She was whooping and waving her arms, jigging from side to side, attracting amused looks from the throng standing around the bar.

"No mistake then?"

Nancy almost shrieked. "Jock, Jock! I had another winning ticket. The Caribbean Cruise. Fly to Florida and then 7 nights for two cruising round the West Indies." She stood still for a moment. "And I just had a pic with the Duchess."

"Show me. The prizes, not the photo."

She brandished two envelopes and the contents proved her point. They stared at them, murmuring about the long odds against winning twice. Suddenly, he gave her a huge hug, his strong arms wrapping round her and with ease sweeping her feet from the ground. For a moment, they were cheek to cheek yet even before he put her down, Jock sensed that a kiss would not be welcome. They stared at each other for a lingering moment, both confused by their reactions.

"Nancy, there was a message from the boss. We're to meet him." He saw her nod but she was already fantasising about the blue waters of the Caribbean.

-38-
Mumbai

Nitin Mithi handed over his imported Model S Tesla to the car jockey who almost licked the ground at seeing his hero. It was a typical day in the life of the Indian captain. Revered in cricketing circles, in his home city of Mumbai it went far beyond that. To the teeming hordes, he was like a God.

Everywhere people wanted a piece of him – usually selfies or to touch his clothes or to shout, wave or whisper invitations to him as if they owned him. In a way they did. Their hard-earned rupees for watching him play had made him rich. It was not just earnings from being a bachelor super-hero with Bollywood looks. It was from TV shows and product endorsement including his brand of men's toiletries. Mithi's friendly smile and gleaming white teeth dominated hoardings in every big city. India's masses could not get enough of him.

Now, after a morning practising his cover drives and hooks in the nets, he was arriving for lunch at the thousand-bedroom Gateway Palace Hotel. The media was still crowing about the three matches to none victory over the West Indies. Though Mithi was tired from playing so much cricket, he willingly smiled and clasped shoulders with fans and hotel staff as he approached the red car-peted entrance.

Today, he was lunching with the owner of the Mumbai Raiders IPL team. The Indian Premier League was where big and easy money was plentiful. Almost alone among the best Indian players, he had never signed for any IPL team but after a couple of useful exploratory meetings in London, the financial attractions seemed too good to miss.

By the end of lunch, he had been astutely non-committal. He knew his worth at next year's auctions and had merely promised to talk to his agent. Anyway, as the wall-clock chimed three, his mind was already on the afternoon ahead. He politely left the table with promises to be in touch.

He was acutely aware that by now movie starlet Keya Gayen would be eager for him in the upstairs suite. He went to the elevator and before entering, he generously tipped the elderly elevator attendant in his scarlet tunic and black pillbox hat. In return, the attendant slipped him a duplicate bedroom key but more importantly, he had bought discretion for the afternoon ahead.

It was certainly needed. Keya Gayen, with the big red lips and pouting mouth was the long-term mistress of Mukesh Jilani, the billionaire commodities tycoon. For the past two years she had been Jilani's regular escort at the city's most fashionable social events. Through his connections, she had landed her first starring role in *Wounded Pride* and was being tipped for Hollywood fame too. Mithi, like everybody, was aware of her relationship with the ageing mogul. He did not care. It made the sex even more exciting. He loved the risk he was taking.

At the seventh floor, he entered the empty corridor on which there were just two suites. His pulse was already quickening in anticipation of the twenty-two year old beauty. As he strode along the corridor, all broad shoulders and long legs, his thoughts were only of her smooth burnished gold skin and dark eyes. Using the key, he entered the seductive ambience of the sitting-room. As usual, the heavy curtains were closed and the room was lit only by four low-powered wall-lights. He closed and double-locked the door and hurried through the dining area to the bedroom beyond. As usual, he expected to see Keya lying on the bed wearing only a welcoming smile and his favoured black negligée.

Not today.

The bed was empty.

The room was empty.

He called her name in case she was in the bathroom.

Silence.

He checked the time on his Longines watch. Reasoning she must be stuck in the crawl of traffic, he went to the minibar. After helping himself to a Johnny Walker Black Label, he plopped in a couple of ice cubes and settled down on the jet-black chaise-longue with his feet up.

He tried calling her but there was no answer. He was unconcerned. That had happened twice before when she had been delayed on the film-set. He flicked through the channels and found *Gabar is Back*, a movie he wanted to catch up with. While waiting for the download, he savoured the whisky, swirling it around his mouth and wondering whether to have another.

After the movie started, behind him, there was a slight movement of the floor-to-ceiling curtain. A gloved hand appeared. Then a small man emerged. He was wearing all black clothes, a black hood concealing his face. Even his trainers were black. From a side pocket, the intruder produced a Maxim 9 pistol with inbuilt silencer. In three small steps across the plush carpet, he was immediately behind the cricketer, who was concentrating on the movie's noisy opening scenes.

With not a word being spoken, he fired a single shot straight into the crown of Mithi's head. With just a slight popping sound, the bullet smashed his skull, ripped through his brain and exited his chin before slamming into his thigh. Though a second bullet was not needed, the killer was taking no chances He waited for the cricketer to slump forward and sideways, blood spurting from his mouth, nose and thigh. This time, he fired into the right temple. A glance convinced him his task was complete.

Seconds later, the killer had changed back into his stolen bell-hop uniform of red tunic and pillbox hat. Moments later, like any other bell-hop, he hurried along the corridor as if carrying a guest's small suitcase. It contained his bloodied clothing and trainers in a plastic bag. Additionally, beside the Maxim 9, there were his jeans and T-shirt for another change when he reached the staff lavatories.

Job done. Mission accomplished.

-39-

London

It was Monday morning and Ratso was still cheered by the funds raised at the golf. He was heading down to the canteen when Nancy stopped him in the wide and brightly lit corridor. They were surrounded by a faint smell of floor-cleaner mixed with a stronger smell of frying bacon and toast. Having finished her granola, she had just been leaving. As they met close to the entrance, Ratso took in her heavy perfume and tired eyes. "A word, boss?" She was looking limp, head down and the merest glimpse of her bleary eyes confirmed that she was hung-over or had slept not at all.

It was not a good moment for him with his mind planning the afternoon's brain-storming but Ratso sensed she was troubled. "I'll grab my scrambled eggs and a coffee. Take a seat somewhere." He joined her a few moments later and sat opposite, taking a metal chair with a sagging blue seat. "Celebrating were you? Excited, eh?"

"Couldn't sleep, boss."

"Two of the best prizes. I'm not surprised." Even as he spoke, Ratso sensed this was not the reason and his mind began running on ahead. He just hoped there would be no allegations against Jock. He saw her inner tension as Nancy fingered a lock of hair that hung down beside her right cheek. Each time, she was about to speak, she faltered. The knuckles on her left hand were whitened. Eventually, the silence got too much for him, so he continued. "Surely, it wasn't the news from India?"

"Murdered! Helluva shock, sir – but no it wasn't that. Thoughts on that, boss?" She seemed to be relieved to be on solid ground.

"When Craig reported that Nitin Mithi was dead, well … of course I was stunned. But based on Lee's final words to Premadasa, a murder was always likely."

"Lee Westdale haunting us from his grave?" Nancy's tired brain struggled to get her thoughts as coherent as she would have liked. "Like I mean, that match in Delhi. Maybe Nitin Mithi failed to fix."

"Same as Mark Rayner? Craig reckons there's no evidence from the black market of strange betting patterns."

Ratso saw the distant look in the DC's eyes and sensed she was just going through the motions. "Look Nancy before we get on to whatever's bugging you, let me just wrap this up. Mithi was executed by a professional hitman who used the staff elevator to enter the hotel. He changed clothes at least twice and slipped out through the staff exit – presumably to pick up his cash." She turned her dead-eyed look towards him as he continued. "The Indian police are looking for motives. Besides being a talented player, he was a hard businessman. He was also a playboy who enjoyed flings with any number of beautiful women." Ratso flourished his fork towards her. "Take your pick."

Ratso put down his cutlery to raise both hands in a shove-away gesture. "Nancy, we never *knew* of any fix. We *knew* nothing." Ratso munched the last of his toast and pushed his plate aside. "So what's bugging you? How can I help? Hell, winning two prizes like that … I mean."

Nancy stared round the room and seeing nothing. At last she looked at him, leaning over the cruet set and sticky ketchup bottle. "This is, like I mean … confidential. Just between us?"

"Unless you confess to some crime. That would mean all bets are off."

She clenched and unclenched her fists and then took the plunge, cupping her hands under her chin. "No crime. It's," she paused. "It's about Jock, sir. The cruise, boss. That's the problem."

Oh shit! "Go on." Ratso was not going to volunteer anything. He swirled his coffee around to mix the milk and then waited, watching the stress crying out from her screwed-up face and quivering hands. Ratso recalled his car journey across northern Spain when Jock had poured out his heart about his wife in Glasgow leaving him for a rich geezer and a Celtic supporter to boot.

"See, boss. You know we've been ... well, rather ... sort of friendly." The words were coming out in slow-motion.

"If you mean singing to each other through a plate-glass window and coming to the Pro-Am, yes I guess so."

"Well, see sir. Winning those tickets to the Caribbean? I mean Jock ... expected to come with me."

Ratso said nothing but another *oh shit* thought went through his mind. He said nothing.

"See, sir. I mean I like Jock. He's a fun guy. Usually, we have a good laugh. We both live alone. So when he asked me to the Red Cow when you saw us dancing, I mean why not? But I mean. That's it. I mean we don't ... er ... y'know..."

"Sure. Platonic. That's the word you're looking for. Or to use the jargon from our Cauldron days, you weren't at it like stoats in a sack."

Nancy grinned for the first time. "But he ... y'know. After the golf, he drove me back and he, y'know ... kind of expected..."

Ratso nodded, his eyes showing solidarity as they met hers. "Men do. We're like that. Lots of women do too. But obviously not you with Jock." He cocked his head to one side and breathed deeply. "There's plenty of it about. Including in the Met." Ratso gave a sardonic laugh, his cheeks colouring.

"I got a bit rat-arsed on Saturday night with him sober, so I said I'd think about it. But poor Jock might have false hopes. I said we'd talk about it today." She glanced up cautiously to test his reaction but Ratso's face revealed nothing. "And last night, I was all boozed up again. Drinking alone. Vodka, a couple of big gins and half a bottle of Campari." She rearranged the cruet set without even noticing what she was doing. "For now, he's expecting to be packing the sun-oil and sharing my cabin." She shook her head and Ratso could see she regretted the sudden movement. "It's not on. Like I mean I don't want to screw up our professional relationship."

Ratso mentally crossed his fingers and hoped for a negative response. "Did you want me to have a word? Do anything? Or did you just want to talk to a friendly face?"

"No, boss you see … well there's more."

"Go on."

Tears filled her eyes. "You see boss, the person I want to join me on the cruise … is you."

-40-

London

Ratso was standing by the whiteboard which was not a pretty sight. As brain-storming sessions go, the team of twelve had barely whistled up a breeze, let alone a storm. The atmosphere was somewhere between dumb insolence and sullen resentment at dashed hopes from India. Nobody had any fresh ideas despite staring at Westdale's note on the PowerPoint and then scrolling down the doctor's statement line-by-line.

Det. Constable Willison had reported that the older bank and credit-cards statements had arrived. Ratso though had reservations about Danny Willison. Under his reddish hair and neatly trimmed beard, he looked shrewd enough but there was a touch of slapdash about him. "Go through half each with Nancy and then swap and cross-check. Nothing must be missed."

"What are we looking for?"

"Use your brains, Danny. If he buys six eggs at Sainsbury's you can ignore it. Now, shall we get on?"

Jock Strang had been unusually quiet and Ratso could guess why. When his intervention came, it was pessimistic and out of character. "Boss, what's the game? To me, we're running aboot like headless chickens."

Given his chat with Nancy, Ratso cut him more slack than usual. "Well, Jock I wouldn't go that far. Take a look at these slides I've prepared." All eyes turned as the first image flashed up on the screen opposite the curtained window that shut out Vauxhall on a wet afternoon. It was headed AIMS & OBJECTIVES.

- **The GOAL: Bring down whoever is behind match-fixing**.
- Lee may have been GOING TO a meeting when killed.
- Check CCTV before the blast. Look for him and any other cricketers or possible sporting contacts he may have met.
- The Indian police are working on Nitin Mithi.
- Investigate Mark Rayner's team-mates … discreetly.
- Liaise with DS Lilian Trasker on the acid and hammer attack.
- Unravel Jupiter. **Mandy doesn't know that we have this note**.
- Check commentators to identify Westdale's contacts
- How did Lee have four million to invest?
- Who else was at the Parabolic meeting? Sportsmen? Celebs?
- Why did he change his flight to return from Miami?
- Who travelled with him to Miami – if anyone?
- Did Mandy know he went there or is she lying?
- Is Mandy involved?
- Did Mandy know he was a fixer?
- Where did he stay in Florida and with whom?
- Hawaladars on Bishopsgate?
- What did Lee do / who did he meet in Dubai?
- His "rented homes" in Barbados and Dubai. Check.
- Watch out for anything WC.
- Liaise with Craig Carter about suspicious betting on every televised cricket match for the last 5 seasons.
- Ongoing checks on Rayner – his travels, contacts, money.

Jock Strang looked at the list and then pointed at the screen. "See what I mean. It's all questions. No answers. Headless chickens, right enough, that's what we are." His gruff tone and rasping Glaswegian made the assessment seem even more provocative until Willison broke the tension by making chicken noises.

Ratso waited for the laughter to die down. "Anyone got anything new or positive to contribute?" He looked round the downturned faces and shaken heads. "Okay then. Jock – I want you to share out these duties. This is real detective work – painstaking. Boring. Detailed. No instant glory. Just the hard slog of endless cross-checking till something creates our eureka moment."

"Can I work from a bath, then boss?" It was a rare comment from DC Ray Booth.

"Yes so long as you prove your middle name is Archimedes."

"One thing boss?" It was Det. Constable Carole Viment, who had only recently joined the team. She was tall, lean and wearing black track-suit bottoms and a purple blouse. Something in her face reminded Ratso of a weekend in Paris and the Musée d'Orsay. So many of the Impressionist paintings featured women with strong, almost manly faces, not least a Cézanne of a woman seated beside a coffee-pot. With her pencil-thin eyebrows and a broad nose perfectly suited to her wide-set eyes, Viment had that look about her – and it suited her well.

This morning though, Viment was not looking her best. She wore no make-up and her brown hair that normally cascaded shoulder-length, was hanging like rats-tails, tucked behind just one ear. Even so, her strong physique and proud bearing commanded respect. Ratso also admired her youthful enthusiasm. It was early days but already there were signs of high-flyer, another Nancy Petrie, in the making.

"Go on, Carole."

"The line between us and Sgt Trasker's investigation?"

"Fair point." Ratso lobbed his empty paper cup, his regular party-trick. Everyone watched as the white cup curled over the four metres to land precisely among the trash. He had never missed, not even when hung-over after a pole-dancing night celebrating Tosh Watson's birthday. "The Deputy AC now agrees the acid attack was probably cricket linked. I suggest you work on that. Trasker is winding down her local nutter enquiries to let us use our specialist knowledge on match-fixing. Trasker's not prissy or touchy. She's a realist. You'll get along just fine. Play it right and the Deputy will probably give us the entire investigation."

"Specialist knowledge? Us? Dinna make me laugh." Jock's face showed his irritation. "So far, our special subject would be wild-goose chases."

"Chickens? Now geese?" Ratso paused for a moment. "Are you into the birds these days, Jock?" Obviously, everyone had some idea of his crush on Nancy. He waited for the hoots of laughter to die down before adding. "If you are, never forget ducks in cricket. They can be a big clue to match-fixing."

Jock's already reddish face turned a shade deeper and for a moment Ratso thought his sergeant was going to say something he might regret but instead, he simply asked that somebody explain what a duck had to do with the daft game of cricket.

"It's when a batsman scores not even one run. I've had a fair few ducks but then I'm in the team as a bowler." He knew it would be a cue for some quacking and he let it die down. "So, everyone – negativity is self-defeating. I don't need it. Not from anyone. Got it?" He rarely showed anger but his voice and glare at the listeners made his views plain to all. "The answers are out there. Go find them."

The burly Scot was first to leave, his shoulders looking heavy with the burden of his thoughts. Even with his iron-grey hair and no-nonsense frame, he looked more mouse than mountain as he slipped out of the room. "What's got into him?" It was Willison. There were no answers, just mutterings and shrugs all round.

Ratso said nothing. Neither did Nancy. They both left the room locked in their thoughts and Ratso almost immediately left the building. There was cricket net-practice, something to take his mind away from his confused thinking. Nancy's astounding confession and the aggro from Jock filled his mind as he dodged between the commuters on his way to the Underground. Maybe hurling the ball at the batsmen would be good therapy. That and sinking a couple of pints of ice-cold Guinness afterwards might help.

He liked Nancy. He fancied her, no question. But as her boss and a dozen years older? Not ideal. Who wouldn't fancy those chubby fresh-faced looks and her generous and ready smile? Together with her sharp brain and bubbly personality, Nancy was a winner. No wonder Jock's dreams had got ahead of him while making cheese toasties for one in his bedsit.

Ratso changed trains to the District line at Victoria to head westwards. While staring mindlessly at the passing adverts and still wrestling with Nancy's outburst, he had an idea, rather a good one.

Yes, he told himself.

It definitely had win-win, potential. *Maybe even four wins.*

-41-

West London

"**N**ancy? Fancy a Mexican in that place near you in Parsons Green – the one opposite the station? I'm starving after my cricket nets. Good. I'll hop on a bus. Ten minutes and I'll be there." Ratso turned away from a weirdo who was earwigging the conversation by the bus-stop. He lowered his voice even more. "And don't raise your hopes. I'll explain."

The excitement in her voice had made the warning essential and he heard her sharp intake of breath. He ended the call and right on time, he carried his clumsy cricket-bag into the Yellow Sombrero restaurant and took a tiny side table, the best on offer. The room was noisy, busy with a mainly young crowd. The smell of enchiladas, tacos, refried beans and grilling meats from the kitchen sharpened Ratso's appetite.

When Nancy appeared, in a black roll-neck with a red waistcoat, black leggings and dark red boots, she attracted a number of second looks as she glanced around and then headed for his table. Ratso stood and gave her a friendly hug, a move he had decided was somewhere in the middle of his options. "Thanks for changing your plans. You've set your TV programme to record, I hope." Nancy nodded in an abstracted way, her face showing that whatever chit-chat they shared, she would only be going through the motions. "Shall we order and then I'll explain?" Ratso continued.

The waitress hovered while Nancy ordered a large vodka and

Red Bull and Ratso a Guinness. When the server had headed for the bar, Nancy removed her leather bag that had been slung across her shoulder. "Sorry about the pong. I bought this in a Morocco street-market. Stinks like hell it does."

Ratso sniffed and grinned. "You're right. Reminds me of camel dung."

"I'm going to have to dump it. Anyway, item one – tell me the worst. Item two – we order. Item three – I get rat-arsed." She gave a self-deprecating laugh. Her tone was definitive. In a sudden but gentle move, she clasped his hand and Ratso found her fingers cool and enticing. Her movement was accompanied by fluttering eyelashes. Ratso guessed rightly that for a few frantic minutes, she had taken considerable care with her make-up. "Tell it to me as it is. I'm not hungry. I'd already downed a plate of pasta." She did not mention the three hefty vodkas.

Ratso stretched out his other hand and placed it on hers, hoping to send the message he wanted. "Nancy, I think you're fabulous. I've always thought that, ever since you first entered the Cauldron wearing that purple wig. That really fooled us! You know, well, we both know that we've had a great and friendly relationship. We work well together."

Her eyes hardened. "Okay. Just tell me the big but."

"And what you said this morning, well I was surprised and not surprised. Not surprised because moving from friendliness into cosy dinners or cruising in the Caribbean could be almost a natural progression." As he spoke, Ratso made a point of looking deep into her eyes, trying to get across his sincerity. "But then I was surprised because you've never really flirted, maybe the occasional hint but never any real reason to expect..."

"Why do you think I transferred to Vauxhall? To follow Jock?" She watched his reaction at the message, his hand still clasping hers. "But I guess that after seeing me cavorting with Jock that night?"

"True." He paused to dismiss the young waitress. "I would love to go cruising with you. We'd be great together, have real fun." He shook his head as if not believing what he was about to say. "So why am I turning you down, and hurting – someone I would hate to hurt?" He lowered his eyes. "It's hard to explain."

"Is it Kirsty-Ann?"

"Look, Nancy. If Kirsty had been working in London, then yes, we'd have been an item. She is, oh … very special to me. But we have an understanding that we can't expect our relationship to survive. Not without one of us changing our lifestyle. And that isn't going to happen."

"That's a long way of saying she's not an obstacle. That makes rejection worse."

Ratso twisted his mouth and the lids of his eyes closed before answering. "Perhaps it does, yes. But deep down I value the way you and me are … or the way we were until this morning. Taking that next step, me over-nighting at your place or you at mine. God knows where it would lead. No happy ending, that's for sure." He ran his spare hand through this hair and shook his head. "I'm your boss for God's sake! Been there, done that. Right bloody mess it was." He fell silent recalling being carpeted.

Nancy played with her empty glass, staring at it wistfully. "Look, I've ached for you. I've dreamed of dinner like this ever since I first saw you – good-looking, big, manly and slightly mysterious – those eyes, I think. When you introduced Kirsty-Ann, like I mean you can't imagine how screwed up I felt." For a moment, Ratso thought tears were going to flow but after biting her lips for a second or two, she recovered her composure. "Why do you think I quit the Cauldron? Why did I transfer to Vauxhall? Because I loved cricket? Or because I..." There was a long pause as she faltered at repeating the *love* word. "Or because ... of you?"

Her point had crossed his mind more often than he was going to admit. He released her hands. "We're a good team, Nancy. Let's keep it that way." He shook his head sadly. "You won't like what I'm going to say but, hell, I'm going to say it. If you've nobody to go cruising with, why don't I buy the cruise from you? I can take Kirsty-Ann. She lives in Fort Lauderdale where the cruise starts and finishes. You can tell Jock you needed the money. That gets you off that hook without screwing up your friendship with him. And I'll tell you this for free – if you and me went swanning off on the cruise, I'd have a shed-load of grief from Jock. My long rela-tionship with him would be buggered too."

She cocked her head to one side and sniffed, her flared nostrils quivering. "I'll have a starter and another large vodka and Red Bull."

After ordering Fajitas Camaroles and a Guinness for himself and a bowl of Guacamole and her drink for Nancy, Ratso decided to move away from the personal stuff. "And the Ryder Cup tickets? I had another idea but it's your call."

This time Nancy twitched her head dismissively as if she didn't give a toss. "I haven't thought about the golf. Only the cruise." She poured glasses of iced water and sipped. "I don't much care whether I go to the golf." Her normally chirpy self was non-exis-tent, her voice flat.

"Nancy, those tickets are gold-dust and there's one guy who would mortgage his backside to be there."

"Who's that, boss? Or right now should I be calling you Todd or Ratso?"

"I like Todd but I'm called that mainly at cricket or away from the Met. I know I'm called Ratso behind my back. Todd works just fine at times like this."

"And your nickname? Explanation?"

Ratso gave a quick laugh. "I've heard so many rumours of how I got it. Not one of my prouder moments. In fact it involved a right cock-up when I was a young detective. Believe every bad version you've heard."

"So you were saying – the Ryder Cup?"

"Tosh Watson. He's always gone bananas over it, gets all patriotic Why not take him? He needs a bit of cheering up. His career path is still ballsed up – at least for now."

For the first time, there was a flash of the usual Nancy. She gave a quick laugh. "And he's got that dreadful missus to put up with. Right bloody shrew that one. I had a fair old ding-dong with her. She reckoned him and me ..."

"You're joking. I hadn't heard that."

"No joke. She came by one day and gave me a right earful. Over nothing. As someone once commented, Tosh's body is designed to put things in rather than into other people."

Ratso had not heard this before and chuckled. "Here's your chance. You can wind her up something rotten by inviting him."

"Todd, the damned golf goes on for three days."

"You take Tosh and you'll spend a load of time queuing for pies and burgers. Other than that, Tosh is fine. Oh except he has the smallest bladder known to man. He has more leaks than the whole of Wales."

"I remember."

The food and drink arrived. Ratso's was steaming hot and the warm aromas seemed to mellow the moment as they chatted like an old married couple about TV programmes, new movie releases and whether or not to download a new version of Windows. But all the while, there was a sub-text to the banter, messages still being drip-fed into her glances and her occasional touch of Ratso's wrist or sleeve. He was well aware of the subtle seduction and at first played along before deciding that was not smart. In fact it was plain dumb. "I had a big thought about the fixing. It hit me somewhere between Earl's Court and West Kensington stations."

"Well good for you, boss." From the slurred sarcasm, it was plain she did not like the change in the conversation's tone.

Ratso spotted this but was not going to be deflected. "Mobile phones, particularly Lee Westdale's. So he's dragged from the rubble with his phone. We know there was another one he used in the restaurant when he met Nitin Mithi." He saw Nancy's resigned look as the topic turned to work but he had no intention of backing off. "The one we sent for analysis came back with not a shred of anything naughty or even interesting on it."

Her vodka had gone and she waggled her glass at the server for another. Ratso waited while Nancy wavered before deciding to contribute more than a bored shrug. With the alcohol, she was now struggling to get her brain into top gear. "You mean this was just his regular phone." The words splashed out.

"Sure. The Samsung that Mandy kept ringing after the bombing had all the flutes and whistles but it held nothing to reflect his hectic business life."

Nancy forced herself to concentrate. "There's nothing new in that thought. He used it mainly to keep in touch with Mandy and send occasional text messages about buying bread or more teabags. His phone contacts list wasn't worth a fart in the bath."

Ratso laughed. "Agreed – just crap numbers like his hairdresser, a travel agent in Wimbledon, his London solicitor, the New York lawyers and companies where he worked as a presenter or columnist." He pushed aside the last of his shrimps and waited for any further comment but she volunteered nothing. "So what's missing? You've ten seconds." Over-dramatically he looked at his watch while she stared at her still empty glass. The Hungarian waitress put the next vodka in front of her and she grasped it without a pause. "Six, seven, eight," he counted.

"Sh…hure. Got it." She downed half the glass before speaking. "No cricketers. No other sporting personalities. No celebs. None of the people he rubbed shoulders with." She finished with an exaggerated look of triumph as she slurred her way through the answer.

Ratso nodded in appreciation. "So the missing phone was for an entire secret life beyond home … beyond Mandy."

Nancy was now enthused, Caribbean islands and rejections momentarily forgotten. "Surely Mandy must have realised he had a second phone." The words rather splashed out. "Sod's law that it got lost" The words splashed out slowly and unevenly.

"Yeah." He moved his head almost imperceptibly. "Fixers and drug-dealers often use several pay-as-you-go phones with ever-changing numbers." He rubbed the day's growth on his cheek before propping his head in his hands. "Lee must have written a zillion emails and vital text messages. He wrote three newspaper or magazine columns. He had no laptop, just that desk-top computer which Mandy said he never used."

"With the hard-drive destroyed." Nancy forced herself to stay on message. "So Lee had his entire secret life on a tiny smartphone or smartphones that he might lose or damage." She saw his nod of encouragement. "So…… oh I see." It was her turn now to prop up her head in both hands, pushing her wide cheeks even wider. "I'm with you now, boss." For the first time, her eyes danced as her face lit up with pleasure. "He was a smart guy. He would have everything backed up."

"If he didn't put everything onto the old computer, then, yup, up in the cloud somewhere."

"But, er … Todd," she clutched her near empty glass. "There,

there must be hundreds of companies offering back-up somewhere … up there." She waved an arm precariously close to her untouched water glass. "We'll never know which one. We'd need that and his passwords, stuff that died with him. Mandy didn't even know – at least, *said* she didn't know of any other phone." Nancy swirled her glass before looking up to see his reaction.

"We have his phone contract. Monthly payments – but for his Samsung only."

She frowned in concentration. "So any second or even third phones must have been funded by someone else."

"Or all cash payments." Ratso delivered his real point with a jabbed finger, happy to keep talking business rather than Caribbean cruising. "So, back to his desk-top. Okay, it was old but our techie guys say a Dell like that would have been reliable." He wiped some froth from his upper lip. "Backing up his missing phone to a computer would have been easy. Easily done overnight. Mandy might never have known."

"Or she knew and trashed the hard-drive. She's convincing but calculating. Least that's my take, boss." Her slurred words did not detract from her input.

Ratso's quick look showed agreement. "I hate it when evidence is destroyed." He saw the server heading their way with more drinks which Nancy must have signalled for. "Nancy, I think you've had enough, don't you?"

She pouted before grabbing the glass with a flash of anger. "You're not in my position, are you?"

"Point taken."

"Imagining you and Kirsty-Ann having it away on a cruise." She pumped her fist up and down in a lewd gesture before pushing both elbows firmly onto the table to get closer. "Imagining that is worth a whole bottle of booze."

Looking embarrassed as her point hit home, he changed tack back to Lee. "He wrote his newspaper articles without a ghost-writer. Would you tap out 2,000 words or even dictate them on a smartphone if you had a computer and decent keyboard?"

Nancy's already slack jaw dropped further and she grasped his arm to show how impressed she was. Her eyes also flashed admiration, one narrow eyebrow raised in respect. "So despite, what, er, what Mandy said – you think he used the desk-top." She slurped another mouthful of vodka and wiped her mouth in an extravagant gesture. "He conned Mandy into thinking it was, it was, it was er … redundant."

"I don't buy that anymore. Maybe she knew all along. We need to *think Mandy*. Be suspicious." Ratso tapped his own phone for emphasis. "He must have spent hours typing. Or he had a secret laptop or … he simply dictated his newspaper columns straight onto his missing smartphone. That is possible. Then occasionally and perhaps overnight, he backed it up onto his Dell."

Nancy had a flash of inspiration. Every facial expression was now exaggerated so that tiny wrinkles circled her eyes and mouth. "Suppose, whatsisname …"

"Lee Westdale." Ratso frowned at having to prompt her.

"S'right. Suppose Lee never had the missing phone with him."

"You mean Mandy dumped it or has it well hidden?" He eyed his empty glass with disappointment, unaware of the speed he had sunk it

"Kept it secret from us?" Ratso did not sound enthused.

"You don't get it, do you darling?" She giggled, covering her mouth with her hand. "Oops, sorry, er boss. Lemme explain. His Jupiter note was hidden in the … the Sam's Song."

"The Samsung, yes."

She managed to wag a finger his way as she leaned onto the

table and tried to sound coherent. "Lemme try again, Detective Inspector Holtom," she giggled. "Surely this agenda, his note, he would have kept inside the back of his secret phone, not the Sam, er Samthingie?"

"Nancy, that's good thinking." He did not wish to sound patronising but failed. Not that Nancy would have noticed as her eyes were looking dreamy as she propped up her head with one hand. "If you're right, then we could conclude that his second phone was not with him."

She rewarded his compliment with a huge wink, her eyelashes working overtime as she started stroking the hairs on his left hand. At the same moment, he felt her knee-length boot caress his leg, stroking his calf muscles in a gentle circular movement. He warned himself to move his leg away but her coquettish smile and her enticing fragrance were too pleasurable. He swallowed hard and as the rhythmic stroking continued, he realised that down below something big was stirring.

She grasped both hands, leaned further towards him and spoke softly as her boot rubbed more urgently against his calf. "Come on Todd. Don't be a wimp! My place. Over the road. I want to feel you, to know you. Come on. I dare you. Let's, oh God, let's, let's … unleash our lust. Really taste it, roll in it. Let's ride the tiger." She almost purred the final words.

-42-

Parsons Green

"**C**ome on, I'll get you home." Ratso's words were met with a sly grin and what Nancy must have thought was another subtle wink. Though she left the restaurant with exaggerated care, she still stumbled, grasping his arm for support more than lust. Despite being burdened with his cricket-kit, he steered her across the road to her basement apartment. At the top of the steep stone steps behind the rusted iron railings, she faltered, rocking to and fro.

"Wait Nancy, follow me." He dumped his bag and descended one step ahead of her, she with an arm on his shoulder. "Keys." In answer, she fumbled in her stinking bag but found nothing. In frustration and with a flourish, she tipped out everything – make-up, perfume, tissues, small change, credit-cards and eye-liner. Even in the open air, the stench of dead camel was almost overpowering while Ratso scrabbled until he found the Yale and returned the other contents to the cavernous sack.

Once inside the narrow corridor, he flicked on the light and saw the sickly grin of triumph on Nancy's face as she leaned against the intrusive ochre-coloured wall. He saw the compact kitchen-diner to his left. It smelled of garlic. He peered into the next room and found it was the bedroom, the sound of Ravel's Bolero playing seductively on the sound-system. A king-size dominated the small space and the air was sweet from a cinnamon-scented candle burning on a table beside the bed. Scooping her up from behind her knees, his other arm around her neck, he lowered her onto the bed, laying her head on the pillow. "I'll fetch in my bag." For that, he was rewarded with a slurred comment which sounded something like *sod the bloody bag. I want it now.*

He fetched in his bag but was in no hurry, dawdling in the kitchen which extended into a cramped sitting area with a small TV. It was all immaculate and oozed Nancy's warm character – from the striped tablecloth through to the subtle lights, to the colourful sketches of somewhere in Italy and assorted interesting collectibles. On the table was a near-empty bottle of vodka while beside the trashcan lay two more empties.

He waited nearly five minutes before tiptoeing into the bedroom. As he had hoped, she was sleeping soundly, her face peaceful, her modest chest rising and falling gently. As a young copper, he had once dealt with a drunken teenager who had died from inhaling vomit. He wanted no repeat of that and though she was not comatose he had no intention of leaving her after the skinful she had drunk. Convincing himself it was the right thing to do, he stripped her, item by item starting with the sleeveless waistcoat. She barely stirred as finally he removed the red bra and matching bikini briefs.

He was just tucking her between the pink sheets when he caught sight of her dark golden bush, much darker than her blondish streaked hair. He had seen plenty enough triangles over the years, some wild and some neatly trimmed but this one, made him do a double-take. As she lay on her back, her breathing now much deeper, he even took a third look.

No question!

She had shaped and shaved her hair into the letters T H.

In the flickering candlelight, he almost stopped breathing at the invitation. In silence, he stood admiring every curve of her shapely

body. Then, after blowing out the candle, he hovered, the temptation to climb in with her now so compelling that he started to kick
off his shoes.

But he stopped.

An image of K.A flashed before him together with the warning when he had dodged a gross misconduct bullet. Back then, he
would never have spurned the chance but despite the pulsing message from his groin, he slowly covered her up and turned away.

Fully dressed, Ratso settled on the too-short settee at the rear
of the kitchen. He dozed fitfully, occasionally reliving the image of
the golden T H. A couple of times, he crept in to check on her but
each time, she was on her side and sleeping peacefully, her face
the picture of contentment. Finally, shortly before dawn, his body
aching and his mouth tasting sour, he scribbled a note which he
left beside her. In his bold sweeping style he scribbled "Thanks for
the best sex we never had." He then grabbed a near-empty Tube to
head home for a long and piping-hot shower.

Amazingly, that morning, Nancy arrived on time for work.
She dropped by his desk shortly after nine with a sheepish and off-
centre grin on her rounded face. Only the extra layer of make-up
suggested she had a late night to conceal. She eased herself onto a
chair and looked across to him. "Drank, y'know, like a bit too much
before you phoned. Sorrows. Drowning, y'know." She forced a
smile. "That's it then – I blew my chance."

Ratso looked at nothing before responding. "Better that way.
But I loved the T H. Tempting that was, I can tell you. You feeling
okay?" He saw an unconvincing nod. "No rush but when you've
got your head together, you'd better decide about Tosh and the
tickets."

"While imagining you shagging your way round the Caribbean
with Kirsty." She stopped abruptly. "Sorry, I shouldn't have said

that. Makes me sound screwed-up – all bitter and twisted – as I am." She stood up and from the pocket of her jeans-jacket she produced his note which she had amended in red – "Here's to the best sex we nearly ever had." He read it and for a moment shared her pain as she turned away, her eyes welling with tears.

"Nancy, I'm really sorry. It's for the best." His eyes slowly emerged from behind the heavy lids to show sincerity. "But I gotta say, it doesn't feel that way right now."

"Keep the note. Souvenir." Then she sighed. "Catch up later. I need a black coffee."

-43-

Newcastle

Alex Anderson strolled into the bar of the Northern Lights pub in Wideopen expecting nothing to have much changed. It had been over twenty-five years. Once it had been a man's pub, designed for sinking pints and talking football or the racing at Gosforth Park. He winced when he saw the transformation to gastropub. Sure the changes were an improvement but he was in no mood for change. He liked familiarity.

After parking his rented silver Nissan, he had stood outside looking at the so-familiar surroundings, remembering staggering out as if he had drunk there just the previous week. The pub had once been on the busy A1 north to Edinburgh, a few miles outside the city centre. Now it was bypassed and those days when it had been pivotal to the mining community were now almost forgotten.

The grand brick facade was still crowned by a clock over the front entrance. Momentarily, he was swept back to living for Saturdays, watching the Magpies and celebrating a win or drowning sorrows. Life had been simpler then – working at the dog-track, sweeping trash. Chasing the hot peroxides in their micro-skirts as they danced around their handbags in the clubs beside the Tyne. As a nineteen year old, that was life – give or take sorting out someone who had not shown sufficient respect.

Now he was wealthy beyond dreams.

Life though was far from simple.

Simplicity had ended when he had taken a job renting out student properties. That had been his first step to understanding what made the city tick. From there, he had started buying distressed properties. Then as his skills improved, he bought derelict sites until finally he was the go-to man, able to deliver major redevelopments around the city.

But not without controversy.

Plenty of that.

Rumours of bribing officials and threatening competitors.

All rumours.

He had quit before they stuck.

Now as he stood just inside the entrance, Anderson remembered the grimy surfaces and the familiar smell of urinals, stale beer and cigarettes. Today, the large bar was almost empty and clinically clean. The air was fresh and the tables all highly polished. He spotted Walter Harvey sitting in a back corner reading the Sporting Life. Walt had aged and not in a kind way either. His once brown hair had almost all gone and what remained hung straggly in a comb-over down to a clumsy looking ear. He either had rapid beard growth or had not yet shaved today. He spotted the familiar scar still visible above the right eye – a legacy of a broken bottle rammed into his face.

"Walt. Another?"

Walt looked across his paper and nodded. There was neither pleasure nor interest in seeing a mate from a quarter of a century before. He pushed across a plain glass. "The usual," he muttered.

"Nothing's changed then – well, except your hair and this pub. Doesn't even stink of puke anymore." If Walter had heard Anderson's comment, he took no notice, returning to his paper. Anderson looked disdainfully at the image. As ever, Walt's stained blue jeans looked as if they would still hang a few inches below his crotch. His dirty white sweat-shirt was crumpled. Three filthy marks, probably ketchup, coloured its front. The short sleeves revealed muscled arms and a meaningless blue and red tattoo.

On the plus side, the guy still looked lean, fit, strong, his eyes as steely grey as ever.

Anderson headed for the bar and bought a bottle of Newkie Brown for Harvey and a scotch and ice for himself. Wearing a lilac polo-shirt with a lightweight cashmere sweater to match, he looked the picture of assured elegance. The contrast was striking and as Anderson eased himself onto the corner seat, the barman was still staring towards this odd couple.

Anderson raised his glass. "What's new Walt?"

He saw the shrug as Walter folded the paper and dumped it on the next table. "I've been in here."

"Not all the time. Not that I heard."

Walt looked at him and wiped his mouth with his sleeve. "Ee, man! You're right, Twelve years away – guest of Her Majesty."

"I heard. Attempted murder."

"You?"

"Keeping my nose clean."

"Not what I heard. That property deal in Ponteland."

Anderson's nose twitched in irritation but otherwise there was no reaction. "Long ago. Business. Just business – Tyneside style."

"You left here."

Anderson's slight inclination of the head was the only acknowledgement. He had no intention of letting the guy from his dog-track days know more than essential. "I heard you're having things tough."

Walt took a slurp and belched. "I get by."

"Costly divorce. She got the house. No regular job." He patted his hand on the razor-sharp crease on his thigh. "I heard though," he paused to eyeball the listener, "you still do things. If the money's good."

"Dinna believe everything you hear. I heard you was in Florida. That was wrong. Ye're here. Wideopen."

Anderson had shared enough verbal skirmishing. "I've ten minutes. You want a job, maybe two jobs?"

"Heavy?"

"The heaviest."

"Anyone I know?"

"Out of your league, Walt. They've never been near Durham prison or the dog-track in Byker."

"Coppers. I'd kill coppers. Hate the fuckers."

"I want an answer. Just yes or no." Anderson drained his whisky to show time was running out. Anderson had no fear of Walt though he knew the man had knifed a youngster on the Scotswood Road and had shot and wounded two drug-dealers on Pilgrim Street.

"How much?"

"Is that a yes?"

"How much?"

"Cheerio Walt. Go back to betting on slow dogs. See you in twenty-five years – if I'm unlucky." Anderson rose from the seat and made a dramatic spin turn as if getting a bit of dog-shit from his foot. He strolled away as nonchalantly as he had arrived, not once looking back. Outside, the sky looked sullen and flecks of rain spattered onto the windshield of the small rented car.

He climbed in and waited for a couple of moments, all the while keeping an eye open for any movement. He was not disappointed as the lanky figure padded out of the main entrance, his left arm waving his newspaper. Anderson fired the engine and started to pull away, enjoying the sight of Walt now frantic to prevent the Nissan from departing.

Anderson touched the rocker-switch and the window glided down. "Did I hear a yes?" He saw the Geordie nod. "Say it Walt or I'm away."

"Yes."

"Then get in and stop pissing me about."

~44~

Putney, South-West London

Outside Putney Railway Station, Ratso's face lit up as he spotted a vagrant that he had come to know. The man was sprawled on grubby cardboard, a bowl with a few coins beside him. The mongrel at his feet looked better fed than him. "Not your usual pitch, Jonno. Shifted from Clapham North?"

"Hello Guv! Yeah. The guy who always sat here topped himself the other week. I reckoned I'd do better wiv more posh geezers about. So I walks here."

Ratso crouched down to be at his level and stroked the dog's ears. "How you keeping?"

"Ain't too bad now," he sniffed. "But the winter, blimey, doesn't half play merry hell, it does. Numb bum an' all. Bones ache."

"Still no chance of a change of luck? Getting a place? A job?"

"Not easy mate. Once you're doin' this, the only way is down, that's my take."

"See you again, pal." With a pat on the shoulder, Ratso slipped him a tenner note. "And don't drink it all." He walked away, head down in thought. He understood, had seen it happen. Ending up like Jonno or Lee Westdale or Mark Rayner was just too easy.

One wrong move and you're buggered.

Some Tuesday evenings, Ratso would drop in for a pint at the Star & Garter on the river by Putney Bridge. The first time had been after reading that mass murderer John Reginald Halliday Christie had been arrested close by on the towpath. Tonight though, Tosh was coming over from the Cauldron and had suggested Bill's Restaurant on the High Street.

Ratso was the first to arrive in the noisy and dimly-lit restaurant. He was a bit early, part of his fad of never being late. Neither Tosh nor Nancy had arrived and Jock Strang, now without the droopy moustache, had declined, no doubt still smarting from Nancy's rejection. He glanced at the menu but while he waited, his thoughts were more about Nancy and the other night at the Yellow Sombrero. He could almost feel the rhythmic rubbing of her boot on his calf with her invite to *ride the tiger*. Judging by her erotic fantasies that evening, the booze had been doing more than just talking.

Nancy arrived next, breezing in, swinging her camel bag. At that moment Ratso had been imagining the ins and outs of the red *his-and-her-vibrating-beads* that she had promised to use on him. She had not been joking. Later, he had spotted them lying on her bedside table. He rose to greet her as she waved a huge hello. Their shared look said everything that a hug might have done as she slid onto the bench across the large plain wood table.

"I'm on Rioja? For you?

"No thanks. I'm trying not to. The booze like, I mean it was taking over. Y'know what with Jock and then you and Kirsty-Ann." Her head cocked to one side, she accepted a sparkling water and moments later they had barely chinked glasses when Tosh arrived, squeezing his belly between table and seat. Despite the Met Police wanting an end to roly-poly coppers, Tosh was not even paying lip-service to any diet. "I always go for the 10oz ribeye with extra fries and onion rings," he announced on arrival. Ratso and Nancy both opted for the chicken skewers and were just awaiting delivery when Jock's bulk loomed large beside them.

"Mind if I join ye?" He saw the surprised smiles and pushed

himself in beside Ratso. As Tosh poured him some red into a tumbler, Jock raced into an apology. "I've been a right pain in the arse. I guess ye all ken why. Sorry guys, especially you, Nancy." He placed an elbow on the table and clasped her arm. She touched his hand briefly.

"Forget it! Like the old days in the Cauldron again," said Ratso chinking glasses all round.

"I hear your investigation's dead in the water," said Tosh.

"Think can you do better?" Nancy's voice showed her resentment as she put Ratso's thoughts into words.

Tosh at first said nothing but his body-language was *back-track* … and bloody quick too. "It … well the word's out there. Like it's going nowhere. But …"

Ratso leaned onto the table. "No offence taken. We're at that see-saw moment, waiting for something to tilt the bloody thing our way."

"We're checking every player that Lee knew well enough to corrupt," added Nancy. "Jock and me, we've spent hours checking televised matches from Australia."

Jock looked at Ratso and Nancy in turn. "Talk about waterboarding torture in yon Guantanamo, I've watched cricket for hours. Like a life-sentence. Fitba' – now that would be different but watching this daft game. Tosh, it'll fair drive me to drink!" They all laughed as he drained his glass with an almighty flourish.

As Ratso ordered another bottle of Rioja and more sparkling for Nancy, he watched Tosh's large eyes rolling as his steak and fries appeared. "This means a lot," Tosh nodded. "Us being together. At work, my career's fucked. At home, Patsy never stops nagging." He stabbed his steak aggressively. "I mean, I like the new crowd in the Cauldron … but they ain't the old crowd. You get me? Know what I mean?"

Ratso could easily imagine the hell inside that marriage. "Patsy's one tough woman and no mistake."

"Sod her." Tosh continued to attack the steak with fierce movements and rapid chewing. "Let's talk about something else. Is this social? Or do you need me to kick-start your enquiry?" As he spoke, his mouth twitched into a grin and then a laugh. Tosh had no illusions – powers of detection were not his strong suit. Solid, methodical plodding was more his style.

"Social!" The three listeners almost chorused the word. Ratso nodded to Nancy who pulled the envelope from her pocket. "Tosh. We thought this might cheer you up. Take a look." They continued to eat as Tosh stared at the Ryder Cup tickets in disbelief. Mesmerised, he laid them down. "Me? Going with you? Patsy would kill me." He sounded like he'd just suffered ten rounds with his wife already.

"Go for it, Tosh. You tell her the way it is. Three days at Wentworth." Ratso's voice was commanding.

"Nah! Patsy will never stop nagging about me and Nancy having it away in the rough."

"Nagging about shagging? Us in the buff in the rough?" Nancy chipped in with a face-splitting grin. "With TV cameras and huge crowds everywhere?"

"Patsy doesn't do logic! Bare-knuckle fighter, that's her."

Nancy pushed her ticket across the table. "Look Tosh. Like I mean, golf I can take or leave. You go with someone else. Take both tickets." Everyone stared at her in disbelief, forks hanging in mid-air.

Tosh looked really moved. "Nah! Can't be doing with that" He put down his glass and reached for the ticket. "Sod Patsy. We're on. You and me." He turned to Nancy and gave her a squeeze.

As Nancy kissed Tosh's cheek, Ratso stole a quick picture. "Just one more please. For the record."

-45-
Caribbean

They leaned on the stateroom's balcony as the giant cruise ship neared Nassau on New Providence Island. It was dawn and they were both skimpily dressed – wearing just enough to view the sun rising. Ratso kissed Kirsty-Ann full on the mouth. "Get dressed to go ashore?" He paused. "Or ..."

"*Or* sounds pretty damned good to me." She snuggled her head against the nape of his neck and sighed. "I'm missing Leon but it sure is a nice kinda miss."

"He's great – a real tearaway. In England I'd have him learning cricket. I guess here he's into baseball."

"Sure but after I started to learn golf at Lauderhill, his aunt gave him a set of plastic clubs. Hits it real good. When he's a top golfer I can retire." They both laughed as they went back into their stateroom. "Walk the deck or the gym?"

Ratso patted her trim butt with affection. "Yeah. The gym. Lapping the deck, it was only seeing you coming the other way, kept me going." Ten minutes later, they were in the deserted gym, Ratso using the step-climber, K.A beside him on the running-machine at 8mph with a steep gradient. Above their heads were three TV screens – one showing CNN, one basketball and the other cooking.

Ratso put on the headphones and tuned his dial into the news-feed. It was the usual diet of political sound-bites and clips reporting global unrest. It helped to numb his brain, every muscle complaining as his ascent got harder. "I'm calling it quits," he gasped forty minutes later. He looked across at K.A as he towelled his dripping face dry. She looked as fresh as when she had started.

As she went into cool-down mode, he watched her lithe figure ripple and bob. until the machine slowed to a stop. "I need a shower PDQ," Ratso volunteered "but you look ready for another few miles."

"Too much Guinness, maybe," she grinned as she draped a towel around her neck. They dropped down several flights of empty stairs to their deck. An impromptu seduction while soaping each other in the shower delayed breakfast before the steward laid out porridge together with juice and coffee. "I really got into porridge in London, "K.A volunteered. "Much better than Deep South grits."

"S'funny," Ratso responded as they sat side-by-side on the sofa. "Remember Jock Strang? The Glaswegian? All Scots are all supposed to get their rocks off on porridge with salt but not him. Goes for the full English – eggs, bacon, sausage, beans, tomato, hash-browns. Not that hash-browns are English."

"They're pretty damned good though. I treat myself occasionally." K.A looked at the TV and flicked through the channels. "Ah! The Ryder Cup. The USA team are well up on the first day." Mention of the Ryder Cup was an unwelcome reminder of the real world Ratso had left behind. For a moment, he imagined Tosh at Wentworth watching the action from behind a bulging greasy burger.

For twenty-four hours, he had parked all thoughts of match-fixing and headless chickens. All he wanted for the next few days was small-talk and loving cuddles as the giant vessel glided through the deep blue waters. Now his forgotten burdens hit him like a ten-ton truck. "I'd put England out of my mind." His voice showed resentment as the unwelcome memories flooded back.

She topped up his coffee, strong and black. "Sorry for the reminder, lover-boy. My fault ... but since I took up golf, I'm really into all this USA versus Europe thing. Been reading up all about it. The PGA's HQ is quite close by me back home."

"The PGA?"

"Professional Golfers Association. We've some great courses." She paused, her nose wrinkling as she thought. "So where is Wentworth?"

"Kirsty, I know nothing about the game but I'm told its twenty-five miles from Central London. Not that far from Heathrow."

"Looks beautiful even in the rain." For a moment, they both watched as Zack Gomez, an American player, chipped into the hole from off the green to excited shouts from the Americans in the crowd. "Look, seeing as you're reminded of work anyway, you said you'd show me the note, y'know, the dead guy's agenda."

Ratso sighed, his thoughts more about wanting to stroke her neck and nibble her ear. "K.A, you're a great detective but what you know about cricket could be written on a pin-head. Let's forget that stuff." He squeezed her waist and snuggled into her neck.

"You talked plenty enough about cricket when I was in London. Try me!"

Ratso's face showed resignation. "Okay but promise me. All fixing talk is locked away? For the next few days, I just want to," he paused searching for a word. "To lose myself with the most beautiful, wonderful and desirable woman I've ever met. Deal?"

"Well thank you, kind sir." She ran her fingers down his spine, making Lee Westdale's note seem even more intrusive. "Spoken like a real English gentleman." She tilted her head back as she laughed before leaning across and wrapping her lips round his. "Deal. Sealed with a kiss,"

He padded barefoot across the cabin and returned with his iPad. K.A watched, her eyes revealing how impressed she was with his dexterity as he switched through his screens. Then suddenly, there it was – Lee Westdale's neat writing. "And this guy had this note with him when the bomb went off?"

"Hidden inside his phone cover." Ratso handed over the iPad and said nothing as she studied each point on the list with obvious care. About halfway through, she cut him a quizzical look but said nothing. "You said the guy was a cricketer, a TV celebrity? Right?" She watched Ratso nod. "That explains a lot."

Ratso twisted sideways to catch her excited smile. His eyebrows almost met as he puzzled at her comment. "Don't tell me you can decipher this?"

"Not if you don't want me to." She gave him a playful dig in the ribs.

"You mean?"

"Sure. I can understand most all of it. Let's talk on deck."

-46-

London

"If we were in a movie, we'd cross the road and spot Lee Westdale's missing phone, just surfaced during rubble clearing." In the dry dusty air, Nancy and Jock had shown their passes and were stumbling between chunks of concrete and charred timber, the shattered remains of Piccadilly not far from the ruins of the Ambassador Hotel.

"Nae such luck. In fact, when the boss gets back from topping up his tan on yon boat, he's going to be downright ratty." He expected some response, perhaps even a laugh at his choice of adjective but Nancy said nothing, looking away as tears filled her eyes. Realising she was not going to respond, Jock continued. "I reckon Lee Westdale was found just aboot here." He had stopped on the corner of Piccadilly looking down Duke Street towards the Cavendish Hotel which was once again open for business, sheltered as it had been from the devastation in the cordoned off zone. He saw Nancy nod her head but still she said nothing, her imagination running wild about Ratso's naked torso writhing in synch with the American blonde. "Tell you what. That's the rain starting. Let's check out the Cavendish."

After an over-long silence, Nancy spoke on autopilot. "We know Lee set off from home that morning, so what's the point?" It was less of a question, more of a resigned dismissal of the idea.

The Scot looked at her profile, confused by her pessimism.

"But we might find a name, someone staying there; someone he might have met." Jock shouted over the roar of a bulldozer that was shifting rubble into a dumpster-truck. "Remember what Ratso said? No negativity. I'm going to try anyroads." He did not wait for her to follow but she did, surreptitiously wiping away her tears before they turned in under the hotel's canopy. At the front desk, they asked for the Duty Manager who, moments later, sat them down with hot drinks while she went to check hotel records. She returned minutes later with a print-out.

"Here's every booking for the night before the bomb and those booked for the night after. We've two-twenty bedrooms plus five meeting rooms. Every room was full but after the bomb," her young face twisted with the hurt. "Y'know several guests did not return." She fell silent at the recollection, looking at the wall behind Jock's head. "We'll have more details, like how the bill was paid or booked." With a sombre glance she was ready to leave. "Take your time."

Nancy turned to the long list, quickly skimming down the names, most of them foreign, many of them companies. When she had finished, she handed the sheets to Jock. "Nothing jumps off the page. Not one big name or sporting personality." She sipped her green tea from the delicate cup while she waited for Jock. She caught his eye. "You agree?"

"Aye. I canna see any names from Craig Carter's list." He was referring to their meeting at Lord's earlier that morning. They had the names of every player in the top-ten most suspicious televised matches in which Rayner had played and where Lee had been commentating. "On each of these English T20 games," Craig had explained "the bookies reported concerns about betting patterns on the result. The older ones included spot-fixing."

Craig had then pointed to his screen. "Look at that. Nearly a million bet on the fourth ball of the over being a no-ball. And, as the bible would say, verily it came to pass. But that was eight years ago. That type of bet won't get accepted now, not here in the legit market, perhaps not anywhere." The former detective had shaken his head ruefully, his eyes looking tired and bloodshot. He pointed to the names and photos of thirteen famous cricketers. "This is raw data. Knowing guilt and proving it is so bloody difficult." He shook his head. "And it's not simply about getting good evidence."

"Meaning?" Nancy was taking the lead while Jock sucked on his cheap pen, his brow furrowed.

"Cricket politics. Government politics and money. All three get in the way of clearing out the shit from the stable. Top administrators don't always want the truth to come out."

"No case even against the guy who bowled the no-ball to order?" Nancy's voice had risen an octave in surprise.

"Granted – you'd think it was easy but he would say – *shit happens. Sheer chance.* Unless we can show he got a big payday and that Mark Rayner, Lee – or someone else fixed the guy, we aren't in with a prayer. No way." His friendly face brightened as he passed around the chocolate-chips. "Dig deeper. You have ways of checking for extravagant lifestyles, learning about money being thrown around. Uncover phone calls, suspicious meetings – join the dots."

Jock shifted uncomfortably, his eyes restless, one eyelid drooping. "I'm still way, way out of this cricket, this T20 game." He leaned forward. "Pretend I'm Lee and I want Mark Rayner to fix. So I pay him. Mark does what?"

Craig was now in his element. "No problem! Todd warned me I could write all you knew about cricket on an ant's arse."

"As long as he didna' say my aunt's arse because that's the size of a pregnant elephant."

After the laughter had died, Craig continued. "Mark would

maybe sound out the captain of the other team. Easy – if they'd conspired before. They could fix who would win and the captains would then fix maybe a couple in one team to bowl piss-poor badly making it easy for the batsmen in the other team to score quickly. Another dodge – Mark might fix an umpire to give some bad decisions like refusing a good appeal that the batsman was out or wrongly giving him out. A bent captain might place his fielders in strange positions to let the opposition score easier. Bent team members might deliberately drop a catch or mis-field the ball to help the opposition."

"Fixing a score?" Nancy prompted.

"Much cheaper. You could pay a batsman to get himself out for less than say ten runs. Or you could fix the speed of scoring."

"Example?" Jock's Sudoko champion brain was soaking up the detail.

"A bet that a team will score under twenty runs after six overs. That's thirty-six balls and an unlikely score so the odds would be attractive. The fixers could make a killing." Craig grinned as he stood up. "Lesson over as I have another meeting." As he showed them out, Craig paused outside the glass-plated doors. "Look – it's not just cricket where it's hard to prove. Tennis – you've got just two players. Easy to prove a fix, huh?" He looked defeated for a moment. "You'd think so, yes? Not so. The bookies reckon fixing has been happening for years – mainly in obscure tournaments – but proving it?" His downturned mouth spoke volumes.

Nancy looked at both men. "And instead of just two players fixing a tennis match …"

"You got it!" He smiled at Nancy. "With twenty-two players plus officials, cricket fixing is far harder to prove. In tennis, snooker, darts both players can agree a fix – one player is bribed to lose or fake an injury. Take College Basketball. Where some giant of a player misses a few baskets. Go on – you prove he was paid off!" He shrugged. "For tennis, at my next meeting, we're checking out criminals from Russia and Italy – organised crime of course. It involves one or two stars, household names – top guys with skeletons rattling in their closets." His eyes seemed to be watching a distant horizon somewhere beyond the Media Centre. "We reckon they got suckered in as youngsters and were left dormant."

"Like sleeper spies, you mean?"

"Exactly, Nancy. The gang let the youngsters go on to become top seeds, big, big names and very likely to win most matches, especially against low-ranking opponents. At the bookies, the ignorant mass of punters pile in on the favourite, expecting to make a good return on slim odds. Then their man loses to a rank outsider."

"So the criminals clean up betting on the outsider."

"Correct, Nancy. And of course they let their bent player win most of the time to make the winnings bigger when they crash out." Craig checked the time. "Guys on the committee reckon they're closing in. But my dream, we nail the ringleaders – whatever the sport."

He pointed to the Nursery Ground just beside them where a friendly match was being played. "We have twenty-two youngsters involved plus the umpires and ground-staff. That's where we're concentrating – warning and educating these up-and-comings. They don't get paid *loadsamoney*. They're vulnerable. They must not get sucked into it. If he were alive, Hanse Cronje would tell you. Fix the youngsters who are in awe of you."

Now, leaning back in his wing-chair at the Cavendish, Jock drained his tea and glanced at Nancy who looked miles away. "Ready to move on? I'm fair famished."

Nancy shook her head as she suddenly rose and headed for the Front Desk. "I've an idea. It might be a good one."

~47~

London

Outside, the rain was belting down, dancing off the line of black cabs and red buses, their lights trying to break through the gloom. Inside the café at King's Cross Station though, Alex Anderson's quiet smile radiated satisfaction. On the train back from Newcastle, his evening meal had included a surprisingly decent red and a couple of malts. Back in Newcastle, Walt Harvey was on-standby for the call to come south All he needed now was good news from Toufiq. Then he would speed west to Trevose Golf Club in Cornwall, a favourite occasional haunt. In the evenings there would be golfing banter over dinner with American friends. By day, they would play the demanding course, wagering hefty sums as they had done at Carnoustie, Royal Birkdale and Troon.

He blew his large Americano to cool it, alert for Youssef Toufiq's arrival and idly flicking through the evening newspaper. After their meeting at the Trumpeters, a couple of days previously, the Moroccan's knowledge and self-confidence had been impressive. Now, though, the whizz who had studied computer science in Portsmouth was twenty minutes late.

Should I have trusted him?

For the first time, he wondered if Toufiq would be a no-show and his deposit lost. Edgy, he put down his paper and drummed his fingers on the table-top, idly passing the time by watching others dunking cookies or shovelling away chicken wraps.

Full of apologies, it was another ten minutes before the sallow-skinned figure with his sinister pointed beard, appeared in a black hoodie and skin-tight jeans, a laptop bag in his hand. "My bus was caught up in the downpour, sir," he explained. His English was good but with a guttural Arabic overlay.

Anderson showed his irritation by a gruff okay and a forceful glance that made the Moroccan look away.

"Sir. You will see. You will be happy. Very happy."

Anderson grunted again as he watched Toufiq produce his Apple laptop and with swift keystrokes, open the private page for HOSS. He saw the familiar screen and logo he had used hundreds of times to obtain the racing selections. "You see, sir. It looks identical."

"You mean?" Anderson faltered. "You mean, this is not really HOSS at all?"

For answer, Toufiq just laughed, showing rather too many zebra-like teeth. "I tell you. Not the same. Not HOSS as you knew it. But your colleagues, they will see nothing different."

"So?"

"Behind here, I have changed the software. The HOSS programme is now fucked."

Anderson gave an encouraging smile and nodded for him to continue. Toufiq twisted the computer around and tapped in *York – 2-30pm* for the previous day. The runners' names appeared, everything normal. "So HOSS predicted Misty Forester would win at 4 to 1."

"Go on."

Toufiq laughed. "It came last." His large, dark brown eyes peered at the screen as his slender fingers flew across the keys. Again the tombstone teeth appeared. "Here, sir." He pointed a narrow finger at the screen. "This page is now accessible only by you with your password. Any other passwords take the users to the dummy. Now you see the original HOSS programme."

Anderson saw what appeared to be an identical page. "Go on."

"I now enter *York 2-30 pm* for yesterday on the genuine HOSS site. See it tips Angelic Delight to win at 9-2."

Anderson stood up excitedly. "I watched. It romped home." He sat down, thumping a fist into his other palm. "Brilliant. Amazing."

The Moroccan handed over a complex twelve number password. "This gets you and nobody else to the original site. Your friend's passwords will only take them to the dummy." They both peered at the screen. "From now on, your friends will be backing three-legged fucking donkeys." In his deep Arabic voice, the expression sounded doubly forceful. "On every race, they will lose their goddammed fucking shirts – as you English say."

"They have a clever guy in India who wrote the programme. He's damned smart. Can he rewrite it? Get it back?"

Toufiq shut down his laptop with a mocking look on his face. "Forget it! HOSS is yours. If their Indian expert tries to repair the dummy or even gets close to the real HOSS, I have inserted a virus, a poisoned-pill to scramble the hard-drive."

Anderson was beyond laughing. He was so excited he had to stand up and pace round between the busy tables, his face radiating triumph. Inwardly, he was imagining Pagano losing his millions backing donkeys. Eventually, he sat down and asked Toufiq to show more examples "to prove your point." He did, showing six more losers that HOSS had regarded as winners.

Anderson had heard and seen enough. From the side pocket of his lightweight case, he pulled out a chocolate box, stuffed with fifty pound notes. "That's five grand there, as promised."

"Thanks, Mr Bristow." The Moroccan surreptitiously looked at the bundles of notes. "A good selection of chocolates. I really like truffles." He laughed as he turned away and within seconds, was gone – lost in the crowds sheltering from the rain beside the plate-glass doors leading out to Euston Road.

-48-

Caribbean

Scarcely able to contain his excitement about what K.A was about to tell him, Ratso strode around the deck, Kirsty-Ann beside him. Before leaving the cabin, he had received a message from Jock suggesting that perhaps Lee's manipulator or contact had also been killed by the bomb. "That could explain why there was no fix in Delhi," Jock had volunteered. It was good thinking but no help on why Nitin Mithi had been murdered.

On deck, the air was humid but they were both dressed for the sultry heat with casual tops and shorts. Way down below them, like a line of ants, a steady stream of passengers was filing off the ship heading for the trinket stores and tourist traps of Nassau's Bay Street. "Come on, K.A! No more know-it-all looks. Give! I'm all ears."

"Golf. Lee's note is about *golf.*"

"What?" Ratso's voice was louder than he intended. "Golf? You're kidding me!" Ratso pulled up and they faced each other. He swallowed hard as a torrent of jumbled and unwelcome thoughts clouted him from every direction. He was met by K.A's calm and confident smile. "Why? How? You're sure?" Already he could imagine another arse-kicking from Mick Tolvey for the hundreds of police hours wasted chasing the wrong sport.

"Todd, I gotta tell it as it is. Lee was a cricketer, so you *assumed* the note was about cricket."

He listened, looking confused, his eyes now blank.

"Explaining will take a while, "K.A continued. "Let's go find ourselves a couple of recliners." Moments later and three decks higher and behind the funnel, they nestled into a secluded and shaded niche towards the stern where Ratso pulled a couple of chairs together.

He looked along the deserted deck. "It's like the Marie Celeste Almost everybody is ashore." He tapped away on his iPad until the note appeared. "Bishopsgate, Dubai? That's about golf?" Then he pointed to the code **+409WGG =SJW 4878903.** "And SJW? That just has to be St John's Wood home of Lord's Cricket Ground."

"Okay, sure I can't explain those – except I guess Lee was talking money and codes. But the rest? The meaty bits." She waved an arm with a manicured hand in a broad expansive sweep. "Honey, like I said, they read like a book."

"Jupiter? Is that a golfing term?"

"My guess Jupiter refers to someone who lives in … well, Jupiter. Just north of Palm Beach, up the coast from Fort Lauderdale. It's a rich man's enclave if you will. Full of famous names."

"Top sportsmen including golfers?"

"You betcha. Plenty golfers."

"Golfers earn more from a winning putt than I ever will. Why cheat?"

"The top ones, sure they do real good." Ratso saw the smile playing round K.A's lips and knew she was tormenting him like a matador about to plunge the sword deep into the bull's neck. Her face radiated excitement, her eyes were dancing and her cheeks flushed with pleasure. "The numbers 6-2 and 10-6. Dead giveaway and the tie. Well that plus September and WC."

Ratso could see she loved his bewilderment. "No more suspense. Finish me off now!"

"This note is about fixing the Ryder Cup."

"What? You mean?"

"Like it's happening now!"

His voice showed disbelief though the date had clicked. "You mean at Wentworth where Tosh and Nancy are?" He took in her confident laugh and her eyes smiled in amusement as he continued. "Top golfers? Representing the USA or Europe? Huge money and bragging rights. Fixed? Tell me you're kidding."

K.A stretched across to clasp Ratso's hand as it hung between them. Her fingers felt soft and cool despite the humidity. "The European team gets paid but not like fill-your-boots. For years in the US camp, there's been trouble and debate, maybe worse, about being unpaid. The team is expected to play good without big bucks."

The faint lines and crow's feet on Ratso's face suddenly seemed etched deeper as he wrestled with the new situation. He stared almost unseeingly at the note on the screen. "So your American team of multi-millionaires from Jupiter could be ... bought?" His worried look reflected a recurring image of a right royal rollicking from Mike Tolvey. "Assuming they don't mind crapping on their egos and selling their fans down the river," he concluded.

K.A undid the top three buttons on her red shirt revealing her black bikini. "Not for you," she grinned though Ratso was unconvinced. "I'm letting in the breeze." She twisted sideways to face towards him, improving Ratso's view of her rising and falling curves. "Most spies don't sell secrets because they hate the U.S. Nor do they love Russia or North Korea. Most do it for greed – because they spot an opportunity and a challenge. They believe they can get away with it. Why not golfers?"

She leaned across and tapped him on the nose with an enthusiastic grin as Ratso found himself looking more at her breasts than her face. He knew at once that she was still toying with him and had yet to deliver the sucker-punch. "Anyway, a fixed result could be great for spectators." This time she tapped the side of her own nose in a knowing gesture. "And even better for your fixers."

Ratso wiped a bead of sweat from his neck. "WC?"

"Wild Cards. See ... each team has a captain – more like a manager. He doesn't play. His role is strategy – selecting which players partner each other in the foursomes and four-balls. Each day, he selects the team, the playing order and chooses whether to partner left and right-handed players. Particularly on the last of the three days, sending out your players in the most cunning order can mean win-or-lose."

"The captains don't share their playing orders?"

"Give away the Crown Jewels?" Kirsty-Ann laughed. "Heck no! They exchange their lists last minute and are stuck with their decisions. Between the two captains, it's real cat-and-mouse psychology."

Ratso's face showed that he was starting to understand. The feeling of having been kicked in the stomach by a stallion was easing. And maybe, just maybe, the fantastic positives would make Tolvey even see the funny side of it.

Or not.

"So you fix one captain or better still both." Ratso saw her agree. "Wild Cards? What are they? The jokers in the pack?"

"Some folk sure would agree with that! Each team has twelve players. During the year, the captains follow the players' form. The top eight Americans who have played the best are a shoe-in. The U.S captain selects a further four players, his choice. They're the Wild Cards. The European team captain may be allowed to pick say three Wild Cards. I gotta tell you – in previous Ryder Cups, Wild Card selections have sometimes raised eyebrows. The media love the controversy as to why a captain has preferred X over Y."

"Corruption?"

"Never. Not a hint of it." She watched an elderly couple shuffle by with Zimmer-frames. "But if both captains have been bought, then colluding over playing order and manipulating Wild Cards – sure, the result could be fixed."

"Fix the Wild Cards?"

"They owe the captain their selection, so sure." She pointed to the screen. "Today is Friday, the first day and if I'm right the score will be 6-2. Tomorrow it will be 10-6. On Sunday, the final day, the Ryder Cup will be tied."

Ratso eased the angle of his recliner so that he could see K.A better. Beneath her scarlet peaked cap, her blonde hair was swept back above her pale bronzed cheeks. Her hair was longer than last Spring. "That pony-tail suits you. You look more sensational than ever."

"Not admiring my brains then?"

"Your inner beauty too." They each leaned closer and he kissed her full on the mouth. "I'm recovering from feeling like a deflating balloon. Christ! I owe you. You are just amazing."

K.A stroked the hairs on his arm. "A Tie. Great finish, eh? Neither side loses. The drama is *terrific*. The crowds will love it going down to the wire. No bragging rights lost."

"So … let me get this. Each day, the captains collude on the playing order and control enough bent players to manipulate a tie come Sunday?" Each word was punctuated by hesitation as he tried to grasp what it all meant.

"Sure. Why not?" She started to sit up. "I'm getting kinda parched. Let's drop by the little bar at the back."

"The stern. It's called the *stern*. But don't ask me why there's also something called the poop deck!" Ratso laughed, his confidence returning. "The media would *love* a Wild Card screwing up. Result a tie."

"You got it! All the *he-should-never-have-picked-that-guy* or *temperament-counts* or *just as I predicted when writing my column last week.*"

"Been a tie before?"

K.A shook her head. "Never and get this – if the score today ends up 6-2, your fixers will get great odds on the tie."

He stood up, stretched and then effortlessly pulled K.A off her chair. "Besides that, they could clean up betting on 6-2 today." Ratso was still thinking aloud. "*And* the captains and those fixed players get a monster pay-day." As he walked slowly, his eyes downturned, he was seeing the picture clearer with every step. "So maybe these Wild Cards, they miss the odd putt or land in bunkers. I mean I guess they have an easy excuse to be nervous."

"Not long ago, a great golfer called Ernie Els seven-putted from about a couple of feet. Even the top guys can be human, get the yips." She clasped his hand while they strolled along the near-empty slatted wood decking to the open-air bar.

"Put like that, disguising a fix is pretty damned easy."

The colourful pastel-shaded bar was empty and the bar-tender looked delighted to have some business. They selected a table with padded purple seats. The view was towards Nassau town. Close to the ship was a tall yellow tower topped with white, like a giant ice-cream cone. The remaining skyline was dominated by white buildings with red roofs in a mish-mash of clashing styles. "I'm glad we stayed on board." K.A licked her parted lips adding seduction to the message. Margaritas and shrimps appeared while they looked deep into each other's eyes as they chinked glasses. "You want to know the score today? See if I'm correct?" There was an impish smile and a chuckle in her deep melodious voice.

"I can guess by your face."

For an answer, she pointed to a TV screen behind Ratso. "Day One has ended. Look at the score." Ratso turned to follow her gaze. He did a double-take as if the ghost of Lee Westdale were tapping him on the shoulder, whispering *I-told-you-so*." Despite the clammy heat, a shiver ran through him as he saw from the ticker-tape that the US team were winning 6-2.

Slowly, he raised one hand to his head and pointed his fingers like a pistol. "Bang." He lowered his hand and his eyes were downcast, sunk deep into their sockets. "God! I've been a right tosser. Blinkered." Every nerve end seemed to be on fire, burning him up. He walked to the rail and looked down at the water far below. Then slowly he returned, head down, hands in pockets and deep in thought. K.A watched him, saying nothing as she helped herself to another shrimp. His head was shaking in bemusement and his hands clenching and opening. "What's the connection between a former England cricketer and a golfer living in Jupiter?" He was thinking aloud, his brain working overtime to reprogramme everything.

"The US captain is a guy called Jake Myerson."

Ratso had heard the name on TV but it meant nothing. "Tell me more."

"In the 1990s until ten years ago, Myerson burned up courses everywhere. Won a fortune. Typically, Ryder Cup captains are former top players – still involved enough to understand the modern game but maybe not up to making the team. I'd guess he's forty-seven."

"And far too wealthy to be bought by fixers. That leaves the European captain?"

"Marcello Baresi. He's Italian. He's won several majors. Similar age. Probably stinking rich too."

Ratso stopped circling and exhaled heavily. "Makes no sense.

Two rich captains. Unbelievable." The barman came across and they accepted his suggestion of same again. "But the score tells it as it is."

"What about blackmail?" K.A prompted.

Ratso's nod was receptive. "I need in-depth on both captains. So rich and yet ..." His sentence trailed away into silence as words failed him.

"You're right!" K.A waved her glass of Margarita. "How in hell would your Lee Westdale get to fix Ryder Cup captains?" Now it was K.A who eased herself from her chair to stretch like a cat. She stood by the TV where both captains were on screen. She beckoned him over. "There you go. Baresi on the left."

There was no sound from the TV as Ratso stared at the two men, both tall, bronzed and self-assured. Baresi was just the shorter and tending to a paunch with wavy black hair swept back. Jake Myerson's face showed his age more, probably from sun damage. The lines were carved deep but did nothing to take away from a face that radiated warmth with pale blue eyes and flashing teeth his prominent features. His sandy hair was flecked with grey but there was no sign of touching-up with hair-dye. If they had been a couple of Iraq war heroes, rather than suspects in a major international fraud, it would have been less of a surprise.

"Mustn't judge by appearances," he said to K.A quietly as if reading her mind. K.A's thoughts though, seemed to have moved on as she was stroking the back of his neck – the lightest of touches and utterly sensual.

She leaned even closer to whisper into his ear, her fragrance compelling. "Tell me, kind sir. For all this help, what's the reward for a hot-blooded Southern gal?" She exaggerated her drawl in every slow-spoken word.

"I'll need to fess-up to Tolvey. I should phone him at once."

There was just a moment of hesitation as she rested her sun-tanned hand against his cheek . "But ... he can wait. So you mean, er, before or after a late lunch?"

"*Both* sounds pretty darned good." She hooked arms. "Let's drink up and move."

−49−

London

When she reached the hotel's Front Desk, Nancy Petrie flashed her smartphone at the receptionist. "Ever seen this man in here?" The young man thought for moment and said no, explaining that he was a new hiring. He beckoned a bellman. "Seen him?"

Without hesitation, he said yes. "Lee Westdale? I reckon I was maybe the last guy to see him alive. He'd only just left when the bomb went off. He wasn't here a lot but was like a sort of regular."

"Stay overnight did he?"

The bellman shook his head. "Mornings usually. He'd arrive alone and leave alone. No luggage. Always gave me a smile. Usually here for an hour, maybe three. I guess he had meetings. Not my business what happens upstairs," he concluded with a wink.

"Thanks." Nancy asked for the Duty Manager who joined her and Jock. With Jock saying nothing, Nancy explained what she wanted. The smart looking woman thought for a moment and bit her lip as she gathered her thoughts. "Lee Westdale? I saw him once, no twice."

"Meeting someone? A woman friend perhaps?"

"That I can't say. He was even more handsome in the flesh than on TV. I remember asking the front-desk if he stayed with us and was told he used a junior suite, not the upstairs lounge."

Nancy drew her chair closer. "So here's how you can help." Twenty minutes later, they were back outside leaving the calm surroundings for the noise and pungent dust that swirled and settled everywhere. Nancy started a Q & A cross-check like pilot and co-pilot before take-off. At first, Jock, five biscuits more replete, was more interested in griping about having to walk but he warmed to it, plodding along, feet sloshing through the puddles.

Nancy made the suggestions and Jock responded. "Mithi's death?"

"Nothing from the Indian police."

"The names in the Parabolic Class Action?"

"There's 14,000 victims. Danny Willison is still working through them."

"Right person for that?"

Jock Strang hesitated long enough for Nancy Petrie to know what the Scot thought. "Aye, maybe I'll take a wee look. Danny's not the sharpest. Says it's tedious. But he's done his share of the old credit cards and bank statements."

Nancy's brow furrowed and she hesitated before asking. "Silly question Jock. Would Danny recognise names of top sportsmen even if they jumped off the page shouting *Howzat* or saying *they were feeling sick as parrots*?"

"You're right. I'll get DC Booth onto it too." He looked at her and they both stopped. "Silly? Not you. Silly was my dreams about you and me. Plain bloody daft. There's no fool like an old fool."

Nancy reached out and clutched his arm. "I'm sorry. We're both bruised right now. Let's bury ourselves in the job."

Jock looked puzzled, wondering why Nancy was bruised. He pointed to Burger King. "I feel a Double Whopper and fries coming on." Yet even as he spoke, he was wondering if maybe Nancy was softening towards him.

Bruised was she?

"I'll treat you." He lengthened his stride towards Burger King.

-50-

Caribbean

As darkness fell and following a deeply satisfying blast of the ship's horn, the 91,000 tons of spanking white vessel slipped her moorings. K.A had dressed in her best slinky black evening-wear with a delicate silver necklace and matching bracelet. Even Ratso was wearing a shirt, linen jacket and tie, a rarity which he tolerated to comply with on-board rules. Though they had Pina Coladas and nibbles in front of them, each was tapping furiously into their devices.

"Sealed with a kiss, Todd, remember? No talk about fixing or work!"

"Fat chance now!"

"Sign of the times," K.A muttered. "You and me hunkered down with these damned things. No conversation."

"We've had our moments," he responded with a raised eyebrow and cheeky grin. "But you're right. When we're done now, we switch these damned things off. Enjoy dinner, a show, maybe hit the dance-floor. After a few drinks, I do a mean Moonwalk."

"That's not what that guy with the weak bladder told me last February." K.A laughed. "I think he used the words *dances like a demented baboon.*"

"Tosh? He's not exactly nimble himself. Anyway, he would never have said *demented.* Too long a word for him."

She flicked her free-flowing hair as she cocked her head in thought. "And he warned me to watch out for waving arms, trampled toes and spilled drinks."

Ratso raised his hands in mock horror. "Take no notice. Just wait for my Lambada."

"I can wait forever, no problem," she kissed in response, then helping herself to a tortilla chip, "I prefer the smoochy kinda stuff."

"Making love standing up? I'll drink to that." He raised his glass while stroking her knee. "You got a deal" He blew a kiss. "Back to reality. All that tapping away, what have you discovered?"

"You realise this is now official? Not me doing a favour for our limey friends. US citizens may be involved. I've informed my boss Bucky Buchanan. Here's what he got for us. Lee paid cash for his Florida flight. He sat next to a Japanese car salesman and a Puerto Rican oil executive. I'm waiting for more on Myerson. And you?"

"I got a bet on for tomorrow and for Sunday's tie. You'd better be right. I've a hundred quid riding on this. Six to one odds on the tie. Tasty!"

She nodded. "Could be a champagne moment. You got more?"

"Besides a message from Tolvey about me being up shit creek, yes – a company name." Now it was Ratso who rubbed his hands, looking decidedly cocky. "A corporation called Thoractic Inc booked a hotel-suite close to the bombing. Westdale used it that morning. This company had made five different bookings over the past eighteen months. I've got the dates."

"Westdale dating someone?"

Ratso looked out at the creamy foam rushing by. "There's not a hint of him cheating on Mandy – so far." He handed over his notes. "Can Bucky check out whether Jake Myerson was in England on these dates."

"Todd, it takes two to tango." She looked at him, her eyes throwing down the challenge. "And I'm not talking of your John Travolta stuff. And answering this question, you can't phone a friend."

He twirled the umbrella in his cocktail. A waiter walked by, balancing a tray of six full glasses, oblivious to the sway of the ship. "Duh!" Ratso hit the table with a satisfying thud. "This Jupiter place kept me thinking American. The Italian guy. We need to check on him."

"Marcello Baresi used to play the American Tour."

"I'll get someone working on that."

She raised a trimmed eyebrow. "This company? Who owns it?"

"Thoractic? Nancy Petrie says it's registered in Tortola, the British Virgin Islands. Nominee directors and shareholders. The Cavendish Hotel bills are cleared by the company, not by Westdale. Unless secretly, he is the company. Thoractic banks in Barnet, just north of London."

"Serendipity or what?" Her excited laugh was infectious and she leaned across to chink glasses. "Todd, Tortola is our next port."

After sipping his drink, he shook his head. "K.A, I hate to spoil the party but Thoractic is registered at Wickhams Quay. I've come across that address several times. We'll be wasting our time. It will be some lawyer's office with a thousand other faceless companies based there. We'll get nowhere. Thoractic will be opaque. Whoever set up this company will be hidden behind fiduciaries with anonymous trusts or more companies."

"Put like that then," she laughed, "we needn't feel guilty bunking off to some sandy cove or eating grilled mahi-mahi."

Ratso disappeared behind his tumbler of Pina Colada. "We'll find out another way." He stretched out an arm to fondle her wrist. "Under KYC standards, due diligence by UK banks *should* mean they know the source of funds."

"Should?" The slightly raised eyebrow did not show much shock.

"Some shyster bankers in the City launder money for a pastime."

"Snouts in the trough? Annual bonuses?"

"You got it. But hopefully we'll get a name behind Thoractic. Plus I like the Barnet bit. Whoever is behind the account might live in that suburban area. Makes the haystack smaller."

"Anything else? Our table's in ten minutes." As she spoke, she was looking intently at her phone and a huge smile transformed her face, her almond eyes saying *wow*.

Ratso waited for her to volunteer something but she signalled to him to continue. "Westdale's credit-cards and bank statements show nothing in Florida. He must have used all cash or he was bankrolled." His thoughts went back to Mandy's gobsmacked look when she had seen Lee's passport. *Was she a great actress, a cool customer or was her shock genuine* "Whatever he was doing was pretty damned secret."

"Well, maybe I have the answer. But … there's a condition."

Ratso's wicked smile of anticipation was a like dog drooling over a lump of meat.

"Don't tread on my toes!"

-51-

Dubai

P.T. had brought Vijay Chetri straight from the airport to the racetrack for the meeting. It was Saturday in Dubai and the early morning desert air was still decidedly chilly. Even so, the smell of dozens of camels drifted towards the grandstand beside the Al Ain Road. Almost immediately on arrival, they had been joined by a tall, muscular figure with a thatch of neatly parted black hair. He was probably just over fifty.

P.T. introduced him as Sandun from Sri Lanka but Vijay didn't buy that, convinced he was a Pakistani – the hair, the thick salt and pepper moustache and the dark brown, nearly black eyes being the main pointers. His English was good and he stood very upright but he never once smiled. Vijay placed him as ex-military and a man not to be crossed.

They dealt with their agenda in crisp exchanges, each knowing what the other wanted to hear. The words *hot money, USA* and *two-hundred million* featured as they stood, surrounded by the shouts and waves of excitable owners and trainers. Above that crescendo of noise were the sighs, groans and roars from the camels themselves. Then, as rapidly as the tall man had appeared beside them, he was gone. His parting stare was accompanied by a wagged finger of warning. P.T. watched him disappear down the steps. "That's good. Yesterday's fix at Wentworth clinched it. At 6 to 1, a tie on Sunday and you'll net 108 million dollars. Sandun, naturally, will make much, much more."

"He's good for the money?"

P.T.'s laugh was mocking at the stupid question. "Sandun's outfit sets the odds. In every corner of India and Pakistan, layer on layer of ever smaller bookies rely on him. He'll offload this today. Some here, some there, maybe even a little into the big UK bookies, the Far East guys. Not enough to raise suspicions anywhere. You'll see how the odds on Europe or the USA winning will change. Like he said, the hot money is now on the USA to hold this big lead, maybe even to increase it by Sunday night. He'll offer good odds on a US win – sucker the patriotic punters towards what looks like easy money."

Chetri looked doubtful. "So long as you're sure. We've bet the ranch on this."

P.T. gave him a withering look. "Relax." He put an arm around Chetri's shoulders. "This market works on trust. You let someone down?" He answered his rhetorical comment with a finger run across his throat. "My friend," P.T. continued, using words that Chetri felt were an exaggeration, "if the score after Day Two is as *you* predict, then you and me?"

"Twenty-five million."

"Shared 50-50 – just you and me. You had better be right." P.T.'s eyes hardened as he shook his head. "That bastard Mark Rayner screwing us on that cricket fix? When Sandun summoned me, I nearly didn't go. I thought he would er … well that I would never return. Sandun's eyes that night. They still haunt me." P.T. looked down and shook his head as he relived the moment. "Hatred. Menace. I knew *someone* had to pay for it. He wanted me, you, Lee and Mark Rayner all dead," he paused for emphasis. "So I told him about the Ryder Cup. You're lucky! He bought it. Last chance saloon, he said." For a moment he was lost in Sandun's warning. "Thank me for you not being found in a ditch with your throat cut.

But," he patted Chetri's arm. "If there's no tie, Sandun will kill this time. Not just you. Everybody involved. We'll all be executed like stray dogs." The words were accompanied by P.T.'s unflinching stare which made Chetri's bowels struggle against free-fall.

Sandun's mention of Nitin Mithi had been sufficient warning without the wagged finger. The Indian swallowed hard as he tried to forget the photos of Mithi's corpse, sprawled across a hotel room floor. P.T.'s squat and almost square shaped figure oozed menace enough. Chetri was left with no illusions. Failure on Sunday meant he would be dead in some gutter. He fought to clear the dryness from his throat. "Just you and me. Sharing 50-50 for Day Two. That's agreed," Chetri confirmed as he stepped from foot to foot, tired from the overnight flight. "We'll deliver, P.T." Chetri concluded with more confidence than he felt as he sipped a sweet milky coffee.

His nagging worry was Marcello Baresi and his Naples background. Sure, the guy had delivered on Day One but with Russian and Italian mafia muscling in on tennis, why not the Ryder Cup? Who better to threaten than Baresi? What if Baresi had received an offer he could not refuse?

No tie on the final day?

It was too late to worry about that now.

But he *was* worried.

Shit-scared actually.

"We missed the first race. Shall we watch the next one before we go to my penthouse? We can discuss the remaining details." P.T. was now leaning against a concrete wall and his voice brought the Indian back to his surroundings. They were looking at the camels chewing the cud, their ungainly jaws chomping from side to side. He pointed to the track. "We used to have kids as jockeys. Come." P.T. strutted closer to the action in his pigeon-toed fashion. "See. That little red lump wearing a white cap? That's a robot jockey."

"You're kidding me."

"No shit," responded P.T., a comment which seemed singularly inappropriate with the stench that mixed with the sandy dust.

"See all those 4x4s? The trainers ride in them, controlling the robots – getting them to whip the camels or to shout just like real jockeys."

Chetri's jetlag and ulcer-like pains from his stomach were not being helped by the noise and stink of steaming urine. "Look, P.T. It's damned noisy here. You're right – we need to talk hawala before I leave. Perhaps we move on?"

The two men turned towards the car park. "As you wish, Vijay." P.T.'s eyes narrowed. "Moving so many dollars to pay the captains and, er, that New Yorker."

"Enzo Pagano," Chetri prompted.

"Yes. Pagano. Maybe you should avoid hawala? Perhaps use that guy from the Indian Embassy? His diplomatic immunity worked well."

Chetri panted to keep up with the short and busy striding figure as they headed for the limo. "That shit got too greedy." He fell silent as they left behind the noise and smell. "I may not move everything. I could invest some here. The rest, we'll use our hawaladars." Then he was again silent, his ears ringing with the sound of Pagano's rasping voice invading his thoughts. HOSS had delivered five losers the previous day. The American's foul-mouthed rant ordering him to get it sorted had only been the first part of the call. "Fuck no," Pagano had shouted so most of New York's 5th Avenue could hear. "We pay nix to that Alex Anderson fucker and nix to Lee Westdale's woman."

"But Lee's cut was agreed." Chetri's tone had been simpering under the onslaught.

"The guy's six feet under. Maggots feasting on him. The bitch knew nothing. Did nothing. So what she never knew about, then sure as hell, she ain't gonna miss."

"Let's pay her, Enzo. For fairness? For a quiet life?"

"Fuck no, you goddammed wuss." Pagano had cut off the call leaving Chetri again regretting involvement with the pig-ignorant New Yorker. It was a relief when his thoughts were interrupted by reaching the long black Mercedes. P.T.'s chauffeur opened the rear door and his host suggested they shared a Talisker on ice during the journey back to the airport.

His hands shaking, Chetri accepted the tumbler with pleasure.

-52-

Tortola, British Virgin Islands

"So, Tosh," enquired Ratso into his phone, "Today's the last day. The USA going to win?" Even as he spoke, he had one eye on the giant screen showing the golf from Wentworth. Incongruously, it filled one wall of Ma Mabel's Sports Bar. On other walls hung an array of stuffed marlins, jaws of giant fish – all rows of jagged teeth and several photos of fishermen holding up barracudas and reef sharks.

"You tell me, guv. The rain's belting down. Me and Nancy, we're soaked even under a bleedin' big brolly."

It was just on 12-30pm and the Caribbean sun was beating down on the tumbledown wooden shack from a cloudless sky. The heat shimmered from its corrugated roof. Down the years, the pink walls had been faded by the heat, wind and tropical rain. Inside though, the temperature was cooled by a noisy air-conditioning unit. "Beautiful day here. Blue skies and birds singing. The smell of conch fritters. *And* I've a great view of Wentworth … but I can't see you." He winked at K.A before adding "and that's good. It means Patsy can't see you two huddled up together either." Ratso's comment prompted a guffaw from Nancy.

"I can't see you neither," Tosh retorted. "Just as well, I expect," he added pushing his luck. "How is Kirsty-Ann?" Ratso gave the bird at the phone and said nothing, leaving it to Tosh to continue. "We're following the last pair. They've just finished the sixteenth.

The way Zack Gomez is playing, he's going to win his match for the US. He's one-up with two holes to play."

"So if he wins, then the USA takes home the Ryder Cup 14.5 to 13.5?"

"Correct."

Ratso thought about playing the smartarse and telling him that Gomez had been picked by Jake Myerson as a Wild Card. That he was probably being paid to blow it, leaving the teams tied. But he said nothing. After all, he *knew* nothing "In those playing conditions, anything could happen."

"It's been blowing half a gale, so the players have found all sorts of trouble. Out of bounds, in the trees, in the water. You name it, they found it."

Nancy chimed in. "The commentators reckon the Europeans are better suited to driving wind and rain, especially Bertie Quayle from the Isle of Man." She wiped a huge drip from her cheek. "Boss, I'm not surprised they've pulled right back in these conditions."

"Lee called it right again, yesterday. 10-6 to the Americans."

Nancy agreed. "Day Two, the Europeans still looked washed up, dead and buried but on TV, they said the Italian fella, Baresi gave a rousing team talk overnight."

"Seems to have worked." Ratso signalled to K.A querying whether she had anything to add but she shook her head. "Let me know if you spot anything strange."

"You mean besides Tosh in his tweed plus-fours and yellow socks, boss?"

"Spare me the details, Nancy. Too early in the day for that image. Text me any news." After ending the call, he ordered more Rum Punch as they settled in to watch the last holes.

K.A pointed to a spectator's soaked cap that was blowing across the fairway. "It's a crapshoot in those conditions. Easy to disguise fixing."

"Easy for a fix to go wrong too." Unusually, Ratso was seeing the tumbler half-empty. "Where's our food? The smells from the kitchen are making my stomach rumble."

"You're sounding like big Jock Strang," she laughed. "This is the Caribbean. Nothing happens quickly. Relax. Enjoy the views. Remember, we're here on vacation. Or we were." She stretched out her long bronzed legs, wiggling her manicured toes out of her flip-flops.

"Vacation?" Ratso's head rocked back in a mocking laugh. "We've been working our butts off ever since you cracked Lee's note." He looked back at the endless colourful umbrellas lining the fairway. "You're right though. Let's enjoy the moment. I've six-hundred good reasons to watch the golf. That's a first I can tell you."

K.A looked at a caddy drying a club. "Imagine what the fixers are going through. They're in it for millions."

"Sod their multi-millions. Think of my hundred quid!" Ratso grinned as he edged along the torn bench seat and flung an arm around K.A's neck and pulled her closer. "Wouldn't it be great if this could last forever. You, me, hot sand, cold drinks and swaying palm trees."

She kissed his cheek. "Sounds good but, heck, I miss Leon. I guess I feel kinda guilty at leaving him. Y'know he's a real little person now. Every day is more rewarding." She leaned her head into the nape of Ratso's neck. "But you and me? Sure, it's pretty darned good."

Ratso was about to reply that it was a damned sight better than that when the commentator's excited voice attracted their attention. They saw a close-up of Zack Gomez standing on the 17th tee. He had a worried look on his face and was scratching his head as he spoke to his caddy. His tee-shot had been long but the cross-wind had gusted it way out to the left, over the trees and out of bounds. "Good on you Zack. Keep 'em coming like that!"

K.A's small nose wrinkled. "I'm not sure he intended that but no matter. After O'Hagan has played, Zack will tee-off again, probably aiming further right."

"But he adds a penalty stroke? Correct?"

"Yup and the Irishman should have learned from Zack's mistake. Billy O'Hagan need only play safe to win this hole and be all-square."

Their spicy blackened fish arrived with piping hot fries just as O'Hagan drove from the tee. Adjusting for the wind and rain, his shot was aimed well right and came to a stop in a perfect position for his second long wood to the green.

"The Americans are in trouble now." K.A added a dash of Tabasco to her fish much to Ratso's amazement. She saw his look and grinned. "It can never be too hot for me."

"And you," he grinned, "can never be too hot for me." Even as he spoke, he realised how K.A changed him. Since his mother had walked out over thirty years before, for too long, smiles, laughs and chuckles had never come easily. Being with Kirsty-Ann seemed to trigger something long forgotten – and he liked it, liked it a lot. She rewarded him with one of her open-mouthed smiles that seemed almost to split her tanned face in two.

"Golf, Todd. Keep your mind on the golf."

Ratso put down his fork to watch Gomez strike the ball with an effortless swing. Yet again, with the swirling wind, the ball veered left, bouncing off the fairway. "Jeez!" She chewed her lip for a second. "He's almost blocked by that huge tree. Now let's see how the Irish guy manages."

Moments later, O'Hagan was on the green in two, barely three feet from the pin. "If it wasn't the Ryder Cup, he could sink that blindfolded." Echoing her opinion, one of the commentators almost parroted her words. The cameras turned to Gomez as he steadied himself for his next shot. It soared high right but the wind drifted it back to land twenty feet from the hole.

"Could he sink that?"

"Sure but even world-class players don't sink twenty-footers every time."

Food ignored for a moment, they watched as Gomez studied the green, the grass sodden and saturated. His putt was good, the ball leaving a halo of water as it sped across the wet surface. But it was not good enough. It stopped just short of the hole and O'Hagan nodded that he need not putt out. After a moment's hesitation, Gomez conceded the hole.

Ratso could barely contain the excitement in his voice as they exchanged excited high-fives. "All-square in the Ryder Cup and one hole to play."

"The 18th is a par 5. If both play safe and get down in five, we have a tie. But the commentators reckon sinking a four is doable." K.A spoke with conviction. "So, either player could go for glory and win."

"Or screw up by living dangerously?" Ratso looked at K.A to see if he had got it right and she nodded yes. "This food, Kirsty! My mouth's on fire. Another rum punch? We'll need them to celebrate anyway."

"Don't count those chickens, Funny old game, golf."

Ratso went to the bar and ordered, his steps slow, his thoughts locked on the battle in Wentworth. K.A was right – *fat ladies singing* came to mind. In fact, when Ma Mabel's husband shuffled over with the drinks, Ratso sank a good half of his almost instantly, his feet now restless and his heart starting to race. When he had reported in after Days One and Two, Tolvey had been purring. Now this would be the clincher.

"Todd, the way I see it, a tie opens up the money trail. The captains collecting their pay-offs, that's when you strike."

"Yuh! We'll need to work on the rest of Lee's note. Work out what it all means."

"If it is a tie."

The warning words prompted Ratso to suck hard on his straw. He drained the last of the fiery alcohol before the ice melted. He headed to the bar to get in another round.

–53–

Wentworth, Surrey

R ed and white umbrella angled in front of them to protect their faces from the driving rain, Tosh and Nancy hurried
to the best viewing spot available. The huge crowd on the lines
of bench seats circling the 18th green had the prime position for
the final agonising putts. However, for those like Tosh and Nancy,
moving from hole to hole, there was a rush to reach the best available positions. Tosh pointed into the distance. "There's a notorious
stream guarding the green. You fall short, you're in the water. Not
funny. You go long, you're in the bunkers at the back of the green.
Not funny."

"You just land it by the pin. Simple, eh?" Nancy was peering way down the fairway where the flag was barely visible under the black scudding clouds. They were standing on the left side
of the dog-leg just beyond where the two drives should land. She
looked back to the tee where O'Hagan was getting ready to drive.
Moments later, his shot landed about forty metres behind them.

Tosh shook his head. "He's left himself one helluva shot to
reach the green. My take – he'll play short of the stream and chip
over. Safety first. Better than being remembered as the guy that
lost the Ryder Cup." They turned to watch Zack Gomez's shot and
heard the distant thwack as he struck the ball. Eyes straining, they
stared into the storm-clouds to follow the trajectory. Without even
seeing where the ball finished, Tosh knew from the groans and

shouts. "Bunkered," he pointed at the ball lying in the sand. "No way will he make the green. Not safely anyway. He'll have to lay up short."

Nancy started pushing her way between the soaked spectators to be closer to the stream. Tosh was just behind, sloshing over the squelchy ground to see where the approach shots landed. All around them was noise – the deep rumble of jets from Heathrow overhead and the whoops and cries of the spectators, all gripped by the prospect of a tight finish.

"Looking good for that tie then, Tosh."

-54-

Tortola – British Virgin Islands

R atso realised that even with the players now approaching their second shots, nobody else in Ma Mabel's gave a fig for what was on the big screen. The few locals who were drinking beer from cans were cackling and hi-fiving as they half-watched American football on a screen above the bar.

"No sign of Tosh or Nancy." K.A was looking at the crowd-shots as the players headed for their balls.

"Hard to tell with that sea of umbrellas. Anyway, there's a high chance that Tosh will be taking a leak and missing the action." Ratso rolled his eyes at memories of all the occasions when Tosh's bladder had been priority business. Their empty plates had now been cleared and Mabel had given them complimentary shots of rum-based Guavaberry liqueur. They sniffed and tasted and their faces showed they would not be standing in line for seconds of the bitter-sweet flavour. Meantime, O'Hagan was talking to his caddy and appeared unsure about choice of club. He started to pull out an iron but after sensing the gusting wind, opted for a wood.

"He's got a tricky shot! Should his third be an eighty yard chip or thirty? Tough call in that driving rain."

"You've lost me. Surely you get as close as you can without hitting the water?"

"Some of these top players find a longer chip easier as the ball stops better. But a high chip in that wind? Risky." K.A swivelled her slender hand emphasising the fine balance. Except for the wind whistling around the microphones, everything fell silent as the crowd watched the Irishman address the ball. Then with a satisfying sound, O'Hagan struck it cleanly. All eyes looked skywards to watch its flight as it soared majestically towards the stream and the green beyond. As the ball started to lose speed and fall, it faded to the right of the fairway. Had it kept straight, it would have been a perfect shot to lie up and chip over the water.

"Heh, he's in trouble." Even as she spoke, K.A could see that with the ball veering to the right, the stream was that much closer. The ball landed about twenty-five yards short of the hazard. Even with the sodden conditions, it took a bounce and then another before trickling over the bank and splashing into the water. "That costs him a stroke," she volunteered but Ratso had guessed that anyway. A huge groan went up from the European fans but from the Americans there was cheering and laughter and ironic shouts of "He's the man!"

"Credit to Marcello Baresi. The order he put out his players, he's pulled Europe right back into this. He's proved himself a mind-reader in the cat-and-mouse game between the captains." The cultured and somewhat hushed voice of Sean Jamieson, the English TV commentator seemed curiously disembodied in the Caribbean surroundings.

"Sure," responded Bubba Bosner, the co-presenter, a veteran American golfer "but the US team still have the Ryder Cup in their sights.

"Agreed! Zack Gomez just needs to play safe."

"But who wants to be in Zack's shoes now? This is when the yips kick in. Your heart pounds, your nerves are jangling. Your brain gets addled. You kinda know the whole country will never forget if you get it wrong."

"Golf fans have long memories. You're right." Jamieson laughed "and you know better than most after what happened to you at The Masters on the 18th."

"Hey! Don't go there! I don't need that memory." Though Bosner laughed, he was barely joking. "It's still painful twenty years on." Bosner fell silent, watching Gomez select his club. Then, with almost unseemly haste, the American thrashed the ball from the sand, racing it towards the water hazard that protected the green. "He's fine; he's safe," Jamieson sounded relieved. "But his next shot across the stream? Not easy from that distance. Not in these conditions. Snorkels would be pretty darned useful and the wind's swirling round like a tumble-drier. Bubba, English summers, don't you just love them." He paused for effect. "No. Don't answer that!"

Ratso squeezed Kirsty-Ann's thigh and was rewarded with a sly smile that contained more than a hint of invitation, so Ratso leaned across and kissed her on the mouth. "So if Gomez gets this on the green next shot...." Ratso left the thought unfinished as Gomez played his approach shot. It landed on the green but stopped quicker than the American wanted. As Gomez chewed at his narrow moustache, the grimace on his face showed he still had much to do. O'Hagan then chipped neatly across the stream and was on the green in four, still one shot more than Gomez.

K.A took a small sip of iced water, wiping the condensation from the side of the glass. "The Irishman should get down in two but so should Gomez even though he's further from the pin."

"Meaning Gomez somehow has to screw up and three-putt to fix a tie."

"Without becoming a laughing-stock or making it look like a fix." Ratso found his hand was sweating even in the air-conditioning and he let go of K.A's wrist. In the stand behind the green,

Enzo Pagano and Chetri had more than damp palms as the rain dripped from their waterproof tops and kept settling on Pagano's tinted spectacles. Some two-hundred miles west at Trevose Golf Club, Alex Anderson was joining in the joshing with the mainly European supporters as the tension mounted. Around the globe, countless millions were gripped by the sight of Gomez and then O'Hagan facing putts they were unlikely to sink in one.

Neither did.

O'Hagan was left a shade further from the hole but he sank an eight-footer, the ball kissing the lip of the hole before toppling in.

"Pressure, pressure," murmured Jamieson. "Most days, Zack could sink his five footer in his sleep."

Bosner's laugh did not come out naturally. "Trouble is today is not most days. Right now is not most days. Worse still, he's not asleep. The guy's in a waking nightmare. He has this putt to win the Ryder Cup for the US team."

"And if he misses, this moment will haunt him for ever." Gomez crouched down to read the green, his famous swan-neck putter gripped in both hands. He walked to the other side of the hole and again crouched down. "That five feet seems like five miles to him now," continued Bosner. "He'll be seeing imaginary bumps, slopes like mountain-sides and obsessed with the speed of the wet green." Slowly, like a condemned man going to the gallows, Gomez' tall figure returned to his ball. "Sink this and every American will be dancing by their seats. Miss it and the US will have to settle for a tie."

"It's been a remarkable European come-back." Jamieson lowered his voice even further as if unwilling to say the words out loud. "And ... perish the thought – if the yips really take over, Gomez might not even make the tie. Remember poor old Ernie Els."

"I pray for him that he doesn't lose us the Ryder Cup." Bosner was about to add something but he stopped as Gomez positioned himself and gently eased back his putter for a smooth push of the ball.

Jamieson's cultured voice whispered into the microphone. "So here it is. Three days of great golf and if Zack Gomez sinks this, America wins the Ryder Cup."

-55-

Fort Lauderdale, Florida

Bucky Buchanan's smile was almost as big as his giant mitt which gripped Ratso's hand in greeting. "Good to see you again, son. Welcome back! You're becoming quite a regular in these parts." He grinned across at Kirsty-Ann. "Not just social either. But I can't tell you a whole bunch more since my call." On the table in front of them was the morning newspaper with photos of Myerson and Baresi, the two Ryder Cup captains, giving each other a hug. Above the photos was the headline: "Golf the winner as US and Europe tie in dramatic finish!"

As soon as Gomez had halved the hole, Ratso had known he was in the wrong place even without Tolvey's cryptic text demanding him back by Tuesday morning. Instead of two more blissful days flopping about on the ship, he and K.A had grabbed an overnight flight from Beef Airport to Florida via San Juan.

Still recovering from Buchanan's fierce grip, Ratso looked enquiringly. "Just run by me whatever you've got, Chief." They were seated in the diner close by the HQ of the Fort Lauderdale Police Department where Buchanan always breakfasted. The air was cool but the room was noisy and the smell of hot waffles drifted across the simple tables. Today Bucky had ordered three waffles, scrambled eggs, bacon, grits, wheat toast, jelly, maple syrup and fruit. Somehow, his physique seemed able to carry the calorie intake, no problem.

"Your guy Lee Westdale got friendly with the US team captain Jake Myerson years back."

"My sergeant has just sent me the same info. They were paired together in a charity golfing event at St Andrews. Back then Lee was the England cricket captain, riding high."

The Chief's face lit up as the food arrived, K.A having granola and Ratso facing a bowl of sub-tropical fruit, his self-imposed penance for over-indulging on the cruise. "Seems they hit it off pretty good and became buddies. Right?"

Ratso agreed. "But the million dollar question?"

Buchanan shook his head. "We don't know. Not yet. But it sure wasn't a million dollar question!" He leaned in. "Myerson lost forty mill." He enjoyed the shock on his listeners' faces. "What's your take now then?"

"Christ! Forty million!" Ratso looked at K.A who smiled encouragement. "Flip a coin but ..."

"Chief," K.A chimed in. "I'd bet it was Jake Myerson got Lee into Parabolic."

Bucky paused to crunch on a piece of streaky bacon. "Didn't a few other Brits invest?"

"So Todd says," she continued "but with over forty million in this bad boy, I'd say he really believed in it and enthused his Brit pal about the riches to be made."

"Greedy Lee." Ratso prodded a chunk of pineapple. "It figures. Nothing we know suggests his bedtime reading was the financial pages. Someone got him involved. Myerson sounds interesting."

The Chief put down his fork and stopped chewing for a moment. "So Parabolic goes belly-up. Both are big losers. The next link?"

"Let me run this by you, Bucky." Ratso had finished his fruit. "Lee flies to NYC for the big hoo-ha meeting with the attorneys. By then he's already been into fixing cricket for some years."

"You know that?" Bucky pounced on the assumption, his tone sharp.

Ratso lowered his eyes and thought for a moment. "No. But somehow he had four million to invest."

"I'll let that pass then. Go on."

"In NYC, Myerson and Lee chat. Because of Myerson's bum tip, Lee's lifestyle had been destroyed. He tells Myerson – *hey pal, right mess you got me into but I've an idea, a win-win for us both. Get you rich again.*" Ratso looked across at Bucky's eyes, now thoughtful in the fleshy face. "Okay so far?"

"Assume yes for now." Bucky spread orange jelly, bacon and maple syrup across his waffle. "Myerson had lost a fortune too. Not bankrupt but the guy had some mighty big problems after kissing goodbye to forty mill."

K.A chimed in. "Didn't Myerson have to sell up his home in Jupiter?"

"Correct. He hunkered down in a rental on the PGA National at Palm Beach Gardens."

"So," continued Ratso liking that detail, "in NYC, Lee suggests they fix the Ryder Cup. Myerson had just been appointed captain. He could select the Wild Cards. Our Brit had the contacts to make a fix happen. Who and how are unknowns. He flies to Florida to talk it through. Mandy, that's his wife, never knew."

Buchanan had demolished every last morsel and pushed his plate aside. "You mean placing the bets."

"Agreed. No way could Lee fund this. There's serious people behind this, gambling huge sums. Knowing of the fix, they would clear multi-millions."

Buchanan pulled out a cigarette pack and looked at it wistfully. "So your boy flies down here and you *guess* he stayed with Myerson."

"And while here, they fixed Baresi."

The Chief opened up a slim folder and showed Ratso photos of two adobe style ranch properties. "Marcello Baresi and Jake Myerson were neighbours in Jupiter – great buddies from their playing days. That's until Myerson was a forced seller." Once again, he saw that Ratso was impressed.

K.A's pony-tail swayed as she nodded her head in agreement. "Chief, like I said to Todd, it takes two to tango. One team can't fix a tie. Baresi had to be in on it – doing his pal Jake a favour – and making big bucks too."

Buchanan tapped the cigarette pack, his need for a smoke kicking in. Then he put it down. "Old habits die hard," he grinned. "You reckon the players bet on the result?"

Ratso laughed. "Unlikely but possible."

"Don't forget the note." K.A's fingers flew over the keys on her Apple as she searched for her copy of Lee's document. "See? The underlined words – No Personal."

Bucky picked up and paid the check. "Yeah. Makes sense, stopping all insiders from betting." He grabbed his rimless spectacles and then peered over them. "But don't you never underestimate temptation, opportunity and greed."

Ratso tried not to grin at the thought of his winnings waiting for him in London. "We've got surveillance teams watching Baresi and Myerson. According to the note, I reckon they had thirty percent upfront, so they're due the rest. We mustn't scare them off."

Bucky stretched out his long legs and tapped his pointed snakeskin boot on the floor. "Jupiter is north of FLPD territory. If your evidence improves, I'd reckon to bring in the Feds. Nailing two big name golfers – that could make some ambitious guy's reputation."

"And," chipped in K.A thinking back to her dead husband's approach, "I'd bet the Feds could throw in corruption, money-laundering, RICO, tax evasion. I bet those guys never declared their upfronts."

Bucky laughed, head rocking back. "But laundering such big bucks?" He shook his head. "Where in the world would they hide this? And how much might it be?"

Ratso had no answer to that and his slight shake of the head was response enough. "Today, the two captains are doing media calls. If the pick-up is in London, they need the media frenzy to die down. But it could be anywhere. Bishopsgate maybe. It's time to revisit Lee's note."

"Son, this pay-off has to be under the radar. They need a *no-questions-asked* kinda banker, art-dealer or realtor to get it cleaned up."

"Being Italian, Baresi, might know how to get cash into Switzerland."

Buchanan picked up his cigarette pack and rose to leave. He nodded to the ciggies. "Can't resist any longer." He stood up, suggesting they kick around some ideas. Then, with a wave, Bucky was gone, a few giant strides taking him to the door.

"Not now because you don't want alarm-bells ringing yet," K.A suggested "Bucky can fix some snooping around Jupiter and Palm Beach Gardens. Check out whether Lee ever visited. Maybe a chauffeur or cleaner might identify him."

"Right. For now, nothing must alert the captains. Nothing." Ratso made a chopping motion with his right hand before nodding at the newspaper. "The media never spotted the fix."

"Gomez sure looked like he wanted to sink that putt."

"Missing by two inches. Was that cool or what!" He motioned to the door. "I must phone Craig Carter at Lord's."

K.A looked puzzled, cheeks narrowing as she pursed her lips. "But he's your cricket guy?"

"Craig sits on the Sports Betting Integrity Forum. It's supported by the PGA and the European Tour but the Forum covers most sports. The big bookies are involved, so Craig can dig deeper on betting patterns."

"Hopeful about that?"

Ratso pushed back his chair and yawned, the uncomfortable night flight catching up with him. "Not unless the Wild Cards or captains got greedy. Lee's contacts would have tapped into the illegal market." He followed her languid swaying walk into the sunny skies and balmy air. The smell of traffic hung over the busy road. "Your plans? Back to your desk?"

K.A stopped in mid-step. "Heh! I'm still on vacation, remember? Today, we should be cruising towards Puerto Rico. And y'know … having fun, cosying up." She pouted to exaggerate her feelings. "My Mom and Leon won't be back from Disney till late. They weren't expecting me home today so…" She tilted her head and arched an eyebrow. "If you have time, kind sir."

Ratso grinned. "Sure. I can make a little time before heading for Miami."

-56-

London

Shortly after Zack Gomez had sunk his third putt for a tie, an exhilarated Alex Anderson raced back to London from Trevose Golf Club. He was glad he had dumped his first instinct to screw Pagano and Chetri by whistleblowing the fix after their bets had been placed. Predicting the precise scores for each day's play to the PGA would have got their attention.

And got a few arrests too.

But Plan B was better than Plan A.

It was his mind that was racing more than the rented Porsche Turbo on the long journey eastwards. The Sunday evening traffic started to back-up even before Bristol and the journey seemed never ending. During the walking-pace progress near Maidenhead, he made a succession of calls and as he left the M3 to enter the sprawl of London's hinterland, he had ticked off nearly every box – Walt Harvey was in London waiting like a coiled spring and his private detectives had just updated him about Pagano and Chetri. Finally, the message from Youssef Toufiq about HOSS had made him laugh out loud before he parked up in the leafy courtyard of The Trumpeters.

It was way after midnight as he sank a Spitfire beer and munched on turkey and stuffing sandwiches. From a late-night TV channel, the solid beat of *Jive Talking* from an old Bee Gees concert drifted across his suite as he eyed a chunk of strong smelling Camembert to follow.

He was still riding on a high as he planned the next moves. Pagano was nothing if not predictable. The agents confirmed he was staying in his preferred London hotel – the opulent surroundings of Claridge's in Mayfair while Vijay Chetri was at home with his family.

Would Chetri have changed the usual channels for pay-off?

Why would he?

Okay, just about maybe yes if that shit at the Indian Embassy took a smaller cut.

Or if Vijay thought I could break into those channels.

Nah! Only if he thought I *could and would* crack his system.

And he doesn't know I could.

Thinks it's impossible.

The thought made his fingers and toes wiggle in satisfaction.

Using the usual channels, nothing would hit London from Dubai before Tuesday. Would it be two-hundred million? Or just Pagano's share? Or only the giant slug due to the captains and their lackeys?

One thing was certain.

There would be nothing for Mandy Westdale.

That thought made him smile for a long moment as he poured another Spitfire.

Bishopsgate?

Tick! His guys would be watching.

Then, using the Lee Westdale route, the two captains would be paid off.

Would Chetri and Pagano keep their profits in Dubai?

Or send the money direct to Monaco? There was no way of knowing.

But there was a way to find out.

-57-

London

"**F**uck you! This is your fault. My hard-drive is wiped," shouted Pagano across the suite at Claridge's. "Those sonovabitches who built HOSS, the goddammed bastards have added a virus." He twisted to pull his legs up onto the sofa.

"Sounds unlikely," responded Vijay Chetri, trying to sound the epitome of cool while wiping his palms on his trousers. Until now, he had been leaning back on a comfy chair, hands clasped behind his head and his voice quiet. Despite his own doubts, he was determined to sound relaxed. "I paid them well." He did not mention the constant bickering about fees for data input. "HOSS is sending crap data but my system's just fine. Your virus probably came from downloading stuff from some kiddie-porn site."

Chetri knew mentioning this would stop Pagano's tirade. "Some of that stuff you showed me in Miami. You could get jailed for looking at it." Chetri rose and poured peppermint tea for himself. "Enzo – HOSS had served us well. It's gone, scrambled, whatever. So we move on. You're like a kid yelling over a lost toy. Forget it! We have just pulled off our biggest fix ever. Let's enjoy the moment."

Pagano's snort showed what he thought of that. "HOSS was biblical – give us this day our daily bread. It did. HOSS fed us." His tone was calmer now until another thought crossed his mind. "Hey! What about Anderson? Reckon he screwed up HOSS?"

Chetri took a long time to reply. The thought had crossed his mind several times. "He's probably moved on. Remember that morning at the Beverly Hills? Such a pussycat." He turned slowly to Pagano who was rotating his hairy bare feet beneath the bottom of his slacks. "If he *has* somehow fixed HOSS, then it's your fault. You cut him out. You refused him any deal. I wanted to share."

"The fucker gets what he deserved," Pagano rasped. "And that's nix!" He wiped some spit from his chin.

"It's not too late to cut him in."

Pagano adjusted the cushion behind his head. "No. NO!" he shouted. "I guess you're right. He'll have moved on."

Chetri was keen to encourage that thought. "He'll be swinging on his hammock in Boca Raton, day-dreaming about the millions we made for him these many months. Forget Alex Anderson."

Slightly breathless, and in a wheezy movement, Pagano swung his feet to the carpet and stood up to grab a plate of large oatmeal cookies. "So when you doing the laundry?"

"The bank draft is being couriered. The cash I pick up after three tomorrow."

"You still got the banker onside?"

"Relax. He's well taken care off. There'll be no Suspicious Transaction Reports here. and Baresi has a bent banker lined up for their cut in Campione."

"Campione?"

"A pretty little money-washing hideaway beside Lake Como. It's between Italy and Switzerland."

"Couldn't the transfers have been done today?" As ever, Pagano was suspicious, his impatient eyes glaring at the Indian as he flopped onto the settee.

Chetri let out something between a sigh and a groan of irritation. "Enzo, like I said, it's going to happen. I do the set-up tomorrow. Baresi or Myerson can collect whenever they want after the media circus has left town."

"I don't like it," Pagano fixed the Indian with a suspicious stare. "Why can't one of these guys come to your place? Pick up the money there."

Chetri shook his head. Even behind his tinted glasses, his dark brown eyes revealed his mounting anger. He crossed the room till he was looking down on Pagano, who was reclining like a fat Roman emperor and munching noisily on another cookie. "Because, Enzo," the Indian snapped unusually sharply, "Myerson and Baresi do not know me or you. They knew only Lee Westdale." He pushed his glasses up his snub nose before continuing. "Baresi has an emergency number that reaches me. But he doesn't know my name or who or where I am. Both his phone and mine are disposables."

Pagano grunted, seemingly satisfied.

"That reminds me," prompted Chetri. "No change of mind? About paying off Lee's wife … er his widow?"

Pagano said nothing but the dead-eyed look was answer enough. He rolled off the couch, farted noisily and headed towards the bathroom.

-58-

Wimbledon

It was just after six-thirty a.m. and Mandy Westdale was eager to catch up with Alex Anderson. She slipped into the twins' bedroom and kissed them goodbye. They would not be awake for another forty minutes but Nena was in the kitchen watching breakfast television. "I'll be out till lunchtime. Lawyer stuff. Tell the boys I'll take them to Bocketts Farm to see the animals. We'll have ice-cream and cakes."

She went from the kitchen into the garage, locking the door behind her. Nena looked at her slightly curiously but Mandy had decided to offer no more explanation for her early start. Dressed in a tight-fit white blouse, figure-hugging black jeans and dark red high-heels, she could scarcely pretend she was going to the gym or the swimming-pool.

Before using the zapper to open the garage door, she put on a pair of tough gardening gloves and delved deep into a large tub of sandy grit that Lee had used in wintry conditions. Moments later, she pulled out a bulky pack wrapped in heavy-duty black polythene. After shaking off the grit, she slipped it into her shoulder-bag and dumped the gloves back on the mower.

In the Range-Rover with its smoked-glass windows, she made good time covering the few miles to Richmond, arriving punctually at seven. Head held high and with a confident stride, she swept into the reception of The Trumpeters, bringing with her a trail of Gucci perfume and eye-catching style and panache.

Alex Anderson rose to greet her. The lightweight black rollneck and matching trousers emphasised his slim physique. Considering his short night, there was no sign of it with his eyes alert and glowing cheeks. His hair was slightly damp and his Florida-tanned skin radiated fitness because only a few moments before, he had been in the sauna, wearing nothing but a contented smile, excited to be meeting Mandy again.

Though he was unsure of where breakfast might lead, as he had towelled himself dry, his expectations were aroused. Now, on seeing her arrival, hips swaying, her hair coiffeured, her make-up immaculate and every move oozing confidence, his hopes rose further. "Good to see you again," he greeted her in his soft tones but in a markedly Geordie accent. "Right on time too. I like that." He leaned towards her and she kissed him on both cheeks.

"I admire punctuality too," she smiled back. "Breakfast you said? I had nothing at home."

"Served in my suite. We can talk there freely." He led her up the wide stairs, the gold carpet thick beneath their feet. As she followed him up, Mandy admired the long legs, narrow waist and taut buttocks. He nodded approval on finding that, as instructed, the maid had already serviced the suite, leaving a faint smell of spring flowers in the air. The king-size had been made along with her other chores while he had been sweltering downstairs in the sauna. Breakfast was laid out on a low table. He turned off the TV and offered her a wing-backed chair looking down to the lawns, a silver sliver of the Thames just visible.

After opening the balcony doors, the room was at once filled with the excited chatter of birds coming from the giant trees that were scattered around the grounds. "Very different from my childhood in Newcastle. There the birds coughed every morning. But you'd love my villa in Florida. There's sandpipers, gulls and plovers along the shore, just below my place."

"I'm sure." Mandy nodded abstractedly, eager to get to the point. "Is everything okay?"

"You saw the result. Jeez! What a finish to secure the tie. You gotta give it to that Zack Gomez. He fluffed his putt so convincingly. You'd never have known he was our man." With casual grace, he eased himself into the matching chair. "From my side, everything is hunky-dory. And yours?" He tried to sound casual about his question.

She poured mango juice for them both and helped herself to a warm chocolate croissant. "Let's get to the point, shall we? The deal we discussed last time? Still on."

"Trust me."

Mandy winced. She hated those words, never quite trusting anybody who had to use them. But she did trust him, at least so far. She had no reason not to. Based on their first meeting over afternoon tea on the terrace downstairs, she had decided that Alex was plausible and could deliver his part of the deal. "Fifty-fifty. Right?"

"Agreed. Trust me." He took a hefty bite from a banana and waved the remains as he continued. "No second thoughts since last time?"

There was a long pause, certainly longer than Anderson wanted. This time, Mandy remembered to play it slow, kicking herself for having sounded over-eager. For many of her waking hours, she had agonised over his proposition. After recovering from the shock news that Lee had fixed the Ryder Cup, what remained was anger and resentment that he was being cheated out of his reward. His proposition over scones, jam and cream had been simple.

Steal from the crooks who were robbing her of Lee's share.

No question, it was wrong. *Christ! It was downright bloody dishonest.* But the upside was incredible and the way Alex had explained it, the downside risk was acceptably low. She could wake up without worrying about debts She could fund the twins' future. "You're sure they won't pay me off?"

He turned towards her and his gimlet stare oozed sincerity. "This scumbag Pagano would never cut you in. You've never heard from him or from Chetri. Enough said."

"There's no way we could get arrested. Correct?"

"Think about it – these bastards can't call in the cops." His face broke into a big smile that became an infectious laugh that set her heart pounding. "Look, Mandy – the fix was never spotted. The huge win was handled through the black market. There's no giveaways for the cops to seize on, least of all to connect anything to you or me."

Mandy gave a reassuring nod, "I just want Lee's cut. Anything more, you can keep." She had no intention of volunteering about Detective Inspector Todd Holtom's visits. After chatting to Alex over tea last time, she had chain-smoked her way to that decision.

Best to say nothing.

Was that unfair to Alex?

No. The detective and that Nancy woman had gone away satisfied.

This was golf, not cricket.

Anyway, I back myself to outwit PC Plod any day.

Anderson lobbed the banana skin onto the tray in front of them and stretched to grab a peeled kiwi-fruit. "Communication between Lee and Chetri was secure, always changing and untraceable. Irretrievable. Lee never even knew Chetri's real name. There's nothing can link you or Lee to this fix. So what's to worry about?" He leaned onto the arm of the chair to get closer. "Mandy, for all our differences, our trio were good – so damned clever, so damned careful."

"Careful? What way?"

"No bets placed by us on the legit market, not by the three of us or by the captains or other players. That was the deal. Nothing to arouse suspicions."

"But the other two, particularly the New Yorker – he sounds like a right bastard. Greedy too."

"You're not wrong there." Now, his expressive eyes showed the depth of his anger as his firm jaw tightened. "Not a clever move. For smart guys, cutting you and me out was pretty damned dumb."

She pointed a delicate finger at his chest. "It drove you to contact me. How clever was that?"

Anderson sat back, almost winded by the incisive assessment. "You're right, of course you are. With what I know and what you *say* you have, we can fix them. But," he karate-chopped above the coffee-pot. "neither of us alone can outwit them." He gave her another wide-mouthed smile, revealing expensively whitened teeth that contrasted with his wind-bronzed skin. "We can be a great team. That's if you have …"

"Lee never told me anything of all this, never a hint." She surprised herself at volunteering this again but his soft voice and clean-cut appearance charmed and calmed her. Had Alex been a famous cricketer, someone would have snapped him up to model their designer clothes. "I thought Lee and I shared everything. I was wrong. " Her smile started off as sad but then turned philosophical. She leaned close to him. "At least I know everything now." She almost whispered the words he wanted to hear, her voice husky. She held his penetrating look and an electric message seemed to pass between them, not in the least driven by money. His fit and lean body, his healthy skin and hair swept forward gave him a confident air that she found uncomfortably compelling. Looking away, she helped herself to wheat toast with chunky marmalade and no butter.

If he would just stop saying trust me, I'd trust him a whole lot more.

"Listen, Mandy. Here's how it works. Lee's cut was delivered using hawala to Vijay. That was usually about thirty-six to forty-eight hours after the cricket finished or the tennis fix was through." He paused, mentally crossing his fingers. "I'm sure, dead positive for the golfers, it will be the same."

"So how did it work?"

"It was like a pyramid. Vijay dropped off Lee's cut for collection. Lee then paid off Mark Rayner. Then Rayner paid off those he had suckered in."

"Lee knew this Indian well?" Mandy was still getting used to the idea that Lee had led such a double life.

"They went back some years, yes – but like I said, Chetri remained anonymous and the golfers only dealt with Lee." Anderson brushed some croissant flakes onto the carpet.

"Got it." A buzz of excitement now gripped Mandy. She half-wished he would stop leaning closer to her with that dreamy look. It was disconcerting and causing her pleasurable sensations deep inside. She wiped her lips with the napkin, leaving a faint trace of pink on the white. Just as when their eyes had met over tea, Mandy noticed strange but compelling feelings pulsing deep inside. She shifted position but the ache continued.

Anderson touched her arm with just a hint of caress. "The payment system was not broken. They'll use it, trust me."

Mandy breathed out deeply, attracting attention to the movement of her breasts in the white blouse. "With what I've uncovered, that makes sense." She found she could resist her inner feelings no longer and reached across to pat his hand. She left it there even as her voice turned business-like. "Time to share?"

"You've brought it?"

Mandy nodded towards her bag.

"You're some woman." He stood up and watched the water tumbling down the impressive stone fountain that was playing midway down the lawn. He turned and gave her a cheeky grin. "You give me what I need. Then you and me – we can have it all." His words were spoken softly.

"We can have it all. Sounds like that Adele recording." Mandy enjoyed his subtle innuendo. Her cheeks coloured and there was a choking sensation at the back of her throat. She swallowed hard. Was he flirting? It seemed so.

She hoped so.

"So how much are we talking about? Last time, you promised to tell me."

By way of answer, Anderson sat down and produced a black and gold Cartier fountain-pen. On the small pad provided by the hotel, he wrote down the numbers in bold, black ink. Mandy studied the line of figures. After a series of deductions, the list ended with an underlined total. Her eyes opened wide and her jaw fell slack. "I didn't know the odds for sure last time," Alex explained. "Now I do. So, the two captains will share at least thirty million, probably much more. Lee was due five."

"Sterling or dollars?"

"Dollars. Always US dollars."

"All cash?"

Anderson laughed but kindly. "Thirty-five million in one hundred dollar bills? You'd need a truck."

Mandy pointed to the bottom line. "One-eighty million? Are you dreaming?"

"Not dreaming. Split three ways, that was our deal. I've lost sixty million. Maybe more."

"I'm worth a lot to you then." Her words were accompanied

by a half-smile as she looked sideways and across to his smooth-shaven chin and smiling mouth.

"What you can give me, yes." He rose to his full height, hand in pocket, looking even more like a male model in a Sunday magazine. He met her look and moved closer to rest his free hand on her shoulder and noticed no resistance. He then leaned down and kissed the top of her head. "We're worth a lot *to each other*." He ran his fingers slowly down her cheek. "We could be good together."

"Business. This is business, Alex." Both knew that her words now meant nothing. Unable to stop herself, she found she was nibbling his little finger. With him so close, she noticed a touch of cologne, reminding her of pine forests and snowy slopes in the Austrian Alps. "Business," she faltered. "Business before pleasure, Alex" she repeated.

She knew now what she had sensed ever since their first meeting. His animal magnetism was too fierce to resist. *Had she expected it to come to this? Had she hoped it would come to this?* As she thought of her red and black lace underwear that was worn to be admired, she knew the answer.

"Business can wait." He reached for her hand and helped her rise slowly from the chair. He was tempted to kiss her full on the mouth, wanting to cup her chin in his hands to upturn her mouth to him. He wanted to squeeze her, impatient to feel her firm breasts pressed against his chest but instead, he led her with a strong grip through to the bedroom.

Beside her wing-back chair, she left her bag on the floor. Inside it was the black package, all thoughts of it forgotten as she melted into his arms, his strength of purpose reaching every part of her. As she was swept towards the bedroom, there was just one word on her mind.

Cathartic.

-59-

London

The comforts of Kirsty-Ann's curves wrapped around him seemed far too distant as Ratso stepped out of the Underground at Vauxhall on Tuesday morning after overnighting from Miami. He started the short but now familiar walk over to Cobalt Square. It was not raining but it might just as well have been with dark clouds hanging low over the impressive yellow and red brick building with its mass of glass. At least inside, the airy atrium and modern layout added cheer compared to even sunny days in the compact and depressing Cauldron, down in the Clapham basement.

The steady rumble and roar of traffic around Vauxhall was ever-present and with the low clouds, there was no escape from the fumes from thousands of exhausts. On the brighter side, the text message that had greeted his arrival at Heathrow had been cheering. He could look forward to the whiteboard session. For a change, the arrows on the board linking the photos and fixed points would be leading towards... well, he did not yet know what or who – but an attractive funnel-shape was now forming.

The first person he saw was Tosh who was scurrying along the corridor, his gait slightly lopsided from his accident during *Operation Clam*. "Been transferred here, Tosh?"

"No decision from the Deputy but I've been told to attend your meeting. Y'know, after what happened on Sunday." He looked uncomfortable. "Must dash. Can't stop."

"Why not?" Ratso grinned, knowing the answer full well. "See you at the meeting." He was clutching a cup of Starbucks bought by the station and plonked it on his desk. As he looked around, he thought of K.A's work-station with its views of blue skies, even if across a nondescript highway. He liked Cobalt Square as a base. It was far better than the stale air down in Cauldron. Even so, the other week, Nancy had spotted a rat scuttling round a corner, causing general merriment. Someone had pinned on the board – "Lost, One Rat. Contact Det.Inspector Holtom for Reward."

He summoned Jock and Nancy and after they were seated, he saw the questions on their faces. "So what do you want to know?" He enjoyed keeping them waiting.

"Not much of a tan, boss" prompted Nancy, an innocent look on her face.

Ratso was not rising to that. "Not surprising. Work, work, work! Sod's law that everything blew up just when…"

"When what, boss?" chipped in Jock, deadpan at first but then with a smile playing around his lips.

Ratso played the dig with a dead bat. "When I was trying to catch some rays." He turned away and fumbled with the zip on his carry-on. "Nancy, this is for you. Jock here's a bottle of Balvenie malt whisky."

Both recipients looked shocked but grateful. Nancy opened the gift-carrier and found a red and green-striped Satchel Bag." She grinned.

"No camel smell for miles," Ratso laughed.

Nancy seemed lost for words. "Thanks. I mean, gosh – well, you didn't have to."

"My pleasure." He saw sadness in her eyes and immediately averted his gaze. "Back to business. Surveillance?"

"Tolvey approved three teams of six operating 24-7. One team for each captain."

"I'm losing track. Damned jetlag. So it's now Tuesday morning. Maybe from now on, it will get interesting. But three teams? Why?"

"The Barnet bank gave a pointer yesterday."

The tiredness left Ratso's face. His eyes flashed satisfaction and something close to a whistle escaped his lips. "You have a name?"

"Aye! Vijay Chetri. His mugshot is up on the whiteboard."

On hearing this, Ratso thumped a fist into the palm of his other hand and hissed a long y-e-e-s. "Get anything from Lord's?"

"Yes and no. Craig is some boy, eh!" The Scot made the *R* in Craig sound like a roll on a snare-drum. There was a toothy grin on Jock's face but he made no attempt to elaborate on his comment.

"Is Mick Tolvey around?"

"He's at Hendon today." It was Nancy who responded.

Ratso was pleased to be dodging the boss. "Chetri? Sounds Indian. What do we know?"

Nancy flipped open her laptop. "He is. And looks it. See boss?" Ratso took in the placid pale brown features and gentle eyes. The neatly trimmed wrap-around silvery beard was cut to the same length as his matching hair. "We're still working on him."

"For what?" Ratso rubbed his tired eyes.

Nancy checked her scribbled notes. "Source of wealth, current occupation, travel movements, banking arrangements, contacts."

Ratso rose from his chair. "Good. Good. You've done well. Time to go. Let's find out what we've got."

"Do you no think we're too late, boss? I mean the captains might have been paid already."

"Jock, don't say that in the briefing. We have to keep optimism levels high. Right?"

"So, between us?" enquired Nancy.

"We have Chetri covered. That's a positive. Our best hope is the two captains have been too busy with the press vultures to collect."

"And your worst fear?" Nancy as ever was sharp and to the point.

"That their cut isn't delivered in London at all. Sophisticated gangs might use some godforsaken place like Vanuatu, or Belize. But I doubt it. Not with those codes in Lee's note."

– 60 –

Surrey

As she drove carefully through the twists and turns with the twins laughing and shouting in the back, Mandy's body still felt on fire. She glanced in the rear-view mirror and thought she could still see a contented glow on her cheeks, a carry-over from her yelping crescendos of passion.

Her neighbour Janie had been right. Moving on *was* cathartic. Two hours in bed with Alex was cathartic – and then some.

"Are we there yet Mummy," enquired Sam intruding into her personal space.

"Not long now darling. Then we'll see the pig-race and maybe get to feed some of the baby lambs."

"Daddy always let us feed them."

"Yes, he did Mummy. Always. Please, Mummy!"

"Of course Daddy did, Roger. Feeding them will be great fun."

"Will Daddy bring us here next time?"

"I … I don't expect so, darling. Daddy's, er … feeding the lamb of God."

"Oh, can we do that one day too? Please Mummy."

"One day, Sam." She glanced back. "Finish your Gruffalo books before we get there." A spasm of guilt ran through her as if she had been unfaithful to them all – Lee, Sam and Roger. For a few moments more, she remained in the real world of small boys' chatter. Gone were recollections of the nerve-tingling gasps and sighs, drowned out by childish giggles and the reality of the crime she was plotting.

Thinking back, she couldn't describe what had happened as love-making. That had been Lee's forte – soft, gentle and cuddly seduction whereas this morning had been all about Alex's bone-rattling power and intensity – pushing, pulling, grunting, heaving, kissing, nibbling, rolling and shuddering in a flurry of animal intensity.

God! How I want more of that – and soon.

Afterwards, Alex had led her back to the French window, the coffee in the pot now cold. After more had arrived, he had looked at her expectantly as she pulled the package from her bag. "Hard to believe I know but *this* is why I'm here," Mandy volunteered. "I can't stay too long as I'm taking the twins on an outing and then my mother picks up them up. They're staying with her in Newbury for a few days. The house will be empty so maybe we can? Y'know." She squeezed his arm and was rewarded with a muted reaction, his attention now focussed on the hard-drive. Using a blue cable, she hooked the drive into her laptop.

"This is not the original? Right?" Anderson's tone suggested suspicion. *Might she have fiddled with the code to dupe him? Surely not? He could trust her, couldn't he? Surely he could?*

"Correct. Some evenings, Lee spent ages in his study. I'd go to bed. He said he needed total quiet while drafting magazines articles or his Sunday paper column. I asked once if he were being secretive again – but he denied it." She watched the screen come alive. "Somehow, I felt sure he was using the Dell but he said not. Deep down, I'm not sure I really wanted to know. I didn't want to believe he was cheating on me or doing something devious. We'd been through enough of that."

"You thought he might have been fixing? Because of the money?"

She closed her eyes and nodded towards the carpet as if ashamed. "I didn't want to know that."

"But you said there was no password, so you could have checked it out."

Again, Mandy noticed the pointed tone. "I liked the money flowing – designer clothes, expensive trips." She clicked on the mouse and smiled. "He kept saying he was going to dump the Dell but somehow never got round to it. Now I can see why. The cunning bastard had been bluffing. But he *had* turned our lives around." She fell silent as the screen lit up. "After …the bomb," she hesitated as she used the word, "I wanted nothing to destroy his reputation. I was worried about his Dell. Late one night after a bucket of gin, I wondered if the hard-drive would be incriminating." She shrugged as they looked at the screen. "After seeing what was on it, I decided to destroy it to protect his reputation. But I made a duplicate and literally buried it."

"Why?"

"In my alcohol-fuelled state, I saw everything differently. I needed to know but never wanted the police, or all his adoring fans, ever to find out. I covered myself. If ever asked, I would be able to prove I had destroyed it."

"And did they? I mean the cops? Did they ever ask?"

"Not a peep from them. They've never been near the house."

"And what I need is on here?"

"Naughty! Not *I*, Alex. What *we* need." She tapped him on the nose. "I checked after our tea together."

"You're right. Sorry, pet." For the first time, Alex found himself using a term of endearment dating back to childhood. "I know the place that Chetri used for Lee's pay-off but not the code. You need the location. We must find the code on here."

"I went to the library and plugged the original into a computer. My God! What I discovered! Talk about destroying his reputation." She pointed to a list of contacts with phone numbers. "With this stuff, the police could bring down maybe a dozen cricketers and umpires, five tennis players, a snooker star, four tennis umpires and Baresi and Myerson. Bloody silly really – he even recorded his pay-offs. But not how he collected."

"So you destroyed the original having made this duplicate?" Alex's voice showed a hint of suspicion.

Her face broke into a sly grin as she shrugged. "Best of both worlds, maybe? I wanted to protect *my* reputation too." She gazed down at the fountain, a dreamy distant look in her eyes.

"But your reputation now? Stealing the money? Becoming a criminal? You're sure?"

She clasped his muscled arm. "I need it. Splitting Lee's five million. That does it for me."

Anderson looked shocked. "Mandy, love, no, no! I meant fifty-fifty of *everything* including the captains' cut. Come on! Take it. I'll help you hide it offshore." He leaned in close to absorb the details on screen.

The warmth of his body filled her senses and she ached to return to bed with him but simply gave him a hug followed by a quick and friendly peck. "That's sweet of you, Alex. Thanks but no thanks. Tens of millions? That would be a burden, a worry. Shifting money around. Bankers are so paranoid." She returned to the laptop, her fingers flying over the keys. She pointed to page after page of photos of cricketers and a former Wimbledon champion. "Ah! Here we are." She stopped at a page headed *Jupiter*. "Photos of both Myerson and Baresi. Plus the scores for each day at the Ryder Cup."

Anderson's face broke into a smile and then a grin followed by a throaty laugh, his eyes racing down the screen. "There it is! The code! That's it!" He pulled her close and kissed her hard, his breathing once again excited. "It's there." He pointed at the screen. "The one detail I was missing."

"You mean? You're sure?"

"Between us, we have the golden key." He hugged her again, rocking her back so that her throat was exposed to his lips. In a sudden move, his other arm cradled her buttocks and she found herself swept up into his arms and being carried back to the unmade bed. "Celebration time!"

"Mummy, Mummy, we're here. Look at the piglets," shouted Sam. "Hoorah, hoorah!"

"Aren't we going to have such fun, darlings?"

-61-

London

Ratso strode through the modern spaciousness, his surroundings in Cobalt Square so different from the depressing dullness of his Clapham days. As he edged between the assembled officers to the front of the packed room, he sensed expectation in the air. Enthusiasm that had been non-existent last time, was obvious from the excited buzz. The laughter and chatter died and eyes all turned his way. At the last briefing, eyes had been evasive, the tone subdued and the hopelessness almost tangible.

As Ratso took centre stage, his mind was racing. A wry smile started to appear and he turned to the whiteboard to disguise it. He now knew how he wanted to play the sensitivity. "We're talking golf, not cricket." He saw there was no sign of surprise. "So I expect you want to know how we had the breakthrough." He grinned at the rows of transfixed faces. "It would be easy to say that it was my smart work. It wasn't." He looked away and paused for a long moment. "This was down to Jock Strang and Nancy Petrie putting their hands in their pockets to support a spinal injury charity. They bought raffle tickets and Nancy got lucky. Without that, this we would still be like blind men looking for a one-legged flea on a cat's neck." He waited for the laughs to die away. "So I went to Florida where by chance a certain detective who I know…"

"Tasty, sir," shouted a voice from the back and Ratso picked up some other wag muttering about the lucky sod getting a hole in one.

"... who I know," Ratso continued deadpan, "understood instantly what Lee's note meant." He looked at each row from end to end. "Nobody here ever think this was about golf?" He checked the blank looks. "No. I thought not. None of us did, me included. We were blindsided because Lee Westdale was a famous cricketer. Let's take a lesson from this. And the lesson is?"

"Learn to play golf?"

"Get to know a sexy blonde in Florida?"

"Come on, come on," prompted Ratso.

"Lateral thinking, boss." It was DC Carole Viment yet again showing promise. Ratso's craggy face creased into a near smile but before he could comment, DC Grant intervened.

"Is lateral thinking lying on a sunbed on a cruise, sir?" His comment was said with a cheeky smile but an innocent tone.

Ratso waited for the laughter to die down. "*Any* thinking from you would be welcome." From the board he unpinned every detail about cricket. "We must never again get blinkered by seizing the obvious."

"Think outside the box, sir. Is that it?"

"If you like American jargon, Digby, yes you're right." He turned to the board and tapped the photo of Chetri. "We'll come to this Indian guy in a moment. For now, tell me this. Who saw anything odd during the Ryder Cup? Show of hands please." Not a hand moved. "So nobody spotted the fix. Not even Nancy and Tosh Watson who were there. That's another lesson. I knew *exactly* what was planned yet saw nothing. A good fix is hard to spot." He tossed the marker-pen from one hand to the other. "And that is how and why the fixers get away with it – international football, tennis, cricket, golf you name it."

Nancy raised her hand. "Sorry boss. I don't want to sound like a smartarse but once you briefed DCS Tolvey that the fix was the Ryder

Cup, well …" She fumbled in her pocket and produced a betting slip. "I bet the correct score on the second day and the tie on the third." She lowered her eyes, slightly sheepish. "I got tasty odds on the tie."

"But you saw nothing strange?" Ratso kept a poker face as he thought of the winnings now due to him too.

As Nancy shook her head, it was Tosh that chimed in. "There *was* a pointer but not from the players. The Ryder Cup often produces big swings. No pun intended. Too many American players don't like the foursomes."

"Go on, Tosh."

"Critics say they're control freaks – wanting to be in charge of every shot. But they can't do that. Having to share strategy and play alternate shots doesn't come easily."

Ratso leaned his buttocks against the brown-topped table. "And in the singles? Sunday's weather?"

"Those Yanks don't get to play too often in conditions like that." Tosh looked at Nancy before continuing. "I'd give Myerson and Baresi both barrels about the playing order on the final day. Can't prove nothing but Jake Myerson should have sent out the four or five most likely winners first."

"Go on."

"To win the Cup you need 14.5 points. The USA started the last day ahead 10 to 6. So if your first players out on Sunday all win, you don't expose the ones who are playing less well or who are more likely to be beaten."

"With you. Go on."

"All twelve of the team play the Sunday singles. The first American players Myerson sent out were more likely to lose because of Baresi's playing order."

"And they had four Wild Cards like O'Hagan and Gomez at the end," Nancy chimed in. "Like I mean … to clean up."

Tosh tapped the side of his nose to great effect. "It worked a dream – pulled Europe right back into it. When quizzed by journalists later, both smooth-talked their strategies."

"Collusion?"

"Boss, the playing order is a poker game. Neither captain knows the opponent's strategy."

"But on Sunday?"

"Not just Sunday, boss. Someone who was suspicious – someone working backwards from the tie," Nancy chipped in with forceful confidence, "might say it looked as if Myerson and Baresi had fixed the order of play."

"Call me Mr Suspicious." Ratso scribbled the word *cahoots* beneath the photos of the two captains on the board. "That fits. Westdale's note referred to *who will play* and to *Order*."

"And not all the players need be fixed," Tosh confirmed as he removed a slightly melted Mars Bar from his pocket. "But I expect they were –enough of them. The Wild Cards, probably."

"So no evidence of daft shots?"

Tosh was hesitant, more because his mouth was full of Mars Bar. "Nothing I spotted. Under pressure, players' brains get stir-fry crazy. I've read the press reports. I've listened to the pundits on the sports channels. Nobody suggested anything unusual."

Nancy was quick to agree. "We need to nail the two captains."

DC Viment looked intrigued. "So, sir, Lee's note?"

"It was his final instructions to whoever he met at the Cavendish Hotel." Ratso now pointed to Chetri's photo.

"First, I want everything we've got on this guy Chetri. Second – we brainstorm the note. These entries." He pointed to just three.

Bishopsgate
Surrey
+409WGG =SJW 4878903

"We assumed Surrey meant Surrey Patriots. But now we need to assume it may be a location."

"Unless the word is *Survey*, boss."

"Lateral thinking, Jock, but let's stick to Surrey. Tosh, this is urgent. List every Surrey in the A to Z for London. From the Yellow Pages, list every business in the London area with Surrey in the name."

"Looking for?"

"Maybe a bank but more likely a Safe Deposit company where the code below," he tapped on it, "could be used. That code also wrong-footed us ... well me. I read it as cricket and that led me up a blind alley." He saw the puzzled faces. "WGG stands for W G Grace, a legendary cricketer in the Victorian era. SJW is short for St John's Wood, home to Lord's Cricket Ground."

"Aye but right enough, it disna' mean that we'll find the money in the Changing-Rooms or lavvy there."

"Correct, Jock. This looks like a password or code chosen by Lee."

"And he told Baresi or Myerson, so they could use it?"

"Makes sense, Nancy." Ratso walked along the dais and back again, tossing the marker-pen even higher from hand to hand. "Let's look at that headless chicken list. See what answers we now have."

"There was a missing question, boss." Again it was DC Viment. "And I have an answer too."

"More lateral thinking?" Ratso looked at her with a warm and appreciative smile.

"Sunbed, sir. Never fails." Everybody laughed except Nancy who stared at her purple finger-nails.

"Go on then."

-62-

Enfield. near London

"It's bad, Eric. I've got a problem." Chetri had just limped in from a taxi, his right arm in a sling, his brow furrowed, eyes almost tearful. His gofer, Eric Sommer, in white overalls, had been whiling away the morning watching TV in Chetri's Enfield home. The plan had been to travel together to do the drop hours ago. "Broken, is it?"

Chetri nodded. "And a sprained ankle."

"I wondered. You were gone nearly four hours."

"My own damned fault – tripping over the kid's skateboard."

Sommer had not seen the accident when Chetri had been waving off his family. "Shame your lady-wife has jetted off with everyone. You'll need help."

Chetri's eyes saddened. "When they told me how bad it was after the x-rays – too late. They were all in-flight to Delhi." His normally pale brown skin was ashen as he hobbled across the garish carpet towards a favourite comfy chair and eased himself into it. "I can get by."

Sommer did not look convinced but it was not his business. "I can stay. I don't have to flog out to Essex. Your call." The house was quiet but from the kitchen came a lingering smell of curry and bhajis. "Taking the van, is we?" Sommer's estuary accent and mangled English rang through the spacious sitting-room with its heavy drapes, maroon scatter cushions and violent splashes of colour from the modern paintings that hung on each wall.

Chetri sat looking pensive, his good hand stroking the curve of his beard. In the taxi, he had been in two minds. He had always handled the big money himself. Eric always drove and would then drop-off the plastic sacks of clothing but Chetri never trusted him, or *anyone* come to that, to pick up the cash in its place.

Should I let Eric do it alone?

Trust him?

Do I have a choice?

With the grandchildren gone, the huge mansion seemed strangely quiet, no noisy shouts or grandkids crying as the Indian's face showed the inner torment. His whole body was telling him to take it easy and relax. His shoulder was aching and his left knee and ankle were now both stiff and swollen. A couple of pain-killers and putting his feet up beckoned. The alternative of being bumped around in the passenger-seat of the ageing Transit van was especially unattractive.

"Listen, Vijay. You don't look too special. Maybe leave it to tomorrow?"

"I've got to deliver today. Should really have been this morning."

Letting Sommer handle the money was the easy option but something, his whole upbringing and instincts kept nagging at him. *Trust nobody with your cash.* The thought of giving the code to Sommer was a leap too far. With a resigned look, he rose and shuffled slowly away from his chair beside the red-brick fireplace that dominated one wall. "I'll come with you."

"I'll dump the plastic sacks in the van then."

Chetri slipped the code into his pocket was ready to leave.

-63-

London

After the meeting broke up, Ratso hoofed it to Tavistock Square in Holborn. The offices he was visiting were on the third floor of a fine red sandstone building that rose nine storeys. In the 19th century, it had housed a merchant family. Now, it was subdivided into offices and the third floor housed the London HQ of Galobetta International, major bookmakers – a group that ran betting-shops across the UK and into Europe. For the past eight years though, its rapid growth had come from on-line betting using a Gibraltar licence and the installation of rapacious Fixed Odds Betting Terminals in its UK shops.

Craig Carter was already seated in the waiting-room reading The Racing Post when Ratso entered. He rose at once and shook his hand. "I had a horse running yesterday. Good odds – five to two."

"And?"

"It took so long to finish the jockey kept a diary."

"I've heard better." Ratso laughed politely but his mind was elsewhere – in fact just outside. Returning to Tavistock Square had taken him back to the terrorist bus-bomber of 2005. He had just walked beside the bus-stop and now he could see it down below. As if it were yesterday, he was reliving the sight of the red double-decker with its roof torn off, ripped open like a can of beans.

The sights, the smell of explosives and the endless wailing sirens as London had been attacked that summer morning had never left him. Before entering the building, tears had filled his eyes so that he had to pause before entering to log-in with the porter. He turned away from the window, his eyes closed against memories that still had the power to rip him apart. Now with the Piccadilly bomb blast, he reckoned nothing had changed or improved. Not for either side.

"Seen that Sorbonne report?" The question was a welcome relief. Ratso cocked his head to one side and said no. "I thought not," Craig continued. "There's £83 billion laundered every year through sports betting."

"How can they know that when so much is on the black market?"

"Good question. I think the word is extrapolation."

"Get you, Craig!" Ratso paused. "Sounds like a posh word for guessing."

"I'll send you an email attachment." Craig Carter put down his paper. "You'll find Morris interesting. I wanted you to get what he told me straight from ..."

"...the horse's mouth?" Ratso was saying when a tubby figure aged under thirty appeared, almost bounding towards them.

"Meaning I'm the horse? You two getting personal about my hairstyle?" The man guffawed loudly at his own joke as he swung round to show off his ponytail. Then, in a hairy fist, he gripped Ratso's hand. "I'm Morris Guyler. Good to meet you. It's Todd, isn't it?" In a flurry of activity, he was already bouncing back along the corridor, arms swaying like a gorilla in search of a mate. He turned into a spacious and airy room with large sash windows and several plastic cups littering his desktop. "Help yourself to coffee, tea, water, biscuits, anything," he suggested dumping himself down by his computer with a vast external monitor. "Or seeing as you're you both coppers, maybe a stiff whisky? It's almost noon."

Both visitors chose water though Ratso reckoned Carter would have gone for the whisky had he been alone. "I'm intrigued," Ratso volunteered. "But I'm racing against the clock."

"We have software – look I'm not a techie. I have no idea what goes on inside this box of tricks but it might be called a neural network… and maybe something called algorithms."

"You and me both." Ratso was none the wiser. "I use a watch to know the time. I'm not arsed about how it works. So?"

"We have a team of guys who write the programmes. Another team read the stats like you read the sports pages. Any betting oddities are thrown up." He grinned cheerfully. "They then reach me, the Luddite General." Guyler chuckled and despite his impatience to get to the point, Ratso found it infectious. "Mainly, reports are computer-generated but sometimes our Far East team spot something – call it gut reaction."

"Like what?" Craig Carter shifted his chair so he could see the screen filled with reds, greens, yellows and blues on the graphs and pie charts.

"Like loadsa money suddenly betting that the world snooker champ will lose to a colour-blind one-legged man with arthritic wrists." He cackled again. "Get my drift? I mean it might be kosher and just be locals who saw the champ pissed out of his brains, meaning there was no fix." He tapped the screen. "The techies can't tell us that. That's when I come in – the human element. I dig deeper."

"So if a guy tries to bet say ten million quid on a cricket result or Premier League score?"

"Not as clear-cut as you'd think. There are some serious gamblers out there, especially on the nags. These whales bet big, like fuck-me big. To them, ten-mil would be pocket-money. But we know them. They bet on-line and their source of funds has been checked out for AML. To us, it would stand out if they bet only a fiver each way on the three-o-clock at Kempton."

"So anything unusual raises red-flags?"

"The Ryder Cup threw up a sodding great red."

"Betting on the tie?"

"Predicting all three end of day scores correctly." He slurped his cold coffee and grimaced. "Okay, it could happen as a long-shot – y'know like some sad loser betting a tenner and getting lucky. I could get the odds worked out. Like Leicester City when they just won the Premiership at odds of 5,000 to 1. It can happen."

Ratso was trying to understand the pie-chart on the screen. "Spoon-feed me."

"Italy. We had a series of bets from our betting-shops over there. Not mega sums – averaging around ten to twenty thousand euros. Enough to do this." He changed screens and a map of Italy showed red flags in Milan, Naples, Rome, Turin and by Lake Como. "Total bets of just over 330,000 euros."

Craig looked at Ratso and pursed his lips. "Someone flitted about a bit."

"Or shared the info to avoid placing one big bet," agreed Ratso. "Baresi was at Wentworth. When were the bets placed?"

Guyler turned away from the screen. "Some just before the tournament but they piled in backing the tie big time after the US team were so far ahead after Day One." He almost seemed to lick his lips as he pointed at the screen. "Great odds if you knew the fix was on. Tasty."

Ratso said nothing while he noted to get Baresi's relatives and contacts prioritised. "Morris, don't get me wrong – this is signifi-cant. Very. If linked to Baresi it would bring him down but I'm thinking big numbers, big chunky multi-million bets."

"We've seen nothing like that."

Craig was quick to chip in. "You don't surprise me. Besides a few well-known whales, the really heavy bets would be in the black market."

Ratso agreed. "The gang insisted that Baresi and Myerson placed no personal bets." He paused for a moment and then fired in a sudden thought. "Vijay Chetri. Know the name?"

Guyler shook his head but then typed a command into the system. "No. He's not on our radar."

Guyler's eyes almost disappeared as his face crinkled when he laughed. "But someone, not Chetri, turned naughty here."

"Greed and criminals? Tell me about it."

Carter swept some biscuit crumbs onto a napkin and then came in heavy. "Morris – you sit on our group. Let's speak plainly. If some fixers had bet a mega sum on the Ryder Cup ending in a tie, would you definitely be aware?"

"Definitely? The simple answer is no – sometimes in cricket we spot unusual betting patterns or pick up a buzz and I see surprising dropped catches or run-outs. But these big–sum fixers don't use us. You're talking about the huge bubbling pot of money swirling around India and the Middle East. If someone there bet three-hundred million on the Ryder Cup ending in a tie, would we know? The answer could well be no. The bookies out there have their own ways of hedging. They rarely lay off with us."

Ratso's phone rang and he listened intently, ended the call and then rose to leave. "Thanks, Morris. Very helpful. Keep me posted on anything from Italy."

After leaving Morris Guyler to his pie-charts, Ratso and Craig stood outside for a few moments close to the memorial to the bomb victims. "Any advance on Piccadilly? If you can tell me," asked Carter.

"No more than you hear on TV. The bomb-makers skipped the

country before the blast. Four of them are believed to be lying low in Molenbeek, a suburb of Brussels. Raids on an apartment found TATP similar to that used in Piccadilly but the suspects had moved on." Ratso sighed and turned away. "Anyway, that call I just took. Talk about a bloody wild goose chase. The surveillance team went into overdrive chasing this Chetri fella in an ambulance to the local hospital and then back by taxi."

"Genuine? He wasn't meeting a contact there?"

"Unless he hid his millions wrapped in a sling." Ratso was so jet-lagged he was unsure whether he was joking or not. "I must get the betting shops in Italy watched. Someone is going to collect those big wins." He grinned, suddenly more cheerful. "After looking at all those pie-charts, what you reckon?"

"You're right, Todd. I do feel a pie and a pint coming on."

–64–

London

Seated by the window in a bedroom of a three-star hotel, the two watchers had a great view across the soulless side-street. One of the two men had a video camera, the other a camera with a powerful zoom. It was early afternoon and they had checked in just before twelve noon.

This was the London of Charles Dickens, not far from his stamping ground of Fleet Street and the Inns of Court. Today, he would barely recognise what remained. The 18th century buildings that had once lined the shabby and narrow street were nearly all flattened to house accountants and lawyers in glittering towers. It was still a work-in-progress – part cranes and jack-hammers and partly three storey buildings being emptied of tenants for more redevelopment.

On a notepad, the two men already had eight timed entries and departures as visitors dropped off or collected from the self-store facility opposite. The drive-through gave visitors ten minutes' parking and they had jotted down all vehicle models and registrations. Two people had arrived on foot with small packages. One person had collected a cardboard box but the rest had used small vans. Two had names and logos for law-firms emblazoned down the side.

"This is where them City types dump their crappy stuff. That's what I reckon."

"Yeah, I suppose." The second and much younger man looked uninterested and sounded as bored as he was. "What time we done?"

"The place shuts seven till seven," the thinner man replied. He had a chin and forehead that both jutted out so prominently that he looked like a caricature of the man-in-the-moon. He glanced over the remains of his burger and fries to the photo of Vijay Chetri and of a white Ford Transit with no markings "But like if this guy would only bleedin' turn up like right now, then that's us done and bleedin' dusted."

"Sod's bloody law. This geezer will come at five to bloody seven. I'm tellin' you."

Less than a mile away in the Templar Inn on Kingsway, Craig Carter had just got in pints with steak and mushroom pies while Ratso sat in a booth of the noisy pub. Their spot was too near the kitchen and the smell of hot cooking-oil drifted around them. "Any news?" asked Carter as he clinked glasses.

Ratso looked at his scribbles. "Tosh Watson and a couple of the lads have come up with a short-list of eight places with the word Surrey."

"Give."

"I've cut it down – like a safe deposit company in Guildford, a bank from Oman operating in Surrey Terrace. There's a Surrey Drive out in the Hackney Marshes with a self-store."

Carter peered down at the four names. "You've got it down to just them?"

"They could all be wrong. Jock Strang is checking out two … and these two," Ratso pointed to the lower two, "are mine."

"Because they're more likely?"

Ratso shook his head and chewed on a tough lump of beef. "Nah, just closer to here." He put down his fork as he gave up on the chewy beef and dumped it on the side of plate. "I'll stick to the pastry. Remind me not to come here again. Good for the figure though." He patted his flat stomach. "Craig – imagine you're this guy Chetri. You receive a load of hot dosh through a hawala dealer in Bishopsgate."

"Or cash from a bank on Bishopsgate?"

"Whatever. Chetri is not going to drive thirty, maybe forty miles to Guildford just so Lee Westdale could collect – when he was alive. Neither would you send Lee or two famous golfers to Hackney Marshes, night or day."

Carter laughed and then sank a large part of his pint. "To collect millions? Not without an armed security truck, no way!"

"We don't know how much the captains will get but it'll be pretty damned tasty. Agreed?"

"Go on."

"I ruled out safe-deposit boxes. Generally they are not very large. They're good for gold, jewels, storing a few documents."

"So you need something big enough for a clunky box or suit-case? Left-Luggage at a station?"

Ratso shook his head. "The code on Lee's note is too complex for that." He tapped on the two names. "That brings us to these two – a self-store place on Surrey Hill down near the river and a place in Greville Street off the diamond area in Hatton Garden called Surry Locksmiths and Self-Store."

"Surry spelled wrong then."

"Near enough and also the closest point to Bishopsgate." Ratso looked at his empty glass but decided against another Guinness. "Around there, a top golfer in a hat or cap might be anonymous. Plenty of foreign tourists mingle with the dealers in Hatton Garden. Almost every shop handles high-value jewellery and gold."

"Go on," prompted Craig his eyes alert beneath a slight frown.

"So Myerson and Baresi could pick up their cash and turn it into valuable jewellery just round the corner. Easier to take back to Florida. Or store it there. Maybe that's what Lee Westdale was doing to hide his wealth too. He could buy gold and store it in the acres of vaults right there." Craig looked and sounded impressed at Ratso's logic. "Shouldn't you be racing off there like the proverbial blue-arsed?"

"The surveillance team say that since getting back from the hospital, Chetri is still at home."

"What about Bishopsgate?"

"We're only guessing there's a hawaladar secretly operating there. You know what it's like with budget cuts." Ratso finished his last corner of pastry. "We haven't the resources to watch every likely corner-shop, newsagent or whatever. The Beatles would call Bishopsgate a long and winding road. That's why I'm banking on Chetri leading us to the pick-up and drop-off."

"I see. And hopefully on Bishopsgate." Craig glanced at his watch which seemed capable of doing everything except play chess like a Grand Master. "I have a committee meeting in Bayswater. Your plan?"

"Check out whether either of these places uses codes like on the note."

"Let me see it again." He waited until it appeared on Ratso's i-Pad. "I'd say it looks like a two-parter – one to access the building and the second the code to open up the personal facility."

"That makes self-store more likely." For a few seconds after Craig had gone, Ratso thought through money-handling, wondering what he was missing and how Jock and DC Viment were doing. Thinking of Viment, he remembered her words at the morning meeting. "Sir, don't you think it was a tad too convenient that a scruffy vehicle repair outfit would have invoiced ten quid for crushing the hard-drive?"

"You mean it would have been cash in the back pocket?" Ratso showed he was impressed. "That makes sense."

"Unless, sir," Viment had continued. "Unless Mandy insisted on a receipt."

"Good point. I like it. We'll need to ask her." Ratso caught Nancy's eye and she did not look happy at Viment upstaging her. Ratso was still debating what Viment's idea might say about Mandy as he loped along High Holborn towards the self-store on Greville Street.

It was less than a mile. After that, he'd grab a bus to check out Surrey Hill. With luck, up on the top deck, he'd get a moment to check the cricket scores from Cape Town.

But a bus might not be needed. Not if Greville Street held the answer.

-65-
London

Eric Sommer was seated alone and reading the sports pages while drinking latte and munching *pain au raisin* in Caffè Nero at Liverpool Street Station. Outside, there was the steady rumble of traffic on Bishopsgate. The white Transit was parked about three-hundred metres away, towards Monument.

Vijay's dizzy spell as they were about to leave had changed everything. Right now the Indian was sedated at home about twelve miles away. In contrast, Eric was edgy and excited. It showed in the way his fingers were restless as he kept checking the time. Never before had he been authorised to do the pick-up; to have millions in cash in his hands.

In my power.

On the slow drive through north London, he had seen no sign that he was followed though he was not expecting it anyway. But Chetri, paranoid to a fault as usual, had always insisted on their regular runs to be aware. No way was he going to start cutting corners now. *It's got to be done proper* he had told himself.

But millions.

In cash.

Soon.

In my hands, under my control.

After parking, Sommer had dropped off the two black sacks of old clothes at the steamy unpleasantness of the laundromat and was now giving it a long sixty minutes before picking up the money. Chetri had always been meticulous about the charade in case the cops had the hawalador under surveillance.

At last!

His digital watch showed it was 16-20pm.

Time to collect. He left the newspaper on the table and threaded his way against the endless streams of people heading for trains or other public transport. The van was in an underground car-park, a thought that made him smile as he crossed at the lights. Chetri always griped at the cost of parking even when collecting the millions of dollars. Sommer stopped, seemingly to look at the display of e-cigarettes in a corner-shop newsagent. Above it towered an all-window office block from which workers were pouring out. Just as Chetri had briefed him, he looked back up Bishopsgate towards the station. There were no familiar faces. There was no sign that anybody had followed him. Decision made, he strolled around the corner and entered the noisy laundromat.

The premises stood in a street of low rise buildings beside a dreary pub that would soon be demolished with few regretting it. Inside, Neil Diamond was belting out *Red Red Wine* above the throb of the machines. Nobody among the customers seemed interested in his arrival. Most played with their smartphones or stared mindlessly at the clothes tumbling inside the long bank of machines. A couple of other customers were standing in line to pick up their laundry which, like him, they had paid extra for the staff to wash. Almost instantly, Sommer was signalled through the strings of beads that covered a doorway at the rear and into a private area. He followed the diminutive figure down the cramped flight of stairs to the basement. It was a first for him and his hands felt damp at the thought of what he was doing.

Money-Laundering.

But he need not have been concerned. Chetri had fixed for him to pick up on producing his driving licence as ID. Fifteen minutes later he left, walking at a steady pace, trying to avoid looking over-burdened. The two black sacks were now treble-bagged for extra strength. At the car-park, he descended two levels to where the van was parked.

The Transit stood out among the swanky BMWs, Mercedes and Jaguars. A couple of city-types were laughing as they got into a sporty looking Mazda with its roof off. If anybody was watching, it was not evident. He dumped the sacks – one on the floor and the other on the front passenger-seat beside the neatly folded clean clothes he had brought in from Enfield. Carefully, anxious not to attract attention as he had been trained, he nosed out and up into the daylight to head west towards Holborn.

Behind him in the storage compartment were three lightweight cases, ready to be filled when he reached the usual quiet corner of Red Lion Square. "This is a good place," Chetri had explained on their first trip together. "Parked here, we can see two sides of the square and be sure nobody is close enough to attack or spy on us." As he progressed through the packed streets, surrounded by buses, taxis and chauffeurs driving executives to their next engagements, Sommer still kept glancing back, his mind filled with thoughts of the millions lying right beside him.

Enough to change my life.

In my power.

As he crossed the busy junction at Holborn Circus, he saw that a powerful motorbike had been keeping pace with him about sixty metres behind. Usually, bikers zig-zagged between the ve-hicles and overtook but this one seemed content to stay in line at each set of lights. Sommer was taking no chances. He decided to take a nomadic route to Red Lion Square and instead turned north beyond Southampton Row and headed towards King's Cross and St Pancras.

A few back-doubles will soon shake him off. Or not. Better to play safe.

Fifteen minutes' walk away from Southampton Row, Ratso crossed Hatton Garden at Greville Street, close to number 88-90, the scene of the great safe-deposit heist of 2015. As he looked at the anonymity of the building, Ratso thought how often loose talk, lavish spending or petty jealousies in London's underworld had led to arrests and convictions This audacious headline-grabbing burglary had soon fallen apart once the twenty-five million had been divvied up. Moments later, he spotted the sign for Surry Locksmiths and Self-Store. His instant impression was that for nearby diamond merchants keeping their stock secure overnight or at weekends, it was ideal but without off-street parking, not suited for dropping off larger items.

Inside the cramped office with yellow walls and a sea of invoices piled on the floor, he spoke to Curtly Roberts. The West Indian manager was in his late thirties, his curly hair receding fast. Almost at once, Ratso sussed that the guy was defensive. His eyes were furtive – sometimes narrowed, sometimes avoiding contact.

Ratso guessed he was worried about what some of his clientele were stashing in the vaults below street level. If police budgets were not so tight, a few days' surveillance would probably throw up some useful pointers to unsolved crimes. "So if I'm a customer with space here, how do I get in? Do I need to check-in with you?"

"No, man. You have a code." He pointed outside to a solid enough metal door with a touch-pad beside it. He then showed the view inside on a screen on his desk. "That's the holding area the other side of the door. You then tap in the next code. That takes you into the corridor with doors on either side." He clicked on his mouse and Ratso saw a corridor about 20 metres long with more metal doors lining both sides.

"Suppose I rent one of your walk-in spaces, what would the code look like?"

The West Indian pressed a set of keys on his desk-top computer and the printer spewed out a number. "We use three groups of numbers. The first two groups, they is the same for all new customers. These third ones are unique to each unit. The second numbers is random, man. They work on your first visit only. Every user must change these numbers to something personal and known only to him."

Ratso looked at the print-out. "And this is typical?"

"Yeh, man. Always fourteen numbers." It was not the answer Ratso wanted and his face showed the disappointment. "Never seventeen or eighteen?"

The gangly figure looked relieved as he grinned and shook his head. Ratso chewed his lip in frustration. Time was running out and he was in the wrong place. "One last thing." He clicked on his i-Pad and displayed a photo of Vijay Chetri and then of Lee Westdale. "Ever seen these two?"

The West Indian shook his head. "Not seen either of them, not here man. But that guy," he stabbed at Westdale's picture "man, he was an England cricketer. He never did come visit me. I'd have given him a few hints on batting." His cackle filled the room as Ratso thanked him and left.

Ratso hurried down Hatton Garden, jostling with dawdling and gawping pedestrians, their eyes glued to their smartphones or on the gold and silverware. At Holborn Circus he grabbed a westbound bus and took an upstairs seat. "Hi Jock! My first visit was negative. I'm heading for Surrey Hill. You?" He listened to the rasping voice. "Both negative? I'm not too surprised." He ended the call and spoke to a sergeant with the surveillance team watching Chetri's mansion. "Anything?"

"No sir. Chetri has not moved since he got back from hospital."

"No other movement?"

"A trader doing some repair job or whatever left some while back. Driving a white van. Loaded a couple of bin-liner bags. He was alone."

"Did you see it arrive?"

"The van? No. Must have arrived early. Before us. The only arrival was a guy in a teal-blue Jaguar. He's still in there."

"When was that?"

"First thing after we arrived. Just after nine."

"The driver of the Jag. Not the same guy who drove out in the van?"

"Can't be sure but unlikely, sir but. The Jag had tinted windows. Pulled up right by the front door. The guy driving the Transit was wearing white overalls, like a painter or maybe a carpet-fitter."

"Give me its vehicle reg. I'll put out an alert for the Transit to be pulled over if spotted."

"And if it reappears here?"

Ratso thought carefully before answering. "If you've heard it's already been pulled over, do nothing. If we haven't stopped it elsewhere, stop it up the street before it gets into Chetri's place."

"Grounds, sir?"

"Suspicion that the vehicle is being used to finance terrorism." Ratso reckoned this was a great weapon. You could beat the ever tighter rules on stop-and-search. Anyway, what the hell! Craig reckoned match-fixing profits were being used to blow up innocent people.

"Get me a full check on both the Jag and the Transit, can you?

Everything you can from DVLA. And if the Transit returns, I want a close-up of the driver – at once too."

"Yes, sir."

"Chetri. Genuine injury?"

"DC Younger saw him trip over a kid's skateboard. He howled with pain."

"Where is Younger? Up a tree? Hot-air balloon? In a crane?"

"Neighbour's house. We're ready to follow when Chetri leaves. If he ever does."

-66-

London

" **H** ello, my son. What's all this then?" The two watchers in the hotel turned to each other with a grin. Down below a white Transit van was parking at U-Do Selfie Storage Limited. "Nice one! We'll be out of here and down the pub in twenty minutes. Done and dusted before five!"

"You're sure? He don't look like no Indian to me."

"Me neither but the vehicle reg – spot-on." He pointed to the notes. "We was told to ID this vehicle and the driver. Start videoing."

They watched as in a single journey the driver carried in three small cases – one in each hand and the other tucked under his armpit. "You get a good mugshot?"

"Nah but watch me when he comes out, no sweat." They sat silently, cameras at the ready. In under two minutes. Eric Sommer came out, the self-locking door shutting behind him. "Stay there, you little beauty. Got you!. Ugly bastard an' all. Full face, every zit, every shag-spot." Moments later, Sommer pulled away and headed towards the river. "I'll phone the gaffer. Then a coupla beers, eh?"

Sommer was not worried about any tail now. Earlier, he'd shaken off the motorbike as he'd entered Theobalds Road. Since then, no other vehicle had spooked him. Delivery of the suitcases now made, he drove along the Embankment drumming his fingers to the music. Then, he stopped to phone Chetri who had been struggling to sleep. "Done it. Delivered, no sweat," he reported.

"Very, very good." The Indian's voice showed his relief. The temptation for Sommer to nick some of the cash, *maybe even all of it*, had stopped him from sleeping. He thought he could trust Eric Sommer but then you never could be sure. "Where are you now?"

"Near Waterloo Bridge, just buying a ham and cheese sandwich and a Pepsi."

After ending the call, Sommer got back in the van and humming along to One Direction on Capital FM, he laboured his way in the rush-hour traffic heading north. There was no easy route, so he headed up Archway, his thoughts now racing ahead to his next moves. At the traffic lights on the long uphill climb, he saw a police car coming from the other direction. Suddenly, its lights started flashing and the siren blared. At the same moment, it U-turned to pull in just behind him, ordering him over.

Sommer stayed put behind the wheel and wound down the window as a uniformed officer approached and peered in. "Good afternoon, sir. PC Dixon, Highbury Valley Police Station. May I see your licence?"

"Is there a problem officer?"

"Just routine, sir. A vehicle answering to this description is suspected of offences involving terrorism. Is this your vehicle?" As he spoke, the young policeman with a wispy ginger beard was peering into the rear of the van but not able to see much. He took in the two plastic sacks beside the driver and the empty sandwich packet as Sommer produced his licence.

"It's not nicked if that's what you're suggesting."

Dixon motioned the driver out of the vehicle as he read the licence. "You have the owner's consent, do you, Mr Sommer?"

"Do me a favour mate. Yeah. 'Course I have."

"And the owner?"

"Mr Chetri – Vijay Chetri."

Dixon walked back and gave his colleague the data who radi-oed it through. He then returned to the Transit and asked the driver to open the rear doors which showed it was empty. "And in the sacks?"

"I could say mind your own bleedin' business but I won't. Law-abiding that's me. Ain't nothing in here, mate." Sommer opened each black sack showing various items of clean clothing.

Dixon's face broke into a cheery smile. "Three saris? Enjoy wearing Indian women's clothes, do you, Mr Sommer?"

Sommer met the quizzical look with a broad grin. "Nah, mate. I'm doing a favour for Mr Chetri. He broke his wrist today. I took his family stuff down the laundrette."

"I see, sir. And Mr Chetri, where does he live?"

"In Enfield."

"And the laundrette?"

"Near Liverpool Street Station."

"Precisely?"

"Blackmore Street just down Bishopsgate beyond the station."

Dixon stood tall, tapping his left foot and scratching his beard. "Yeah! I heard there were no laundrettes in North London. What you reckon, Mr Sommer? Maybe a thirty mile round trip to wash a few clothes? Passing perhaps a dozen laundrettes on the way?"

Sommer shrugged. "Like I said, Mr Chetri said to use this one. Belongs to his cousin."

"And the name of the laundrette?"

"There you got me, officer." Sommer did not like where this was heading. "Mr Chetri just told me the address – number 3."

PC Dixon showed no surprise at the answer as he made a note.

"So what's this all about, officer?"

Dixon filled out a short report and handed a copy to Sommer. "Here are the details."

"You finished? I'd like to get on with the rest of my life."

"Did you go anywhere else on this trip?"

"Nah! Just the laundrette – oh – and Caffè Nero while I was waiting for the load to finish."

"Thank you, sir. You're good to go."

-67-

London

Ratso bustled through the giant semi-circle of the Aldwych and cut down into Surrey Hill. He had never been down the narrow street before but it was obviously a popular rat-run between the Aldwych and the traffic beside the Thames. The smell of bygone days rose from excavations on a building-site. Swirling dust mixed with diesel fumes grabbed at his throat as he spotted a garish yellow sign for the U-Do Selfie Storage, on his right and further down the steepening gradient. As he went to the swing-door into the Manager's office, his spirits rose. The customers' pull-in facility looked more promising than Greville Street. He felt the place just seemed right. Was that coppers' instinct? *Or am I getting ahead of myself?*

Wasting no time, he was in and out in less than five minutes. He dodged a speeding taxi as he crossed into the sparely furnished foyer of the Travecono Hotel just opposite. He ordered English Breakfast tea and grabbed a table far removed from some Japanese and African tourists who were surrounded by mountains of luggage and noisy kids running everywhere. Along the wall were clocks showing the time in seven different international cities. In London it was 18-20 pm.

"Stop digging, Jock. We got it. Surrey Hill," He forced himself not to pump his fist in the air. "Same code format. I'm telling Tolvey."

He speed-dialled his boss. "I need surveillance on U-Do Selfie Storage, Surrey Hill. Starting before seven tomorrow. Best spot will be from the Travecono Hotel."

"Not too late?"

"The manager recognised Chetri from three or maybe four visits but nothing since the Ryder Cup. Anyway, Chetri broke his wrist this morning. He's laid up at home. This place shuts soon. He won't get here in time."

"Lee Westdale?"

"The manager was Polish." Ratso checked his note. "Piotr Wozniak. He wouldn't know a world-famous cricketer from a sea-urchin's bollocks. But yes, he recognised him. Westdale had made several visits but none for some months. He didn't even know the guy was dead."

"Good work, Todd." Tolvey ended the call leaving Ratso wondering how, even in London, kitchen-staff could screw up English Breakfast tea. He stared at the grey hot water in front of him. *Looks like gnat's piss*, he decided, wanting something deep brown and rich in flavour.

He was still scowling at the dirty water costing £4.25 when his phone rang. After he ended the call, his mood was blacker, his fleeting moment of pumped–up euphoria forgotten. "I'm not paying for that" he told the Rumanian waiter. "It's undrinkable. Tell the kitchen to use a tea-bag next time." He stormed out with no idea where he was headed or what to do next.

The call had made his stomach churn and had left him with a look on his face as if his bollocks had been rammed up his arse. He had suffered moments like this all too often but he knew this was a detective's life – a fleeting moment of orgasmic high almost drowned by a shit-load of fuck-ups, dross and depression.

He needed somewhere to explode. Even with the wind

sweeping up from the river, Ratso felt as if his body was on fire and he yearned to punch someone, anyone, anything. He turned downhill, fists clenched, lips pursed and eyes glaring at nothing. He never even noticed the sharp drop in temperature and the wintry chill in the wind. What he needed was space to gather his thoughts, to rethink the strategy. Further down the hill, an empty KFC bucket lay in the gutter. He gave it a hefty kick and felt only slightly better after watching its upward curve before it tumbled back into the dusty builders' rubble.

-68-

London

As instructed, Det. Inspector Jimmy Morrison and DC Ivan Jenkins were parked on Mortensen Avenue when they got the message that the Transit driven by a Mr Eric Sommer had been stopped and searched. Disappointed not to be getting the opportunity himself, Morrison instructed Jenkins to take him back to the house beyond Chetri's. This was now established as a base. There, after being briefed by DC Younger that nobody else had come or gone from Chetri's house, he returned a message from Ratso.

"This is a five-star fuck-up!" Ratso opened his rant. "The Transit was stopped coming up Archway. That driver owns the Jag parked at Chetri's. He's not a carpet-fitter or tradesman. He runs a chain of betting-shops. He was our man, Chetri's gofer. He had been to a laundrette off Bishopsgate. Your lot should have been following him, tighter than a mouse's arsehole. This is some fucking snafu, I'm telling you."

"Sorry. Chetri was the target. I never thought we had to follow…"

Ratso wanted to say that Morrison never ever did think but he stifled the words. He had considerable respect for Morrison's usual efficiency. "You knew Chetri had broken his wrist. Sommer did the business for him. You never saw the Transit arrive so when it left, you just *guessed* it belonged to a tradesman who had been working there. We wanted to know where he went from the laundrette … *and* what he was delivering."

"So the stop and search revealed?" Morrison's thin face had taken on a hunted look as if his bowels were poised for free-fall. His face was flushed as he realised he had nobody to blame but himself.

"Clean laundry." Ratso spat out his reply. "Just clean bloody laundry. He'd obviously been to the drop-point. And your team should have been with him wherever he went, not slurping tea and wolfing down biccies."

"Sorry." There was a long pause. "My fault."

Ratso felt better for the apology. He knew that surveillance was a thankless task, laden with chances for a right old cock-up. "Okay, subject closed – for now."

As he sat on a bench by Temple Underground, Ratso decided to fess-up to Mick Tolvey while he waited for Sommer's DVLC mugshot to come through. His boss was calm about the setback. "Shit happens, Todd. You know that – especially with surveillance. Chetri's injury threw Morrison."

Ratso was in no forgiving mood and he raised his voice over the traffic noise and clatter of a train beneath him. "It was crap judgement. He had resources to follow Sommer." Even as he said it, he knew he was being unfair but could not help himself. Jetlag and the ticking-clock had him fighting to stay fair and alert.

"So what now?"

"Due to Morrison, we can guess but don't know that Sommer picked up cash from the laundrette. Did he deliver to U-Do? All we got was some clean bloody saris. Once I've got Sommer's mug-shot, I'm going back to U-Do."

"And the laundrette?"

"It's called Anil's Automat. I'm sending DC Petrie with her bag of smalls."

"Todd, we're closing in. I can feel it.. Anything known against Sommer?"

"No boss but him being a bookmaker hooks him into Chetri."

"You going to interview Chetri?"

"Not sure, boss. Tough call."

"Let me know what you decide."

-69-

London

S wigging from a bottle of sparkling water, Ratso looked at Younger's surveillance shots as they came through. Sommer had driven in to Chetri's spacious front-drive timed at 18-48 pm. In shot now were the Jaguar and the Transit whilst a panoramic view showed the gravelled forecourt and open double gates between twin brick pillars. From the upstairs room, Younger had captured somewhere between anxiety and panic on Sommer's face as he carried in the sacks of clothing. Ratso was just enjoying the haunted look in the man's eyes when seconds later, he saw the same face come through on the guy's driving licence.

The immediate priority was the manager at U-Do Selfie Storage before he shut down for the night. He needed to move at once. As he dodged between gridlocked vehicles and a couple of speeding cyclists, his frustration was returning and his cheeks were working like bellows as he climbed the sharp incline towards the yellow sign. *Should I door-step Chetri?*

Not yet, he decided, convincing himself this had nothing to do with cricket practice at 8pm.

Better to let Chetri relax.

Let him think Sommer had talked his way out of the search.

But suppose Baresi or Myerson had already picked up their pay-off?

No! No! No!

Wake up, Ratso!
They had been nowhere near Surrey Hill.
Unless.
Unless their surveillance teams had screwed up.

Arms pumping, he strode up the hill towards the manager's cosy but cramped office. He looked for the KYC bucket to kick but even that small pleasure was gone as he spotted it now flattened by a passing vehicle. Still, the prospect of hurling a red leather ball at a batsman's chest gave him a lift, especially anticipating the batsmen ducking and weaving to avoid being hit.

Ratso entered Wozniak's office and sat down on a tubular steel chair with sagging canvas. "Seen this man?" He put the mug-shot onto the counter.

Wozniak would have made a lousy poker player, his face showing recognition but no instant confirmation. "Ja," he murmured eventually. "So, for sure. Today. Maybe around five." His accent was thick but Ratso spotted the hesitation in his tone.

"Carrying?"

There was less hesitation as he relived what he had seen. "Three small cases."

"Vehicle?"

Wozniak looked an old forty and his face was a mass of wrinkles as he thought back. "A white van. Not big." He shrugged. "Ordinary."

Ratso was just imagining kicking Morrison's backside twice around the whole of Greater London when he realised that it no longer mattered. He now had the evidence he needed. "Which lock-up did he use?"

The transparent look told Ratso that he was hearing the truth. "Inspector Hatton," the Pole got the name wrong but Ratso let it pass. "I not spend day watching monitors." He pointed to a small mountain of invoices and contracts. "My in-tray. For sure, like sometimes I am watch down below." He pointed to the flickering grey image of an empty corridor.

"Yeah! It's not exactly Game of Thrones down there, is it."

"So you don't know which unit he went to?"

The Pole shook his head as Ratso flicked to a different screen on his i-Pad. "This guy been in today? Or this guy?" He showed shots of Baresi and Myerson.

There was no hesitation or flicker of recognition. "I say no." He twisted his lip upwards as he shrugged. "Or maybe yes. Maybe I not notice them."

"You recognise them? They're public figures."

"Politicians? Hot cash?"

"No matter," Ratso laughed. Inwardly, he was fascinated that two world famous golfers who had been media fodder for days could still be anonymous. "Phone this number if they appear."

After leaving U-Do, he dropped into the hotel and got quiet satisfaction from pissing away their lousy tea in the men's room. From a chair in the lobby, he briefed the sergeant who would head up observations from the hotel. "And don't drink their tea," he ended the call only for it to ring again. "DI Holtom," he responded.

"Inspector Ryan Floyd at Highbury Valley Police Station. We've met a couple of times."

"The heroin mob. I remember. How can I help?" Ratso remembered the square-shouldered Welshman with warm feelings.

"It was PC Dixon from this station stopped Eric Sommer."

"He did well. He got more details for me?"

"Sorry. No but a Mr Vijay Chetri has complained that his van was stopped under suspicion of being used for terrorism."

"The cheeky sod!" It took Ratso's tired brain a few moments to decide what to do but then he briefed Floyd in a few crisp words.

"Ryan, you're just the person to handle this. Right away, if you would." He then called Morrison to expect Floyd to drop by.

Calls finished, Ratso hovered, forcing his brain into gear. With Floyd's news of the complaint, quizzing Chetri tonight was a non-starter. Anyway, reports had Baresi browsing the fine wines in Harrods and Myerson strolling along Burlington Arcade with his wife. Nothing would happen tonight.

He checked the time and smiled for a nano-second. There was just time to make it to the last indoor-nets of the year. Ratso hurried to Temple Station, grabbing a westbound Tube to collect his cricket gear from home.

While hot-footing it to the cricket club, he called Nancy Petrie. "How's it going?"

"I'm in Anil's laundrette now. Nothing so far."

– 70 –

London

Marcello Baresi was exhilarated as he pushed his breakfast remains to one side and started to pack. The previous evening, his wife, Karina, had taken the flight to Florence where he would catch up with her but before then, he had bankers and contacts to meet in Monaco and Campione. Then it would be over the Italian border to join her.

As he busied himself in his Regency-styled suite, everything seemed to smell of his breakfast kippers and wheat toast. Ever since playing at St Andrews in Scotland, he had loved the taste but their lingering smell was a price to pay. From the closet, he pulled out and packed suits, jackets, shirts and roll-necks, every carefree movement revealing his anticipation of the day ahead.

Today was pay-day and his sun-weathered face radiated excitement. In his fine tenor voice, he sang along to Rod Stewart's *Beautiful Morning,* playing full blast on a music channel. The scattering of newspapers on the table had made good breakfast reading – no suspicion about the result and no serious blame of Myerson for team selections and tactics. Generally, the golfing journalists were crowing about the tense finish being great for the game.

As the Italian packed his gold cufflinks, Jermyn Street shirts and hand-stitched shoes, he thought back to the 2012 Ryder Cup at Medinah Country Club in Illinois. Lee Westdale's sales-pitch to him and Myerson had been brimming with talk of Medinah.

"Remember that day?" Lee had asked the team captains over sundowners on Baresi's shaded terrace in Jupiter. "Medinah?"

"Remember!" Baresi had exclaimed. "Lee, how could I *ever* forget? I was there, standing on the edge of the green." Baresi's reaction had been instant. "Unbelievable. The media called it the *Miracle at Medinah.*"

"I watched on TV, added Jake Myerson. "That last hole, my butt was on the edge of the seat and my bourbon was sinking faster than a coyote with its ass on fire. Can you believe? That final day, we were winning 10-6."

Baresi had taken up the memories. "So of twelve singles that Sunday, you needed to win just four matches and half one to take the cup. Europe needed to win eight and halve one."

"But, like crazy, man, Europe did just that – winning eight and halving the very last match between Tiger Woods and Francesco Molinari."

"14.5 to 13.5 to Europe. Some turnaround, eh?" Lee had enthused, still not quite ready to move in for the kill.

"Sure," Jake Myerson had agreed with a solemn shake of his head. "Worse still, that last match, we could still have tied the Cup. But losing? My God that hurt." He turned to the Italian who managed a consoling smile.

"Pressure!" Lee's eyes also oozed sympathy as he took a slurp from his frozen margarita. "It even got to Tiger! You know it, I know it. Any sport! Pressure can fry the brain, freeze the fingers, blur your vision. When Tiger Woods missed that three foot putt on the 18th, I really felt for him." He put on his most sincere look, cocking his head. "But for us, for Europe, it was bloody magical."

"Come on, Lee," Myerson laughed. "I'm sure Marcello wants you to get to the point." He wagged a friendly finger. "Give!"

Lee laughed but was still not quite ready as he acknowledged

Myerson was right. "The bookies went apeshit. Fucking apeshit! Having failed to win for the USA by missing a sitter, Tiger did the gentlemanly thing."

"Too darned right he did!" Myerson's face showed his worry-lines as he relived that moment.

"S'right," Baresi was as eager to intervene. "Molinari's final putt to tie the hole was the same length as the one Tiger had just missed."

Myerson brushed some crumbs from his slacks. "Yet Tiger, ever the great sportsman, told him he needn't putt out. So their battle ended up all-square but we lost the Ryder Cup."

"Knowing hundreds of millions were watching, Molinari could have missed," agreed Baresi. "Tiger should have made him putt."

Lee put down his drink and drew his chair closer, eager now to deliver his big point. "Guys, especially you, Marcello. Let me ask you something. Guess who the real losers were... and the clue is ... that it wasn't the US team." He saw them flick glances before remaining silent. "Okay, I'll you. It was the bookies. They'd have cleaned up with a tie but Tiger conceding that putt screwed them up something rotten. Multi-millions that cost them."

Myerson rubbed the side of his cheek. "It was a great sporting gesture by a great player."

"Guys, guys! You're missing my point!" Lee spoke slowly, his commentator's voice deep but melodic. "That Ryder Cup wasn't fixed. Nobody ever suggested that the result was fixed or that Tiger missed on purpose or deviously gave Molinari his last putt to win it for Europe."

Myerson looked at Baresi and saw a flicker of a smile break through until it became a broad grin. "So you're saying," Baresi then murmured "that us fixing the next Ryder Cup, wouldn't attract suspicion – because shit happens."

"Too damned right I am. Nobody ever mentioned a fix or thought there was anything suspicious."

"Rightly too." Myerson stood up to stretch. "There was no fix. In their wildest dreams, nobody ever thought about it."

"Or even in their quiet moments," Lee added trying to contain his excitement at the way it was moving. "You're right and so that means ..."

"Our fix wouldn't be spotted either."

"S'right!"

After Lee had left them alone for a few minutes to talk it over, the Italian, as he busied himself now with packing, could still recall continuing his debate with Myerson. "Lee's right. I saw the result for what it was. Great fighting spirit by our team and a beautiful gesture from Tiger – a spur of the moment act of generosity to Molinari."

Relief had shown on Myerson's face as he sensed the Italian's enthusiasm. "Sure, buddy, nobody never considered a fix, so let's do it. This fucking Parabolic had me fucked and then some. You know I'm in deeper shit than that Black Hole the astronomers discovered. Fixing this thing, the Ryder Cup... heck – it sure would help me out."

"Okay, Jake. Let's screw the best terms we can."

"Without us, Lee ain't got nothing," the American had agreed.

Baresi recalled how for several more minutes, they had debated risk and reward – weighing up Lee's outrageous plan against the size of the bribes they could demand. Now, as he filled his final matching case, Baresi laughed aloud as he recalled Lee's re-joining them and the high-fives all round.

"You two, you've a unique opportunity," Lee had enthused. "You'll be like conductors of an orchestra – in total command of the big calls. Medinah was living proof. Shit happens. Players crack under pressure. Under your captaincy, nobody will smell a fix at Wentworth. Why? Because it's unthinkable."

Twenty minutes later, Lee had agreed their terms. "You don't come cheap but the returns here on delivering a fix? They're good. My people will agree. Deal"

For Baresi and Myerson, it had been a great deal.

And today, like this morning, was payday.

The Italian paused beside the window looking down on the early morning calm of the London street, Too restless to relax as he thought of the millions coming his way, he jigged to the rhythm as Rod reached a crescendo. The Italian's handsome Lothario face oozed satisfaction as he relived Gomez on the final green at Wentworth. He glanced at his Rolex and his pulse raced faster. Even now Jake would be on his way to the pick-up.

After pouring more coffee, he anticipated the pleasure of stepping into the leather seat of his Bentley Grand Convertible – destination the Channel Tunnel and then France and Italy. Millions richer, he would be away, certainly before lunch. He looked in the mirror and saw himself grinning like a madman. And tonight? An overnight stop at a five-star hotel near Rheims.

And yes.

Perhaps the concierge could arrange some *discreet entertainment* to round off the day. He licked his lips, almost rubbing his hands at the prospect.

Again, he checked his watch.

Right now, *at this very minute*, Jake would be doing the pick-up. Soon he would be here, dropping off the cash and bank draft. After dividing his share between the six open suitcases, he'd walk the draft to the Davies Street branch of the Monaco-Monégasque Bank. Almost instantly, that money would land with a thud in Monaco. There, on the Rue Grimaldi and then in Campione, was where his key role would begin. It would be no sweat, not given his business associates in Milan, Turin and Naples. He would be arranging transfers to the five golfers before splitting the rest with Jake.

As he packed expensive after-shave and cologne, he thought warmly of Myerson. He and Jake trusted each other without hesitation. Now it was working both ways. He trusted Myerson to do the pick-up alone. The American trusted him to launder so that Jake's fingerprints would never be traced. Using his powerful Italian friends, Baresi had agreed to bury Myerson's cut, hiding it deep down and anonymous in a Naples wine export business, far from the prying eyes of the American IRS. Better still, the generous dividends Myerson would receive would never ever cross the Atlantic.

He clicked on the TV and flicked through the channels, pausing briefly at one discussing the fine arts to be seen in Florence. He thought of Karina, missing her cute ass, her perfume and her lust for life. For now though, her presence was impossible. She had to be far removed from his dark side of which she knew nothing. It was better that way.

-71-

London

The early morning traffic from South London into the City was building as Mandy drove onto Waterloo Bridge. "No! No car. Not even a taxi. I'll walk." Alex Anderson twisted to stare across the front-seat while his tone made plain this was an order. Mandy flinched and gripped the steering-wheel harder. This was a side of her lover she had never before seen.

Mandy took in the change of plan, her cheeks sucked in and her mouth twisting upward as her nagging doubts about Alex returned. "Alex, I'm not disagreeing ... but reasons?"

"Chetri will be a very unhappy little Indian. We must assume there'll be security cameras protecting the depository. Your vehicle reg is a dead giveaway. Even a taxi could be traced."

"The police?"

"Why would they be watching? Anyway, if they were, your vehicle would be noted." His voice had softened, the hand on her arm was reassuring. "Look, pet. I'm not known to them. Especially when I morph into an old man."

She said nothing, just for a moment feeling guilty about never admitting Inspector Holtom's interest. She changed the subject. "So I park up and wait?" Her thighs aching but her body still basking in the after-glow of a night of squealing and yelping sex, Mandy wanted to believe that she could trust him. But what she knew of him wouldn't fill a postage-stamp.

Why is he off to Newcastle today?
Surely, we should be celebrating?
Candlelit dinner.
Champagne!
Sex.
Champagne and more sex.
What isn't he telling me?
After he's picked up the money, will he vanish?

"Alex, I'll come with you. I can help. "

"No need. I'll use the rollalong," Once again, there was a commanding edge to his voice as he waved a dismissive arm. "Anyway, you've no disguise." He pointed to the kit on his lap. "With the beanie, the stoop, the limp, the glasses and the moustache, even if Chetri ever gets to see the recordings, he'll never recognise me."

Mandy shifted uneasily as she waited for the lights to change at the Aldwych. "If you're so sure the cops won't be there, I should do it. Chetri doesn't know me, beanie or no beanie."

"I said no," he snapped. "Got it? Park just along here. I'll be fifteen minutes, max."

She pulled in and after a flicker of hesitation, forced a smile and then blew a kiss as he climbed out. She watched him slope away, looking so different from his usual tall, elegant self. He disappeared, turning left down Surrey Hill, trundling the suitcase behind him. It was hard to believe this hunched figure was her relentless lover; the guy who for hours had her tossing and turning every which way on the king-size back at her home. In the long grey raincoat and purple beanie, he was leaning forward, shuffling slowly as if the suitcase were already full.

To take her mind off Alex, she called her parents in Newbury. Her mother answered, putting the two noisy boys on speakerphone. For a second she felt pangs of remorse as the boys shouted over one another in their excitement to pour out their adventures. After sharing their chatter and hearing about Legoland, ice-cream and hot-dogs, she ended the call. "See you soon darlings. Missing you lots and lots. Be good boys and give grandma a big kiss from me. Love you darlings. Bye!"

As she tuned in to Heart Radio, of Alex, there was still no sign, her other hand restless on the leather-covered steering-wheel. She had no regrets about using Alex to get back what should have been Lee's. This was for the twins, about securing their future. She took a deep breath and fumbled for her first cigarette of the day. As she lit it, she saw that her hands were shaking. Alex had been gone over seventeen minutes.

Relax.

Alex would not do a runner.

Would he?

-72-

London

Ratso had slept well after his Guinness and a couple of glasses of cheap port with a chunk of creamy Stilton. His feet aching after a long bowling stint in the nets, he had flopped into his favourite chair and, with no cricket to watch, had played Van Morrison at a lower decibel level than he would have preferred. At just gone midnight, his eyelids drooping, he had hit the sack, the stained carpet showing past occasions when he had nodded off, spilling the full glass from his hand.

Earlier as he was dumping his sweaty kit for washing, Kirsty-Ann had skyped for a seductive chat, interspersed with an update about Baresi and Myerson. "Trust me, we'll have uncovered much more by tomorrow," she had promised.

Before dawn had broken over the soulless rooftops, Ratso had showered and hurried to Hammersmith Station. During the journey to Cobalt Square, he had checked his messages in the near-empty carriage. Nothing had happened overnight, for which he was mightily relieved. Now he was seated with Jock and Nancy in the canteen, the Scot with his piled-high plate and Nancy nibbling at muesli from the canteen's Deli.

"These daft rules," muttered Jock attacking a sausage like it was still alive. "Dixon having to play the terrorism card to justify the stop. Tipping off thon Indian and his gofer." His eyes looked tired. "In the good old days ..."

Ratso thought of the message just in from Inspector Floyd. "Agreed, Jock but ..." he gave a sly wink, "consider it fixed." His wolfish sideways glance was not missed by either listener. Both guessed that, not for the first time, the boss had been dancing on the edge.

After debating whether to explain, Ratso decided to open up. "Inspector Floyd visited Chetri. He reckons this Vijay Chetri's a cool customer. Anyway, he owed me one and so did me a favour. He told Chetri that, during a terrorist investigation near Holloway Road, a van thought to be his had been spotted. He apologised telling him the vehicle reg had been slightly different."

With the efficiency of a mechanical digger, Jock had emptied his plate and now pushed it aside. "A wee bittie humble pie then?"

Ratso thought of joking that surely Jock did not want more food. "Chetri swallowed it – not the pie, Jock ...the explanation. Floyd then asked if he or Mr Sommer wanted to continue with a formal complaint." Ratso shrugged, one eyebrow arching more than the other. "You got to laugh! Chetri said he had always respected the police and so would drop his complaint."

"Nice one, boss," said Jock from behind his mug of tea.

"And Anil's laundrette, Nancy?"

"Boss, if you're a sad and lonely loser, you sit there staring at nothing or playing games on your phone. If you're a busy City-type, you drop off your stuff and it gets done for you. You collect later."

Ratso looked at his watch. "I can tell you're getting to the point. Go on."

"One customer arrived with a rucksack and a carry-on bag. He filled the machine from the rucksack. Then this Indian guy came from behind a mesh of dangling beads and offered him some Chai. He took the carry-on and they went through the beads and disappeared downstairs. Came back maybe twenty minutes later."

"And in the bag?"

"Aw, come on boss." Nancy laughed.

"Just kidding. You did well. We'll give this Anil guy the works. But not yet."

"And Chetri?"

"Still under observation."

"Aye and the Essex boys are visiting Eric Sommer's home."

"And U-Do?" Nancy stroked her hand across her hair which today was gelled and spiky. Ratso wasn't convinced it was an improvement.

"Coupla guys on Surrey Hill now, hoping to spot a Myerson or Baresi pick-up." Ratso looked at his phone. "Ah! Right on cue! Myerson is on the move alone.. Looks interesting. The surveillance guys are with him."

Nancy shook her head. "Christ! Watching out for international golfers! It seems unreal – and a bloody long way from where we started with the hammer attack."

Ratso nodded. "And maybe we'll never prove who ordered that. Or the scumbag who did it."

"So, boss? Right now?" As usual, Jock wanted action.

"Get Carole Viment down to the laundrette. Stand by to visit Baresi or Chetri. I'll go to Central 3000 and watch on the big screens with Mick Tolvey. If I'm right," Ratso's nod exuded confidence, "Myerson's collecting their pay-off from U-Do. Baresi checks out this morning. My guess? They divvy-up their cash, maybe at Baresi's hotel."

"Aye assuming Chetri hasn't warned them off for a wee while." Jock's growl again showed his irritation with rules and procedures.

Ratso agreed but his shrug was dismissive of the notion. "We need to nab the captains with the money and then raid Chetri."

"Reckon the golfers will squeal?"

Ratso looked thoughtfully at Nancy. "Against us, they're not famous golfers, not celebs. They're amateurs. Shit-scared frausters. If we catch them with the money, they'll need a damned expensive brief to explain away the money."

"Aye but what will they know?" Jock patted his stomach as he eased back from the table.

"Meaning *who* will they know besides Lee Westdale?" Ratso pushed back his chair and led them up the stairs. "Good question. Let's hope we find out" He checked his watch. It was just eight-twenty.

-73-

London

Jake Myerson would not have been a top-ranked golfer without the brash self-assurance for which he was renowned. Like any winner of the Masters and five Opens, he had suffered occasional self-doubts when his putting skills went AWOL or his irons were erratic but over twenty-two years at the top, he had grown increasingly arrogant. After retiring, he played only the occasional charity event but it had been his ego and greed that had then ensnared him in Parabolic – cocksure of his own judgement and hungry for the big returns.

His huge loss had done more than dent his bank balance. His self-confidence had taken a hefty blow. Losing his palatial ocean-front mansion in Jupiter and the Maserati being replaced with a Honda meant that snide digs and cheap jokes were plentiful from those who relished his deflating ego. However, awareness of what people were saying and thinking had only made his desire to fight back even stronger.

Marcello Baresi had stood by him, lending him occasional wads to tide him through the worst times. By maintaining his dignity and writing a best-seller about the history of the Ryder Cup, Myerson had once again earned increasing respect, so that his appointment as captain had been generally well received. Nobody doubted his understanding of the game, especially given that he had played in two winning teams.

He had first met Lee Westdale when they had been partnered in a Pro-Am charity event at St Andrews in Scotland but they had also partied after playing at Royal Birkdale and at Rye in Sussex. When, over drinks in Edinburgh, Myerson had explained the great returns he was getting in Parabolic, Lee had jumped in, both feet.

Now, as the American pulled on his baseball cap and black parka to visit U-Do, he relived memories of the life-changing day at the Parabolic meeting in New York. Far from Lee being abusive and mad at him over his lost four million, the guy had been crazily upbeat and had promised to explain later. That evening, at Patsy's Italian restaurant, he had been treated to dinner with unlimited Barolo "while we lick our wounds, drown our sorrows and plan for a better future" – as Lee had put it.

Over clams, calamari and filet mignon in Frank Sinatra's favourite restaurant, Lee had made his pitch. "This litigation will take forever. Years of uncertainty. My way, we're rich within days of the last putt sinking. By we, I mean you, me, Marcello Baresi and a few of the players."

As they rounded off their evening with Black Sambuca, Myerson's initial shock had turned to sneaking admiration for the Brit's escape plan. "Okay, Lee. Come on down to Jupiter. Let's chew the fat with Marcello. The guy's loaded, doesn't need more money but I reckon he'd play along to get me out of this hole." Then he looked doubtful. "But fixing other players? That's a whole different ball-game."

Lee had leaned across and clasped his wrist. "Simple. Pick the right guys as Wild Cards." There was a pause. "And remember – neither team loses. Think of it – the first tie in Ryder Cup history. Great drama. No shit'll stick to you." The sincerity in the Brit's eyes had been persuasive. By now, the image of the multi-million pay-off was busting the listener's brain. "Just think of the money,

Jake. You'll get your life back. The guys behind me, they'll provide the dollars to fix everybody."

He kissed Shelby, his much younger wife, as she slept off last night's dinner at The Greenhouse. She stirred momentarily but then he was gone, not wishing to speak to her now. As he slipped out of the hotel's side entrance still thinking of the three of them drinking on Baresi's terrace, he could almost relive the sound of the seabirds and savour the fragrance of the sub-tropical shrubs at that moment when the Italian had finally agreed.

"Best thing we ever did," Jake had whispered to the Italian at a snatched quiet moment as the throng at Wentworth dispersed. The nod in response had been enough.

Outside the hotel now, there was no fragrance – just a damp and murky London morning greeting him like a misty shroud. He looked around. Curzon Street was still quiet, just a few financiers and hedge-fund gurus starting to arrive as dawn turned to daylight. The last of the high-rolling gamblers had returned to their penthouses around Knightsbridge and Regent's Park. He turned towards Berkeley Square, cursing that there was no passing cab but his parka and cap kept out the worst of the drizzle. It was only when he reached Half Moon Street that he heard the familiar purr of a diesel engine and saw the orange glow of a vacant cab's light penetrating the drizzle.

Once out of the rain, he asked for U-Do Selfie Storage on Surrey Hill. The driver looked as if he wanted to chat about whatever gripe had already most irritated him that morning but Myerson was in no mood for small-talk. Since the cryptic message on the throwaway phone had confirmed three packages to collect, he had never felt such emotions since easing into the green jacket after winning the Masters. As he tried to tell himself to relax, his racing heart and moistness on his palms reminded him of teeing off on the 18th at Augusta with everything to play for.

Relax
This is a no-sweat situation.
Arrive.
Type in the code.
Exit with the money.

As the driver started to whinge about Uber and the new cycle-lanes, Myerson slammed the glass partition shut. On the two mile journey, skirting north of Piccadilly where cranes and bulldozers were still working 24-7, he never once looked back. That some-body might be following him was far from his mind. Not that he would have spotted the motor-cyclist or the BMW 3 Series that maintained contact with others in the Met's surveillance team.

Over last night's dinner with his petite wife, he had forced himself to appear calm despite wanting to leap up and shout a giant *ye-e-es* loud enough to reverberate from wall to wall. As they had demolished Limousin Veal with a magnificent Premier Cru Beaune 2011, he wanted to boast of the coup – but not just to Shelby. He wanted to *tell the world* how he had fooled them all. He wanted to crow about the riches now awaiting collection. Interviews, photos and media attention had followed his every triumph yet now, his most audacious win ever, he could never again mention.

He leaned back in the cab and adjusted his seatbelt. One thing was for sure – Shelby must never know. She would have loved the audacity and not given a shit about the illegality. But Shelby and secrets? *Forget it!* Within days, her Starbucks coffee crowd and half of Florida would have known.

Occasionally, as the cab crawled down Lower Regent Street and around Trafalgar Square, Myerson wiped the condensation from the side window, uncertain of where he was headed and whether he had reached the destination. Suddenly, after the fifteen minute journey, Myerson was interrupted by the gruff cockney voice as the driver slid back the partition. "Here you are, guv. U-Do."

"Wait here, cabbie. I won't be long."

Across the river, in Central 3000, Ratso clutched a machine coffee as he looked at the ever-changing camera shots. He was receiving a flow of updates from the surveillance teams who were secreted away, the luckier ones inside, the less fortunate outside, their hair matted and faces shiny wet.

"Baresi seems to be getting a lie-in, boss," Ratso volunteered as Tolvey walked in, rubbing his big hands expectantly. "We have Jake Myerson nearly at the facility. But I just heard – what went wrong over Eric Sommer? Nobody watching him after what we'd agreed?

"Resources, resources," Tolvey sighed. "Lack of resources. Like you said, he should have been watched overnight but the Essex boys had a major drug bust climaxing in Southend." He shrugged as if the problem was all too familiar with Government cutbacks on front-line policing. "They're dropping by his property any moment. News on Chetri?"

"No movement. Jake Myerson is just reaching Surrey Hill. There, see." He pointed to the aerial shot of a taxi dodging a cyclist before turning into the cramped parking area at U-Do. Seconds later, the tall figure of Myerson stepped out of the cab under the covered zone.

Ratso spoke to the hotel team. "Contact. Contact. Target exiting taxi. Cap and black parka."

"Positive. Positive for subject black parka," came the instant confirmation. High overhead but just beneath the dark grey clouds, the police helicopter circled, ready to follow the taxi to the next destination. "We have the taxi registration." From his position behind the rain-flecked window of the hotel, DC Giles Smith read it off and Ratso scribbled the number on his pad.

Tolvey cradled a cup of Darjeeling in his hefty mitt. "Where do you think Myerson will take the money?"

"God knows. Not into the USA, that's for sure. Cash ain't king any more. Harder to shift. Specially the amount these two bastards will be getting." Ratso turned to the view from the camera in the hotel as the taxi waited under the drive-through's crimson awning. "Hopefully, he'll meet Baresi. We'll arrest them both with the cash in their hands." Ratso was about to add something when he saw movement.

It was Myerson appearing from inside the building. "Ah, here we go then."

-74-

London

On arrival **at** **U-Do,** Jake Myerson produced a sticky from a yellow pad. He spotted the keypad and read off the first part of the code, tapping in+**409WGG**. The first time, he screwed up, his shaking fingers pressing 8 instead of 9. He took a deep breath, told himself to relax and tried again. At the second attempt, the heavy metal door a few metres from the manager's office clicked and opened inwards. As soon as he entered, the door clattered shut behind him.

Myerson took in the compact and almost cell-like area with the elevator beside him. The powerful overhead lights lit every corner of the bare cream walls. To his right was a small and empty waiting-room with four chairs, a table and some magazines for those waiting their turn to descend. On the wall by an elevator was the instruction that on no account should any customer descend with someone unknown. Beside the notice was a panic button.

Myerson entered the elevator and pressed in the next part of the code =**SJW.** Now he was secure. Only the manager could reach this lower level until he used the same code to ascend. The door shut and he went down one level before the door slid open with a gentle hiss.

He was alone in a corridor that smelled musty, deep down beneath a London street that dated back to the days of The Great Fire, nearly five-hundred years before. As he stood there, taking in the surroundings, the silence and solitude were both eerie and comforting. He was standing in a corridor about three metres wide, once again with a Panic Button on the wall beside him. Large powerful bulbs lined the walls, lighting up every crack and crevice of the ancient cellars. Overhead he saw a pair of small black cameras, one pointing in each direction.

The original brick walls had been painted cream and the stone-flagged floor was mainly covered in thick carpeting, giving everywhere a clinically efficient appearance. Along the corridor, on either side were lock-ups of varying sizes, some designed for just a few valuables but most were walk-ins with stout metal doors and locks controlled by touchpads.

His breathing uneven, he padded slowly down the long corridor and turned a corner looking for unit 3, the final digit of the code. It proved to be second to last and close to where the cellar ended in an impregnable wall, almost forty metres from the elevator. He noticed that the yellow note in his hand was trembling as he stared now at the door in front of him.

"Gotcha," he muttered as he saw the number stamped beside the narrow door. It was not a walk-in but was tall enough and sufficiently wide to hold several sets of golf-clubs.

Or better still, enough money to be rich for ever.

Desperate not to mess up again, he tapped in each number **4878903** with meticulous care. Seconds after the final digit was recorded, there was a whirring sound and then a click. Suddenly realising that he was not wearing gloves, he hesitated for a second. *Too late now*, he muttered as he grabbed the solid brass handle and eagerly pulled the door open, triggering the internal light.

For a moment he stood transfixed, confused by what he saw.

Or rather what he did not see.

No suitcases.

No packages.

Nothing.

Zilch.

Just three bare walls.

His confusion mounting and gasping for breath, he crouched down as if lining up a putt, checking if the emptiness was like an illusionist's magic box and the contents were really there lurking in a back corner.

Nothing.

Angrily, he swung the door shut and typed in a random number to lock it though why he bothered he had no idea.

In the still air, the silence was total, not a creak, not a rumble from a nearby tube tunnel. "Fuck! Fuck. Fuck." He pummelled his fists against the door, yelling into the silence. His voice boomed around the confines, echoing down the corridor, bouncing off the walls and metal surfaces. Despite the cool temperature, he suddenly noticed sweat breaking out and his heart started to palpitate, beating fast and heavily. His chest tightened and breathing was difficult. Beads of sweat started trickling down his lined forehead and he felt faint as his head and the walls around him started to spin.

For a second he wondered if he were having a heart attack as he steadied himself against the wall, his back leaning against the chill of the door. He remained still for three minutes or more until gradually, the light-headedness subsided. Then the surroundings stopped spinning and he found he could stand without support.

Pull yourself together.

He took more deep breaths and closed his eyes, trying to cut out the haunting image of the empty locker. It was another couple of minutes before he felt able to step into the middle of the corridor and turn to face his exit route. As the sweating eased, he wiped his forehead and then without a backward look, walked slowly towards the elevator, every step as if his feet were leaden.

Empty!

There had to be a mistake.

The packages had yet to arrive.

That was it.

Had to be.

Crap!

Don't kid yourself.

Yesterday's message was clear.

Delivery had been made.

Across the Thames and about twenty minutes' walk away from U-Do, in Central 3000, Ratso was waiting impatiently for Myerson to reappear. A message had arrived from Kirsty-Ann. It confirmed that US Border Security had eighteen recorded visits by Chetri in the past two years, mostly to New York, Miami and Los Angeles. As destinations, he had named expensive hotels like the Pierre, the Bel Air, Bellagio, Turnberry and the Beverly Hills. A big smile came over his face as he read on. *Christ, she's smart!* She was now check- ing for other guests who had visited the same hotels on those dates.

Ratso tapped his foot, impatient for Myerson to emerge. Another ping alerted him. This time it was Jock reporting that Carole Viment was watching suspicious activity at the laundrette and that Nancy Petrie had uncovered that Sommer had visited Mumbai and Dubai more than once. Five minutes passed and then seven. He had assumed the collection would be all over in a couple of minutes. "They can't be that heavy," he muttered to nobody in particular. His Nike trainer was now drumming the floor even faster.

"Maybe he's counting or checking it's all there," suggested Tolvey as he turned round from his seat beside Ratso.

"Ah! Here we go then." Ratso saw the door slowly opening and Myerson appeared under the canopy, his face looking pallid and confused. Ratso thought back to when he had watched him from Ma Mabel's bar in Tortola, just a few days before. Even then, in the fire of the Ryder Cup battles, the team captain had been the picture of nonchalance – languid, hand in pocket, laughing and chatting to his team or the media.

"Christ! He's got nothing with him." It was a statement of the obvious but Ratso felt better for saying it.

Mick Tolvey stared at the monitor. "Not what Myerson expected either. Look at his clenched knuckles and the wild look in his eyes. The guy's tormented." They watched him grappling in his pocket for his phone before he clambered into the taxi.

"Looks like he's just been rogered by a particularly randy stallion." Ratso was already on the move. "Boss, I'm going there. And fast."

"Fancy the stallion, do you?"

Ratso found a hidden reserve to give a rueful grin. "Something has gone very, very wrong. Like fucked with a capital F."

"Look on the bright side – maybe it's Shergar down there!"

"We'll need SOCO, boss. Fingerprinting everywhere."

-75-

London

After an early start, Eric Sommer reached Stansted Airport just after nine. He parked his Jaguar in the Long-Term car-park and two hours later was in a Boeing 737 accelerating down the runway. Once airborne, he relaxed, shutting his eyes, at last able to distance himself from unwelcome images of PC Dixon pulling him over. Now, he could look forward to a sausage and egg bap washed down with coffee to while away the short flight across northern Europe to Ljubljana, the capital of Slovenia.

As his flight was crossing the Julian Alps and about to start its descent, back in Wimbledon, Mandy eased her buttocks onto a high stool by the kitchen table. She was alone and the house was still and silent. She thought back to the last few hours, a spiral of smoke from her cigarette drifting over her latte as the enormity of what she had done sunk in.

It had been twenty-five minutes before Alex had returned from U-Do. By then, she had finished another cigarette and had been debating just how long she should continue waiting for someone who was never coming back. But then suddenly there he was, limping slowly towards her, head bowed and lugging the rollalong.

Only after he had clambered up beside her did his face burst into an ear-to-ear grin. "Let's go somewhere quiet till the bank opens," he laughed. Puzzled about the reference to a bank, she drove to a multi-storey in Judd Street where she knew that Lee had sometimes parked. She shivered at the recollection but knew that Lee would approve of what she had done, no question.

In the gloomy half-light and with nobody else parked close by, Alex stripped off his disguise and was quickly ready for the bank. They went round to the back of the Range-Rover and he showed her the cash. "Impossible to know how much but certainly into millions of dollars – plus this." He removed an envelope and from inside produced a bankers' draft for thirty million dollars.

"Can you do something with that?"

"Sure we can." As they climbed back into the front, he rapidly explained that a bank draft was equivalent to cash and that his bank would accept it from him without query.

"And all these laws?" Mandy had asked as they sat together killing time till the bank opened. "Money-laundering. Suspicious transactions? You know, banks making reports, enquiries?"

Alex had swatted away her concern. "I'm well known at my branch. I've paid in bigger than this on land deals. My Relationship Manager knew I might be closing a big deal. By City standards? Thirty million?" He shrugged and clicked his fingers. "Peanuts. In that branch, they deal in multi-multi-millions, even billions. Russian oligarchs, wealthy Arabs, you got it. So relax." He ran his fingers up her inner thigh sending ripples of excitement through her. Then he leaned across to kiss her. "Sure you don't want to split the thirty as well? The offer's still on. I don't need the money. I just wanted to dump Chetri and Pagano in deep shit." For a moment, Mandy thought he was about to add something but he changed his mind.

She hugged him, wondering why she had ever not trusted him. "I'll think about it. After we've counted the cash."

Now, as she swung her legs from the kitchen-stool, she relived Alex exiting his bank in Fetter Lane. "Done. That thirty million is now in accounts I control in Dubai, Mauritius, Singapore and Hong Kong." Twenty minutes later at King's Cross Station, she had pleaded to go to Newcastle. "I'm alone for two more days. We could have a great time. Please Alex."

"You wouldn't enjoy it. Me, seeing the Byker boys, some of me mates," as he had put it. "A lads get-together, supping Brown Ale till we all fall down." He looked deep into her eyes. "You get that cash home and we'll sort it when I get back. Tomorrow night, promise." His goodbye had come with a deep and lingering kiss. "Oh and be sure to wear that flimsy red thing with the black tassels. You look terrific in it – a real turn-on that is." He grinned. "Not that I need one with you." Then he was gone, striding confidently towards the ticket-hall, leaving her with the rollalong.

On getting home, Mandy had wheeled it inside. After tipping out the torrent of dollar bills, she felt overwhelmed. Was it two million? Five million? She had no idea and had no wish to count it on her own. They could do it together tomorrow night. She stashed the hoard back into the rollalong and pushed it among her other suitcases in the hall closet.

Now, after lunching on a couple of Ryvitas with cream cheese and a hefty gin and tonic, she broke her own rules by lighting up again in the kitchen. *But what the hell?* The twins were away and this was a moment to savour – a chance to think of the cash under the stairs and what it meant for their future.

Would that future include Alex?
A place in Florida?
A villa in Italy?
Or were they both just opportunists, hungry for sex?
Was their shared purpose the only glue?
She was unsure.
Of him.

And of herself.

She stared at a photo of Lee, uncertain even of her own feelings. Did she feel guilt? About what? Stealing what Lee should have received? Or guilt because of being seduced by Alex so soon after Lee's death? She drew on the filter-tip and exhaled a steady stream of smoke. *Cathartic.* That's what Janie had promised. She had been right about that. The last few days had been cathartic in spades.

After yawning and stretching, she looked through the window towards the back garden. The night had been short with little sleep. Alex had been beside her, beneath her, on top of her, all over her and as dawn broke, she had still been eager for more. Now, everything seemed so peaceful. The early morning rain had passed and a late autumn sun was catching the glistening lawn. There was a wistful smile on her face as she got off the stool and slowly walked through to the conservatory to daydream of the fierceness of their passion and of the money that would secure her future.

With the sun shining in, the heat in the conservatory was too much in her black slacks and matching tank-top. She opened the sliding door and a gentle autumnal breeze drifted in. The pleasing smell of damp grass hit her as she stood for a moment or two in the doorway. For the first time since Lee had been murdered, she felt truly at ease, listening to the chatter of the starlings from the birch trees beyond the lawn. The credit-card debts, the loans for the furniture, the worry of school fees would soon all be history. And for now, whatever the future held, she had Alex, someone who had proved he could be trusted.

Slowly, she turned away and with a contented smile spreading across her face, she eased herself onto the plush depths of the recliner.

After stubbing out her cigarette, she lay back, looking up at the wispy clouds. It was time to catch up on some sleep.

And after that?

Talk dirty to Alex.

Now that would be fun.

In the cosy warmth and comfy, stretched out full length on the recliner, sleep came quickly after the sleepless night. Soon her chest was rising and falling in an even pattern, her face calm and lips slightly apart. A few minutes later, from somewhere not far away came the sound of something breaking.

But she never heard it.

Never even stirred.

–76–
London

Alex Anderson had no intention of catching any train. For what he was planning, Newcastle never featured. All he needed was Walter Harvey to arrive from there. With time to kill, he took a short taxi ride from King's Cross to the Vue Cinema at The Angel in Islington where he whiled away a couple of hours watching James Bond sort out a megalomaniac hoping to rule the world.

For what he now had in mind, he needed focus which meant time and distance from Mandy. It was not the moment to relive her sighs and whimpers or to gloat about outwitting Chetri and Pagano. For what lay ahead, he needed a clear head and time to think. After Bond had saved humanity, Anderson walked up to Islington Green and ordered Cottage Pie in the Slug & Lettuce. While waiting for his food, like he always did, he wrote out scenarios on a scrap of paper, gradually deleting them until just one remained.

The clock on the top of the pub showed it was three-fifty pm when he headed for the hotel by the station. He had never stayed there but had occasionally downed pints or whiskies in the bar before catching a train. Today though, he ordered only a strong tea and biscuits.

As soon as he walked in, he knew that the cleaners had been busy, the air smelling of pine-forests. There was not an ashtray in sight, unlike the old days when he had propped up the bar, smoking roll-ups before catching the last train. Impatient for Harvey's arrival, the piped music that came from every corner was an irritation. With its floor-to-ceiling burgundy drapes, mirrored ceiling and huge chandeliers, the bar would have looked more at home in Paris.

When Walter Harvey walked in, staring around suspiciously, he too looked out of place. He spotted Anderson and in a few rolling strides, joined him. He reeked of alcohol and Anderson wished that he had banned drinking on the journey south. With no handshake and just a curt nod, Anderson offered him a seat and bought him mineral water. "No more alcohol. All ready?" Anderson quizzed. "You got what you need?"

Harvey patted the inside-pocket of his faded denim-jacket. "Ee, man, when we gannin'?" He asked in his heavy Geordie accent.

"When I say so."

Ratso had cuppasoup and a cheese and pickle on brown in front of him. They had been untouched for several minutes as he struggled for a new plan. His chin was resting in his hands, his eyes shut but his eyelids showed his speed of thought. A uniform from Essex had confirmed that neither Eric Sommer nor his Jaguar were at home. The neighbours had not seen him leave. From Enfield, Det. Inspector Morrison had sent through a photo of an arrival at Chetri's. He was a shortish, fat man in his fifties with a green polo shirt and jeans which his bottom amply filled. The face meant nothing to Ratso, so he had sent it to Forensics and on impulse, a copy to Kirsty-Ann.

Jock, with a chicken pie and beans, dropped himself onto a chair opposite. Ratso looked up from DC Viment's message that she reckoned Anil had a few "specials" who got invited into the back. "Ah, Jock, I've watched every minute since 7am until Myerson arrived. Only one person could have beaten him to the store this morning and removed as much stuff as the manager reckons Sommer dropped off. Three small cases, that was." Ratso pointed to the film of a stooped figure trundling a suitcase up the hill. "Let's call him Mr Rollalong. You'd get three small cases in there. Just."

"Sommer went to the correct locker?"

"Users choose a random code but always ending in the locker number, so we know it was three. SOCO confirm it was empty."

"Mr Rollalong. Maybe a disguise?"

Ratso stretched and yawned. "Forensics are onto it." He flicked forward to Myerson leaving.

Jock watched the brief clip. "Right enough, he looks shit-faced. Like he'd seen a ghost."

"Here's a positive, the only one, seeing as we can't nab them with the cash. He went straight to Marcello Baresi's hotel nearly three hours ago. He's still there." As he often did when his mind was trying to join elusive dots, Ratso found he was doodling concentric circles.

"We could drop by the hotel? For a cuppie tea and a nice wee chat?" Jock did not sound convinced. "Or maybe whoever dropped off yesterday left no cash there."

"Sommer left empty-handed."

"Anybody else collect last night?"

"We had nobody there watching but the manager said nothing bulky was removed – not that he noticed, anyway."

"Visiting the hotel? Doesn't do it for me. With no cash-mountain, some smart-arse lawyer would dream up a defence." Ratso sipped the soup and found it had gone cold and pushed it aside. "Someone ... Mr Rollalong knew the code."

"Could Mr Rollalong be Baresi or some guy he's hired? Double-crossing Myerson?" They both leaned forward and studied the enlarged photo of the stooped figure on the screen.

"Baresi never left his hotel. Someone helping him? I don't buy that. These two are great mates. Let's stick with that." Ratso fell silent thinking back to Carole Viment's comments about Mandy and the hard-drive. Peering over his big mug, Jock saw from the doodling and rapid eye movement that it was a time to say nothing. He took a noisy slurp of his dark brown tea and waited for whatever was about to emerge. Then he saw a flicker of a smile as Ratso thumped his fist into his other palm. "Lee Westdale knew the code. We have his note."

"Boss?"

"Mandy must have been lying."

"She crushed the hard-drive. Remember I checked."

"So what if Mandy took Lee's stuff off it first. Maybe Nancy was right and Mrs Mandy Westdale is a right little vixen. Nancy never did trust her."

The Scot's chuckle was infectious. "Well, she canna be Mr Rollalong."

Ratso was not to be deflected now. "So she sent someone." He stared at the littered table-top but was seeing nothing. "I'm bloody daft missing this." He looked up and saw Jock's blank look as his sergeant mulled over whether to agree his boss had been bloody daft.

"But the note never mentioned Surrey Hill or U-Do."

"You're right, Jock. So we have nothing better than an *assumption* that Lee had told her about U-Do. Or that detail was also on the hard-drive."

"Aye! If Lee had been alive, he'd have needed the location *and* the code to collect his dosh."

"Here's the story." Ratso counted off the options on his fingers. "One – Mandy was in on it all along when Lee was alive. Two – she wasn't but was intrigued and so destroyed a different hard-drive or thirdly she made a copy first or jotted down the best bits. Whatever … she is the one person besides the two captains who *could* know the code."

"There's a fourth. There's Eric Sommer in disguise?"

"It's a thought. Good call, Jock. We don't know where he's been today. He had the code so we can't rule him out." Then he frowned as he scanned through the images from Enfield. "Get forensics onto it but looking at this shot of him, I think the height and shape are wrong."

"Leave it to me."

"With her sexy glances and wiggling bum, I'm thinking Mandy's played me for a fool."

Nancy had walked up behind Ratso and had heard the exchanges. She joined them, a tray in her hand. Her face and eyes looked tired but she sounded alert. "Mandy? I still reckon she knew all along, straight from Lee."

"Nancy. We're going to Wimbledon. At once."

She looked at her tray. "My latte and salad?"

Ratso picked up his sandwich. "Bring them with you. We just might find Mr Rollalong too." He turned to Jock. "See how SOCO have been getting on down at U-Do."

-77-

Enfield

Vijay Chetri looked across at Enzo Pagano and wished the American was anywhere but here. "You needn't have come. Everything is under control." He poured himself a soda with difficulty.

Sitting on a sofa, surrounded by scatter cushions encrusted with multi-coloured jewels and sequins, Pagano glared, making clear that he did not agree. "I need a wrap on this. HOSS is still fucked with no explanation." He pointed a hostile finger and saw Chetri shake his head. "And I'm here because I don't want no fuck-ups on Jupiter."

"Someone hacked into HOSS. That's what my guy says."

"The sonofabitch had better have life-cover." Even as the New Yorker spoke, his mind had raced ahead. "Besides your guy who designed the programme, just three of us knew about HOSS." He snorted some phlegm from his throat before continuing. "Alex Anderson then. It has to be."

"No it doesn't have to be anything like that. A hacker is a hacker, a third party who stumbled on HOSS."

"Crap and you know it."

Chetri sat down and folded his arms defensively. Confrontation was not his style but this one was inevitable. "Remember at the Beverly Hills? You cut Anderson out of everything. HOSS, the Ryder Cup? His share would have been over $80 million." He glared at the American. "Maybe that bugged him like I warned."

"The guy had broken his deal with us."

"Enzo, you were so damned mean you never let him have his upfront back." He rose and moved closer and still closer till Pagano looked away, seemingly more interest in looking at his thumbnail. "If Anderson destroyed HOSS, it was your fault."

"The guy deserved all he got. That was nothing." Much to Chetri's disgust, Pagano searched for his cigar holder and lit up, each movement slow and deliberate. "Where do I find Anderson? He's dead meat."

"Leave it. We made plenty enough from HOSS."

"Where is he? That was my question." The hard-edged guttural voice bridged the gap between them as if it were not there.

"Golfing in Florida or at his Italian villa maybe. How would I know?"

Pagano said nothing for a moment, his eyes on the ornate plasterwork of the ceiling. "Okay. I'll track him down." He exhaled noisily. "So. Jupiter. Where's our winnings? Monaco?"

"Yours was transferred yesterday. I left my cut in Dubai. I might invest in a new marina project on the Black Sea. No questions asked there about hot money." His laugh was forced and nervous.

"Baresi and Myerson?"

Chetri's face twitched with irritation at every detail being checked. "Job done. Delivered yesterday to the depository." If his arm had not been in a sling, he would have clapped his hands together to emphasise finality.

Pagano twisted to put his feet on the sofa. "HOSS then? We gonna repair it?"

"I've had enough, won enough. After Jupiter, we're superrich." He spoke quietly so that Pagano had to strain to hear. "I'm too old for all this now. If you want to fix Anderson because of HOSS, count me out. I want a quiet life."

It was not the answer that Pagano wanted. He looked around and saw no ashtray so he flicked the ash onto the carpet and scuffed it in with his feet. Chetri's sallow brown face darkened with anger but before he could say anything, the phone rang. Looking concerned, he rose from his chair to one of four phones lying on a heavily patterned Oriental chest. Pagano saw the concern on his face.

"This number is emergency only," Chetri explained as he stood beside the phone, his brow furrowed and his eyebrows almost meeting. He picked it up and clicked, putting it on speakerphone. "Yes?" Close by and standing nearly three metres tall was the front half of an elephant, cast in heavy metal, its trunk raised as if ready to charge. He waited for a response.

"Jupiter."

"Yes." Chetri spoke with caution and a question in his voice.

"The lock-up was empty." The Italian accent was apparent to the listeners. The tone was big-time pissed-off.

"Impossible. It was delivered. Yesterday afternoon." Chetri tried to sound more confident than he felt. *Christ! I should have ignored the pain and gone with Sommer.*

"You delivered it? Yourself?"

"Yes. Personally." Chetri tapped his foot as Pagano shoved his cigar deeper into his mouth and rose to stand closer to the phone.

"Who else knew it was delivered yesterday?"

"Nobody. I told nobody."

"Then you lie. Don't fuck with me." Despite the Italian accent, the message was stark. "Lee Westdale knew. He gave me the code the morning of the bomb."

Chetri's nervous laugh fooled nobody, least of all himself. "He's dead. You know that." He noticed that the phone was shaking in his hand. "There must be some mistake. By you or Myerson." *Yes. My mistake trusting Eric.*

"I am coming over. You are going to pay up or regret it."

Chetri turned off the speakerphone and cupped his hand over the mouthpiece. "So?"

Pagano's eyes bulged and his face reddened. "Tell him to go fuck himself. He doesn't know who you are or where you live."

"It's not convenient today. Maybe tomorrow." Chetri absent-mindedly was stroking the elephant's raised trunk as he waited for a response. There was none, just a click as the line went dead. For a few seconds he stood staring at the phone in disbelief.

Pagano waddled across to the sideboard and poured a bourbon and lobbed in a couple of ice-cubes. "You delivered yourself, huh?"

Chetri licked his lips and his head nodded from side to side. "Yesterday afternoon. Around five."

"Then Baresi is bluffing. Trying to get paid twice. He don't know you live here?"

Chetri was sure of that. "How could he? Lee Westdale asked but I never told him, not even my real name. I said I lived over in Southgate. We rarely met anyway."

The American nodded in satisfaction. "So those two can go fuck themselves. No way are they conning us with their lies." As he drained his drink, he turned towards the kitchen. "Something smells good." He followed Chetri into the spacious kitchen where a pot was simmering on an Aga. "You delivered to the store. End of story."

Chetri used his good arm to lift the lid. The aroma of chicken dum biryani that his wife had left for him burst out stronger than ever. "As you say. End of story." He ladled out the chicken and a mountain of rice. "Help yourself to a beer. Or more bourbon."

"So long as nobody knows you or your address."

"Relax, Enzo."

-78-

Wimbledon

Mandy was unsure what caused her to stir on the recliner. Perhaps it was the sound of the sliding-door moving. She did not open her eyes, just shifted position as the sun was blocked out and a chill fell across her. She shifted again, thinking that the sun must have gone behind a cloud.

"Wake up bitch!" The voice was sharp and rough, London at its worst.

She opened her eyes and was about to scream when a gloved hand was pressed hard across her mouth. Leaning over her was a hooded figure, eyes barely visible between the slits. Her own eyes though were now wide open, petrified by the hooded man and the gun pointing at her head. "The money. Where's you put the money?"

The intruder had come from the nearby station wearing a baseball cap pulled low over his swarthy features. Only then had he switched to the fearsome hooded appearance. Now he removed the dirty black glove from her mouth. It smelled of diesel. "No scream, right. Otherwise …" he waggled the gun to make his point.

Mandy tried to think straight.

Who knew she had the cash?

Alex.

This wasn't Alex and he would never have set this up. It made no sense. He could have stolen everything at Surrey Hill.

"Who are you? What money?" She surprised herself at getting the words out because suddenly her throat was like parchment.

"Don't mess." The gun moved nearer.

"You've come to the wrong house. I'm Mandy Westdale. I live here. I don't have money." She paused and shook her head. "There's maybe ten or fifteen pounds in the kitchen. Take that. Take my jewellery. Just leave."

"Lee. He knew where to collect the money. You collected it."

"Lee? Money? Collect? From who? From where?"

Only Alex knew the cash was in the house.

It made no sense.

"This morning. You collected it."

"This morning?" She shook her head and forced herself to stay calm. "I was at the Health Club. After coffee with friends, I came home." She met his unflinching eyes with a cool steady look, stunned at how calm she felt with death from a snub-nose just inches away. The gunman wavered as he thought of the urgent briefing that had dragged him from his bed in a New Cross high-rise apartment. "The Indian. Lee's contact. Give me his name and where he lives."

Whoever the guy was, he knew something.

On Lee's hard-drive she had found an entry naming an Indian called Kirmani who lived in Southgate. Lee had added – *if I believe that*. Should she name him? Or should she point him to Vijay Chetri – the name Alex had told her only yesterday evening. Previously, he had only spoken about two *devious bastards who had shafted him*. Last night, over Chianti, steak and salad, Alex had explained that his agents had traced them both months back and "had the full nine yards on them."

"Enzo Pagano lives in Bel Air. He's a convicted criminal from New York with nothing good going for him" he had explained.

"Vijay is clever, cunning and well connected but scared of Pagano. He lives in some style. A huge three-storey mansion in Enfield. It has a pillared entrance leading into a gravelled drive between lawns and Hindu statues."

Later, while Alex had been watching snooker on TV and she was in the kitchen, she had scribbled down the two addresses – *just in case*, as she had thought at the time. Even now with her heart pounding, she could remember the details.

He won't kill me. He needs me.

"I'm counting to five." He jabbed the gun forward till she felt the cold metal against her forehead. "The Indian," he repeated.

"Okay, okay. The Indian. Vijay Chetri." She tried to change position but his other hand moved swiftly to pin her shoulder hard against the seat.

"You drive. No crap neither or you ain't ever returning. You wiv me?"

"I'll tell you, I'll tell you. He lives in Enfield. Mortensen Avenue. The house is called Shamoon."

"If you're pissing about and it's not the right geezer ..." the rasping South London voice left the threat hanging.

"It's true. That's him. Lee told me. Just go. Leave me alone. I'll not run. I won't tell the police. Just go will you?" The words tumbled out.

The gunman laughed but it was mocking and dismissive. "Think I'm stupid? Well I ain't. You or this Chetri geezer has the money. One of you is handing it over, right? Or you're both dead." He motioned her up and then slowly walked her into the house, gun behind her skull. For a moment as they crossed the hall, she thought of the money hidden beneath the stairs.

Should I tell him?

No way.

It belonged to Lee.

It belongs to us for what Lee did.

With her fingers trembling, she picked up her handbag with the car-keys and phone and led him into the garage.

"Got a number for the Indian?"

"No."

He pushed her into the front seat and climbed in beside her, immediately jabbing the gun into her side. "Now drive." Then he gripped her arm. "No. Wait. Got your phone?"

"Yes."

"Turn it off," he commanded making it sound like *orrf.* He removed the balaclava and from a sideways glance, Mandy saw her captor was just under forty with jet-black wiry hair, swept back. He looked like many a guy she had seen on public transport. His nose had been broken in a fight and his cheeks were pockmarked but clean shaven. She could not see his eyes but the firm chin made the profile strong.

It was not a face to mess with. Not with a gun in your ribs. As she reversed out, she tried to think straight.

Should I crash at a junction?

Pull into a police station?

Admit I've got the money?

But destroy Lee's reputation?

Lose the money for ever?

Go to jail.

Not see the twins for years.

Tough it out when confronted with Chetri?

Chetri will not blame me.

He'll blame Alex.

And he's safe in Newcastle.

That's good!

That's bad!

"Use the M25," he commanded with a jab in the ribs. She took a couple of lefts and rights, heading for the A3 and the motorway at Junction 10. Only after they were speeding down the dual-carriageway towards Guildford and the M25 did she sense him relax. He took out his phone and speed-dialled a number. She strained to hear the voice at the other end but could make out nothing. "Target One secured. No. She ain't got the money. She's given me Target Two. She's driving me there now." She listened as he passed on Chetri's details. A long silence followed as he listened to his instructions. "I'm cool with that. No sweat." Once again, he jabbed the gun into her ribs. "Both? Whatever it takes," he laughed.

Mandy gripped the wheel harder, biting her lip at what lay ahead.

God! If only Alex wasn't pissing Brown Ale against a wall in Newcastle.

-79-

London

Everything looked normal as Ratso and Nancy Petrie walked across the drive to the front-door of the Lee and Mandy's home. There was no car in the drive. No surprise. On every visit, the Range-Rover had been in the garage. The door-bell chimed cheerily but nobody responded. They walked around the side of the house and Ratso was tall enough to peer into the slit of a side-window of the garage. "Car's out."

"Shopping. Cinema with the kids. Who knows? She wasn't expecting us." Nancy had continued walking to the side gate leading into the back garden.

"Boss, take a look." The gate was half-open. She was pointing at the bolt on the garden-side of the door which had been forced. The receptor for the bolt lay on the ground still attached to a chunk of wood from the gate's frame. "Breaking and entering?"

Ratso said nothing, just brushed past her and into the garden. Nancy saw the urgency in his set jaw and in his quickened pace. The smell of fresh cut grass filled the air and Ratso absorbed the perfect lines where the mower had patrolled. He reached the door into the kitchen It was shut but he was hesitant to touch the handle. He continued crossing the crumbling red-tiled patio until he reached the sliding-door to the conservatory.

It was open. He looked around the garden. Nobody was sunning themselves or doing the weeding. "Locals round here would never go out leaving a door open."

"*And* they would set the alarm," Nancy added as she peered in. By the entrance was a stubbed-out butt tinted by pale lipstick. Ratso nodded to Nancy who immediately followed him into the warmth beneath the glass roofing. Today's Daily Mail lay on the floor beside the expensively padded green and white striped recliner. A ceramic ashtray lay on the floor and someone had trodden on it so that ash and another butt had spilled onto the sandy-coloured tiles.

"Not like her. Not leaving it like that."

Nancy was quick to agree. "House-proud to a fault."

"You know the upstairs. Take a look around. I'll check down here."

Despite the empty garage, Ratso was half-expecting to find ransacked drawers and mayhem, if not a battered body. He moved in slow steps, ready for whatever he might find – the study first, the kitchen, the dining-room and then the sitting-room where he had instant playback of Mandy using her long legs and short skirt to flirt with him. Nothing that looked ransacked. He waited for Nancy to return. She appeared looking excited. "Her vanity kit, make-up, washing-kit – all that stuff is there. She hasn't gone away but I reckon the nanny has. She had a suitcase when we came before. That's missing."

"The kids?"

"Unusually tidy room. I'd say they might be away with the nanny."

"Trace the grandparents. Check if she or the kids are there." Then Ratso saw the widening grin on Nancy's face. "Come on. Give. You're holding out."

She cocked her head beckoning him upstairs and he followed her into the airy en-suite bedroom with a huge California king-sized.

It was unmade and the sheets on both sides were twisted back. "She had someone here, presumably last night. The sheets are still damp. Could have been a one-nighter while the kids were away. There's no sign of any men's clothing or shaving-kit."

"Never play poker, Nancy. Your face is a dead giveaway. There's more."

Holding a tissue, Nancy pulled open the bedside drawer and pointed in. "I didn't want to touch it."

Ratso looked at the note and memorised the details. He also took several photos of the unit, the open drawer and then a close-up of the note. "That links her to Chetri. Enfield here we come." Already he was onto the stairs and they were bounding down as Ratso continued. "Nothing explains why she went out leaving the door open, a spilled ashtray and a broken side-gate."

"Meaning," Nancy descended the last two stairs, "maybe she left here with someone – but not whoever slept here last night?"

The slight nod and the raised right eyebrow was answer enough. "Get a uniform here. With the forced entry into the back, this is a crime scene." He stood in the hall with its parquet floor-ing and wood-panelling, debating which exit to take. As he did so, he spotted the cupboard under the stairs. An image of sports gear and suitcases filled his memory. In a sudden move, he opened the door and turned on the light. The tennis racquets, clubs and cricket-bag were still there, leaning against one side. But at the rear were the suitcases just as he had recalled, one of them a grey rollalong.

"Nancy – look at this." He held out his i-Pad and was flicking through the screens. "There," he said, triumph in his voice as he played the video of U-Do. "Snap!"

"Maybe it was the hunched-up guy that got his wicked way in the California king."

"An old bloke with a stoop and a limp? Not her style. That's someone like me," he grinned.

"Especially the limp bit, boss." Nancy grinned as Ratso's chuckle showed he had got her point. "So he was disguised. But who is he?" Ratso ducked into the closet and after wrapping his hand in a handkerchief, pulled the large suitcase towards him. It was heavy but moved freely on its four wheels. After tipping it on its side, he unzipped and stood in silent awe looking at bundle after bundle of US dollar bills.

"Change of plans. I want you here. Get Danny Willison here and the SOCO guys. Don't touch the suitcase till forensic have crawled all over it." He gave her a rare big grin. "Or nick a few dollars either. Tempting, eh? You could be set up for life." He turned to head for the conservatory. "We need Mr Rollalong's DNA."

"If it's him, there's plenty of DNA on the sheets. You going to Enfield?"

"Jock will set it up."

Once in the car, he briefed Mick Tolvey, trying not to sound like an over-excited schoolkid. "We'll raid Chetri after dark."

"An armed-response team?"

"These are white-collar guys. There's no evidence of weapons. No known violent history. Except for the possible abduction. But that may not involve her being taken to Chetri's place anyway."

Tolvey changed the subject. "Pity this woman wasn't under surveillance like you wanted. My bad call. As usual, resources. Well, lack of."

"Can't blame you for saying no, boss. We had nothing to justify it. Not with everyone else we're watching."

"Is she in danger?"

"Can't say for sure, sir. We don't know when the gate was

forced. My guess is yes because of the open door. But she *could* have left suddenly to collect the kids."

"Leaving an open door and millions in dollar bills?"

"Get your point, boss."

"This guy Eric Sommer. There's been no sign of him. Maybe him and Mandy had something going on? She wouldn't be the first to want a bit of rough, being a vulnerable widow and all."

"Not the way I see her. Vulnerable? Not Mandy. More like Lady Macbeth."

"Oh?"

"Boss, I'm thinking she's bloody lied all the way. She fooled us." He stopped to correct himself. "Well, me, actually. I'd mark her card as hard, devious, ruthless. But maybe now into deeper shit than she expected." He watched a patrol car appear, *on the noise.* "Another thing. Sommer isn't tall enough to be Mr Rollalong. Besides which I don't see Mandy overnighting with an ugly bastard like him. PC Dixon's report puts Sommer in the *scum-made-good* bracket."

"I'd heard that she'd made eyes at you, so she's not that fussy."

Ratso laughed. "So, try this – maybe it was Sommer who broke in, took her away?"

"If he thought she had the cash."

"But he never got it. There's no sign the place was turned over."

"Anything else, Todd?"

"If she *was* abducted, the guy must have arrived on foot and left in her Range-Rover. There's no parked vehicle nearby. DC Petrie will get some door-to-door going but I'm not hopeful of sightings. The houses are too well set back behind walls or hedges." Ratso was about to end the call when he had a final thought. "Baresi and Myerson. Any movement?"

"Not unless they've slipped out unseen."

"Hell, those two ought to be zapping about, all guns blazing. Wouldn't you if someone had nicked your millions?" Ratso ended the call still puzzling over that. It made no sense.

Unless they didn't know as much as he had expected.

-80-
Enfield

Vijay Chetri went to the central console in the kitchen where the remains of lunch were stacked ready for the maid in the morning. As the clock in the hall chimed five, he selected the button he needed. A single press and every curtain or blind in the house slid across or fell to a close. Lights appeared in rooms both upstairs and down.

He cursed himself for trusting Sommer who was not answering either of his phones. Screwing Baresi was bar none the dumbest game in town. Just thinking of the Italian's links to Naples had brought on stomach cramps. Okay, Marcello Baresi had been a top golfer. But coming from Naples? With Italian match-fixers linked to organised crime, who were his friends?

He shovelled down a couple of Buscopan tablets with some iced water before returning to the sitting-room. The wide open spaces resonated to the sound of Pagano snoring off his third helping of chicken and a half bottle of bourbon. He glared at the slob, bitter at his error in ever letting him be involved.

As he looked at the rising and falling stomach and the slack-jawed mouth, he hated the New Yorker and wanted him out of his life. *Or what was left of it.* He returned to the kitchen and phoned a limo company to get him picked up. His satisfied smile lasted only until he thought about Eric Sommer. Again, he dialled both numbers but only heard the rasping voice telling callers to leave a message.

Gone abroad with all those millions?

His stomach churned at the thought. In the sitting-room he prodded the snoring figure who jumped up with a startled grunt. "Your limo will be here any moment. The Sofitel at Heathrow Terminal 5, right?"

"What's that? Sofitel? Sure." Pagano's eyes slowly opened and he looked around confused. Then he removed his feet from the sofa and plopped them on the floor with a thud. His eyes were bleary as he gradually eased himself up to grab a final drink for the journey. The ice had melted but he slopped some icy water onto a generous Wild Turkey. He had barely taken a sip before a scrunch from the gravelled drive penetrated the room.

Chetri's face brightened. "Limo's here. I'll be in touch." He forced sincerity into the lie.

As the bell rang, Pagano picked up his travelling-bag. "You sort Baresi. Got my drift? Like fix him. Not my problem. I'm outta here."

-81-
Enfield

"**W**hat an unexpected pleasure seeing you, Enzo. Two for the price of one. Suits me. Going somewhere, were you?" Even as Alex Anderson spoke, he was into the hall followed closely by the thuggish menace of Walter Harvey who shut the door with a hefty push. Chetri had been a pace or two behind the American, eager for his departure and Anderson at once spotted the arm in a sling. Terror was written all over the bearded face at the shock intrusion. The Indian's dark eyes were flicking left and right and he was speechless, instead licking his lips.

Now he was inside, Harvey pulled out his compact Colt pistol and aimed it at Pagano. With a flourish, he forced both men to retreat across the polished wooden floor and back into the sitting-room. Anderson noted with distaste that it smelled stale, heavy with lunch, joss sticks and cigars. "I said, Enzo, are you going somewhere?"

Pagano shifted his weight from one foot to the other as he stood close to the wall where he had been corralled by Harvey, a pace or two from the elephant. "Heathrow."

Anderson laughed. "There's going to be an empty seat on your flight then."

Chetri had recovered a little poise and wanted to ingratiate himself though his voice sounded a good octave higher than usual. "No need for guns. Whatever your problem, we can sort this."

Anderson stood tall, steady and unflinching, his eyes fixed on each man in turn. "Me? *I've* no problem. That's you. Vijay and of course Enzo. When Walt has finished, your bad arm won't seem so bad after all. That's the good news." Anderson's open-mouthed smile was like a Bengal tiger about to eat its prey. "Anyone else at home or expected?"

Pagano leaned his bottom against the wall, a sullen look on his boozed-up face while Chetri answered quickly. "No. Well, yes. Enzo's limo. That's due."

Harvey now had both Chetri and Pagano forced back against the sitting-room's furthest wall between the elephant and an ornate jewel-studded plinth on which stood a massive bronze of Shiva, the Dancing God.

"Cancel it." Anderson beckoned Chetri over to the four phones. "Nobody is going anywhere. Ring now."

"The number is in the kitchen. On the table."

"I'll fetch it." Anderson was back in no time and handed over the card.

As he dialled, the Indian's hand was shaking. "The limo for Mr Pagano?" The Indian gabbled out the instructions, "Yes,collection at Shamoon. It won't be needed just yet. Cancel please. Yes. We'll need it later."

Anderson shook his head. "I don't think so. You two bastards thought you could fuck with me. Well you can't." He walked back and forward in front of them. "You stole everything from me." He grinned. "Well no guesses what I want. Transfer every last dime you won on the Ryder Cup to my accounts or I want you both dead." He moved closer to the listeners. "Three-hundred million you won? Would that be about right?"

"But."

"No buts Vijay! That's my figure, right or wrong." He paused.

"Transferred right now!" He barked out the words causing both captives to press back harder against the wall. "Agreed? Or shall I let Walt start causing pain." He turned to Harvey who looked eager to start at once, his cold-eyed look breaking into a smile and an exaggerated nod.

"Your own fault," retorted Pagano, some of his usual bravado returning. "Chickened out of our deal."

"We'll know who's chicken when Walt gets started on you." Anderson motioned to Harvey who rammed the gun against Pagano's chest. "I'm so pleased you were here as well, Enzo. Much more pleasure. I only expected your Indian toy-poodle. So … all the money or two stiffs for the price of one."

His sinister grin was wide-mouthed as he moved closer, smelling the fear dripping from the Indian's armpits. "Okay, Walt. Mr Pagano is going to place both hands above his head. Now!" He shouted the final word and watched as the American raised his podgy fingers.

Throughout, Walter Harvey had uttered nothing more than a primeval grunt, adding to his aura of demented and trigger-happy psycho. Suddenly, in a swift move and without warning, he smashed the butt of the Colt hard across Pagano's cheek with such force that for a second his entire face was lop-sided. A second pistol-whip smashed down onto Pagano's bulbous nose. A howl of pain filled the room and blood gushed from his mouth and distorted nostrils. Seconds later, as Anderson and Harvey towered over their much smaller prisoners, Pagano spat out two smashed teeth from his lower jaw and they fell with globs of blood to be lost in the pile of the multi-coloured carpet.

Anderson turned now to the Indian. "Arm problem, then Vijay?" Chetri was now unsteady on his feet, his legs trembling. The sight of blood spattering from Pagano's face had him shrivelling against the wall for support.

"No. No. Stop. Not me. We'll see you right. I always wanted that."

"Don't give me that crap. Your friend Enzo wasn't yet ready to transfer the money. You lose." Anderson nodded to Harvey who did nothing for a moment as if assessing how best to inflict maximum pain. Then he handed Anderson the gun. In a swift and violent move, Harvey ripped away the sling and grabbed the plastered arm. Chetri howled, his eyes rolling heavenward, as the pain ripped through his body.

But Harvey was not yet done.

He twisted the small figure around and pulled the injured arm backwards, twisting it up higher and higher behind Chetri's back. As Chetri screamed in agony, his legs momentarily left the floor under the force of the attack. Then, almost drowned out by the screams, there was a sharp crack as the little man's humerus burst free from its socket.

Harvey gave a satisfied grin as he let go. The Indian's arm fell heavily to hang useless by his side. Almost instantly, Chetri's knees buckled and his eyes rolled upwards as he slithered down the wall to lie helpless on the bloodied carpet.

"Your turn, Enzo." Anderson handed back the gun and relished the sight of the New Yorker's wrecked face, blood now staining Pagano's bulging green shirt. He signalled to Harvey. "Enzo is right-handed. He may need that to sign the money transfers." He nodded the go-ahead and, eyes bulging with pleasure, Harvey rotated Pagano's left hand so that the palm was pressed against the wall. This time the pistol's butt slammed repeatedly into the tufted dark hairs, pulverising the knuckles hard against the wall.

Anderson leaned forward as Pagano's involuntary tears trickled down to mix with the bloodied cheeks. "Ready now to sign?"

Like a parent with a toddler, he gave the American's sweaty skull a paternal pat and then stood back to leave Harvey in charge.

Pagano wavered, still reluctant.

"Not a wise move, Enzo." Anderson's curt nod to Walt was all that Harvey needed. He slammed a hefty knee into Pagano's groin, crushing his testicles and smashing his pubic bone. For a second, the American looked bemused, his eyes glazing over before he doubled up, hitting the floor with a thud. There he lay groaning, spewing more blood, his knees pulled up towards his bloated stomach. Seconds later, with a cross-eyed heave, he jettisoned a torrent of chicken lunch which spattered down his clothes and across the carpet.

"You will sign now, won't you?" Anderson heard a muted grunt from the squirming fat heap. "I'll take that as a yes."

Meanwhile, Harvey pulled across an austere hard-back chair and sat down. A dead-eyed look on his face, he held the gun across his lap watching the two crippled victims, one writhing in a pool of vomit, the other gradually recovering consciousness.

"I'm taking a look round," volunteered Anderson. He crossed the hall into a front room which served as a small study for Chetri. A heavy safe attracted his interest. There was bound to be cash but more probably gold valuables. With Walt's help, Vijay would give him the code. In the drawers of an oak desk were several cheque-books and a heap of papers that looked like banking data. He stacked them to use when Chetri had come round.

The dining-room had a table which seated fourteen but otherwise Anderson saw nothing of interest. He was just turning to check upstairs when a car entered the long drive and eased to a stop close to the portico. He dimmed the room lights and eased back the edge of the dark golden drape to peer out.

-82-
Enfield

R atso studied the map on the i-Pad as he was driven through Central London. At White City Tube, he had picked up Jock and two DCs. They were now on the noise to beat the Kilburn traffic, swerving and swaying as they raced towards the North Circular.

"Mortensen Avenue is about three-quarters of a mile long and Shamoon is about midway on the south side." Ratso pressed the symbol on Google and took in the street view. The avenue was just wide enough for three vehicles to pass and tree-lined with a tarmac surface in poor condition. It ended in a turning area beside a magnificent property with a green roof. He clicked on the arrows to see the kerbside view of Chetri's home. He held it up for Jock to see in the gloom as the sun disappeared to their left. "Not short of a few bob is Chetri."

"Right enough. We'll need big back-up to surround it. Beside those double doors at the front, I bet there's a side-door, one into the kitchen and another into the garden."

Ratso switched to an aerial view and saw the expanse of lawn stretching south from the building. "That garden must be two acres. At least." Then he pointed to the add-on at the rear. "And you're right. There's what posh folk call an Orangerie. That'll have an outside door too." He laughed. "If they bolt for the garden, neither the fat stranger nor the little Indian shrimp could clamber over that boundary wall. See?" Ratso switched to the 3D aerial view.

"Aye but see, the wall is only high at the back." Jock peered closer. "At the front it looks half the height. And there's plenty wee hidy-places, all thon trees and bushes. And a kiddies' play area. "

"Look on the bright side, Jock. Even you could run faster than these two."

"I just had a fish supper. I'm no so sure." Everybody laughed.

"It's some house. I reckon it sleeps twenty with never sharing a bed." Ratso switched off the i-Pad and checked his messages. "We know the family left. It's just Chetri there and this fat bastard – ID not known."

"Timing?"

"I've not decided – after dark for sure." He looked out of the window and spotted a distant view of Wembley Stadium. *One day, Fulham will make it there! Win the Cup Final. One day*! "We'll reach Shamoon in about eight minutes, give or take. Morrison can update us and then we cordon the place. There's twenty-one coming. Three TSG carriers are on their way." Ratso's phone bleeped an alert and he clicked on the message. It was from K.A. He read it to himself. "Enzo Pagano. Aged 61. Born New York. Sentenced to fifteen and served ten for timeshare scam in 1980s. Money never recovered. Now lives quietly in expensive home in Bel Air, Los Angeles. No record of violence but I am checking his old NYC connections. Passport photo attached. Taken two years ago."

Ratso refrained from adding a kiss to his thank-you message before explaining the new information to the other occupants. By now their Audi had crossed under the M25 and was almost immediately into the myriad of residential roads and leafy lanes that formed London's outer suburbia.

Between the rows of executive homes, Ratso took in the occasional park or golf-course. It was not an area he knew well but he guessed that as the road climbed north-west, increasingly upmarket homes would start to appear. Using the satnav, the DC driver had no trouble finding the destination. As they turned into the quiet but dimly lit avenue, Ratso called Morrison. "Any news? We're nearly with you."

"Next house on the left after Shamoon. Pillared gates. The TSGs are about a mile away. Ten minutes ago, a blue Honda Saloon arrived and two men were admitted. It looked friendly enough."

Moments later, the Audi was driven quietly beyond Shamoon to turn between the pillars of the millionaire's mansion next door. There were three vehicles in the open spaces of the courtyard. "Rich boy's toy," muttered Jock as he nodded towards a silver Aston-Martin.

"Never seen one parked at Cobalt Square, that's for sure." Ratso saw DI Morrison hunched in the passenger-seat of a 5 Series BMW. He joined him and was introduced to DC Ivan Jenkins who was in the driver's seat. Using effectively crisp headlines, Morrison briefed Ratso who in turn reported on the ID for Pagano. "Any advance on these other two guys?"

"The Honda is rented. We are working on who rented it from where. No names yet and the profile views of the men aren't perfect."

Ratso looked at the stills of the two men taken beside the portico outside Shamoon's grand front doors. "Good pics though."

Morrison nodded up and beyond the Aston-Martin. "Our guy is in that upstairs bedroom window. Lucky sod is being fed choccie biccies and mugs of tea." He was about to continue when a message bleeped in. There was silence in the car as Morrison studied the message and then showed it Ratso. He tapped the photo of a tall lean man. "There's nothing known of him. ID unknown but his mate – not nice at all." As a picture of a lived-in face appeared, he read off the screen: "Walter Herbert Harvey. Aged forty-three. Born

Newcastle-on-Tyne. Long-term criminal. Multiple offences including manslaughter reduced from murder and also GBH."

"That changes the dynamics." Ratso asked to see a close-up of the tall man which Morrison sorted with a couple of swift moves. "It's not Baresi or Myerson. They left the hotel and have just entered the Sexy Fish restaurant on Berkeley Square. I doubt they'll be opening the bubbly." Ratso then displayed a close-up of Mr Rollalong, head bowed as he stooped his way into U-Do. "What do you think? Same guy?"

Morrison thought for a moment. "Could be. Difficult to be sure with the beanie, the glasses and the moustache I'll get them sent through the Face Recognition programme."

Even before the first Carrier with the Territorial Support Group had slowed to a stop beside them, a message from one of Morrison's team reported that a Range-Rover had just turned into Mortensen Avenue. To Morrison, this meant nothing but Ratso's voice showed his excitement. "Mandy Westdale owns a Range-Rover. We feared she had been abducted. Looks like we were wrong."

"If it is her, she's turning in next door." Morrison passed on the news to DC Younger. "Standby. Maybe Mandy Westdale arriving." Almost immediately Ratso and Morrison had a photo of her in the driver's seat as she parked.

As usual when pumped up, Ratso thumped a fist into his other palm. "This must be a celebration – the big meet to divvy up. That's five of them."

"Make it six. Younger reports she has a man walking in behind her." Morrison sounded excited. And maybe ... shit! Yes, he's putting on a balaclava."

Ratso's moment of elation was killed stone dead. "Christ, that's not good! Not friendly. That shoves abduction up the list." He looked at Jock who just shrugged as he continued. "But no Baresi and Myerson. It's strange they're busy feeding their faces with posh nosh." He paused. "I'll get ready."

"Are we clear on Silver, Bronze?" Morrison turned to Ratso as he readied to exit.

Ratso's response was immediate. "Superintendent Enwright is Gold. It's my operation. He's made me Silver for the raid. I'll be in charge with Detective Sergeant Strang as Bronze and you as Bronze on surveillance."

-83-

Enfield

"Walt. Quick! Come here." There was urgency in Anderson's voice.

Harvey appeared, gun in hand, lumbering at a speed that he thought was fast. He saw Anderson pressed against the wall of the unlit dining-room peering through the gap he had made at the window.

"What's up?" As he spoke, two car doors slammed.

"Keep your voice down." He moved from the window towards the hall. "There's a woman coming in. Defend her with your life. The other guy I don't know but he's just put on a black balaclava. My guess is he has a gun in her spine. Here's what you must do." In less than ten seconds the plan was created and Harvey loped away with his curious rolling gait. Moments later the door-bell ding-donged. Anderson peered through the spyhole which confirmed his fears. Mandy looked petrified, her eyes gaunt and her hair hanging damp and limp.

He was about to open the door when he had a better idea. "Who is it?"

After an overlong silence, during which she must have been prompted, she replied. "Mandy Westdale to see Vijay Chetri."

"Mandy! It's Alex," he shouted. "I'll open the door. Those cheating bastards Chetri and Pagano are here."

Mandy felt the gun jab in her back. "Okay. Let me in."

Alex slid back a deadbolt and then turned a strong lock. He swung open the door and pretended to be shocked at seeing the swarthy masked man. "Hey! What the fuck? Who's this?"

On feeling the prod in her back Mandy came inside while the man in the balaclava said nothing. "He wants to sort Chetri." As she answered, her face showed her confusion. *What in hell was Alex doing here rather than swigging beer in Newcastle?*

Anderson laughed again as he shut the door. "Sort Chetri? Don't we all! Join the party." He turned to the gunman. "Who sent you? Someone that Chetri double-crossed?"

"They dead?" The man sounded concerned.

Anderson wanted to keep the conversation going as they stood in the hall, a curious looking group. "Not quite. Not yet," he pointed back over his shoulder anxious to let Walt get in position. "Anyway, who the hell are you and what are you doing?"

"Where are they?" The man who stood a head taller than Mandy jolted her forward so that she stumbled across the hall and into the lighted sitting-room. "And you," he rasped at Anderson. "Keep walking backwards and keep your hands held high where I can see them."

Anderson did so with not even a show of reluctance. Treading carefully, he did as ordered almost face to face with Mandy who looked better than she had just moments before, the colour in her cheeks returning. As he moved, he was figuring out what had happened to her. It took only a few shuffled backward steps for him to assume that the gunman had been hired by Baresi or Myerson.

Did this guy know Mandy had their U-Do money?

He assumed not.

That was curious.

She must have said nothing.

Impressive.

As they entered the huge spacious sitting-room, the stench hit them all as Mandy spoke. "Alex," she faltered. "This man says I stole money belonging to some golfers. Tell him it's not true."

Alex stopped but kept his hands above his head. He knew now what to say. He was just over a metre from the gunman's intimidating headgear. He fixed the eye-holes with a determined stare. "Buddy, you're just so wrong. It's these two down there by the elephant. The fat one's been wriggling around since his bollocks disappeared up his arse. He'll squeal any time soon. So will that fucking shrimp Chetri when he's stopped crapping himself. They stole my share. I guess they double-crossed the golfers too."

Anderson stepped to one side. The new arrivals could now see the squirming figure of Pagano lying in a mess of puke and blood. Chetri was groaning as he rubbed his eyes using his good arm. The hooded figure nodded with obvious satisfaction as he took in the scene. "Next, until you interrupted me," Anderson continued, his confidence now sky-high, "I was going to discover where the money was and get it signed over. Sounds as if you need cutting in on the deal." He risked lowering an arm to point at the figures by the far wall, Pagano's noisy breathing filling the air. "There's your enemy. Stop threatening the lady."

The slit for the mouth moved more than the eyes. "Chetri is the little guy. But that fat oaf? What's he in this?"

"Enzo Pagano. The boss. Pulls Chetri's strings. Together, they screwed me." Anderson turned to stare into the holes in the balaclava where just a hint of pallid skin was visible. "So what you here for? Who sent you? Why are you holding Mandy at gunpoint. Her dead husband was never paid." He spat on the floor. "Lee got nix, zilch. Nothing. Let me put my arms down. You and me, we're on the same side. And stop aiming at Mandy."

"No."

"So why is she here? She's been screwed by these two as well." He liked the way the hooded man was admiring his handiwork, studying the wrecked figures, Pagano wiping blood and vomit from around his mouth.

"Shut the fuck up, will you." The sinister figure motioned Mandy and Anderson to stand by the wall, just a few feet from the blood and evil-smelling puke. He then stood looking down at Pagano, his Glock at the ready. Anderson spotted that the man's hand was steady, not a sign of nerves.

Impressive.

Dangerous.

"Don't you fucking kill my prisoners. They need to squeal first." Anderson glared at the gunman, adding emphasis to each word. "I intended killing them in the morning but only after the money has been transferred. You can kill them then if you want."

What the masked man was thinking was lost behind the balaclava. Chetri though, had started to regain focus and from his slumped position, he looked sideways, head tilted against the wall. His dazed eyes first spotted Anderson but then as he looked up, he spotted the Glock. He seemed to shrivel even more, wincing as he tried to move. panic and confusion obvious from his wild-eyed look.

Beside him, Pagano, still breathing heavily, was now trying to regain a sitting position, his face a mix of dried and wet blood, his nose pulped and off-centre. The bleeding had slowed to a trickle but as he levered himself up with both hands on the carpet, they both became bloodied from the red mess in which he had been rolling.

Anderson caught Pagano's eye as he tried to make sense of the much changed scene now confronting him. "This guy in the mask reckons you greedy shits never paid Baresi and Myerson." Anderson wanted to remain in charge, calm and relaxed. "Has *anyone* who fixed the Ryder Cup been paid, you shitty double-crossing bastard?"

For the first time, the gun was switched to the American. "You two never left the money at U-Do and you're gonna pay for that." The gunman's voice was pure Camberwell, rough to the core.

It was Pagano who spoke, his breathing laboured. "Go on Vijay! Tell him. You delivered yesterday. Correct?"

"Right," Chetri's voice was shrill and faint. "I did. Yesterday afternoon."

"I don't believe you." The gunman turned to look accusingly at Mandy. "Someone here is lying. And I am going to find out who." He waggled the gun towards each person in turn.

Again there was a long silence. For a split-second as they waited, Anderson caught Mandy's eye but no message passed between them. The gunman continued to stare through the small peepholes at Chetri. "Like the guy says. You delivered yourself? Yes or no."

Chetri grimaced as another spasm of pain racked his body. Then with a shake of the head, the word somehow emerged. "No." Whether he was about to add something was lost in the furious re-action from Pagano. He leaned on one elbow and spat at the Indian, a glob of sputum striking him just below the left eye. "You lying sonofabitch. You stole their money!" Even as Pagano's shouted words filled the room, the gunman saw a puzzled look flash across Pagano's battered face.

He swivelled round.

Now, just a few feet away he saw Walt Harvey, a scary lop-sided smirk on his face. He saw the Colt aimed at his chest. The Geordie had taken a handful of silent steps across the carpet from the kitchen intending to creep up from behind and force the man to drop the Glock. Pagano's reaction had spoiled that. A single shot rang out and the hooded figure was jolted backwards, his feet catching Chetri's outstretched leg. He crashed down landing mainly on the American. Blood immediately spread across the dying man's black top and his gun fell free.

"It was him or me." As Harvey spoke, he was already leaning down to pick up the Glock before Pagano could grab it. Meantime, Mandy almost fell into Anderson's arms as she saw the corpse of her captor close to her feet. The only movements now came from Chetri and Pagano as they tried to wriggle free from the dead weight on top of them.

Anderson motioned to Harvey who walked around the trio lying on the floor and ripped away the balaclava. Considering his swarthy physique, the face was rather thin and the chin even more prominent beneath the swept back black hair. His eyes were wide open and lifeless. "He broke in and kidnapped me," sobbed Mandy as she fell onto Anderson's shoulder. "Thank God you were here."

"Explanations later." He gave her a squeeze but his attention turned to Chetri. "So, Vijay. You were telling us the money was never delivered."

Chetri tried to shake his head but the pain was too great. "It was. My gofer, he delivered it."

Pagano was unimpressed. "I don't believe you," he panted "you lying lump of shit. You told me you delivered it." He wanted to punch Chetri's face but with the pain plus the corpse straddled across him, he couldn't reach. "You ..." Whatever Pagano was about to say was interrupted. He never got to finish the sentence.

-84-

Enfield

The message from Superintendent Enwright was clear. Baresi and Myerson were still in deep conversation in Sexy Fish. A small team was in position to arrest them as soon as "you've sorted Enfield."

"So no golfers invited to the party in Shamoon," Ratso commented to Jock as they put on their body armour ready for the assault.

"Any weapons in there, boss?" Jock was gathering his Taser, baton and CS Gas canister.

"Not sure. Morrison reckoned that guy with Mandy might have had one, the way they walked so close. Harvey, the thug from Newcastle, has form but using a knife and broken bottle." Ratso checked the Taser that he had recently been trained to use. Satisfied it was good to go, he joined the TSG now gathered staying silent outside their carriers.

Jock could tell Ratso was tense and uneasy. He had seen his boss in action often enough but he knew from his rapid hand movements and chewed lip that he was concerned. Jock was right. Ratso was trying to predict events inside. What had started out as a simple raid on Chetri was now something that he could not fathom. A cosy drinks party celebrating the coup? Counting out money? Or had the moving parts fallen out?

Sometimes, raids could be planned with inside knowledge and

surveillance reports – perhaps even after bugs had provided every detail, hours or days ahead. Now was not like that. Rapid decisions had to be made based on very little information. What had been a plan to arrest Chetri now involved six people, including Mandy. Once inside, nothing was known of the geography and even faster decisions would be needed depending on whatever was happening.

It was less than ideal.

Far less.

Three ambulances drove past to park at the end of the cul-de-sac. To Ratso, they provided reassurance and sharp reminders in equal measure as he looked at the gathered officers, most of them young, keen and enthusiastic. Some, if not most, would have wives, partners and probably kids. At least, they all carried batons and shields and were kitted out with ballistic helmets and body armour if events turned nasty. As they listened to Morrison's surveillance report, before he handed over to Ratso, their faces showed tension.

Nothing I'm going to tell them will make them feel any better. Here goes.

"Listen closely – there's an Indian guy called Chetri – probably low risk. There's a woman – Mandy – unarmed and probably low risk. There's a fat older American guy – Pagano – probably low risk. There's a big thug aged around forty – Walter Harvey from Newcastle – dangerous and probably a strong Geordie accent. There's a tall guy, big build and possibly in a balaclava – dangerous and assumed armed. There's a tall slim, fit looking guy aged around forty – unknown quantity and so assumed dangerous."

Ratso took less than four minutes to add the finishing touches about the cordon he wanted and what to do once inside. After the briefing, the sinister looking group filed out between the gates, turning right towards Shamoon. There were about seventy metres to cover but their progress was swift and silent as they walked on the lush grass verge. The night sky and their surroundings were intermittently black whenever a cloud scudded across the moon. Occasional moonbeams reflected off helmets and visors, adding an eerie aspect in the hush of the empty street.

As they reached the gate, Ratso had the familiar feeling that always hit him when a raid was soon to start. It reminded him of when he had once been waiting to bat against a huge and powerful West Indian bowler. The hulk could hurl any delivery at 90mph and had the speed and bounce to inflict pain, concussion or even a lethal head injury. Then and now, his throat was like sandpaper and whatever outward bravado he tried to show, inwardly he could not ignore the shivers that every few seconds raced through him. Whatever was going on in there was far from clear.

Yet, when the action started and the bowler had thundered towards him, a sudden calm took over, all fear evaporated. He needed a repeat of that tonight as he approached the front doors beneath the white stucco portico.

Action please – the sooner the better.

-85-

Enfield

Total silence was impossible in the front yard once they had crossed the well-trimmed lawn. It was then gravelled right up to the portico. Nevertheless, in their rubber-soled boots, the team sounded less like an army regiment stamping around Horseguards Parade as they filed off around the house in different directions, treading lightly as directed.

At moments like this, Google's aerial shots had been invaluable and Jock headed straight to the side door into the kitchen. With him was a youngster in uniform who was ready to deal with the side-gate but it was unlocked and no problem, being designed only to be child-proof. Jock was followed to the rear by another sergeant, also with a Taser, and another slightly older constable tasked with guarding the Orangerie.

Morrison had briefed everyone that nobody arriving had triggered security lights so that Ratso and his team grouped under the portico without creating any obvious clue of their presence. As Ratso leaned against the pair of solid doors, he strained to pick up any conversation but for all he could hear, the house could have been empty. The only noise came from his stomach which was growling discontent. Imagining the pizza places they had passed on the journey made matters worse. Breakfast seemed a long time ago – and it was.

Ratso waggled his fingers and shuffled his feet, anxious to keep his circulation going. It was not wintry cold but lack of food and standing still, exaggerated the dropping temperature. He motioned to the officer trained in using the big red key to position himself to batter down the door. He was about to give the signal to swing the hefty enforcer when from somewhere inside there was a gunshot, no question and a woman screamed. Without losing a moment, the enforcer, packing a three ton punch smashed into the double-doors. Most would surrender with a single blow but the locks on these doors took two almighty swings before Ratso had radioed that they were going in.

The smell of curry hit Ratso as the doors burst open and the torrent of officers stormed in and making as much noise as possible to cause panic and confusion. To the left Ratso saw a downstairs cloakroom and empty study and to the right was a dining-room. Straight ahead beyond the hall and the stairs, were open double-doors leading to a well-lit room. He led the charge into what was the sitting-room, its size suitable for a Departure Lounge at a small airport. Behind him others scattered in different directions, some heading upstairs, all the while adding to the sound of pounding feet and shouting.

Taser at the ready, Ratso could see Mandy Westdale clinging to the shoulder of the tall slim man. Neither showed any sign of fleeing although both turned to face the noise and fast-moving action as Ratso raced across the empty space towards them. "Get down! Get down! Show me your hands" Both crouched and then fell prostrate, arms spread out sideways, Mandy rather quicker than Anderson.

As Ratso was shouting the command, he took in what seemed to be three victims lying in an untidy heap beside a wall covered in flock wallpaper. Surrounding the trio were bloodied footprints, smeared blood on the wall and a spreading stain from one figure's chest. A second glance showed that Chetri and Pagano were alive but covered in blood and incapacitated. Both were partially pinned beneath a corpse with a hate tattoo on his neck. He was staring lifelessly at the richly patterned ceiling. Beside him was a balaclava.

"Both clean, sir," came the reassurance as a woman constable finished frisking Mandy. Now handcuffed, Mandy and Anderson were lying close to Chetri's brown loafers. "There's one person missing," Ratso shouted to the officers in the room. It had to be Walter Harvey. Ratso sent out a message warning that an armed and dangerous male subject was somewhere in the house or might exit. He ordered a sergeant and a constable to take control of the room while he moved on. The scene made no sense – not three victims from a single shot but there was no time to check out what had happened because the shooter had disappeared.

From upstairs came more heavy thuds and shouts of Clear as the rooms were searched. Ratso looked around for other doors from the room. Among the expensive furnishings and larger than life ornaments including the charging elephant, he saw only one and he raced towards it. The only way Harvey could have bolted was into the kitchen. Levelling his Taser as he advanced to the open doorway, he had not even reached the entrance when he felt a blast of cold air. The outside door to the garden had been opened. He moved cautiously peering into the designer kitchen which was as big as Ratso's entire apartment. There was the usual array of white-goods, a red Aga and a large microwave all positioned on different walls.

In the centre of the room was a lengthy breakfast bar with a granite top. Beyond that was the back door, now open. Beside him was what he took to be a larder and he swung open the door not expecting anybody to be lurking among the herbs, spices and bags of rice and lentils.

Clear.

Suddenly from outside, came shouting followed instantly by two shots in quick succession. He knew that Jock and a youngster had been guarding the kitchen door. Racing round the table Ratso shouted instructions into his radio that the subject had escaped via the kitchen and was shooting. He called for support to guard the front entrance and to prevent Harvey escaping by car.

"Deploy stingers." Ratso wished that the armed boys were here to use their Hatton rounds to pulverise the tyres but at least stingers would shred the tyres if Harvey tried to steal a car to escape.

As he peered outside, he heard another gunshot from somewhere in the darkness to the rear of the house. In contrast to the mass of lights in the kitchen, the darkness was opaque and Ratso paused till his vision improved. Then he heard a groan and as his eyes grew accustomed to the blackness, he saw two of the team lying on the ground, one motionless and the other writhing but very conscious. "Two officers down. Kitchen entrance." Then he heard Jock's familiar voice.

"That way boss," Jock Strang raised his arm with an effort and waved vaguely towards the garden. Then it dropped back. "I'll be just fine and dandy. Go get the bastard."

"The medics are on their way." Ratso checked the other victim who was still breathing but very laboured and uneven. There was nothing he could do for him and with a killer somewhere around, he assessed his next move. He thought again of Google's aerial view and of the high perimeter wall around the huge expanse of garden. Taking a chance that Harvey would have taken refuge somewhere among the trees and shrubs further away from the house, Ratso decided to check something out.

It could be a plan.

However, unseen between the trees, Walter Harvey was making a plan of his own.

-86-
Enfield

Taking hesitant steps, Ratso left the patio and headed for the side boundary of the property. Using his torch would have invited a bullet. He counted the paces, anxious not to get disorientated for his return. He found he was moving slightly downhill across sloping flower-beds, filled with unseen plants, shrubs and roses. The ground fell away with each step. Twenty-two paces came and went as he imagined the distance between the stumps on a cricket pitch. In the end after thirty-five steps he reached the wall. It was dark brick and felt to be in good repair.

He stood on tiptoe and stretched one hand as high as he could and no way could he reach near to the top. A thinner cloud permitted a glimmer of light suggesting that it stood at least eleven feet tall, well over three metres. Unless he was an expert pole-vaulter, Harvey could not hope to scale it. Only at the front of the property was it lower.

That convinced him.

Keep Harvey in the back.

A caged lion – and best left alone.

He re-counted his steps back, helped by the distant light from the kitchen door. Desperate to use his radio but unable to speak or risk revealing his position in case Harvey was lurking nearby, he quickened his pace. He had to reach the house and to resume command.

There was no sign of the gunman as he neared a large bush that he had not even noticed on the outward journey. Under the moonlight it appeared like a giant shadowy form. Only then did he realise that somehow he had meandered a little more off-course than he had noticed.

He stopped.

Was that a movement ahead?

There to the left of the bush.

Ratso paused, unsure whether it was just the slight breeze moving the branches. He decided to play safe and to skirt round the other side of the bush, Taser at the ready. He shuffled silently to his right towards the kitchen and safety, ducking his body forward and treading as lightly as he could. Then the quiet of the Enfield night was broken by the sharp crack of a single shot. The bullet narrowly missed his left shoulder. A figure broke cover from beneath the bush and ran downhill, heading away from the house, bounding over the rolling lawn and out of sight.

Now you're trapped.

Only you don't know it.

Ratso raced between the rose bushes, the thorns ripping harmlessly at his protective gear. He headed for the light and within a few seconds was inside the glare of the kitchen where a curry dish simmered enticingly on the Aga. At that moment, the paramedics arrived with their torches, guarded by three TSG officers, all with Tasers. He called up Morrison and explained the situation. "I'm creating a fortress along the back of the house. He's trapped somewhere in the garden but it's too dangerous to go looking for him. I want the armed response boys and a helicopter overhead with a searchlight. If need be, we sit it out till daylight."

"No point chasing this mad bastard," Morrison agreed. Ratso then radioed ordering a blockade from the back of the house to the front.

One-hundred-and-thirty metres away and out of sight, hidden by the drop beyond the sloping lawn, Walter Harvey was prowling slowly around the perimeter cursing his luck that the wall was too high to scale. Though he had never passed a single exam in his life, he had learned a thing or two during his long term prison sentence. One of them was that scaling prison walls was not possible without help or special equipment. He cursed his mistake of running down the garden rather than to the front where the rental car was parked.

He continued his circuit of the wall, far removed from the lights of the house. As he took another step into the blackness, his knee struck something solid and he overbalanced. As he tumbled head-first over a low metal fence, he shouted an obscenity more from shock than pain.

For a moment, as he lay on the damp ground, he felt like surrendering but then recollections of prison life struck hard – the bacon-heads, the rub-downs, the razing-ups, the screws and the endless mindless routines.

No way am I going back without a fight.

No cops is gonna stand in my way.

He forced himself to stand before scrabbling around till he found his Colt on the soft surface beside him.

-87-

Enfield

Satisfied that the police line was rock solid and with Tasers every few paces, Ratso went out through the kitchen door to catch the two gurneys being moved to the waiting ambulance, its blue lights flashing off the other vehicles. He broke into a trot and as the gurneys were being raised into the vehicle, he asked one of the green-suited paramedics for news.

"The Scot. He's going to be badly bruised. The bullet hit his upper thigh but didn't penetrate the protection. The young lad, he's not so good but he'll live. The bullet hit him in the chest. Looks like he was felled and hit the back of his head on a low stone wall. He's starting to come round."

The paramedic clambered into the back and as the doors closed, Ratso saw Jock ease himself up, one arm waving. "Boss, you owe me a good drink." By the lights of the ambulance as it pulled away, Ratso saw the stinger across the gate being replaced after the ambulance pulled away, its siren sounding all the way down Mortensen Avenue. Satisfied, he went back into the house where Anderson and Mandy were now cuffed and seated in separate chairs.

Ratso was about to arrest them both when he realised that cuffed and sitting on two other hard-backed chairs were Chetri and the American called Pagano. Both were covered in blood and in obvious pain judging by their eyes and groans, The Indian's arm looked strangely lifeless and misshapen. "Get an ambulance crew,"

Ratso ordered. "They need to get to hospital under close guard." He saw a feeble flicker of relief on Chetri's gaunt face when he heard the instruction.

After the two men were slowly led out by paramedics, only then did he turn to look at Anderson full-face. He thought back to the stooped figure with the limp. He was sure he was now looking at Mr Rollalong. "Busy day you've had – and quite the actor. Collecting the money from U-Do and leaving it with Mrs Westdale." Ratso got no reaction, except a look of contempt. Mandy's tears had now stopped and he saw just defiance and hardness in her eyes.

He arrested them both on suspicion of money-laundering and warned that other charges would follow. While he informed them of their rights, Mandy's eyes fixed him with hatred, so different from when she had flashed soft and doe-like glances towards him. She too said nothing. As he watched them being led away, he was already looking forward to the interrogation. Who was this man now identified as Alex Anderson? Maybe an old cricketing mate of Lee's? When had he and Mandy become friendly … and why? And Walter Harvey? Why had Anderson brought him? Who had given Chetri and Pagano a right going over? Harvey? Or Anderson? The dead man who still lay on the carpet? And why? What was it all about?

"Sir, it's D I Holtom," Ratso reported in "Four arrests, one dead suspect and one target trapped in the grounds as we await support."

"It's heading your way," responded Enwright. "Our boys? News of the casualties?"

"Two, sir. One minor and the other unlikely to be fatal."

"Keep me posted."

"Myerson and Baresi?"

"They won't finish their puds. Arrests are imminent."

Ratso went back outside and informed the sergeant in charge of the line that he was now Bronze. "Any movement?"

"None sir but there was a shout maybe five minutes ago. Like of pain. Down there." He pointed way down the garden. "Since then nothing."

"Stay alert. This guy has killed already tonight." He listened, hoping to hear the distant sound of the armed response unit racing to the scene or a helicopter approaching to take up station overhead. Nothing. He checked with Central 3000 and was told they were both some minutes away.

As he looked down the garden from the house, all he saw was blackness and a distant orange glow of the night sky over London as a backdrop. Yet somewhere out there was the guy who had tried to kill him just minutes ago. Was he still skulking way down there or planning to shoot his way through to the front? He looked across to the next door property and noticed that the security lights were on, illuminating the rear of the house which was Morrison's HQ. "When did they come on," he asked the sergeant.

"Maybe a minute ago, sir."

Ratso's brain raced through the possibilities. The owners were exercising their poodles? Not so. They had orders to remain under lockdown. A passing fox or cat had triggered the sensors? Possible. Or had Harvey escaped the cage? Impossible ... or so he had thought. So? Unlikely but not impossible. He radioed Morrison.

No reply.

He ordered eight men from the line to follow him and started running. They hurried to the front of Shamoon, pounding down the drive, leaping over the stinger and turning left along Mortensen Avenue. In their bulky clothing, it was less of a gallop and more of a fast trot. Usain Bolt would have left them for dead over the seventy metres to the next house. Still breathless, Ratso stopped near the next entrance for a briefing. "Subject could be anywhere, even close by. We are not going looking for him. We had the front security lights in here disabled but not at the rear. Something triggered them. Armed response will arrive soon. Till then, we prevent Harvey leaving by car or on foot. Stingers are positioned. Understood?" He heard a muttered yes. "You – four of you – continue to next door in case Harvey scales another wall into that property. Deploy a stinger. I need to reach Morrison and Jenkins. They're not responding."

An ambulance had moved into the drive and was parked just in from the entrance, the stinger now blocking any exit. With three of the team Ratso took cover beside the ambulance to assess the position.

Overhead, the moon was struggling to penetrate the cloud cover. From somewhere came the distant sound of a baby crying but otherwise, all was quiet. There was no sign of any movement around the driveway. No sound either.

Harvey is no pole-vaulter.

How in hell could he have got out?

It must have been a fox.

He's still trapped next door.

Where's that damned helicopter?

Where are the armed response boys?

The BMW was parked nearer the house, some twenty-five paces away. In the silvery half-light, at first he saw nothing unusual. Then, just as he was about to race to join Morrison in the car, a chill ran through him and he swallowed hard. The BMW's front was facing them. He looked again and was sure. Someone was moving close to the passenger-side where Morrison had been seated. As he peered again, it looked like there was more than one person moving. Then the sliver of moon was gone leaving almost blackness and a vague impression that the moving silhouette looked wrong for just one person.

No radio contact from Morrison and Jenkins.
Nobody beside the BMW was speaking.
Morrison and Jenkins out of their car?
Why?
Morrison and Walter Harvey?
Jenkins and Harvey?
Is there even a third person at all?

He raised his Taser knowing that a five second burst at this range would take down any target. At that moment, the Beamer's passenger door was thrown open and the internal light came on and he saw movement. He knew then that Morrison must be clambering out. Or had been ordered out.

He wouldn't do that without good reason.

The two figures had to be Jenkins and Harvey.

Jenkins the driver being held at gunpoint?

But which man was which? Assisted now by the light from the car, Ratso watched Morrison's shape rise to create a shadowy trio.

Would Morrison try something?

Unlikely.

Not if Harvey had a gun at Jenkins's head.

The two figures merged into three. As the car door shut and the light faded out, the three figures then skirted the front of the vehicle and grouped near the driver's side. "Fucking pigs. Get down. Kneel. There." The strong barked command carried across the short distance and Ratso was now sure. This was Harvey, his Geordie accent unmistakeable.

Yet Ratso saw no sign of movement. "Get down you bastards. Now." This time, Ratso saw the group break up and two shapes slowly sank from sight, hidden beyond the bodywork. A scudding cloud moved eastwards and thinned improving a side-on view of the standing figure.

Still not good, not good enough.

The angle and the vehicle's roof prevented a clear target.

Missing was not an option.

Then, dimly seen, Harvey seemed to turn away to stand directly over the unseen kneeling figures. It was now or never. Instantly, Ratso left the protection of the ambulance and ran fast but moving left for an unimpeded shot at the bulky figure. As he drew closer, he saw then that the gun was now just inches from someone's down-turned head. Might tasering cause Harvey's trigger finger to spasm and fire?

He dare not risk that.

The gun had to be pointing his way.

"Harvey! Drop the gun!" Ratso's rasping shout ripped through the silence when he was just a dozen paces away. Surprised by the intervention, the figure swung round and for a moment, his gun no longer pointed at the captive. He started to raise his arm to aim at Ratso's running figure, Ratso squeezed on the bright yellow Taser. 50,000 volts surged out. Almost instantly Harvey suffered loss of voluntary muscle control. Harvey fired too as he was struck but he was already falling from the force of the impact. The bullet flew harmlessly skyward as Harvey was hurled off his feet.

In a couple of seconds, Ratso was beside the BMW. He looked at Harvey writhing on the ground, his legs and arms flailing out of control. He shone his torch and quickly spotted the gun close to the car. He kicked it way out of Harvey's reach but the man was helpless anyway. "You okay, mate?" Ratso watched as Morrison pushed himself up from his kneeling position.

"Shit! That was close. Thanks, Todd."

Ratso helped up Jenkins who was shaking uncontrollably while two of the other officers had now raced forward to stand over Harvey. As his gyrations slowed they then cuffed him. "How in hell did Harvey escape from Shamoon?" There was no blame or accusation in Morrison's tone, just bewilderment. Morrison peered at Ratso, hoping for an explanation.

Ratso had no answer to that and said so. "I'll check that out. Unless you were Houdini, it looked impossible."

"When this thug appeared beside Jenkins, there was no time to lock the door. He came from nowhere. Jenkins was forced out at gunpoint. The car's internal light then came on so that Harvey then he saw me. That's when he warned that one peep from me and Jenkins was dead."

"But there was radio silence for at least a couple of minutes while we raced here?"

"Brave lad, Jenkins. He tossed the key into a bush over there and Harvey forced him to look for it with him. After finding it, they returned but I still saw no chance, couldn't risk anything. Not knowing he'd killed already. Then he ordered me out."

Ratso heard the sound of a revving engine speeding closer on Mortensen Avenue. "Thank God! Here comes the cavalry. Just in time." He laughed as he put an arm across Jenkins' still trembling shoulder

-88-

London

Jock had not even been kept in hospital overnight but was still limping three days later as he joined the team in the upstairs room for the latest debrief. As he strolled back and forth on the small podium, Ratso's eyes and voice showed that he had not slept much these past seventy-two hours but even so, his movements confirmed that he was still fired up. It was as if his body were fist-pumping a never-ending *ye-e-es*.

"Firstly, I'd like to thank all of you. This was a team effort." He strolled towards his sergeant. "I'm delighted to see that Jock is okay though his top speed now is even slower than a one-legged centipede. Even when he recovers though, the difference will be imperceptible." He got plenty of laughs at that, not least from the Scot. "As for Constable O'Reilly who was concussed from hitting his head, I've visited him in hospital and he's doing just great, no lasting ill-effects."

He looked over the heads to the back of the room. "We got lucky – but we deserved it. Great effort by all of you. So here's the position." He sipped a double espresso in a carton that he had just bought at Starbucks. "Myerson and Baresi have both been charged. Neither is saying anything. They were refused bail, despite their hot-shot lawyers."

"Evidence, sir? We solid?" It was DC Carole Viment.

"We have a treasure trove called Mandy's hard-drive. She's

saying nothing but the hard-drive shouts loud and clear. "Either she knew all along or was suspicious of what was on Lee's desktop computer. My take is the little vixen made the duplicate and covered herself by getting the original certified as destroyed."

"Where was it?" It was Viment again.

"Credit to DC Petrie." He waited for eyes to turn towards her and he saw her cheeks colour, adding to an attractive smile. "Nancy saw grit spilled around a sack in the garage. There had been no spillage on our first visit." Ratso laughed. "Okay the weather hasn't been like Vegas but there's been no need to grit. The hard-drive was deep down in the sack." He paused to let the congratulations die down as Nancy beamed at the sixteen officers surrounding her. Mick Tolvey breezed in and heard the compliment. He shook her hand before taking an empty seat towards the back. What she did not yet know was that, having completed the first three stages, she had just been approved for the final stage of the promotion process to sergeant. Tolvey reckoned that this was Ratso's moment and now was not the best time to tell her that for the next twelve months she would be an acting-sergeant.

"The hard drive named names – Baresi and Myerson of course. The Wild Cards too. We now know the cut for Lee had he lived. Better still, it included who he was bribing in the cricket world. Mark Rayner we knew. But Craig Carter owes us a good drink – we got the names of two umpires, several ground-staff and fourteen players including Nitin Mithi. We even got some bent team physios passing on info about fitness and team morale."

"Mithi's murder, sir?"

"I've given the Indian CBI details of payments he received from Lee but who killed him? No decision yet." He checked his notes before continuing. "In English cricket, I'm working with Craig. You'll be busy enough. There's a load of guys out there crapping themselves following news of Mandy's arrest. I want at least nine more arrests over the next few days."

"Mark Rayner? His wife and baby?"

"As you know, we had nothing on him. He had stripped, destroyed or hidden anything linking him to fixing."

"Aye but what about the hard-drive?" It was Jock Strang who still felt bad at not being more suspicious over its destruction.

"You're right. Lee's hard-drive showed Rayner was paid just under three million in cash. Where it went?" Ratso shrugged. "That secret died with him. Lee's notes show that Rayner was full of remorse, so he tried to persuade Chetri to let him go. He refused. You know the rest."

"Aye but what about the attack on the wife and wee bairn?"

"Jock, I'll come to that."

Ratso went over to a low table and clicked on the laptop. "Most of you will not have seen this." It was a photo of a plank and a large segment of an oak tree lying in some long grass. He clicked and showed it again, this time as a makeshift see-saw in the kiddie's playground, the plank balanced over the large log. Beside it were a small metal rocking-horse, its spring set in concrete and a double swing. "Here's what Walter Harvey used to escape." He clicked to the next shot and there was a ripple of admiration and gasps. "That wall is three-point-three metres high. Nearly eleven feet. I had assumed he was caged." The photo showed that Harvey had taken the plank and leaned it high up the wall and secured it at the foot by the weight of the slab of oak.

"You charged Harvey, boss?"

"Yes, Nancy. This morning. Murder and attempted murder."

He looked at his jottings before continuing. "Mandy? She's proving to be a tough nut, not saying anything. Alex Anderson, on the other hand, is talking plenty. Having brought Walter Harvey to Shamoon, if he wants to avoid a life sentence, he needs to talk plenty." He pointed the control and revealed the dead man lying on the carpet. "The guy in the balaclava. His name was Piero De Campo. Sounds Italian, huh?" Ratso lowered his eyes as he shook his head. "Not so. By chance, D S Tosh Watson had come across him. Rated him as pure evil. De Campo is, well was, a second generation Italian living in a rough part of Camberwell. He mixed with a south London mob." He looked at Tosh for comment.

"Don't go shedding no tears for this sod. We couldn't never get the evidence but this punk was an enforcer used by Italian mobsters and linked to laundering Brinks-Mat gold."

Jock lowered his sandwich for a moment. "Hired by Baresi?"

"Good question," Ratso responded. "We're getting there. We have Baresi's phone and records. We'll prove Baresi phoned Naples for ten minutes that morning and then called De Campo. They spoke for over twenty minutes. I'd say we'll prove that someone in Baresi's home city of Naples gave him De Campo's details. We'll be working on that with Europol."

"Did Baresi place those bets in Italy?"

Ratso shook his head no. "We were wrong about that, Jock. I'll get there." He lobbed his empty cup high across the podium and as usual, it landed precisely in the waste. Those in the audience who had never seen his party trick laughed. "Anderson has also spilled about why he teamed up with Mandy. Each had half a jigsaw."

"They weren't doing jigsaws all the time. The SOCO guys reckoned they went at it like stoats," Willison called out, a dirty grin splitting his face.

"Jealous Willison? Not getting enough?" Ratso glared at him. Coming from someone else, he might have laughed. Too often, he found Willison irritating. "Anderson has confessed to using their pooled knowledge to steal from Baresi and Myerson. Seems that Mandy was furious that Pagano would not pay Lee's cut."

"And Harvey?"

"Anderson was not expecting trouble. His idea was to use Harvey to scare Chetri shitless and get him to transfer his Jupiter winnings. He was not expecting to see Pagano and certainly not De Campo or Mandy. Harvey will say self-defence, him or me. Anderson will support that."

"Aye, right enough, a jury might wear that."

"Is Enzo Pagano a mobster?"

"Italian name but the Feds say there's no evidence that he ever frequented Little Italy or other Cosa Nostra hangouts around New York, Queens or Brooklyn. If you believe Anderson, Pagano is just a greedy fat slob." He put up photos of Enzo Pagano and Chetri. "We're on the money trail. Pagano, mobster or not, follows omerta on the advice of his solicitor." Ratso chopped his hand across his body. "And his sodding brief is as bent as a banana."

"Are we solid against Chetri and Pagano without relying on Anderson?"

"Carole, Lee's hard-drive will nail Chetri but not Pagano. "But my guess, Chetri will start singing." The listeners could tell there was something underpinning Ratso's confidence. "We're working on his laptop even as we speak. We already know who wrote the HOSS programme. That earned them multi-millions. Nothing illegal in that. But it raises tax crimes and laundering."

"Dubai, boss?" It was ambitious Carole Viment again, eager as ever to raise her profile in front of Mick Tolvey. Ratso could see from her penetrating stare that she expected to strike a weak spot.

"Anderson couldn't help on Chetri's links. I believe him. But we have names seized at Shamoon." He changed screens and put up mugshots of Hanif Qasim and Rustomji Amarnath. "Craig Carter says these two names tally with his undercover research. He says India's Central Bureau of Investigation are trying to link these two with the Mumbai murder of Nitin Mithi – but that may have been related to sex rather than fixing. Amarnath, by the way, was nicknamed P.T."

"Mr Piss Toff," suggested Nancy. "You know like a joke – pissed-off."

"No need to explain the pun, Nancy." He paused and glanced at the lines of faces. "Actually, second thoughts – looking at the guys near the back, maybe you did." He waited for the laughter to die down. "Anyway," he put up a photo of Chetri with Amarnath who was wearing a grey suit, a white shirt and navy tie. "This was taken by an agent that Craig Carter had hired to follow P.T. during the Ryder Cup. Look at his legs – or rather his feet. Pigeon-toed ... or what! P.T? Get it? This was Chetri's gateway to the black market betting."

"This guy still in London?" Nancy Petrie looked eager to make an arrest.

Ratso's hangdog look was answer enough. "He is now believed to be in India. He certainly flew there but he's now lost, somewhere under the radar. – but anyway P.T. is not the top guy."

He changed the picture and Qasim, now featured. He was a tall, fit and muscular figure and was chatting to Chetri and Amarnath. "Hanif Qasim, a Pakistani aged fifties, is reputed to be top of the shit-heap – his syndicate operates what Craig reckons is the subcontinent's biggest and most dangerous illegal empire. With his billions, this guy funds terrorists and organised crime. In the USA, he would be the Godfather, *il capo di tutti capi*." He paused to let that image sink in. "Black-market betting is just one arm of the businesses he operates. Craig reckons Qasim's lieutenants set or influence the odds for Premier League football, limited-over cricket, golf, tennis even including the occasional Grand Slam tournaments, you name it."

"Sorry, boss but I dinna get it."

"Jock, if Qasim knows the Ryder Cup result is fixed, he sets attractive odds to lure in suckers who are then making what he expects to be a guaranteed losing bet."

"They think easy money?" suggested Viment.

"Exactly! Chetri tells P.T the result will be a tie. Amarnath deals with Qasim. A tie in the Ryder Cup is not a popular bet. When the USA was winning easily, Chetri and Pagano got damned good odds. Qasim, though, lures in billions on the mugs who thought America or Europe would win."

In an effortless move, Ratso swung himself onto the table-top and sat for a moment swinging his legs before continuing. "The CBI will arrest Amarnath when he surfaces. Qasim? I've no great hopes. He's too powerful and well-connected to be convicted, let alone jailed. His outfit has a long history of murder and intimidation. But he sails over every bit of shit thrown his way."

"He'll walk free?"

"If he's ever arrested, then yes. That's the difference between knowing and proving to a jury, Nancy. Nobody messes with Qasim and lives. He also uses witness intimidation, bribing or blackmailing judges and corrupting the top brass in Government. With those weapons at his disposal, Qasim will never see a jail."

He changed the screen to a photo of a tiny spice store. "This is in Calcutta. Imagine a pyramid with Qasim at the top. All over India, Sri Lanka and Pakistan in tiny cafés, above corner shops like this and in fashionable Delhi restaurants, thousands of small and bigger illegal bookies set and adjust their odds, taking a lead from Qasim's men. Millions of little guys lose their rupees suckered into backing results that were never going to happen." He tossed the remote to his other hand. "The legit market in Europe and the USA was no different. Plenty enough backed the USA to win."

"You looked confident that Chetri would sing, boss?" It was DC Samuel, a young West Indian who was showing promise. He had raised his hand from his position in the front row.

"Noah – yes and no. Mainly yes."

"Ark at him," Willison called out. Samuel turned round and grinned at the group and gave a big thumbs-up.

"Your joke was only funny the first time, Willison." Ratso's mouth twisted upwards on one side, his exhaustion showing. "Shall we get on? Vijay Chetri is smart but without guts. Craps himself at the mention of P.T or Qasim. P.T. has been linked to several missing or murdered sportsmen. With our help and from Craig Carter, the CBI may build a case. So far, Chetri denies even knowing anyone called Qasim." He grinned. "He hasn't seen Carter's photos yet. They'll nail him."

"So the order to attack Mark Rayment's wife and kid?"

"Came from P.T. after Qasim lost millions on two failed fixes."

"Confirmed by Anderson?"

"No, Nancy. He denies knowing either name. Again, I believe him."

"So who was the bastard who attacked them?"

Ratso tapped the side of his nose. "I'll get there." He looked around the eager faces. "But first, here's where Chetri is spilling. He's nailed Anderson and Pagano in fixing cricket and of course what he called Jupiter. He blames Pagano mainly. That's bollocks of course. Even a Southwark jury won't wear that."

Ratso eased himself off the table and, hand in pocket, swivelled to patrol the podium. Despite his fatigue his relaxed pace gave away that he was enjoying himself. He knew the best was still to come. He put up a passport photo of Eric Sommer. "Sommer was arrested last night as he flew into Stansted with a suitcase full of cash. His car had been spotted at the airport." He chuckled. "We had assumed Baresi had placed the tie-bets around Italy. It wasn't. It was this bastard."

He clicked on to a series of shots of Sommer with P.T. in Dubai. "He was a gofer for Chetri but couldn't resist making a few extra thousands by placing bets in Italy. He avoided flying there direct, routing himself though Slovenia and then driving across the border to collect his winnings."

"Why Italy?"

"Good question, Jock. Sommer owned betting shops around London. Italy permits British style high-street bookies. I'd say he thought he had a better chance of getting away with it over there."

"Except he didna'."

Three new pictures then filled the screen. "Correct – thanks to a great tip-off from Craig's betting geek I met in Bloomsbury. When Sommer disappeared, I had his photo sent to Italy to see if he might be collecting winnings." His hooded eyes turned down modestly. "It was a long-shot but the Italian police got pics of Sommer at bookies in Turin, Milan and Florence."

"There must be more, boss. About Sommer. Not just these sneaky bets." It was Nancy who could see from his rapid eye movement that Ratso was about to shoot the big gun.

"I told you Chetri was tight-lipped about P.T. and Qasim. He also denied any knowledge of the hammer attack." He slammed a fist into his other palm. "But Chetri's denial won't wash, will it Carole?" He moved towards Viment. "Tell them about your hard graft."

Viment came to the podium and somewhat hesitantly faced the group. "My main focus has been the attack in Richmond Park. After PC Dixon stopped Sommer driving Chetri's Transit, I checked reports of vehicles in the vicinity. Two witnesses remembered a Transit parked close enough to be interesting. Not far from the pond."

"And at around the time Yvonne and baby Emilia Jane were attacked," Ratso chipped in.

Her voice more forceful now, Viment continued. "The forensic report on Chetri's Transit revealed traces of blood in the rear – perhaps from the hammer." She managed a shy smile. "The blood matched the baby's DNA." The listeners broke into spontaneous applause. "We confronted Chetri last night with the forensics. Excuse my French but he shat himself faster than after a Vindaloo. You could almost hear his bowels rumble into free-fall. He of course denied authorising the attack. Blamed Eric Sommer."

She went to the laptop by the screen and clicked. The words "You were warned." appeared on screen. "The note from the windscreen," she explained. "Found in Mark Raymer's briefcase." She clicked to the next screen. It was Eric Sommer's driver's licence application. "Our handwriting expert says the same person wrote both." She returned to her seat amid noisy congratulations and a handshake from Mick Tolvey as Ratso added. "Chetri and Sommer will be charged later today for these vicious attacks."

"Proceeds of Crime Act recovery, boss? Any chance?" enquired Jock.

"Work-in-progess. I've got the Criminal Finance Team working on tracing the money. It won't be easy. Not with hawala and shady jurisdictions. We'll likely press more money-laundering charges too., I intend to get after a few bankers who ignored reporting laws on suspicious transactions. For starters, Alex Anderson's bankers seem complicit and complacent about suspicious transactions. Not easy though. Juries can be gullible when there's white-collar crime."

"Bankers aren't exactly popular though," chimed in Tolvey. "But you haven't mentioned the Wild Cards?"

"We got names from the hard-drive but we need better

evidence." Ratso for the first time looked hesitant and uneasy and avoided Nancy's questioning look.

"Todd is off to Florida." It was Mick Tolvey who had risen from his seat and who now came forward to the podium. There were several laughs at the word Florida. Someone muttered *randy old goat*. Ratso suspected Willison but knew that he always blamed him for everything. "Quiet, please," continued Tolvey. "He's to brief the Feds and Fort Lauderdale Police Department. Besides searching Myerson and Baresi's homes, the FBI wants to net the Wild Cards. Zack Gomez lives close by in Coral Springs. They'll squeeze his balls so hard he'll cut a deal and spill everything on Myerson, Baresi and the other Wild Cards."

"And, as ever over there," Ratso chimed in, "the Feds will be looking for wire-fraud, money-laundering and RICO offences. They may even want to extradite Anderson and Pagano. I also want to check out what sounds like solid identification evidence of Lee Westdale's visit to meet Baresi and Myerson in Jupiter." He looked at the sceptical faces and continued. "With that schedule, I'll be too busy for relaxation." Somehow, he maintained a deadpan straight-face. He was about to thank everybody and leave the podium when Tolvey touched his arm to stop him. Ratso looked even more un-easy now, embarrassed by thanks or congratulations.

"You did a great job, Todd. Led the team with distinction, okay maybe in the wrong direction at first – but you got a great result." He saw Ratso's eyes close and then open to look down at the cord carpeting. "I'd like you to know that Detective Inspector Morrison and young Jenkins have asked that your name go for-ward for the Queen's Medal for outstanding bravery." He waited for the clapping to subside. "That is beyond my control but I have been delighted to support such a recommendation to the Commissioner."

He shook Ratso's hand and in his embarrassment, Ratso missed his footing on stepping off the podium and stumbled. Were there tears in his tired eyes? Nobody could be sure as his rapid strides sped him out of the room. Alone by his desk, there was no time for Ratso to bask in the afterglow. He had a flight to catch. He picked up his tote bag, next stops Miami and Fort Lauderdale. As he bounded down the steps into the swirling dust and noise of Harleyford Road, he was already texting Kirsty-Ann to expect his arrival.

As he bounded down the steps into the swirling dust and noise of Harleyford Road, he was already texting Kirsty-Ann to expect his arrival.

****

Thank you for reading DEAD FIX the second in the Ratso series. Ratso, his team and Kirsty-Ann Webber return in DEADLY HUSH. Following the murder of LGBTQ+ people around London, Ratso puts his career on the line to catch the serial killer.

Click Here to read DEADLY HUSH

Did you enjoy DEAD FIX?

Please click here, leave a Review and let others know!

Want to know what happened on the French Riviera involving Ratso and Boris Zandro before *Hard Place*?

- Sign Up here for my NEWSLETTER to receive your free copy of *HARD PLACE-THE PREQUEL* and regular updates and other exclusive offers.

FIND ME ONLINE

Facebook
Website
Instagram
Email

BOOKS BY DOUGLAS STEWART

Fiction
The Ratso Series
Hard Place
Dead Fix
Deadly Hush

Other Mystery Thrillers
Deadline Vegas
Undercurrent
The Dallas Dilemma
Cellars' Market
The Scaffold
Villa Plot, Counterplot
Case for Compensation

Contributions
M.O. – a compendium
Capital Crimes – a compendium
Death Toll – a compendium

Non-Fiction
Terror at Sea
Piraten (German Language market)
Insult to Injury
A Family at Law

ABOUT DOUGLAS STEWART

I was born in Scotland but raised in England. I have lived and worked as a lawyer and writer in London, Las Vegas, Cyprus and the Isle of Man. *Deadly Hush* is my sixteenth book and the third in the Ratso series, *Undercurrent* was a WH Smith Paperback of the Week. An earlier book topped the charts for 24 weeks as did a Compendium to which I contributed. Whether fiction or non-fiction, my books reflect my legal background and my love of interesting locations, whether distant or closer to home.

Printed in Great Britain
by Amazon